SIR ARTHUR'S LEGACY  BOOK 5

Henry's Honor

SARAH EDWARDS

Cover: Deranged Doctor Design
First Electronic Edition: October 2019
ISBN: 978-1-990731-11-2
ISBN: 978-1-990731-10-5

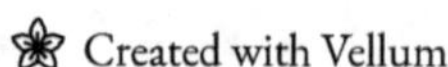 Created with Vellum

Chapter One

A mix of dust, goat, and the spices of a hundred evening cook fires infused the air. Cumin, coriander, and cinnamon twined together and made English's mouth water. Sunset splashed the sky above Cairo in burnt orange, growing brighter closer to the fiery ball sinking behind the soaring minaret. He tried to remember the name of that mosque, but his head didn't work like it used to.

After herding a small flock of goats into their pens for the night, he ended his working day with the soft click of the latch.

From the city beyond the walls came the wail of a *muezzin* calling the faithful to prayer. "Allah is great; Allah is great."

The inner courtyard emptied as people sought their prayer matts.

"I bear witness that there is no divinity but Allah," the muezzin called.

English bore witness to no divinity, and he did not pray. At one time, in another land and to another god, he might have.

Drawn to the heat the stones gathered during the day, he pressed his aching back to the wall and waited.

Like him, she did not pray. The girl on the wall. He knew her name as Alya, had heard it called often enough, but to him she remained the girl on the wall.

Curtains fluttered at the open doorway on the roof balcony. Here she came. For certain, she remained unaware of him concealed in the deepening shadows and watching. To be caught with his eyes on her now would mean Bahir and his whip. Still he waited, would not move from this spot until he saw her.

There. A slim figure shrouded by her *hijab*.

The girl on the wall stopped at the parapet and faced the street. She pushed aside the *niqaab*, which concealed all but her eyes. Then, she lifted her hijab and shook her hair free. It spilled down her back as she raised her face in a silent blessing to the day that passed. Dying sunlight rushed to pay tribute to her loveliness. Her hair dark and lustrous as the wood of the wild cherry that grew in a thicket he had once walked, her skin like crushed almonds.

Not that he could see from this distance, but her eyes above her niqaab were lighter than he would have expected. A mix of green and brown that he had only glimpsed in passing before she hastily lowered her head. He wouldn't call her beautiful in the way of other women now hazy in his mind. Her chin held too firm a jut, her nose slightly hawk-like. The strong slash of her cheekbones bore testament to her mixed blood. She had a strong face, fascinating, and in her private moment on the rooftop her elemental fire drew him like a starving man to a feast. Her very essence called to that barely living part of him that remembered life in abundance.

In her evening ritual, she discarded the modesty she showed during the day. She believed the rest of the household to be at prayer and took these forbidden moments before she would be called in or admonished by the older woman who always accompanied her.

In her stolen moments, English became a man again.

* * *

"Come in, Alya." Nasira beckoned from beyond the curtains. The old woman knew Alya well enough to end her prayers early and drag her back inside before anyone else saw her. Creases on Nasira's craggy features meant another lecture on the way.

As Alya reached the point on the rooftop garden where her hoarse whisper could be heard Nasira started. "You show your face like a street woman." Nasira shook her head. "What will people think when they see you like so?"

"Nobody sees me." Alya pushed the gauzy curtains aside. A stiffening evening breeze sent them dancing around her. "I only do it when nobody else is about."

"Somebody is always about." Grabbing a brush Nasira motioned for Alya to sit. "Especially now."

"Why especially now?" Nasira's tone gave Alya pause. She tried to turn and look at her.

Nasira rapped her on the head with her brush. "Stay still. Your father has called for you to attend him after prayers."

"He did?" They always ate the evening meal together.

Huge frown creasing her brows, Nasira nodded. "There has been trouble *habibti*. In the *souq* today."

Trouble in the souq hardly deserved the look of doom on Nasira's face. Trouble blew perpetually through the souq like the desert winds. One merchant squabbled with another, buyers quibbled over prices, and the constant thieves threaded through the place like snakes, always looking for the chance to strike. "What happened?"

"I will let your father tell you, but it is bad. Bad." Nasira lowered her head in obeisance. *"Inna lillahi wa inna ilayhi raji'un."*

"Did someone die?" Alya swung about on the stool, wincing as Nasira's hold on her hair tugged at the roots.

"You ask too many questions." Nasira grabbed her shoulders and turned her about again. "Your father will tell you all you need to know."

Her nurse should know better than to think she would leave it there. "But someone did die?"

"Come." Nasira bustled to her clothing and grabbed a fresh tunic. "I sent the boy for water, you must wash and attend your father."

A new tunic meant the news her father bore was weighty. She washed and dressed quickly, flinging her veil over her shoulder as she trotted out of her chamber and down the stairs to the small, inner courtyard shaded on one end, where her father and she shared their evening meals. The table lay set for their meal but her father sat beside a small pond, staring into the water.

Skin darkened by the sun, a stranger could never tell he had not been born in this land, but had come from somewhere beyond the sea.

"Alya." Holding his hands out he smiled and drew her forward for a kiss on both cheeks. "Nasira tells me you have been on the roof again."

"The sunset was particularly beautiful today." She could always get around him with a bit of teasing. He smelled as he always did of silk and spices, and fruit tobacco from his *hookah*.

Tonight, he turned from her and went back to his study of the pool. "You need to be careful, Alya."

"What happened in the souq?" Father dressed, ate, spoke, acted and even prayed as a son of this land, but he had raised her differently. Nasira warned his indulgence of her would come to no good, but Alya had always been encouraged to speak openly with her father.

"A merchant was killed." Father trailed his fingers through the water. Flashes of light glimmered beneath the surface as fish darted away from him. "A foreign merchant. He was murdered."

"Why?" Alya sank onto the low stone lip of the pond. Her father acted not as himself this evening. Dread prickled across her skin and sunk deep into her belly. "What are you not telling me?"

"The tension between the local merchants and the foreigners grows worse." With a sigh, he sat beside her and rubbed the back of his neck. "And the Sultan does nothing to aid the foreigners. What, with the same battle taking place in his palace, his hands are tied."

"But why?"

"You know why" Father looked up at her. She had her eyes from him, a mix of green and brown that marked them clearly as not from here.

Alya nodded, she did know why. "The army of unbelievers."

Even now, years after the Nile had risen and forced the invaders to flee, the distrust lingered.

"You must be more careful than ever." Father captured her hand and squeezed. "Eyes are everywhere and looking for a way to discredit us."

When dripped with venom from the wrong tongue, her simple act of freedom on the walls at sunset could take on the worst of connotations. She nodded. "I will be more careful."

"Let us enjoy our dinner." Father smiled but the worry lingered. "And then I must see Bahir."

Chapter Two

Bahir had it in his head to be a whoreson this evening. At the completion of prayers, he had English fill the water barrels beside the house. Not a duty English minded because it meant a trip outside the walls to the well at the end of the street. After that Bahir had him sweep the courtyard within and then bring his broom and follow him to the master's private courtyard.

Night had fallen over Cairo. Above him the velvet black sky threw out a glorious mantle of stars. Countless needle pricks in the vast fabric of the night. With night came the sudden cold, but English did not mind the cold. At times, when he lay on his bare pallet in the slave's quarters the chill on the air took his mind to a white blanket of snow, and blurred faces huddling around great hearths.

"Bahir." The master greeted the giant Eunuch.

"*Sahib*." Bahir bowed low. With skin as dark as night, Bahir's oiled scalp shone in the flickering oil lamps.

"We must speak." Master gestured to him. "We should send him away."

Both gazes swung his way and English went about his business of sweeping.

"That one." Bahir snorted like a giant bull. "The English does not speak our tongue. One too many blows to the head with steel."

Except English did speak their tongue. He kept his head over his broom. The gentle *whisk whisk* over the mosaics broke the silence. Bahir used the French tongue with him and, in a small rebellion from which he drew a measure of satisfaction, English guarded his secret understanding of Arabic.

"You heard the news from the souq?" With a groan, Master sank onto the cushions. For a man not accustomed to resting his ass on the floor, the Arabic custom of cushions before low tables played havoc with the knees.

Bahir poured the fragrant jasmine tea into cups so fine they caught the light behind them. "Amadore was not well liked, but his reputation was unblemished."

"They grow bolder." The master sighed and broke off a piece of *basbousa*. Once over *Ramadan*, English had been given the sweet treat. "But there is more."

Bahir folded his hands in front of him and waited.

"The news has not yet reached the streets, but they killed Amadore's family as well."

Bahir bowed his head. "*Inna lillahi wa inna ilayhi raji'un.*"

"God save us all." Master chewed his basbousa and stared into the night. "It was brutal they say."

When amongst those he trusted, Master dropped his piety and reverted to his former religion.

"The Sultan does nothing." Master drank his tea. "He cannot risk being seen to take sides in this conflict."

Bahir refilled his tea and stood back again, huge hands folded before him. "Your mind is troubled, Sahib."

"They will come for me." Standing, Master brushed crumbs from his tunic. "Someone will remember me as the Genovese merchant Pietro D'Onofrio. We can no longer pretend it is not so."

"You cannot be sure of this," Bahir said. "Cairo has known you as Alif Al-Rasheed for longer than twenty years."

"People have long memories. Amadore lived here before I even arrived. He showed me how to go on in those first days." Hands clasped behind his back, Master strolled to the pond. "It is not for myself that I worry and I cannot take the chance I may be right."

"Alya." Bahir nodded.

Alya. English moved closer, his broom stirring the dust beneath the arbor that provided shade in the midday heat. Moonlight through the vines cast ghostly shadows on the mosaicked floors.

"She is different," Master said. "We both know this. God forgive me, but I raised her that way."

"What is it you wish from me, Sahib?" Whispers spoke of the master having purchased Bahir from a harem in Acre and bringing him to Cairo. Stronger than an ox and able to swing his curved blade with deadly precision, his lack of ballocks had not tamed Bahir any.

"Take her away, Bahir."

English stopped sweeping. Aware Bahir's gaze had swung his way, he bent as if to pick something up from the ground.

"Sahib?" Bahir strode closer to the master. "Take her where? To Damietta?"

"Further." Master raised his head and met Bahir's hard look.

"Acre? Damascus?"

"Further." Dropping his head, Master slumped. "Take her back to my kind, my old friend. Take her where her strangeness will not stand out so much."

"Will they welcome her?" Bahir ran his hand over his face. "She has not been raised one of them."

English worked his broom into the corners so he could stay and hear the rest of their conversation.

"I am aware." Master shrugged. "But at least I give her this chance at life."

"But she is your daughter. The moon in your night."

"She is my everything." Master cleared his throat and straightened his shoulders. "I will remain here. I have not in me the strength to begin my life a third time." When Bahir would speak, he held up his hand. "Nay. I am decided in this. I will remain here. At the least it will take them time to realize she is gone."

Bahir stood, staring at the master.

"You are decided in this?" Bahir said.

"I am." Master nodded. "I have a ship waiting for you at Alexandria. It will take you wherever you need to go. I have loaded it with everything you will need. Most of my wealth goes with you."

* * *

His girl on the wall was leaving. Bahir was commanded to take his light away. English laughed at his own idiocy. A slave had no place in his life for bright dreams.

"Hssst!"

English stopped. Huge protruding eyes holding his gaze as she chewed her cud, a she-camel stared back at him. The master's fears must be affecting his mind. Next, he would see haunts in the deep shadows around the beast pens.

Louder this time, more insistent. "Hssst!"

The habits of a lifetime had him reaching for a weapon that had not ridden his hip for three years. He bent and picked up a rock. "Who is there?"

"Henry?"

The beast pens dimmed, and English reached to steady himself on an upright. A name he had not heard spoken in many years and a voice that drove lance-like into the raw center of him.

"God's balls, Henry, are you just going to stand there?"

His mother tongue came unbidden to his lips. "Newt?"

"Who else would it be?" A figure emerged from the shadows.

"What other poor sod would think it a fine idea to hide out with these disgusting beasts."

"Newt?" Dear God, he might unman himself and faint. English dug his fingers into the wooden upright and tried to right the tilting world about him.

"They spit." Newt scrubbed globs of partially digested cud from his tunic. Three years had changed much about the lad. Taller, broader, his face grown finely hewn. His hair hung longer, possibly concealing those ears that stuck out from his head like jug handles.

"Newt." English drank in all the details, small and large about the man standing before him. A man he had once called friend, loved as he loved his blood brothers. A strange urge rose within English. Laughter! It came from his throat rusty and disused and he hung on tighter to his support.

"Henry." Newt beamed at him. "It took me long enough to find you."

"Newt." It could not be possible to have Newt standing before him. This was a memory from another time come to taunt him, come to break him. English stepped away.

"Aye, that is my name." Sharp gaze sweeping English from head to toe, Newt frowned. "Are you addled?

How many times in the past had Newt asked him that? Worn that same expression, a small part quizzical, but for the most part scornful. "It is you."

"Aye, Henry, it is me." Newt glanced about them. "Can we find somewhere less open to speak? That big ebony whoreson has eyes in the back of his head."

"Bahir." Still not sure his eyes did not deceive him, he led Newt behind the beast pens into his secret place. The same place he used to watch his girl on the wall. Not for much longer.

Newt crowded into the shadows beside him. Now at least as tall as he, their shoulders brushed and fought for space.

The enormity of it hit Henry and he hauled Newt into a rough embrace.

Newt stiffened, it was not his way, but then relaxed into his hold. Fastening an arm around his back, Newt pounded his shoulder blades. "Sweet Jesu, it is good to see you, Harry."

Henry scrunched his eyes closed. He would not disgrace himself with tears, but they built anyway and he held onto Newt as much to hide his disgrace as to assure himself he had not imagined the man.

After a while Newt disengaged. He stepped back, cleared his throat and straightened his filthy tunic. "I have come to take you home."

"Home?" He did not even know what home meant. After he heard the news that Frederick's army had withdrawn, leaving him here, cut off from his home, he had forced that word away. "You have come to take me home?"

"By the rood, Henry. You are addled for certain." Newt shook his head. "Why else would I be here?"

"I know not." He might go home. Swift on the heels of the hope came the fear, washing away the hope. He had learned not to hope. Hope brought with it only the pain of being dashed and trampled beneath uncaring feet. "I will never go home."

Newt gaped at him. "Aye, you will."

"Nay."

"Aye." Newt's face grew taut. He stepped forward. "You will go home because I am here to fetch you."

"I cannot." He could not risk it. This long he had survived on the ruthless annihilation of hope.

"Aye, you will." Newt shoved him. Hard enough to send him crashing into the wall. "You will go home because I promised Roger I would find you and bring you home." Another shove sent him back against the wall. "You will go home because Sweet Bea will still be crying for you, or I do not know your sister. And you will go home, or I will die getting you there, because we both know I failed you."

English pressed his bruised back to the wall. He would like to explain but he had not the words. In this land, he had lost himself.

In this place of a new god, strange food and customs he had learned his lessons at the end of the whip. Henry had become English. He had no more god, no more hope. He was nothing more than a slave. So, he shrugged and said again, "I cannot."

"By God's aching blisters, you will go home, Harry." Newt hawked and spat. "You cower against the wall if you wish, but Newt has a plan. And if Newt must drag your ass all the way across that perishing desert to do it. You. Will. Go. Home."

Chapter Three

Henry followed Bahir into the main hall, the one they kept for formal occasions. He couldn't say he was overly surprised to see Newt there. Polished up and clean, Newt looked older than his years as he faced the master.

"Is this the man?" The master gestured to Henry.

"Aye, that's him." Neither did it surprise him that Newt had learned to speak Arabic, the boy had an uncanny knack for languages.

"Come closer." The master turned his gaze on Henry.

Bahir shoved him forward. "Move, English."

Henry. He was a man and his name was Henry. Just once, Henry would like to match the sod with steel and pay Bahir back in kind. Keeping any emotion from his face, he bowed his head before the master.

"This man...er...Newt is here to purchase your freedom." Master hefted a clinking bag in his palm. "He tells me you are of noble blood."

So softly only Henry heard it, Bahir snorted.

"I am." Henry straightened his shoulders. Yester eve Newt had ripped open the wound and now the memories refused to be suppressed. Henry rose up from within English and demanded his rightful place.

"He offers quite a tidy sum for your freedom."

"Which according to the holy *Qur'an*, you are obliged to accept." Newt oozed affability. "For by freeing the slave, you become a companion of the Right."

The master's eye flashed. "Do you presume to quote the holy law to me?"

"Nay." Newt bowed. "Forgive my eagerness, but Sir Henry has a family who long for him. I am under a sacred blood vow to return him to them."

The master rested his chin on his palm. "Tell me of this family, this Anglesea."

"Sir Arthur, Sir Henry's father, is the greatest knight in all the kingdom. Nay." Newt struck a pose, chin angled up, one leg before the other. "The greatest warrior in the Christian world."

Spreading it a trifle thick there and Henry threw him a sardonic glance.

As if he drew his words from the sky, Newt raised his hand. "He has amassed for his family great wealth. He holds the ear of King Henry."

Henry stifled a snort. Held the king's ear, his ass. A king hadn't set foot in Anglesea Castle since Father had joined the Army of God against King John. Had matters changed? Undoubtedly. When he had left, Father had been whoring William out to the highest bidder. William could be married by now, perhaps even with a babe or two. The weight of his longing hit him broadside, and it was all he could do to stay standing. Damn Newt for opening the hidden chest within him, because now all the faces flooded out. William, Roger, Faye, Bea, Mathew even bloody Garrett. His father, and his beautiful mother. Nurse. So close he could almost believe he would see them again they hovered before him.

The master rubbed his mouth. "Yet, all this time he said nothing?"

Bahir poked him in the back. He half turned to punch the piss out the bastard before he collected himself.

Eyes glittering a challenge, Bahir smirked.

"The army had retreated." Henry found his voice. "I was felled in battle, an old couple found me and nursed me back to health. I hit my head and it took me a while to recollect who I was. They kept me to work off my debt to them, and then sold me when they needed the money. By the time I reached the market in Cairo, my people were gone."

The master nodded, a look in his eyes that told Henry he understood something of being alone in a land not your own. He straightened and turned to Newt. "Your visit is rather timely, as I have a delicate problem of my own."

"If it is within my power to help you." Newt laid a hand over his heart. "Perhaps we can help each other to a mutually agreeable outcome."

"Indeed." The master's lips quirked into a smile. He tossed the bag of gold back at Newt. "What I require of you is not money. I will take my payment in kind."

Newt snatched the bag out of the air and tucked it away. "Indeed?"

"My daughter needs to travel back to Genoa, to my family." Behind Henry, Bahir shifted. "I am sending Bahir along with her, but she is a stranger to my native land. She has been raised here."

"Ah." Newt nodded. "You fear for her safety."

The master scowled. "What do you know of this?"

"I have ears." Newt shrugged. "I keep them low to the ground."

"I am sure you do." Snorting, the master shifted in his seat. "Your Sir Henry could be of service to me. To my daughter. He could provide her an introduction to my family and more importantly, teach her much on the voyage to Genoa."

The question escaped Henry before he it had truly formed in his mind. "Teach her what?"

"How to go about in Genoa. Customs." The master shrugged. "Manners. All those things you were raised knowing."

His girl on the wall placed within his grasp by her father. Henry's pulse quickened.

"When you say voyage?" Newt cocked his head. "Are we to infer that travel arrangements have been made?"

"You are." The master rose. "My fastest ship awaits Bahir and my daughter in Alexandria. It would be a simple matter to have them sail you home once they are done."

"Not to doubt your word." Newt spread his hands wide. "But how are we to know you will not simply strand us in Genoa."

Bahir grumbled.

The master's face reddened. "I hand my daughter into your care. I have nothing more binding to offer as my bond."

"I will protect her." Henry stepped forward. The knight he had once been rose hot in his blood. "I vow this to you, or I will die trying."

* * *

Alya pressed her palms into her eyes to stem the flow of tears. It did no good because the more she tried to stop crying, the harder she cried. Her father decreed she would leave Cairo and journey to Genoa. Father assured her his brother would welcome her, love her as he did, but she did not know these people.

Since her mother's death it had been only her and Father. Unlike other girls who were sheltered and separated from the larger world, Father treated her as a son. He taught her to read and write, he showed her mathematics and made sure she knew it well. He had Bahir teach her the stars and how to navigate by them. More than his daughter, she was his helpmate and his confidant. Now, in one staggering blow, he had made this decision without her. Made a decision about her future without consulting her and none of her cajoling, wheedling, and begging had made one ounce of difference.

All through her long, sleepless night she had waited for him to come to her, and tell her of his change of heart.

With the first touch of dawn, the camels stood ready in the courtyard. Bahir shouted orders to the hired guards who would travel with them. Her stomach churned as they loaded her litter onto the largest camel.

She was leaving. Leaving Cairo. Leaving her father. Who would make sure the cook made Father's favorite sweet treats, or prepared his mint tea for him after his meal? When he looked to speak of his life before he came here, who would wonder at his stories of strange customs and foods?

Camels brayed from the courtyard as the sky lightened. A lone cockerel announced dawn to the city. Beyond the walls, a sleepy peddler pushed his barrow of wares down the road.

Her life was here, and when she left, her heart would remain.

"It is time." His face tired and drawn as if he too had spent a bad night, Father stood in her doorway.

She left the tears trickling down her cheeks. Maybe if he saw how he broke her heart, Father would relent. He never could bear her tears. "Please."

"Alya. My heart." Father held his arms out. "I would not do this if I did not think there was no other way. You cannot stay here. I cannot keep you safe."

"But who will keep you safe?"

Sad eyes gouging her heart, Father dropped his arms. "I will be careful."

"Why can I not stay and also be careful?" She refused the traveling robe Nasira held out to her.

Nasira sniffed and wiped her eyes. She had been crying most of the night with Alya.

Father dropped his head. He took a deep breath and looked up again, straightening his shoulders. "It is decided," he said. "Bahir will travel with you. When you arrive in Genoa you can decide to send him home or keep him with you." He cleared his throat. "I hope you will keep him with you. You will find no greater champion than Bahir."

As Nasira tugged the traveling robe about her, Alya stood rigid. She refused to participate in this.

"I am also sending the English with you."

The news shook her out of her black mood for a moment. "Why?"

"His people have come to buy his freedom. It seems he is an important lord in his country. He will teach you how to go on amongst our kind."

"They are not my kind."

"They are." Father strode toward her. "You must work hard to become who you are. Listen to the English, mind what he tells you, and you will make it easier for yourself."

"Imagine." Nasira gave a choked titter. "An English lord sweeping our courtyard, minding our goats." Nasira attempted to lighten the air, but Alya refused to be cajoled like a sulky child. Like a discarded fruit rind, her father tossed her away.

Father took her by the shoulder. "Come. I would have you out of the city before the sun rises."

This was happening. He was sending her away. Alya's tears welled again. "Do not do this, Father. Please, I am begging you."

"I must." He turned and stalked for the door. "If you are not down in a few moments, I will send Bahir to fetch you. He will tie you to your camel if he must, but you will go to Genoa."

* * *

Henry ducked his head and hid his smile. The look on Newt's face was beyond price.

Newt grimaced. "I am not riding that."

"Then you walk." Bahir checked the straps on the litter one by one.

Even if he did want to run the bastard through Henry admired his thoroughness. It galled him they would share this journey. Even more so knowing they shared a mutual goal. They had both pledged their lives to protect his girl on the wall.

Alya. He whispered her name, trying it out on his tongue. It meant heaven, divinity, and so she had become to him. The lofty deity he scrabbled beneath. Dear God, Roger would kick his ass for that one. His breath hitched. His oldest brother, Roger, whom he had thought never to see again.

"Why can I not ride a horse?" Newt followed Bahir around the camel. "You have horses here. Not terrible stock either."

Drawing himself up, Bahir glowered at Newt. "We have the finest horses of anywhere. Bred light of foot, soft of mouth, and faster than the wind."

Snorting, Newt crossed his arms. "Aye, but how good are they at stamping a foot soldier into the ground. Or biting a sword arm off?"

"You English." Bahir shuddered. "Savages."

"Savages who don't ride camels." Newt smirked.

"Then you are destined to be a footsore thirsty savage." Bahir smirked back.

Dear God, they would still be arguing when the sun set. "They are not that bad to ride," Henry said. "They sway a bit, and smell but they don't need to stop for water nearly as often as we do."

"Aye, but I—"

"Get on the bedamned camel, Newt."

Hidden by her hijab, Alya stood in the doorway. Shoulders slumped, she dragged her feet to the litter.

Her nurse kept an arm about her shoulders. "All will be well, habibti. You will see. Your new family will love you just as we do."

The master entered the courtyard, his expression an open wound as he stared at his daughter. They might never meet again. Henry understood some of his pain.

"Will you not say goodbye to your father, habibti?" They stood less than two feet away from him. Closer than Henry had ever been to the girl on the wall. Subtle notes of night-flowering jasmine twined around his senses.

"He sends me away." Her niqaab muffled her sniffles. "I have nothing to say to him."

The slave wanted to bow to her pain, let her feel his silent support. However, Henry understood only too well what she risked by not making her parting sweet.

He slipped around the camel to stand beside her.

Bahir stiffened. "Get away from her."

"Wish your father God be with him," Henry said.

Her gaze flew to his face. Eyes like the dappled shade of the woodland, part green, part golden stared at him.

He shook off Bahir's grip on his shoulder. "You cannot know what the future holds, or if you might get this chance again. Tell him now that you love him. Carry that memory with you."

Chapter Four

Newt's face amused Henry endlessly. His *keffiyeh* hid the smile that came more easily as the distance between them and Cairo widened.

"What manner of beast is this?" Newt pushed the keffiyeh away from his mouth. Sitting stick straight in the saddle, his legs cinched the camel's sides in a death grip. "And why can I not control it?"

"She follows the lead camel." He pointed to Bahir's back. "Sit back." He tapped the backrest behind him. "See how Bahir hooks his legs up? Do the same, you will be more comfortable."

"Is this English you speak?" Bahir turned his head to speak over his shoulder. "You are an interesting man, Henry." The way the big sod said his name dragged it out ceaselessly into Hen-er-ree. "You speak your mother tongue, French and, apparently, Arabic."

It only surprised him it had taken Bahir most of the day to mention that he had used her language with Alya.

"You bear watching." Bahir nodded. "You appear to be a man of many secrets."

"You asked me no questions." Henry envied the ease of the big man atop his saddle. He swayed with the motion of the beast beneath him. A slow, somnambulant sway that blended with the silken swish of the camel's feet on the sand.

Bahir grunted. "How long have you spoken Arabic?"

"Long enough." Three years in which he had counted the days despite himself. "Ask me why I learned it."

A long silence followed, and then Bahir said, "Why?"

"So I could tell you how much I want to rip your head off and shove it up your ass."

* * *

Alya's cheeks burned at the English's language. Hen-er-ree. She formed his name on a whisper. Did it have a meaning? Could it refer to his mind-stealing eyes. Blue as pure lapis lazuli, bluer than the merciless sky arcing above them. She had never seen eyes that color. They were wasted on a man who tended her father's goats, and used his mighty shoulders for nothing more than toting rocks, sacks, and whatever Bahir bade him carry.

Except, Father had said he bore the title lord in his own land, which made him one of the infidel knights.

She had caught a glimpse of them once when they rode into Cairo to speak with the sultan. With metal tunics and massive horses, and long, straight swords they had made her breath catch. In that moment, she had known a spine freezing fear of the foreign invaders. Had Hen-er-ree a horse so large, and had he sweated beneath all that metal in the desert sun?

Sir Hen-er-ree. This is what they called themselves, Father had told her. Sir this and sir that. Did they call their women thus? Sir Alya. It made her giggle.

Ears always pricked for the slightest sound she made, Bahir's head swung in her direction.

She shrugged to indicate it was nothing, and went back to scouring the desert landscape for something of interest.

With midday heat trapped within its fabric confines the litter grew unbearably hot. She tied one of the curtains back. The first breeze of evening fluttered through the silk tassels and made their shadows dance across the desert floor.

Bahir rode in the front. Behind him came Henry and his pretty friend. Newt. What manner of name was Newt? If she dared she would ask them. Perhaps somewhere on this trip Bahir would allow her near enough to do so.

Her eyes ached from crying. Dry and gritty now that she had no more tears to shed. Behind her lay Father and Nasira. Her beautiful chamber draped in sunlight silk that her father had given to her when she became a woman. Her peaceful rooftop courtyard where she stood to watch the sun set, or sat beneath the canopy and painted. In the heat of the day she might lay upon a bright bed of cushions content to drowse and dream.

In her wake came the heavily laden camels with her baggage. Filled also with gifts, Bahir told her, for her new family. Spices, silks, costly perfume oils, ouds and attars, and rare myrrh. Costly, precious gifts to buy their love for her.

Bahir thought her ignorant. In faraway Genoa, her family would view her as strange and the enemy. Had they not sent their brothers, fathers, husbands, and uncles to fight her kind? To bring them the word of God. Her father had raised her Christian, so she had that in her favor, but not much else. They would not see a niece or a fellow Christian when they saw her, they would see a hated foe, a nonbeliever.

What did Henry see? Or his pretty friend?

They saw a mound of dark fabric. A pair of eyes peeking over the top of her niqaab.

She tweaked the front curtain for a better view of Newt. Near as tall as Henry, but younger and narrower across the chest and shoulders. His dark hair fell to his shoulders. He had the sort of face to make a girl sigh and pine like the descriptions of the poets. Only now he did not look so poetic, perched like a nut atop his camel. He would be bruised by the time they stopped to rest.

Bahir planned to travel well into the night, to take advantage of the coolness. They would stop to rest through the hottest time and travel when the sun lost some of its blaze.

Henry swung in his saddle and looked at her. Even from here she caught the pure blue of those eyes. His keffiyeh concealed the rest of his face. A mercy, as covered in grime and dirt as it was. His people called hers savages. Hah! At least they were savages not frightened of soap and water. She lifted her chin at Henry and dropped the curtain closed.

* * *

As much as he sympathized with Newt's pain, Henry stood ready to pound him into the desert by the time Bahir called a halt midway through the next day. They entered a small oasis, barely more than a few palms sheltering a deep well.

"Jesu and his ever-loving Father's balls." Newt tumbled off his kneeling camel. He arched his back this way and that and hobbled a few steps forward. "I have never ridden anything more uncomfortable."

"You get used to them." Henry watered the animals as Bahir got Alya settled.

Bringing down her litter, Bahir made a makeshift tent with the coverings for her to crawl inside and sleep through the heat of the day.

"I will never grow used to that." Newt stood beside his camel and sneered at her.

Eyelids closing against the bright heat of the day she chewed her cud.

"Here." Henry showed Newt how to drape his keffiyeh over the camel's saddle, and prop it to make a shady patch. "You need to sleep now. We will move again once it grows cooler."

Newt eyed his small tent. "Will we eat, or is the big bastard determined to starve us as well as break our asses?"

"Later." Henry tossed him a small sack of dates. "Put those in your cake hole and stop whining."

Alya had crawled in beside her camel and out of his view.

"English!" Bahir stalked toward him. "Keep drawing water. You smell like a goat, and I will not be subjected to your stench all the way to Alexandria."

Solely based on who made the demand, Henry considered objecting, but he suspected he did smell like a goat.

The fabric surrounding Alya twitched. So the lady wanted to see what happened all about her, did she? If Bahir knew he'd probably slap a blindfold on her as well as the rest of her swaddling.

In a desert, you never wasted water, so he drew a small pail for himself and moved between two date palms.

"Here." Bahir tossed him a bag of sweet sand.

Henry caught it. "Would you like to wash the crack of my ass for me?"

As he'd said it in English, Newt snickered.

Clever enough to catch the intent of his comment, Bahir glowered at him.

Henry met his stare.

With a sneer, Bahir turned away and yelled orders at the guards. A few baleful looks tossed toward him gave Henry a childish surge of satisfaction. The big turd might need to watch his back.

Stripping off his tunic, Newt joined him. "God's wounds, it's hotter than hell."

"You grow used to it." Henry shucked his loose linen pants and hauled the tunic over his head.

"Nay, you don't." Newt wet himself and spread sweet sand all over his body. "Been in this sodding place for more than a year looking for you. I'll never fancy being baked alive like a loaf of bread. Give me the cool rains of home over this sweat hole."

Henry tried not to remember cool autumn rain that brought the promise of winter. Fresh April showers auguring spring. Wintery, hard-driving tempests straight off the freezing sea. Nay, he had not allowed himself to remember. At the end of this journey they waited for him. He could almost taste the rain on his lips. Sweet sand stung the cuts and sores on his arms but he worked it into his skin. Bahir insisted the servants bathe regularly, but working like an ox meant many cuts and scrapes.

Newt hissed. "What happened?" Staring at his back, Newt's expression grew clouded with anger. He jerked his head at Bahir. "He do that?"

"Only one or two." Henry shrugged. "The worst came before him." He had not seen his back, but his obedience had come slowly. Mostly at the hands of the couple who found him and nursed him back to health. A few more from the slave traders who objected to his attitude. Bahir had whipped him in the beginning, trying to beat the resistance out of him. It galled Henry most that it had worked. Sooner or later every man's head bowed beneath the pressure of wanting to live. The big bastard tended to threaten now more than whip. The memory of Bahir's whipping had kept every servant in the master's courtyard under control.

"I'll kill him." Rigid, gaze locked on Bahir, Newt stood.

Henry used the water to wash the sweet sand off. "Not if I get to him first."

* * *

Alya should turn her head and not watch as the men cleaned themselves. Bahir would be displeased. When she had gone with Nasira to the souq, she had been forced to drop her gaze away from the partial nudity of the beggars and ignore the mostly naked slaves herded into pens.

Well, if Henry did not want her to look he should not stand where she had a clear sight of him. Even now, darkened by the sun, Henry's skin remained fairer than the men about him. Would his fairer skin feel cool to the touch? Or would it be warm and dry, surprising her like the skin of a snake she had touched when the charmers came to perform for Father.

Muscle bulged along the length of his arms as he spread sweet sand over his chest. Strong ridges cut across his abdomen. Two lines of muscle dipped inside his hip bones and disappeared beneath his loincloth. His legs were long and powerful.

An odd prickling sensation spread over her skin. She tightened her stomach against the tingle of excitement.

Nasira had lectured her about these sensations, warned her that a pure woman did not look upon a man who was not her husband and feel these things. Nasira was far behind in Cairo, and Alya did not want to look away, or stop the sensation. It climbed from her belly to her breasts, tightening her nipples to points.

Henry dampened a cloth in water and wiped the sweet sand off. Water glistened along every fascinating ridge, snaked in droplets over his belly and thighs.

Lust. She lusted for the English with the beautiful eyes, and the man's body.

She closed her eyes and forced them to remain that way. This would never do. His blue eyes held some manner of sorcery.

Chapter Five

Henry sat beside Newt as they shared a meal before the caravan got underway. With the sunset came the cool of the desert evening and he wrapped his keffiyeh tightly around his head to keep the wind off him.

Bahir prowled the outskirts of the small oasis. He stopped, cocked his head, tense and alert.

"What's up with him?" Newt jerked his chin at Bahir, who slid like a wraith between the date palms, his attention intent on the dark expanse of nothing all around them.

Henry's nape prickled. He sensed it too. It ran like ants across his skin, tightened his belly, and made him uneasy. He rose, his hand reaching for the sword that no longer rested at his hip. "I am not sure."

Wind whispered and hissed through the palms, the deep silence pressing in on them from all sides.

A wild dog yipped.

Bahir whirled and shouted. "Arm yourselves!"

"Bedamned!" Newt whirled. "What is happening?"

"There are no blasted wild dogs this close to Cairo." With no sword, Henry ran for Alya. "Give no quarter."

Swords flashing, the escort clambered to their feet,

Rising out of the sand like smoke, the attackers swarmed out of the desert. Desert nomads. Fast, deadly, and merciless.

Alone, Alya beside her camel.

Bahir engaged three men, and cut down two almost immediately.

Henry reached her before Bahir. "Have you a dagger?"

"Aye." Eyes huge, she looked fearful but calm.

"Use it."

Shrouded in dark clothing and difficult to see, men surged around them. The nomads knew the desert well. Knew how to use it to their advantage.

A figure lunged out of the shadows.

Alya screamed.

Henry ducked the sword. He rammed his shoulder into the man's gut, driving them both to the ground.

Hard packed sand jarred his knees and elbows.

The nomad twisted beneath him and got his hands about Henry's throat.

Henry tossed sand in his eyes, grabbed his turban and pounded his head into the sand until the man's grip about his neck relaxed.

Another two headed for Alya, making no sound on the soft sand.

"Henry!" Newt yelled. A sword winged through the air toward him.

Henry snatched it and swung. Steel bit into flesh and the first man dropped. The other bastard skidded to a stop. His blade swaying like a cobra.

In his hand, the pommel fit like a gauntlet. Henry curled his fingers about it. Another man converged on them from the right.

The first attacked. Henry swung double handed, striking blade against blade. Sparks flew. He found the bind, twisted and wrenched the sword from the nomad's hand.

Dancing back, he dodged the blow from his right. Cutting up, his metal bit into cloth and then stuck in the man's chest.

Henry shoved with his boot, and the man dropped to the ground.

Years and years of training took over. Dodge, cut, thrust, parry, strike. Weight balanced on the balls of his feet, searching constantly for the next attack.

Behind him, Alya. Before him they came in a steady flow, one man after another. Metal clanged against metal, grunts and hoarse cries, the stench of sweat, the sharp coppery tang of blood. Battle. His blood surged in response.

His breath tired first. Rasping through his chest as he danced with his sword. The fatigue spread to his arms. Still their attackers came out of the darkness. His footwork grew sloppy. His responses slower. Henry shook sweat out his eyes.

Then, Bahir was beside him. Carving that deadly curved sword of his through nomads. Shoulder to shoulder they fought, until Newt joined them. Henry drew on his last reserves, his arms shaking with the effort to raise the sword.

The attackers dwindled to a trickle.

And then they were gone.

In the aftermath, the silence rang like a bell.

Henry dropped his hands to his knees and tried to catch his breath. Breath seared through his chest, his heart pounding so hard it drummed in his ears.

"They are gone," Alya whispered.

Bodies littered the oasis, crumpled over like cloth poppets. Camels brayed their alarm. Their handlers clucked and soothed, speaking to them in harsh guttural grunts.

"Bastard dogs." Bahir spat. He strode to the nearest body, grabbed its head and lifted, only to drop it back onto the floor. "Find one of them alive."

Metal whispered against leather as Newt sheathed his weapon.

Henry straightened, his body aching like an oldster.

"That was close." Newt hauled his headscarf off and wiped his brow. "You fight like an old woman."

Henry wanted to brain the little turd, but Newt spoke true.

He had fought like a sodding farmer. Three years of herding goats had cost him his speed and his endurance. Thick spit and sand coated his mouth and he snatched the water skin Newt held out to him. He rinsed his mouth and spat.

But Alya was safe. Behind him she moved in a silky swish of cloth and the scent of jasmine oil.

"An old woman who taught you how to fight." He punched Newt on the shoulder, nearly crying with the effort it took. But a man had his pride after all.

A strangled cry arose from where Bahir dragged some hapless fighter up and threw him against a boulder.

Only then did Henry allow himself to look at Alya.

Her gaze moved across the oasis constantly. Beneath her covering, he could not tell what expression she wore but she held her shoulders tense. She raised her head when she caught him looking. Something fierce flashed in the green-brown depths of her eyes. "My thanks, Hen-er-ree."

She knew his name. It surged through him hot and sweet. Not trusting his voice, he nodded and tightening his grip over his pommel followed Newt.

Bahir had the injured man pinned to a boulder. His keffiyeh lay in the sand at their feet. Through the grit, sweat, and blood a young, clearly terrified, boy stared up at them.

So fast that Henry barely caught a word of it, they spoke in the language of the desert tribes.

At the end of which, Bahir shoved the boy away. The nomad stumbled and fell, righted himself and ran out into the night.

"Should we be letting him go?" Newt examined the metal of his blade.

"He's a child. We do not kill children." With a harsh grunt, Bahir spun on his heel and stalked across the oasis to where a small band of the escort crouched. "We have bigger problems than a dirty tribal boy."

"What sort of problems?" Newt followed on behind him.

He needn't bother. Bahir would deem it beneath him to share

the information with them. Henry wanted to punch the bastard in the small of his back, right at the tender spot that would bring him to his knees.

He followed Bahir anyway.

Bahir and the leader of the escort spoke urgently to each other. From the look on the leader's face, he would not be joining Bahir's band of admirers. Thus far, the only person who seemed to tolerate Bahir was Alya.

For the escort, Bahir had switched to Arabic. "How many?"

"Three dead." The leader rose wearily to his feet. "Five injured."

"Pack up, we need to move." Spinning again, he marched away.

Henry stepped into his path. "Would you care to explain?"

"Nay." Bahir squared off.

One of these days, Henry promised himself, there would be a reckoning between them. "I gather there's a problem. Her father gave her into my care as well as yours. I suggest we try and work together on this."

Bahir curled his lip back. "She is nothing to you, English. You purchased your freedom with this journey."

"Tell me anyway." Henry stepped back into his path.

With a grunt, Bahir scratched the back of his neck. "I see you found a sword."

"Aye, and I know how to use it."

Newt snorted and muttered something Henry did not want to hear.

"I do not have time for this." Bahir stepped around him.

"Feisty bastard, isn't he?" Newt watched him go. "He probably bleeds sour piss if you cut him."

Henry turned to the escort leader. He jerked his head at Bahir disappearing form. "What did he say to the boy?"

"That one." The man spat. "The Devil! He said we need to leave. Now."

"Why?"

"These men." The man gestured to the desert around them. "They did not find us by chance. They were sent here. They want the girl."

He might have guessed. Desert nomads tried not to involve themselves in the business of the cities. Unless a strong incentive was provided for them to do so.

No need to bury the dead because the desert scavengers would make short work of them. The injured were being loaded onto slower camels to return to Cairo. May luck be on their side, because they had a nightmare journey ahead of them, and always the chance the nomads would decide to avenge their dead.

Henry strapped his sword to his pack aboard the camel. He had a sword now and Bahir could pry it out of his dead hand.

"Why her?" Newt joined him in packing up their belongings.

"It's political." How to describe the shifting quicksand of Cairo politics? "The Genovese have been here for a while, even before our bedamned foray after glory. When Frederick came with his army it upset the balance. There are those who are angry with the sultan for being so conciliatory with Frederick's army. Still others who feel he should have chased us down and finished what the Nile started."

Newt nodded. "Why didn't they?"

"It's against the rules of war." It still baffled Henry, this society. So many contradictions within contradictions and all governed by Allah. "The sultan is a devout man, he follows the rules of war."

"Which are?" Newt grimaced at his camel.

"Far more honorable than ours." Henry threw his leg over the saddle. "Mount up. We'll be riding hard for Alexandria."

* * *

Pushing their animals, they rode fast through the night. As much as it galled Henry to admit it, Bahir knew his desert and he moved them across it with eerie skill, finding landmarks in the seemingly unbroken expanse.

They ate as they rode.

The men formed a tight unit around Alya's litter. Tense and alert, Bahir on his faster camel rode patrols into the desert.

As dawn broke over the silent city, they reached the outskirts of Alexandria.

"This city gives me the willies." Newt shuddered and glanced about him. "All these old buildings, now ruined."

Henry nodded. He had not travelled through Alexandria with Frederick's army but instead come from Acre overland in a brutal journey that had killed many fine men and beasts.

Great, ancient edifices loomed on either side of the wide roadway they traversed. Strange and unknown statuary adorned the buildings belonging to a people they could only guess about. Unworldly creatures wrought of finest white stone, paying homage to pagan gods.

The city grew livelier as they approached the docks. The stench of fish, oil, and bilge reached them first. Newt muttered profanities as they wended their way through the early morning travelers to the dock.

"Allah akbaru, Allah akbaru." The muezzin's haunting call wailed over the city.

The caravan moved to the side, along with a pair of silk traders pushing their wares along in a cart. Prayer mats appeared, laid out facing east. The traders and the devout in their caravan paused to pray. Standing first, hands crossed before their chests, eyes closed, they chanted. Like a ripple, they bowed from the waist, rose again. The soft sung chant rose and fell as the men at the roadside bent their knees, pressing foreheads to the ground.

Silent out of respect, he stood beside Newt. He remembered a time when prayer had been the most important part of his day. The hours he'd spent in silent communion with his God some of his most cherished memories. In his moments of deepest anguish, when he had first been sold into slavery, Henry had believed God had turned his back on him, forsaken him in this place.

Now he understood an opposite truth. Henry had turned his back on God. In the face of all the evil he had witnessed he could not give his faith and his obedience. Sometimes he felt as if the evil had seeped through his skin into his very bones and lay waiting there for the day he would turn to it. He could not face any god with the blood that stained his hands, the deaths that stained his soul.

With prayer over, the men stood, packed away their mats, and life resumed again.

Bobbing like apples in a barrel, the ships rode the harbor tides, their barren masts skeletal against the lightening sky.

Bahir led them straight to a large ship close to the harbor entrance. A man came out on deck and he and Bahir exchanged greetings.

In a squalling mass the camels were brought to their knees, and the party dismounted.

The man Henry guessed as captain by his rich raiment and air of command crossed onto the dock and spoke quietly to Bahir. The conversation seemed to go on for a while, the captain gesticulating and Bahir shaking his head. Eventually, Bahir turned wearing a face like a smacked ass.

"Unload the camels," he yelled. "Put everything on the ship."

He went to Alya's litter and handed her out.

Above her niqaab, her gaze darted about, alive with curiosity.

Keeping his hand beneath her elbow, Bahir trotted her onto the boat and took her down below.

Newt sighed. "I do miss seeing a saucy smile on a pretty wench's face. How is a man to know what a girl looks like?"

"Alya is beautiful." The words escaped him.

Newt looked at him sharply and raised a questioning brow.

Henry turned and went to help unload the camels. He chose not to share his girl on the wall with anyone.

The captain oversaw the stowing of the cargo. As the sun rose and brought with it the heat of the morning, he and Newt worked side by side.

"You." For a big man, Bahir moved lightly on his feet.

Henry straightened from stowing a tightly wrapped bale.

Looking pained, Bahir gestured to him and Newt. "I would speak with you."

Just because it galled the big man, Henry took his time joining him near the empty litter.

"We have a problem." Bahir folded his arms. "The captain tells me we are at low tide and must wait for high until we sail."

"How long?" Henry didn't need him to spell it out for them. Whoever had attacked in the desert might be looking for such an opportunity. It must infuriate Bahir to approach them with this. It made Henry a lot more amenable to helping.

"An hour after noon." Bahir frowned up at the sky. "He insists that is the earliest we can leave."

No doubt, were it within Bahir's power to command the sea, he would have bent it to his will already.

"The escort will stay with us until then, but..." He glanced about him.

Alexandria's harbor had woken in a teeming cacophony of sound, people, and smells. Spotting a foe in this melee could prove impossible. A young beggar slid closer to them, wheedling for food.

Bahir sent him about his way.

"A fast camel will have reached Alexandria hours ahead of us." Henry spoke his thoughts aloud.

"And the captain is well known here." Bahir nodded. "It would not be hard to find us."

"We're sitting here like blind men." Henry wanted to punch something. Bahir's face tempted him.

"Well." Newt rubbed his hands together. "Allow Harry and I to shed some light."

"Harry?" Bahir frowned down on Newt.

Newt jerked his head toward Henry. "Henry, Harry to those who know him well."

"Or those I like." Infantile and strangely satisfying, especially when Bahir's shoulders tightened.

"Nobody is looking for us." Newt glanced between him and Bahir. "And harbors are great places if you have your ears wide open."

Bahir shifted, and his eyes narrowed. "You will gather information?"

"Aye." Like a dog with a bone, Newt perked up. "It would help if there was someplace around here where a man could wet his throat."

"You speak of intoxicating drink." Bahir curled his lip back.

"A man with a tankard in his hand is more inclined to share." Newt nudged Henry. "And I wager it's been a while since you got a little something down your gullet."

Bahir pursed his lips, glanced from Newt to Henry and then nodded. "I will ask the captain. This port is filled with all sorts from all parts of the world."

* * *

Henry pushed away his tankard of ale. Three years since his last drink, and this horse piss didn't come close to tempting him to lose his wits.

Of the three taverns Bahir had directed them to, Newt had chosen this one only after carefully considering the other two. What he looked for, Henry knew not, but Newt had slithered his way through the roughest parts of London and knew his way around the shadowed fringes of any city.

The tunic Newt had forced him into itched in a way that made him not want to enquire after the source. Although he had grown accustomed to the stink of it, the way people walked a wide path around him, assured him it remained.

"Eyes down, ears open." Newt had instructed him as they had made ready to enter Hektor's Harem. Hektor, a thick-armed brute, leaned his elbows on the bar and yelled at his weary-looking wenches. As far as Henry could see, Hektor scowled and the wenches worked.

Tallow smoke oozed along with the stench of greasy goat meat and the fumes from myriad pipes in an eye-searing layer above his head. The noise near deafened him. A babble of languages from every corner of the world and all of them near shouted at their companions.

Looking perfectly relaxed, Newt had his paw around his tankard as he yelled good-natured insults with some fur-shrouded trader from the east. Henry had never known there existed so many things that could be done to a man's mother. They'd now progressed onto each other's dubious bloodlines.

"Wench." Newt pounded the rickety table, and Henry grabbed his rocking tankard. "Bring my camel-tupping friend here a drink."

Off they went again, Newt and his new bosom companion.

So far, Henry's open ears hadn't caught much. Mostly whining around the new tariffs the harbormaster had put in place.

"...Genovese blood..."

Henry searched through the noise, trying to locate the source.

"...good money."

Newt clinked tankards, spilling beer all over him and his friend, but beneath the table his boot nudged Henry.

Aye, they'd both heard it. Beside the oil-skin covered casement two men huddled over a table.

He strained to hear over the other conversations.

"...called himself Alif Al-Rasheed but I recognized the sod right off...got me a nice fat purse..."

Newt pressed his toes.

"...bitch went missing."

A sudden lull in the conversation around him, and the next words reached him clear as a bell. "She has to be in Alexandria."

Newt lurched to his feet, and grabbed his crotch. "Need to piss."

"Jesu." Henry grabbed him by the tunic front. "You'll piss all over yourself. Come on."

"Harry." Giving him a toothy grin Newt patted his chest. "Wanna hold my rod for me? Maybe give it a stroke?"

Huge guffaws greeted him, along with a thump on the back from his drinking partner that sent Newt stumbling into him.

With a rough jerk, Henry yanked Newt toward the casement.

They drew closer to the men. With a masterful stumble, Newt crashed through a bench and landed nearly at their feet.

The tavern noise dimmed and then resumed.

"Hey!" Hector's bald head gleamed as he straightened. "You'll pay for that."

Henry motioned that he'd heard and handed some coins to the nearest wench. He doubted all the benches in this place together amounted to the money he gave her.

Using the table Newt swayed to his feet.

He spoke so quietly to the men at the table Henry almost missed it. "Word is you're looking for some information."

The men tensed. The bigger one went for a knife at his belt.

With that puckered scar dissecting his face, the bigger man looked to be a nasty sort. Henry slapped his hand on the long dagger at his waist and shook his head.

Sneering, the man kept his hand where it was. "Word is wrong."

"A pity." Newt pushed away from the table. "Because I have some to sell."

"Get away with you, you drunken sot." Not quite as broad, the man with his back to Henry shoved Newt away. "You have nothing I want to hear."

"Huh." Newt blinked at him. "Guess I must not have seen a caravan come in from Cairo this morning."

Henry dragged him into the street. "What, in God's name, are you doing?"

Newt winked at him. "A little bait and trap, my friend, a little bait and trap."

He straightened his tunic.

The street the tavern occupied was narrow and dark, twisting this way and that between the larger trading squares. It stank of stale beer and piss. Henry wanted out of here and back to the boat.

Newt set a brisk pace away from the tavern and turned into a darker, noisome alley.

"Hey!" A man shouted after them.

"Keep walking," Newt whispered.

"It's the men from the tavern."

"Of course, it is." Newt grinned. "Now keep walking and we'll pick the place of meeting."

They quickened their steps.

Behind them footsteps came faster.

Newt ducked into a darkened archway, and pulled Henry in after him.

They drew their knives.

Running footsteps grew louder, and then their pursuers passed their hiding place.

Newt slipped out first, grabbed the man closest to him and shoved his knife against the man's pulse. "Looking for someone?"

The scarred man from the tavern lunged, but Henry pressed the tip of his sword to his chest. "Do nothing stupid and your friend will be fine."

"What do you want?" Newt's man's gaze flicked between the dagger and Henry.

"Heard you were looking for someone." Newt pressed the tip into his skin.

Blood snaked down the man's neck.

"Heard that someone was a girl."

"I do not know what you are speaking of." Sweat glistened on his forehead.

"Really?" Newt said. His smile raised Henry's hackles. "That's not what I heard at all. Is it?"

Drawing the tip of his sword over Scar Man's tunic, Henry shook his head. The fabric melted beneath the blade, leaving a thin red line on his chest.

Scar Man paled. "Jesu, Aldo, tell them."

"Fine." Aldo licked his lips. "But only if you vow to let us go."

"Nah." Newt pressed the dagger deeper into Aldo's flesh. "I cannot do that until I hear what you have to say. If I find it useful, I might let you go." He sighed. "Unfortunately, my big friend has a nasty temper. It's going to take something special to appeal to his better nature."

Henry slashed another line, dissecting his first cut and making a cross.

"Aldo!" Scar Man screamed. "He will cut me to ribbons. I am bleeding."

"Harry." Newt clicked his tongue. "Must you always be so impetuous?"

"There's a rumor," Scar Man yelled. "Good money to be made from getting the Genovese out of Cairo."

"By out your friend means dead, does he not, Aldo?" Newt went a trifle deeper with his blade tip.

Sweat running in his eyes, Aldo blinked. "Aye."

"Did you make one of these Genovese dead?"

"Nay." Scar Man sobbed. "We did not touch them. By the time we got there, it was too late."

"Tell me about Alif Al-Rasheed."

"We didn't do it." The man's chest labored, blood pouring down it. "We swear to God we did not do it. Rumor says some berserker bastard got to him first."

"He is dead?"

"We do not know. This is only what we heard."

Henry cut the sod again, just because he was the sort of whoreson seeking to make coin from killing an innocent girl. His girl on the wall.

The man screamed and dropped to his knees. "I will tell you what you want. Anything. Just don't cut me again."

Anger surged through him. The master had been a good man, and Alya had loved her father dearly. "And now you are after the daughter?"

"Everyone is." Snot streamed from his nose as he bawled like a baby. "The price on her head is double."

Chapter Six

Leaving the two men in the alley, Henry and Newt hurried back to the boat. These would not be the only two looking to make some gold from Alya's blood.

Alert and watchful, two sentries stood guard at the gangplank. Around them the docks heaved with activity. Busier than when they had arrived earlier. A couple of passers glanced at the two sentries before hurrying on.

Arms crossed, watching the activity around them Bahir stood on the deck.

"We have news." Henry stepped onto the boat. "And none of it is good."

Bahir raised his brow.

"There is a price on Alya's head, and the hunters have found their way to Alexandria. We encountered two, but I am willing to wager there are more of them."

Nodding, Bahir said, "It was as we suspected. What other news?"

Henry hesitated. He could merely pass the news of Alif's possible death on to Bahir and have the man tell Alya. Everything within him, however, rebelled at the notion. It seemed cowardly and callous. "I need to speak to Alya."

Stiffening, Bahir shook his head. "That is not possible. Tell me what you need to tell her."

Any notion of giving the information to Bahir first disappeared at that. "This news is for her to hear first."

"It is not possible." Crossing his arms, Bahir planted his feet apart as if he would stand as a human barrier between Henry and Alya.

"What is it?" Alya slid from behind Bahir, her beautiful eyes intent on Henry.

"I must speak with you."

She gave a soft laugh. "You are speaking with me."

"Alone." Knowing he would cause it to end, her laughter shook him. Telling her of her father with the entire crew staring was also not something he was prepared to subject her to.

"No." Bahir stepped between them.

"Come if you must." Done with Bahir's ridiculous guarding of Alya's modesty, Henry shoved past him. "But she needs to know this."

Alya's glance flickered from him to Bahir and then Newt. "What is it?"

Henry motioned her to precede him below decks.

The air down here clung stuffy and damp to his skin, carrying the smell of tar, sweat, and the caskets of precious spices.

Immediately Bahir positioned himself beside Alya, huge fists clenched.

Dear God, give him patience. Did Bahir think he would fall on her in a lust frenzy? Not with the news he had to impart now. Instead he desired to hold her and stand as a barrier between her and the pain he was about to cause. As Henry knew of no other way over difficult ground but at a gallop, he spoke quickly. "It is your father."

"What of him?" She clenched her small hands together in front of her. "Tell me."

"We heard in the tavern that he could be...dead."

Alya stood, so still he could not be certain she breathed. Her eyes above her niqaab bored into him as if willing him to unsay his words. She shook her head. "Nay."

"Where did you hear this?" Bahir stepped up to him, and twisted a hand in his tunic.

"The two men we found." Henry fastened his hand about Bahir's wrist. He did not care for the manhandling, but Alya concerned him more. "They mentioned him by name."

"Dear God." Alya swayed.

Bahir leaped back and caught her beneath the elbow. "We cannot know for certain it is so," he said. "Men in taverns are drunk and they lie. These men are murderers and we cannot take their word as truth."

"That is true." Henry would agree with the devil himself if he could ease the torment from Alya's face. Chest tight, he stepped toward her. Her pain rippled through him as if it were his own. "But the news from Cairo is not good. There is a price on the head of all the Genovese merchants."

She blinked at him. "Why?"

"I know not." He held a hand out to her, then dropped it to his side. She was not his to touch. "People are angry. In their anger, they are not always mindful."

Her breath hitched on a soft sob. "My father?"

"I am so sorry, my lady." He wanted to say more. To tell her he understood the agony of losing those whom you loved. "If not already dead, your father has been targeted."

Standing between them, Bahir glowered at him.

Alya crumpled.

Bahir caught her and hoisted her into his arms. "I will deal with this."

Dismissed, Henry turned and stumbled up the ladder back into the daylight. Everything in him demanded he go back down and comfort her. Like a fresh gash through his chest throbbed the knowledge he had caused her pain.

Newt came up beside him. "Did you tell her?"

"Aye." Reason shouted down his burning desire to be the one with her now. It was not his place. "Bahir is with her."

"This is a bad business." Newt shook his head. "And here we sit with a target on our foreheads."

Not as long as he had breath. Henry strode to the railing. While his girl on the wall wept below decks, he could and would make sure nobody got near her.

* * *

Alya sobbed but no tears fells. Tears might be a relief from the tearing agony within her.

Bahir continued to whisper that it might not be true. He would send a man to Cairo to find out for sure. Allowing herself a brief flicker of hope, she nodded her agreement at his suggestion.

"But we must sail with the tide." Bahir assisted her out of her hijab and niqaab.

The damp cloth clung to her wet face and nose, and made it impossible to breathe. Alya flung it away from her. "Then how will I know?"

"I will instruct him to follow us to Genoa." Bahir picked up her hijab and smoothed it over a crate. "But it may be a while before he reaches us."

In the meantime, her loss seeped, raw and angry within her. Her father. The man she loved above all others. Devoted, funny, loving, indulgent some had said, but her father.

And she had not allowed him to embrace her in parting. She had turned her back on him and climbed into her litter.

Another sob rattled through her. The pain grew so intense, Alya folded her arms about her middle and hunched over. It felt as if her heart would burst from her and tear her asunder.

Dear God. She should have turned and told him how much she loved him. Now she might never have the chance to do so again.

A long, low wail escaped her.

Bahir drew her to him, folding her in his arms.

Clinging to him with all she had Alya dug her nails into his tunic. She pressed her face into his chest and cried.

* * *

Despite Bahir's protests, Alya spent most of her time on deck. Every morning she would wash as best she could with the water Bahir brought her, dress and go above deck. Huddling in the dark only made her more aware of the gaping hole inside her. She clung to the hope that Bahir's man would deliver the news her father lived.

She kept her niqaab in place but the temptation to throw it off and feel the cool sea breeze against her cheeks grew. The voyage forced her out of her worry for precious moments. The sea never looked the same any two days in a row. Going about their tasks with quiet competence the sailors fascinated her. Coiling ropes, furling and unfurling the great, billowing sails, scrubbing down the deck. When not working, they sat in small groups, laughing and talking, some of them occupied with hand work, others playing games of dice and stones.

Then there was Henry.

Her gaze found him wherever he stood on the boat. The sun darkened his face making his eyes appear otherworldly. Fine stubble covered his head now that he no longer shaved it. It caught the bright sunlight and glinted. Eyes of lapis and hair of gold, like the prized concubines in the sultan's harem. She giggled a little at her own thoughts.

Her isolation wore on her. Glowering should anyone approach, Bahir stood always beside her. At home, she would have spoken with Nasira or one of the other maids, joined her friends at their homes for sherbet and gossip. Not that she had that many friends. She had always blamed Father for being over-protective, but now, perhaps, he'd had other reasons for keeping her separated. That he had been so hated because of his birthplace, she could not fathom. Her father was a good man, a kind one.

Stripped to a vest, muscle playing along his arms and shoulders Henry coiled a rope at the front of the boat. Beside him, perched on a barrel and eating dried fruit sat Newt. She had asked Bahir what a newt was. A kind of lizard. What manner of man took his name from such a creature? As much as she would like to ask, she felt tongue tied around the Englishmen. They spoke often in their language, shutting her out of their world.

* * *

Henry felt her gaze on him. She watched him often, striking eyes above the black of her niqaab. Those eyes held shadows and he wanted to speak with her, enquire how she went on. Always, Bahir guarded her like a jealous dog.

Newt filled the long, warm days with news of home. It no longer felt like a part of him. He had left Anglesea as one man, and he no longer knew who returned to them. William had married a lady called Alice, and they lived in the north with their children. He tried to picture his middle brother as a father, bearing the responsibility of a demesne. A glib tongued diplomat who eased his way through life with charm, William had been the carefree brother.

That Roger had married came as no surprise. Although Newt's description of the fiery Kathryn whom Roger had wed had Henry shaking his head. Roger had married a woman who would rather be a knight than a chatelaine. He had pictured Roger with a serene, calm woman. Someone who could smooth the rough edges off his oldest brother. It seemed Roger had changed in the years since Henry had left with his gut afire with visions of bringing the light of God to the dark heathens. What a naive boy he had been.

"Your father has stepped down from Anglesea in all but name." Newt spat a date pit into the water.

Some things you could not change, and as much as he itched to cuff Newt for spitting, he did his best to ignore it instead. So far and no further Newt changed. The news from home Henry could not have predicted. That the father he had last seen as a strong, vital man, full of piss and vinegar had released control of his beloved Anglesea Henry could not fathom.

"Seems your mother wants to spend time visiting her grandchildren." Newt chewed and spat his pip. "He'd thump anyone who suggested it, but I think your father was ready to hand over the weight of Anglesea."

Perhaps. Father had been fighting one war or another since he was little more than a boy.

"Garrett functions as Roger's right hand," Newt said.

"Garrett." Henry stopped and let that sink in. "Beatrice's Garrett?"

"Aye." Newt shook his head. "Could have knocked me over with a feather when I saw it. They get on, those two."

"Huh." Last he'd seen, Roger and Garrett were at each other's throats. "And they sent you to find me?"

Attention on Alya, Newt nodded. "Imagine telling Beatrice she had to wear that lot?"

Henry smiled. His sister Beatrice had a sweet but determined will all her own.

"Harry?" Newt frowned, and pursed his lips. Sure signs the man had something niggling in his mind. "Did I hear they are taking her to Genoa, to her father's kin?"

"Aye." Alya caught him staring and dropped her eyes. "They are all she has in the world."

"That could be a problem." Newt hopped off his barrel.

Henry took his meaning. "Aye."

If her father's family rejected her, Alya would be cast adrift with only Bahir. Not if he had anything to do with it. Henry dropped the rope and strode across the deck.

As he drew near, Bahir stiffened.

"Her father wanted me to teach her how to go on in Genoa," Henry said.

Alya's head came up. She glanced at Bahir and back at him.

Henry held Bahir's glare. "She needs to learn."

Finally, Bahir uncrossed his arms and nodded. "You will teach her."

"Teach me what?" Alya's voice had a slight husk, deeper than most women's, and rich, with a rasp that brought to mind good mead.

He crouched in front of her. "Things are different in Genoa. Different to the way you were raised."

She tilted her head and studied him.

"Your hijab and niqaab." He pointed. "They will find it strange. Women do not go about covered in Genoa."

Her eyes narrowed. "I am aware."

He waited, giving her time to reach the inevitable conclusion.

First she removed her niqaab. Slowly, she unwound the hijab from her head, then lowered it to the deck.

She bore the skin of her father's people, a shade or two darker than his sisters' but still pale as thick poured cream. Above a full mouth, her straight nose turned up slightly at the end. Ringed by thick, dark lashes, her eyes tilted up at the corners. Whatever they made of her in Genoa it would not be because she lacked beauty.

Under his scrutiny, she went pink, ducking her head to hide her face from him.

He lifted her head.

Bahir stiffened and stepped nearer.

"You have no need to hide your face," Henry said. "You are beautiful."

"English." Bahir's deep rumble warned him away.

Henry dropped his hand, and not because Bahir bristled beside him, but more to conceal his reaction to her beauty. "We will need to buy you some other clothes when we reach Genoa."

Alya nodded. "What else?"

Where to start? His mother, the perfect lady in all matters, had corrected, cajoled and, on occasion, nagged his sisters into proper decorum. When he said nagged, he meant Beatrice, because a simple correction had always been sufficient for Faye.

"The way you are sitting." He indicated her cross-legged position. "Ladies always keep their...um, knees and ankles together."

"Why?" Alya frowned down at her legs.

"Skirts." Inspiration struck him in a dizzying wave of relief. "Skirts confine your movement and you will find you cannot keep your...um, knees parted."

A low growl emanated from Bahir. If he believed the man capable of amusement, Henry might have called it laughter.

Shifting, Alya sat on her hip. Knees tightly pressed together, ankles stacked. "Like this?"

"Not exactly." What had possessed him to give his vow to Alif? "Ladies, in general, do not sit on the floor."

He read the question building, and dragged a crate to her. "They sit on benches and furnishings."

Now Bahir frowned and stepped forward. "No cushions?"

How long would this voyage take? "Let us start at the beginning."

Newt slunk closer, leaned against the mast, and smirked. A little help from that quarter might not go amiss, but Newt looked to be enjoying Henry flounder too much.

"Where we live—"

"Angle land?" Bahir said.

"Well, aye, but nobody has called it that for years, hundreds of years. Now we say England."

"England." Alya rolled the word slowly over her tongue.

The Good Lord knew how she did it, but somehow, she made it sound seductive.

"England is colder," Henry said. "We built our castles... homes...first of wood, and then we replaced it with stone because of the winter. They are more like your palaces."

Bahir snorted. "Stone is cold."

"Aye." Henry shivered at the memory of his breath icing on

the air through midwinter. "But it also keeps the worst of the chill out. And it's safer against attack. Easier to defend.

Narrowing his eyes, Bahir appeared to think that over. Then he nodded. "Better against fire."

"Exactly." Henry saw his first glimmer of hope. "Anyway, as Bahir pointed out, stone is cold, so we do not sit on the floor." Now came the part that made him cringe after all these years in Egypt. "Also, the floor is covered in rushes and dirty."

Sucking in a soft breath, Alya wrinkled her nose. "Dirty?"

"From things people drop." Henry waved an airy hand, not wanting to delve too deeply into that. "Animals."

"You allow animals in your homes?" Bahir's chest swelled. "To live where you eat?"

Alya looked a little sickened, but she said, "I am sure you bathe them before you allow them within."

Newt threw back his head and guffawed loud enough that a gull startled from the mast.

Mother and Nurse had always insisted on bathing within Anglesea, but some did not see the value in it. Indeed, most believed it to invite illness into the body. In Egypt, even the slaves bathed daily. Perhaps the Genovese had a different custom. He hoped for Alya's sake that they did. "We do not bathe the animals."

Her face fell.

"But the bigger ones, are not allowed within the keep. The horses, the cows, and the sheep all live outside in barns and pens. Mainly we keep the dogs within the keep."

"Dogs?" Bahir spat. "You allow filthy creatures who eat their own waste in your homes?"

"They do not eat their own waste," Newt said. "But they do eat the waste of everything else."

Alya pressed her hand to her mouth as if she might be ill. "I do not think I will like England."

"Which is fine." Henry put some cheer into his voice.

"Because you will be living in Genoa, and I am sure it is very, very different."

Newt straightened from his slouch. "Actually—"

"Very different." Henry glared his point home and held out his hand to Alya. "Now, if you will stand."

Bahir growled.

"It is custom for a man to assist a woman to stand." Henry kept his hand outstretched. "Skirts hamper the women's movement."

She stared at his hand. "Then why do they wear them?"

"Modesty," Henry said. "Just as you wear your hijab for modesty, so they wear skirts."

Nodding, Alya took his hand.

She gasped, glanced at their joined hands and then up at him.

Henry felt the jolt down to his toes. Her small, soft palm fit his as if crafted just for him. Henry resisted the strong urge to curl his fingers about hers and hold on. Their gazes locked and Henry lost himself in the sweet heat in her eyes.

Bahir cleared his throat.

With a blush, Alya dropped his hand and plopped onto the crate.

"Knees." His voice rasped and he cleared his throat. "Keep your knees and ankles together. Also, when you have skirts you will sweep them to one side to make room on the bench."

She shifted, looking up at him, a silent question on her face.

"Exactly." His smile, rusty from disuse, creaked across his face. "Now, back straight, chin up, shoulders back."

With a slight toss of her head, she complied. She peered at him from between her thick, dark lashes, a glint of mischief in her eyes.

And Henry laughed.

Chapter Seven

L essons with Henry enlivened her days and helped push back the heavy press of her father's fate. He taught her many things, most of them strange, but he did not seem to mind her questions. Or even her laughter when she found something absurd.

When Henry laughed, which he did not do often, the skin around his eyes crinkled and deep grooves formed on either side of his mouth. When he laughed, his eyes lit from within like the heart of a sapphire held up to the sun.

He spoke little of his family. From what she had gathered, he had two sisters, Faye being the older and Beatrice the younger. Both sisters were married and had borne children. He also had two brothers near his age; Roger and William, and a much younger brother named Mathew. When he spoke of his mother, his harsh expression gentled in a way that made her sad for the mother she had never known.

Bahir relented enough to walk about the boat during their lessons, but his gaze returned always to them. Some days Newt joined their lessons, and he and Henry spoke only in French for her. When they spoke to each other, they reverted to their mother tongue. It fell strange and harsh on her ear, as they clipped the words at a rapid rate. She dearly wanted to know of what they spoke. Especially when Henry would get that distant, cold look on his face, as if he held more secrets and regrets than one man could contain.

She wanted to smooth the frown from his brow, soothe away the sorrow and make him smile again.

Newt, she liked. He made her laugh by teaching her silly words in English. Henry glowered at him when he did, and said something in English, which Newt ignored. She had the feeling Newt did what Newt wanted most of the time anyway.

As they entered the port of Genoa she stood at the railing between Henry and Newt. To their right, and surely high enough to touch heaven, a huge stone tower guarded the harbor mouth.

The harbor was busy, and they stayed out of the sailor's way. As they navigated the narrow strip of sea into the calmer waters of the harbor the captain bellowed a stream of instructions at his men. Closer to the dock sailors broke out oars and brought them in.

Alya tried to take it all in, and failed. Buildings of undressed stone crowded the waterfront, square and narrow with mean windows cut into their facade. Instead of minarets, great crosses stretched into the achingly blue sky. Mountains surrounded the city and crowded it toward the sea.

Even busier than Alexandria, a mind-bending array of people hurried back and forth along the cobbled streets in front of the ships. So many ships, their bare masts spiking up and down as they bobbed at anchor.

Some ships looked like theirs, whilst others could have been magical vessels to carry their cargos to the far end of the world. Plain hulls rode the tide alongside lavishly ornamented figureheads.

Gazes trained on the bustle all about them Bahir and Henry murmured to each other. They spoke of her, and she wished they would say what they needed to aloud.

As he surveyed the port Newt's eyes sparkled.

A woman in skirts such as Henry had described to her sauntered closer to the boat. Boldly she eyed the men aboard and called something out to Newt. Then she tugged down her tunic and showed her dark-tipped, heavy breasts.

Alya froze. Her face flamed. Never could she have imagined such a thing.

Bahir immediately sprung toward her and turned her about. "You should not look."

"Bahir." Alya desperately wanted to have another look at the woman. "Did you see what she did?"

"I imagine the entire harbor saw that," Bahir said.

"Is she selling her body?" She tried to turn.

He blocked her. "You should not know anything of such women."

Bahir could be such a dried up old lemon at times. "I know about concubines, and you were the one who told me, so why should I not know about her."

Newt leaned his hips against the railing and laughed. "She has a point, big man."

"You." Bahir jabbed his finger at Newt. "Should keep your mouth buttoned."

"Or what?" Shoulders taut, jaw locked, Henry straightened.

Bahir stiffened. "Do you fancy your chances now, slave?"

"It does not matter." Alya put herself between them. Henry and Bahir hissed at each other like cats on a rooftop nearly all the time. "How should we proceed?"

Now they had arrived, nerves fluttered in her belly. The family of whom her father had spoken lived in this city. Somewhere in the mass of honey-stoned buildings lay her future.

"We will need to see you properly attired." Henry held himself stiff, and his face had grown remote and cold. "We will need to visit the market and find you something."

"Henry and I will go." Bahir put his hand on her shoulder. "Newt will remain here with you. Henry assures me he will be able to protect you."

Of that Alya had no doubt. Despite the relaxed way Newt lounged about the boat, and his ready jokes and smiles, he had the air of a fighting man. More than that, his eyes held a cunning she would not want to cross.

"Keep her safe." Henry nodded at Newt. "Do what you have to."

Newt nodded.

"You should stay below deck." Henry turned to her. "We do not know if the danger has followed us here, but it is better to be safe."

Alya did not relish a day spent in the stuffy, smelly confines of the ship's belly, but she nodded her agreement. She would spend the time preparing for her meeting with her father's family. Her family now. She needed to think of them as her family too. Soon she would be one of them.

* * *

Henry almost pitied Bahir his dilemma. The stupid cur did not want to leave Alya alone with Newt, but neither would he trust Henry with the coin to purchase the necessary items.

From Genoa, the boat would take him and Newt to England. Bahir might be a miserable sod, but he kept his word, and the instructions had already been passed on to the captain.

When they sailed, he would say goodbye to his last connection with Egypt, his girl on the wall. She would never know how she had provided a brief glimmer of hope in his pitiful existence. He would never forget her. Not her cat eyes or her midnight hair. The dark honey of her skin would haunt him for a long time. That he had never gotten to touch it and see if it was as warm and velvet as it looked would be a regret he took home.

He followed Bahir onto the busy dock.

A passing sailor stared at Bahir, spat and made a wide circle around him. Here Bahir was the oddity, the stranger. The tide had turned.

Henry stopped a woman carrying heavy baskets of fruit and asked her for directions to the nearest cloth market. She kept her wide eyes on Bahir as she gave him directions. It seems even in Genoa, famed for being the center of trade from far and wide, Bahir's dark skin marked him as other and suspicious.

"I should lead." It gave Henry no pleasure to make the suggestion. The way people whispered and stared at Bahir made him feel an unwelcome empathy for the man. Bahir dropped a few steps behind him as they wove their way through the narrow, cobbled lanes leading up from the harbor.

The lane they followed wound around a church and opened through a pair of arches into a bustling market. The dull murmur had been growing as they walked, and now burst over them in a roar of voices. Color abounded from every direction. Bright cobalts and scarlets, yellows that shone brighter than the midday sun, cloth shot with gold and silver that glinted and sparkled jostled for notice with subtler jewel tones, burnt oranges and pristine whites.

As they slipped through the narrow gaps between vendors Henry marked four different languages being spoken. The common tongue here was trade, and it was spoken over the jangle of coins and the exchange of markers. In the far-right corner of the market Henry found the merchants he sought. Weavers and tailors had suspended their wares on ropes beneath the soaring arches. Quieter commerce took place here as wealthy residents strolled between the merchants. Women for the most part, faithfully dogged by a household guard or a male family member.

He stopped to admire a bliaut of peacock green shot with gold. Delicate beads glistened along the bodice. He could picture Beatrice in a gown like that. The more sedate but lovely rose pink three bliauts across spoke to him of Faye. He would see his sisters again. It hit him in a dizzying wave. He would live to see his sisters wear these gowns. He attracted the attention of the merchant. At Anglesea seamstresses made all the gowns for the castle womenfolk. How they would stare at the notion of buying a gown from a market.

"Not those." Bahir nudged him and pointed to a garnet red bliaut at the merchant beside them. "She would look better in that one."

The merchant held both bliauts before Henry. Short and swarthy, he wore a flat cap over his head, the tassels danced around his ears with each move he made. "Excellent taste, sire." He spoke in French. "From the hands of nuns these come."

Bahir nudged him harder. "I said the red."

Henry inspected the bead work on the green gown. The beads formed delicate flowers joined together by finely stitched gold thread. "How much?"

Bahir growled.

Honestly, if Bahir would use words instead of the nudging and growling like a bad-tempered bear, Henry might feel inclined to explain. Since Bahir did not bother with civilities, Henry saw no reason to. Mother would give him one of her gentle lectures about the behavior of others having no bearing on his own. So long since he had admitted a thought of his beautiful mother into his mind, it twisted now in a sweet-sharp pain.

The merchant named the ridiculous sum of fifty marks.

Henry laughed. He waved the gown away and bent to examine the pink.

"For years, the nuns labored." The merchant held the gown out for him again. "I could accept no less than forty."

Henry turned to Bahir. "Show me this red gown you love so much."

"Thirty." The merchant leaped into their path again.

"Thirty?" Henry glanced at Bahir and folded his arm. "Thirty for this and the pink one."

The merchant gaped. "Sire! Now you would rob my family of food. And my youngest laid down with a hacking cough."

Rubbing his hands together as they moved his way the second merchant rose from where he sat. Tall and slim, his skin a shade lighter than Bahir, he bowed. "I bring you silks from Damascus. Woven by the hands of the Sultan's concubines."

Bahir snorted and pinned the man with a stare.

The second merchant took a hasty step back. "Not the concubines themselves, you understand." He gave a toothy grin. "But their serving maids."

Henry hated to admit it, but Bahir's bear behavior made a useful cohort as they worked. While Bahir grunted, glowered and growled, Henry haggled. Together they came away with the green and pink gowns, the red one, and two others for Alya in blue and amber. Bahir had excellent taste as well. They moved on and acquired three silk chemises so fine they could see the light through them.

Alya's slippers would be fine beneath them, and they wove their way back through the market.

Grabbing Henry's arm Bahir hauled him to a stop.

Henry clenched his fists, his laden arms the only thing stopping him from plowing his fist into Bahir's face.

"There." Bahir jerked his head at a tailor who sold men's tunics and chausses. "For you."

"For me?"

Shifting his packages, Bahir cleared his throat. "I have been thinking."

"Blessed day!"

With a frown, Bahir cleared his throat. "I cannot present Alya to her family. You must."

Bahir's jaw clenched so tight, Henry feared for the man's teeth. From what they had seen this morning, Bahir might be greeted with the same hostility they saw all about them. Henry glanced down at his raiment. Serviceable, but the dress of a servant. He chose a plain pair of leather chausses and a sedate black tunic. Bahir added a rich surcoat and they left the market.

In silence, they walked back to their ship. What would Alya's family make of their foreign cousin? Henry's vow to see her safe weighed heavily on him.

* * *

It required a sketch from Henry before Alya could dress in her new clothes. Bahir proved adept at the lacing. Eager to show Henry her new finery she took a step.

The skirts tangled in her feet and Bahir caught her before she went tumbling.

"I believe you must hold them up." Bahir held his hands before him, thumb and forefinger pinched together, little finger raised.

"Like so?" She pinched the skirts between her fingers. Her ankles and legs showed beneath the hem.

"I think not." Bahir frowned as he stared at her exposed limbs. "From what the slave said of modesty, I do not believe you should show your ankles."

"Henry." She grew tired of the constant sniping. "His name is Henry and he is no longer a slave."

Bahir gave her an assessing look and then nodded. "As you wish."

"What I wish—" Alya took a halting step forward "—is to be able to walk."

"I shall fetch the sla—Henry." Bahir disappeared up the ladder to the deck.

A large amount of her chest spilled over the bodice of the dress, and it clung to her breasts and stomach in a way that made her feel naked. Strange that a woman could show her top assets, but beneath her skirts needed to remain a mystery.

Heavy footsteps sounded above and then clattered down the ladder.

Henry entered, caught sight of her and stopped. His gaze swept her from head to toe and back again. The glint in his eyes bolstered her confidence.

Holding her arms wide she swiveled for him, preening a little. "What think you?"

Henry cleared his throat and shoved his fists onto his belt. "I think Bahir was right about the red. It looks well on you."

Well on her? He could do better than that. She straightened her spine and pushed her shoulders back.

Henry's gaze went straight to her breasts.

She liked that. His gaze tingled across her exposed skin like a touch.

"Alya requires your help." Bahir stepped between them, his back to Henry. He glanced at her bodice and then raised his brow.

Alya refused to be admonished. Bahir insisted she dress thus, and he had no say in how much of her it left bare.

"I cannot walk." She peered around Bahir. "I feel there must be a way to do it without looking silly."

Henry smiled. He did it so rarely she could count on one hand the amount of times she had witnessed his smile. Every time it weakened her knees and brought a flush to her skin.

"The skirts are too long," Henry said and stepped around Bahir. "Normally you would get someone to raise them so they did not tangle in your feet." Warm and calloused, his hand clasped hers. Tingles shot up her arm. His voice grew rougher as he placed her hand on her skirts. "My sister's will hold their skirts until they skim their slippers."

His chest pressed against her shoulder, and some devil within her whispered to keep him close. She gripped the skirt three inches above where he showed her.

Clasping her hand, he moved it. His breath a whisper against her cheek. "Here."

"Here?" His face hovered so close, eyes containing heat that shot right through her and made her shiver.

He dropped his gaze to their clasped hands. His lashes feathered dark against the strong lines of his cheek. "Right there."

"I believe we have this now." Bahir cut through the moment.

Henry stepped back, his face hard now. He gave her a curt nod and strode back above decks.

"Alya." Bahir's deep voice rumbled over her. "Do you know what danger you court?"

Chapter Eight

Henry needed some air. When Alya was near him the air felt too thick to breathe. His entire infatuation with her careened into ridiculous. Soon they would track down her family and he would leave for home. Then she would be a distant, jasmine-scented memory.

"Everything good?" Newt leaned his back on the railing beside him.

"Aye." Henry kept his gaze on the port. Newt saw too much most of the time, and he'd already caught Newt's sharp gaze assessing the situation. "She looks well."

"Well?" Draping an arm about his shoulders, Newt chuckled. "Harry, Harry, Harry. A girl like the lovely Alya always looks more than well. Beautiful. Sensuous. A lovely exotic bloom. As you well know."

Irked by Newt's description of Alya, Henry shrugged his arm off. The idea of Newt lusting after Alya galled him more than it should.

"Indeed." Newt stretched his arms wide. "If you have no further use for me, I intend to make a trip along the waterfront. Make some new friends."

Henry did not bother to hide his distaste. "You will catch something nasty tupping whores on the dock."

"I do not tup." Newt looked affronted. "I take a woman to new levels of pleasure."

"They only say that because you pay them." Henry lost his battle not to smile. The man he used to be had spent months trying to bend Newt's moral character back into shape. Unsuccessfully. Now, Newt amused him.

"How about you, big man?" Newt called out to Bahir, who had stepped onto the deck. "Fancy a little carnal adventure? Want to get your leg over?"

"Um, Newt." Henry nearly laughed aloud.

Bahir merely folded his arms. "I think not."

"Nay." Newt grimaced. "I suppose you are like Harry over here, too good for the fine ladies who walk these docks."

"Newt." Henry should have tried harder to stop Newt, but he derived a certain evil enjoyment from the situation. "Bahir does not enjoy the pleasures of the flesh."

Newt gave Bahir a sharp look. "Why?"

Henry pitched his voice low. "Bahir is a eunuch."

"A what?" Frowning, Newt stared at Bahir.

"A eunuch." Bahir closed the distance and loomed over Newt. "They cut off my balls."

"Dear God." Newt paled and caught the deck rail for support. "Nay. Who? Why?"

"Due to my size I was deemed suitable to guard the harem," Bahir said.

Having never seen such an occurrence, Henry could not be certain, but he thought Bahir might have actually been approaching a smile.

With both hands, Newt cupped his crotch, and grimaced. "That is monstrous."

"I can assure you it was not by choice." Bahir leaned beside them against the railing. "Go and enjoy your whores, young Newt."

Newt stepped closer to Bahir and lowered his voice. "You mean you have never..." He waggled his eyebrows.

"I have never." Bahir waggled his eyebrows. "But let me tell you a secret. The loss of balls does not entirely remove the desire, and there are many ways to pleasure a bored and lonely concubine."

"What?" Newt reared back. "You mean the non-roosters found a way to raid the henhouse?"

"Indeed." Bahir actually smiled.

Henry knew he stared but couldn't stop. When he smiled Bahir almost appeared human.

"Bahir." Newt clapped Bahir on the shoulder. "I shall mount an extra whore on your behalf."

"I am much obliged, Newt."

As Newt trotted down the gangplank Henry stood shoulder-to-shoulder with Bahir.

"He amuses me," Bahir said.

"He has a certain charm." Henry still found it hard to believe that he and Newt had drifted into a friendship. "He will also discover where Alya's family are to be found."

"Ah." Bahir nodded.

Henry was not sure why he asked, but he wanted to know. "What will you do when she is safely amongst them?"

"I will stay in Genoa for a while." Bahir kept his gaze on the busy dock. "I vowed to make sure she is safe, and I will not leave before I am certain. And then..." Bahir shrugged. "I have been a slave since I was barely a man. For the first time in my life, I will go where it suits me to go."

After Bahir strolled away, it occurred to Henry that their conversation had been civil.

* * *

Alya placed her hand upon Henry's arm. Hewn muscle flexed beneath her fingers as he led her through the port. He and Bahir had come up with the idea that she may as well practice being amongst her father's kind while they waited for Newt to return.

Tired of being stuck below decks, she readily agreed.

"Raise your chin," Henry murmured.

All very well for him to say. He did not walk with yards of fabric tangled in his feet. "I will fall if I do not watch my skirts."

"Then I will catch you." Henry touched her hand. "You are a lady born and will be expected to carry yourself as such."

Behind them, Bahir lurked like a large moving pillar.

Without her veil, she felt ridiculously exposed. Men looked at her, unabashed in showing their appreciation. Some even went so far as to smile and wink. A permanent flush heated her cheeks, but at the same time she enjoyed it.

"Some girls are told to keep their eyes downcast," Henry said. "It is believed to be modest, but my mother never held with that."

"What is she like, your mother?" Alya wanted to know more about Henry. He seemed to hold so many secrets.

"Beautiful." His voice warmed and he gazed at something only he could see. "Gracious and serene, but with a backbone of steel. My sister, Faye is much like her."

"Faye." Alya tried the strange name out.

Two young girls, dressed much as she was, walked toward them. One of them looked at Henry and whispered to her friend. They both blushed and giggled, peeking at him from beneath lowered lashes.

Alya wanted to bang their heads together. Henry escorted her and not them.

Henry did not appear to notice, but looked about them constantly, alert for any danger.

Henry and Bahir had talked about the danger before undertaking this outing. They spoke with the crew to establish if there had been any whispers to suggest the men from Alexandria had followed. Thus far nothing. Their ship was one in amongst many others moored in the port.

Tall stone buildings rose on either side of the narrow streets, almost blocking out the clear, blue sky. The heat in Genoa lay over her in a humid blanket. It felt thicker than the dry desert air of Cairo. The smells, too, reminded her how far from home she had traveled. Genoa smelled of horse, leather, and human waste. Occasionally the delicate floral scents from the brightly colored window boxes would provide a reprieve, but otherwise the city stank.

Like tangled thread, the streets wound up from the port and into the hills beyond. Up there, grand stone edifices peered down their noses at the braying, brawling city below them.

The greenery amazed her. Growing over walls, trailing down from window boxes, choking up small gardens and squares. The tall, spindle-like trees Henry called Cypress trees abounded, wafting their woodsy-herbal scent throughout the city as Henry led her up toward the elegant villas.

The streets grew quieter the higher they went. The flood of people slowed to a trickle of elegantly dressed men and women strolling in clusters of two or three. Liveried, another new word, servants bowed their heads in passing and carried on about their business. Henry told her they wore the colors of their masters.

In his new tunic, Henry looked very fine this morning. Fine, but different and as much as she admired his broad shoulders and trim waist, his new clothes marked him as separate from her. Not the man who used to stare up at her in the courtyard at twilight. She did not think he knew she had seen him there in the shadows, always watching her with stark hunger on his face. A sharp pang shot through her middle. She missed that man and their secret connection. Now he spoke a different tongue, dressed as another, and even carried himself like another man.

"In your tongue, how would I greet you?"

He smiled at her, his golden hair framing his head. "You would say, 'good morrow' if it was morning. Or you could say 'good day'. If we were particular friends, you could say 'hello.'"

Her breath caught when he smiled at her. Like a stray beam of sunlight wandered into her day. "Are we particular friends?"

He laughed. "Hello, Lady Alya."

Shyness beset her but she tried anyway. "Hello, Henry."

"Perfect." He tightened his grip about her fingers. Bahir did not like that Henry touched her to lead her through the city, but this was how they did it here. Even Bahir must see she was not the only lady walking about with her hand resting atop her escort's.

She looked over her shoulder at Bahir. "Hello, Bahir."

Bahir tried to frown, but ended up grinning instead. "Hello, Alya."

"Lady Alya," Henry said. "Only her family or her husband may address her simply as Alya."

Bahir tensed and glared at Henry.

Henry sneered back.

These two would come to blows any moment and today they irked her. She did not want their constant enmity to ruin her day. "Bahir is my family," she said. "So, he may call me Alya. He is all that I have."

Clearing his throat, Bahir stared above her head. "We should walk."

"How do you say that in English?" She turned back to Henry.

English turned out to be a funny language, full of new sounds and ways to contort her mouth. For the first time since leaving Cairo, Alya felt light and happy. The weight of her father and her journey lifted long enough for the girl she used to be to come out and play.

Bells pealed the hour as noon, and the heat drove them back to their boat. Voices rising and falling in prayer, a solemn procession of monks crossed their path. Alya stood beside Henry and waited for the men to pass. Sunlight bounced off the gleaming pates of their tonsures, the heavy incense smell lingered in their path. She had followed her father's faith since birth, but this was the first time Alya had heard the mass sung. She wanted to follow the monks to the tall, forbidding church at the end of the square, but Bahir shifted beside her. Soon, she would not have to conceal her faith from those about her.

The activity on the docks receded as the devout went to prayer. Their ship bobbed at anchor in its place amongst all the other tall masts.

Newt lounged on the deck looking rumpled and smug. As they climbed aboard he rose. "Did you have a good walk?"

"We did." Alya answered before Henry or Bahir. Her head buzzed with all the things she had seen. Later, when the heat of the day drove her to rest, she would unpack all the sights in her head and examine them.

Henry approached Newt, his shoulders tense. "Did you find what we were looking for?"

"Aye." Newt straightened his tunic. "Alya's family has a villa in the city. They are at home."

Chapter Nine

Today Henry would lose his girl on the wall. Below deck, Bahir took her morning bathing water and saw her dressed as he and Newt waited to escort her. The dull blade in his chest twisted again, widening the aching cavern. In his years in Cairo, she had stood as his beacon of hope. A beautiful star in his dark firmament. Those twilight moments a bitter-sweet reminder that he yet lived.

He would return her to her family and safety so that after today she would no longer stand alone in a hostile world. The rightness of it did not alleviate his ache over losing her.

Newt strode toward him, a bundle of dark cloth tucked beneath his arm. He surveyed Henry from boot to crown, and nodded. "You look more like the Sir Henry who used to box my ears."

"They were an easy target." Henry couldn't stop his grin. When Newt had come to him as a lad on the cusp of manhood, those ears had stood out and begged to be cuffed.

Newt chuckled and held his parcel out to Henry. "I found this the day you were taken. It got trampled beneath hooves, but I had it repaired. It is time for you to don it again."

Henry took the surcoat from him. It shook in his hands and

he held it open before him. Dragon head proper upon argent. The colors of Sir Arthur of Anglesea. His colors. The ones he had worn so proudly on his chest as he rode to join the pilgrimage. Colors he had seen so stained with blood and corruption they made him feel sullied. He shoved them at Newt's chest. "I will not wear this."

Newt squared off. "It is time, Sir Henry." He labored the "sir" and pushed the surcoat back.

How to explain that it would never be time to wear these? That man had died long before he'd been pulled from his horse in battle. The Henry who wore these colors had ridden out, despite his family's vehement protests, so sure he understood the rights and wrongs of the world. Wrapped in more than a silk surcoat. Enshrouded in his sense of righteousness and holy fire. One by one his dreams of glory had drowned in a wave of vice and cruelty. The man he had become blazoned no colors, held no faith, and had no right to those things anymore. He shoved the surcoat into Newt's chest. "Nay."

"Aye." Newt pushed him back a step. "This is who you are. Son of Sir Arthur of Anglesea, knight of the realm, and the man who taught me how to hold my head up."

"Sir Henry?" Alya took his breath away in the red silk. Her sooty hair lay in a gleaming sable cascade down her back.

Newt punched his shoulder. "A lady such as that, deserves a knight by her side."

Henry donned the surcoat. It had grown snug across the chest and shoulders. Bloody thing near strangled him, and he tugged at the neckline.

Alya touched the dragon's head. "What is this you wear?"

"They are my father's colors." Her fingers burned through the layers over his chest.

Stepping back, she tilted her head and studied him. "You look very fine, Henry."

"Sir Henry." Bahir came to stand behind her. "You must call him Sir Henry now."

"Sir Henry." Her full mouth formed the words like a caress.

"My lady." He bowed over her hand. Stupid sod that he was, but the action came naturally to him. One he had performed many times in his past.

* * *

Dwarfed by the honey-hued stone wall, Ayla stood in the shadow and felt no bigger than an ant. Massive arched wooden doors guarded the manor house. At the apex of the arch a large, ornate coat of arms stared down at all those who dared seek entry.

Henry pounded on the door. He stood back, hand over his sword pommel and his shoulders straight and proud.

She wished she could wipe her sweaty hands on her skirts, but she would stain the silk, so she wound them in the stifling drape of her cloak.

A small door opened within the large door and a swarthy face appeared.

"We seek Ugo D'Onofrio." Henry spoke in French.

The face peered at them, eyes narrowed. "Who seeks him?"

Henry's shoulders rose on a deep breath. "Sir Henry of Anglesea, and Ugo's niece, the Lady Alya."

"That should light a fire under his ass." Sweating in his mail and surcoat, Newt stood behind her. Beyond Newt, Bahir carried a chest filled with gifts her father had sent to ease her welcome. Gifts? More like bribes to accept the interloper.

The little door slammed shut and running footsteps grew fainter on the far side of the wood.

With a reassuring smile, Henry turned to her. "You look beautiful."

"They will be proud to welcome you," Bahir said.

He insisted he remain a few steps behind her. It was better that he appeared her servant, he had said. Henry had agreed with him, but had taken no pleasure in his agreement. Perhaps one day they might—what was she thinking? After today they would all part ways.

A grinding noise sounded from the door, and then it swung open on a loud, pained creak.

Sir Henry offered her his arm.

Alya's finger's shook as she placed her fingers on his wrist. She drew comfort and courage from the power of the arm she held.

"Chin up," he murmured. "You are a lady born."

Raising her chin, Alya stepped through the doors.

The gate boomed shut behind them.

They walked through a short, dark passage that smelled of mildew before it opened into a courtyard beyond.

Arched balconies stared down on them from all sides as Henry led her across a bright courtyard full of lush greenery. A fountain gurgled and splashed in the middle, sunlight catching on the water.

Their footsteps sounded loud against the flags.

A serving man waited in a doorway at the far end of the courtyard. He peered down his nose at her, and motioned them to follow.

The cool of the manor provided a blessed reprieve from the hot day without. Large, tapestries awash with vivid color hung from the walls. Beneath her slippers, mosaics created bright splashes of color against the stone floor.

The servant motioned them through yet another set of doors. How many could they need? A man sat at the far end on a carved wooden chair. As they approached, he rose.

Stamped across the hawkish bones of his face, the resemblance to her father was unmistakable. This man stood taller than her father, and slimmer beneath his scarlet tunic.

"Sir Henry." The man spoke in a melodious voice. "I welcome you."

Henry bowed with his fist to his chest. He moved his arm in a smooth arc to indicate her. "I present to you the Lady Alya, daughter of your brother Pietro D'Onofrio, formerly of Cairo."

The man stiffened. A hard stare raked her from top to toes. "Is this her?"

"Indeed." Henry's tone grew cold. "The Lady Alya speaks French."

Alya curtsied as Henry had taught her. She rose again, relieved not to have caught her foot in her hem. "Good day, Uncle."

The man flinched. "You do not look like Pietro."

"Nay." She forced a smile to her frozen face. "I believe I look most like my mother."

"An infidel?" Ugo sneered.

His rudeness left her momentarily speechless. She glanced at Bahir.

He gave her a tiny nod.

Alya took a bracing breath. "My mother was not of your faith."

"And you?" Ugo stepped nearer to her, his arms behind his back, a nasty sneer twisting his face.

"I am of the one true faith," she said. "My father insisted on it."

Ugo grunted. "I take it my brother is dead."

Said so abruptly, the words stabbed at Alya. Her gaze found Henry and the comfort she sought. "We do not know yet."

Ugo walked around her in a slow circle.

Alya forced herself to stand still beneath the scrutiny. Chin high, shoulders back, just as Henry had shown her.

Bahir coughed and jerked his head at the chest in his arms.

Her throat felt too tight to manage any words. Her heart beat unsteadily and robbed her breath.

"We are not sure of your brother's fate." Henry stepped smoothly into the building silence. "We believe he may have met with a foul end after we fled Cairo."

Ugo stopped barely two feet in front of her and scowled. "He sent her to me?"

"Aye." Henry gestured Bahir. "Along with a large portion of his wealth. This is but a small sampling."

Bahir bowed low and laid the chest beside Ugo. He flipped open the catches and let the lid drop open.

Ugo gasped.

"We bring you gold." Bahir dribbled the coins through his fingers. He brought forth a glass vial and unstopped it. Jasmine oil twined in the air. "Rare oils and spices from the east."

Staring at the chest, Ugo licked his lips. "There is more?"

"On the boat that brought us here." Bahir drew forth a drape of silk so fine, his hand could be seen through it. "My master wanted to be sure his child would place no burden on your household."

"My brother was a fool." Ugo spun about and threw himself onto his chair. "The family did not support his decision to leave Genoa."

Alya wanted to defend her father. He was a good man. One of the most respected and wealthiest in Cairo. She dug her nails into her palms to stop herself.

Ugo clicked his fingers and four guards appeared. One of them strode forward and gathered the chest in his arms.

Hand going to his pommel, Henry stiffened.

"Do not be stupid, Sir Henry." Ugo smirked. "I can call more guards in a moment." He draped his leg over the arm of the chair and sneered at her. "My brother was twice the fool to think I would welcome you here. You are a dirty heathen. I would no more take you into my home than I would take a pig. Get out."

Alya froze. Her mind rejected what she had just heard.

Ugo motioned his guards. "Throw them out."

Henry stepped in front of her. Voice vibrating menace he said, "Do not lay a finger on her."

The guards glanced at Ugo uncertainly.

"We will leave." Henry said. "But touch Lady Alya and House D'Onofrio will lose its scion."

Surging to his feet, Ugo went red and spittle flew. "Get out. And take that filthy girl with you."

Tense and alert, Newt stood beside Henry.

Bahir tugged her away.

Her limp legs did not feel as if they would hold her. Nobody had ever spoken to her thus. She still could not believe they had. It made her sick to her stomach. Part of her wanted to protest her innocence, another to abrade him for his rudeness.

With Bahir half carrying her, Alya somehow made it onto the street again.

Swords at the ready Henry and Newt flanked them.

The door rattled shut.

Alya collapsed.

Bahir caught her. "Do not listen to them, habibti. Their ignorance marks them as not worthy of you."

"Let's move." Henry drew his sword. "Before he finds his ballocks and comes after us."

"Can you run?" Frowning, Bahir searched her face.

She could and she would. She nodded, and they set off.

As they ran through it, the city blurred for Alya in her Bahir, Newt, and Henry cocoon.

Ugo's words kept clattering around her mind. The contempt on his face. How could anybody hate her that much? Especially a person who knew her not at all. He had called her dirty, a heathen.

People scattered in front of them. Faces swung to stare.

The numbness wore off, and suddenly she wanted to grab Henry's sword and stab Ugo's sneer off his face. Run the blade across his scornful expression. He had no right to treat her so, speak to her in such a manner.

A man veered into Henry's path.

Henry punched their way clear.

They reached the docks and barreled straight through the throngs. Henry used shouts, fists, and his sword hilt to clear the path before her.

Sword catching sunlight, Bahir breathed down her neck.

Newt roved around them, providing extra menace.

Her legs shook as they bustled her up the gangplank and onto the boat.

Henry stepped away from her and drove his fist into the mast. "Whoreson!"

"Be easy." Bahir stepped between Henry and the mast. "You will break your hand, and he will still be a pig wallowing in his own filth."

Tense enough to snap Henry scowled at him. Then he blew out a long breath and nodded. His gaze swung to her. "Are you all right?"

Alya struggled to answer because nay she was not all right. She wanted to smash something. She wished she had never gone to Ugo at all. And now she was well and truly alone in the world. Barring Bahir, she had nobody.

Her legs gave way and she sank onto a coiled rope. "What will I do now?"

Chapter Ten

Henry propped his shoulder on the mast. On the docks, the day folk had given way to the darker, more sinister souls who crawled through the night. Whores, drunkards, and smugglers used the dark shadows to their advantage.

Cool night breeze rustled at his back, carrying with it the tang of the sea. The smell of his childhood. Mighty Anglesea, perched on an isthmus, the tide had provided his lullaby, the cries of the gulls born his childish wishes up to a God he had still believed in.

Newt appeared next to him. "Got aught I need to do. I will return."

Henry nodded. He'd known Newt long enough to know when not to ask questions. Newt had been wearing that grim face since they had returned from Ugo's. He hoped whatever Newt had planned involved the removal of Ugo's innards. What a miserable cur. God's Balls. His sword hand still itched with the need to run the sod through.

Bahir came onto deck and leaned his shoulder on the other side of the mast. He folded his arms and stared up at the scattered stars. "What now, English?"

A question that had nagged Henry since they returned to the boat. "I made a vow to protect her."

"As did I." Bahir rubbed his nape.

"Any ideas?"

A stray dog sniffed at the boat's dock lines. He raised his leg and pissed on them.

His sentiment on the day exactly. Henry almost chuckled. "Well." He straightened. "We have a boat and men to sail her."

Bahir grunted. "Men who are now well aware of what lies in the hold."

A good point. "Do you think they will try anything?"

"Who can be sure?" Bahir shrugged. "Who can truly know what drives any man?"

"It will be the point of my steel if they try."

Bahir chuckled. "English, how did you manage to last as a slave for as long as you did?"

"Shame." The answer came from his heart. So many layers of shame that he could not penetrate.

"Ah." With a wry smile, Bahir nodded. "I know it well. Shame creeps into a man's soul and rusts it until he can no longer remember who he was."

"You too?"

"English." Bahir huffed. "They captured me as a boy, cut off my manhood and threw me amongst women to guard them. Then, when I became troublesome they put me to market like a gelding. What do you think?"

Verily, Bahir had felt the bitter burn through his vitals. These three years working beneath the man and hating him, and only now Henry saw the similarities. An idea came to him and he blurted it. "You could come with me."

"Eh?" Bahir gaped.

"To England." As the idea bloomed in his mind, it made a ridiculous amount of sense. So much sense that he should have considered it before exposing Alya to her pox-souled uncle. "You and Alya could return with me to Anglesea."

"English." Bahir shook his head. "You have seen how people react toward us. You propose to arrive at your home with a big, black man and a lady from a land your people believe to be heathen."

"You do not know my people." Even as he said it, Henry pictured the Anglesea folk. Most born and raised between the sea and the shadow of the mighty keep, and had never been further than Calder. Still, the offer hovered out there now. "You know not how they think or how they would treat you."

Bahir stared at him, still as the mast. Then he dipped his head. "You are right, English. The offer is generous."

"I make the offer to Alya," Henry said. "You, I would toss over the side into the sea."

Bahir's teeth flashed white as he threw back his head and guffawed. "Ah, English." He shook his head. "I believe you would try."

Bahir certainly knew how to take an insult. Henry's answering smile surprised himself. "You have nowhere to go with her. No place you will not meet with hostility. If you came with me, you would be safe."

"Why would you do this?"

Henry had no true answer, so he shrugged. "I made a vow to her father and I would stand by that."

Staring out to sea, Bahir seemed to consider the notion. "What then, English?"

"Eh?" Henry hadn't really thought the plan through.

"We come with you to your home." Turning, Bahir folded his arms. "And stay for how long? A month? A day? Long enough for your people to chase the infidel away?"

"I..." The offer had been impulsive and Bahir picked it apart with the ease it deserved.

"Nay." Rubbing his hand over his head, Bahir sighed. "I needs find a more permanent solution for her. Someplace she will be safe."

An idea popped into Henry's mind, so audacious he shied from examining it closer. "She could marry me."

"Eh?" Bahir choked.

"Alya needs to come to England as my bride." Perhaps the idea was not so insane. He must marry eventually, and why not a girl of his own choosing? This girl, the one who fired his imagination, fed his starving soul and coursed like raw flame through his blood. The more he thought on it, the more sense he made. He could go home and marry a stranger or marry a woman he desired right down to his marrow. And Alya needed a home, a safe place. Their needs fit together like a lock and a key.

Clearly Bahir would take more convincing as he gaped at Henry. "Are you mad?"

"Nay." He stepped closer to Bahir and lowered his voice. "Married to me she has the protection of my name. It will assure her welcome at Anglesea. As my wife, she will no longer be foreign or an infidel."

Bahir grabbed his tunic front in his meaty fist. "She was never those things."

Henry shoved him back. If they could remain civil for long enough, he might get to explain his reasoning to the stubborn cur. "You have no right to make this decision for her. Think about it. And at least do Alya the courtesy of presenting it to her."

"Never." Bahir sneered. "I will never tell her of this."

"What are you never going to tell me?" Alya said from behind them.

Bahir scowled and crossed his arms. "Nothing."

His first proposal and Henry hadn't ever imagined it would take place this way. "We were talking about what you were going to do now."

"English." Bahir's growl held a wealth of warning.

"Nay, Bahir." Alya's hand lay pale gold against the dark of Bahir's arm. "I want to hear."

Dark shadows clung beneath her eyes. She looked tired.

"I have a suggestion," Henry said.

Alya motioned him to continue. She leaned her slim frame against Bahir's side like she sought comfort from the contact.

"You could come back to Anglesea with Newt and me." Best to get to it.

Alya frowned.

"The English wants you to marry him," Bahir said, and made it sound like he'd offered to drop her in camel piss.

Alya gaped, and jerked away from Bahir. "What?"

"I said I thought it would be safer for you if you were under the protection of my name." Henry tried to recover the ground Bahir had cost him. "As long as you are unmarried, and away from your family, you are subject to the sort of insult you suffered this afternoon."

She bit her lip and stared at her bare feet peeking out from the bottom of her gown. "Bahir." She raised her head. "Can you let Henry and I speak of this? Alone."

"Nay." Bahir's chest swelled.

Henry took a moment to recover from his surprise. He had expected to receive an instant dismissal. That she even considered it caused a strange reaction, part trepidation and part victory, to surge through him. As a husband, he was a poor choice for her. A man without a soul. He nearly recanted his offer right there. Then again, the selfish side of him saw only his girl on the wall and how much he hungered for her.

"I'm not a child." She took Bahir's big hands in hers. "My situation is precarious. Whether my father lives or not, I cannot return to Cairo until it is safe for me. I have only you, and a boat full of wealth that makes me a target in so many ways."

"I can protect you." Bahir's tone came as close to imploring as Henry had ever heard it. "I will protect you. There is no need for you to promise yourself in marriage to a man we know nothing about."

"Ask me what you would know." Henry spread his arms wide and tried to appear non-threatening. "I am from good family. I have wealth. In my country, my name would provide the sort of shelter she needs."

Bahir turned to her. "You cannot be consider—"

"Please, Bahir. I need a few moments with Sir Henry." In her calm lay the woman of substance beneath her lovely face. Her serenity struck him, and Bahir too it seemed, as the big man nodded and went below decks,

Sea breeze tugged tendrils of midnight hair over her face. Alya tucked them behind her ear. "Your offer is most generous, Sir Henry."

"Henry." He could not bear his title on her lips. Sir Henry had died on that battlefield beside the Nile.

"Henry." Her sweet smile almost made him want to be that man again. "Bahir only seeks to protect me."

Henry nodded. He did understand that. Some part of him even admired Bahir's dedication to his vow. "I too vowed to your father that I would take care of you."

She tilted her head. "You did?"

"He loved you."

Hunching her shoulders, she folded her arms about her middle. "I will always regret my leave taking from him." She glanced at him before staring out at the night sea. "It is what you tried to tell me, wasn't it?"

"Aye." He wanted to comfort her, but it was not his place. "I left my family with anger between us. They did not want me to go on pilgrimage."

Profile dark against the moonlit water she nodded. "You spoke from experience."

"Aye."

"And now you have a second chance." She sighed.

So it would seem. What would his family make of the man he had become?

Water slapped against the hull, gently rocking the boat.

"Anyway." She turned back to him. "We cannot change the past, but must needs look to the future. I cannot return to Cairo." Her chuckle held an undertone of bitterness. "I am not welcome here. I must go somewhere."

"You consider my offer?" Before he could stop himself, he took a step nearer. She drew him.

"It is the only one I have." She gripped the rail and sighed. "Now I sound ungrateful and I do not mean to."

Against the wooden railing, her hand appeared impossibly delicate. Henry covered it with his own.

She started and looked at him.

"My vow to your father demands that I ensure your future."

She stared at his hand over hers. "Aye, but marriage." She took a deep breath. "That seems a dire step, even to honor a vow. Could I travel with you to your country until I know where I want to go?"

"You could." Henry threaded his fingers through hers. "But that would make you open to scorn and disrespect." He raised their joined hands to his chest. To speak what his heart held seemed nigh impossible. Her hand against his chest provided a small measure of comfort. "I have not much left of the man who I was, Alya. That man would never have dreamed of dishonoring a woman, and there is still enough of him deep within for me to know that the only way I could take you to my home was as my wife."

"Oh." She tightened her fingers about his. "I think there is more of that former you than you believe within you."

If only she knew. He forced a chuckle past his lips. "Be that as it may. I offer you the protection of my name."

"Is there no sweetheart you left behind?" Moonlight kissed the clean lines of her face. "No lady who awaits your return?"

"I was never one to chase skirts." Would her skin feel as cool to touch as it looked? Smooth like marble. Her beauty was made of the earth, elemental and sensual. He imagined it would warm the cold place within him. "But I shall do my best to make you a worthy husband."

"What will your family say?" She grimaced. "They will not be happy with your infidel bride."

If Henry could break Ugo's face, he would do it. "My family will open their hearts to whoever holds mine."

"But I don't." She pulled her hand free, leaving his strangely cold. "I don't hold your heart, Sir Henry."

He defied anyone to look into her eyes and lie to her. "I am not sure I still have a heart, my lady. But you hold my respect and my esteem and I know of several marriages that do not even have that."

She gave a wry laugh. "This is the truth."

"Marry me, Alya." He had not William's pretty way with words. "If we do not suit, you can go whither you desire, and still carry the protection my name affords you."

"And Bahir?" Mischief played across her expression.

"Bahir." Henry barely kept it above a growl. "I understand well that where you go, he goes. I cannot like it, but I will tolerate it."

"He is a good man. His heart is pure," she said.

He did not wish to speak of Bahir. "Take the remainder of the night and think about my offer. Come morning, we will need to decide where we are going, because we cannot safely remain here."

Looking out to sea, she said, "I do not need the night."

Failure, his old friend banged on the doors of his mind.

She turned back to him with a gentle smile. "I will marry you, Henry."

Chapter Eleven

Alya hadn't been one of those women who pictured her wedding throughout her girlhood. Still, even she could have conjured something better than a grimy little church beside the docks.

How Newt managed to find a priest who would marry them the next morning Alya didn't know. Yet, here she stood, in front of a priest as he droned his way through the mass. Food stains covered the straining girth of the priest's hassock, and he smelled of strong spirits. Still, he knew the words well enough to bind her life to Henry's from this day forward.

As if he feared she would run, Henry held her hand in a firm grasp. Sunlight streamed through stained glass windows and kissed the gold of his hair. The gravely beautiful lines of his face looked like one of the saints depicted in the windows of the small church. His nose bent a little to the right as if it had been broken a time or two. Blazoned across his chest, the snarling dragon seemed to challenge all about it.

The priest had fallen silent. He looked at her.

Henry looked at her.

Even Bahir stared.

"Will you or will you not," Newt whispered.

"Will I what?"

With a grimace, the priest asked her again if she would be Henry's wife.

"Aye." Alya nodded. "I will."

Newt snickered.

Best she pay better attention to her wedding. It seemed unreal.

Since last night Bahir had said no more about the matter.

Braced to counter all his arguments, she had been surprised when he merely asked her what she would wear.

He lowered his head for the ceremony. Perhaps he planned to abduct her and carry her away from Henry. Except the priest continued. Incense filled the hot, heavy air and then Henry slid a ring on her finger.

There had not been much time for self-examination since she had told Henry she would marry him. At any point, she could have balked, and she felt sure Henry would have accepted her change of heart. All through the sleepless night before, she had waited for doubts to assail her. Instead she had spent the hours watching the moon cross the sky and thought of life in England. What would her life there be like?

She blamed it on her practical nature. Marriage for a girl such as her was an inevitability. By extracting Henry's vow to protect her, perhaps her father had given this marriage his approval. Regardless, she had always known she would marry, and that she would accept her father's chosen groom.

Bahir cleared his throat.

Alya forced her mind back to the present.

Henry stood over her, looking at her as if he sought her permission.

She had missed something. Again. Verily, Christian marriage ceremonies seemed shamefully lacking in color and celebration.

"You may kiss your bride," said the priest.

Henry slid his hand behind her neck.

She glanced at Bahir.

Bahir stilled.

Face lowering to hers, Henry pulled her closer until his lips touched hers.

Alya froze.

The priest grinned and waggled his eyebrows.

"May I?" Henry smiled.

"You are already." Alya stood as still as she could. What a strange custom. Strange, but definitely exciting.

Henry's lips returned to hers. A soft brush that ended before it had even begun and Henry straightened.

That was it! Alya felt cheated. She had been expecting something more than the dry peck and retreat. She wanted to demand he do a better job.

Henry tucked her arm in his and turned them.

Down the aisle they marched, with Bahir and Newt following.

Bright midday sunlight stung her eyes as they left the church.

Did Henry not think she was beautiful? Did he not want to kiss her? Such an idea had never occurred to her. Back in Cairo, Henry had stared up at her with such stark hunger. She had thought, for certain, he would want her in that way.

Newt stepped in front of her. "Let me be the first well-wisher to kiss the bride."

Grabbing her shoulders Newt planted a kiss on her. A far more enthusiastic kiss than that which she'd received from her husband.

Henry growled.

Instead of growling, he might consider doing a better job of the kissing.

Newt retreated with a smirk. "You will excuse me, I have a little matter to attend to before we sail."

"We sail on the tide," Henry said.

Newt nodded and slid into a group of people walking away from the dock.

"Where does he go?" Even as she watched, Newt disappeared like smoke. He would have made an excellent spy master.

Bahir and Henry exchanged a look. So now they chose to keep secrets from her.

"Come." Henry gently pulled her along. "We will return to the boat, and perhaps we can find a goblet of wine to celebrate our marriage."

Her first taste of wine. Alya allowed herself to be hurried back to the boat.

They arrived to find a grim-faced captain waiting for them.

"Go below." Henry nudged her toward the hatch. "I will talk to the captain and then we will have that wine."

Alya opened her mouth to argue, but Bahir took her arm and led her below decks.

"I will sleep above now," Bahir said.

The nerves she should have concerned herself with the night before chose now to put in an appearance. Henry now had the right to sleep beside her, and to do those other things.

"Habibti." Bahir took her by the shoulders. His stern face looked so sad she wanted to offer him comfort. "You are a woman grown now."

Not so very grown. Suddenly she wanted to protest that she remained a child. She clung to his forearms. Bahir was all that remained of her past life. Her future loomed ahead of her, full of uncertainty. The ring Henry had placed on her finger seemed tighter.

"You have a husband and he will take my place in many parts of your life." Bahir kissed her forehead. "But I will be with you for as long as you will have me."

"There will never come a time when I will not want you beside me."

Shrugging Bahir cast his gaze down. "That may not always be your decision. You have chosen this man to be your husband. I would counsel you to submit your will to him. Make of this marriage a blessed union, Alya. For your sake." Then he winked.

"And if you cannot, know that you always have a champion in me."

"She will not need it." Henry stood in the companionway from the deck. He jerked his chin at Bahir. "We must speak."

Bahir followed him up.

Alya was alone. On her wedding day.

* * *

Henry slammed his fist into the mast, and wanted to do it many times more. Sailors had big mouths the world over. The captain had grim tidings to share. Only half of his crew had reported back to the boat, bringing with them the news that the remainder had thrown their weight behind a couple of trouble-stirrers.

The contents of the boat's hold had started the murmurings amongst the crew. That much wealth, floating in the harbor had attracted its share of notice. Added to which, Ugo felt it behooved him to collect more of his late brother's amassed fortune. Rumor in the dock taverns had him gathering his men as they stood here. It wouldn't take long for them to find the right boat.

"How long before we can leave?" Bahir's gazed moved over the busy docks.

The captain sucked his teeth. "Tide is turning. Maybe another two hours before there is enough water over the harbor mouth to cross safely."

Two hours! Henry eyed the mast. His fist gave an unenthusiastic throb. In two hours, they could all be dead.

"We could drop anchor in the bay," the captain said. "It would make it more difficult to reach us."

Bahir turned to Henry and raised his brow.

Was the man actually asking his opinion? Henry resisted the urge to check behind him. "How many more men do you expect to return?"

"One or two." The captain squinted at the docks. "For the most part, those who sail are already onboard."

Henry motioned Bahir to follow him to the stern. "Newt is not here yet," he said.

"You know where he has gone?"

"I can guess." It's as much as he intended to tell Bahir.

Gaze searching the dock, Bahir nodded. "Then we wait."

"We need to be through the heads before dark." Head lowered, the captain approached them.

Dear God, if he sucked those rotten teeth stumps again Henry would remove the temptation by shoving them down his throat. "We wait."

"But—"

Looming over the man, Bahir scowled. "We wait."

Midday brought relative quiet to the docks. Many merchants closed shop and went home for their midday meal.

The sun baked down on him and Bahir standing by the railing.

Faces concealed by lowered caps, a pair of men stood near a stack of bales. Henry had spotted them earlier, and still the men stood there with no apparent reason for their presence.

The ship beside them weighed anchor in the creak of ropes and wood.

Bahir stiffened.

Oars hit the water. A slow drumbeat underscored the slap of oars through the water. Rowed by slaves and bound for Damascus, according to their captain.

Henry wiped away perspiration. No wind broke the midday heat.

Their boat neighbor crept away from the docks.

The two lurkers were joined by a third who leaned against the bales, arms folded.

"They wait," Bahir said.

Aye, Bahir had his eye on them too. Canny bastard hadn't missed much in Cairo, no reason to believe salt water had dulled his wits now.

"Aye, but for what."

"This, English, I do not want to discover."

Henry choked back a laugh.

Shouting out her wares to the passers-by a young girl wheeled a barrow down the dock.

The sun slunk passed its zenith.

By the bale the group had grown to five now.

Jesu, Henry wished for his hauberk. Stolen from him by his 'rescuers' after the battle.

Bahir shifted and wiped sweat from his pate. "I hate waiting."

"Aye."

A faint scream sounded from the city.

Then a shout, louder now.

Through the jumble of buildings, people ran, arms raised.

"English?" Bahir tensed.

The running crowd wound behind the line of warehouses fronting the harbor but their shouts grew closer.

A man shot across the gap between two buildings, the crowd close on his heels.

Newt. God's Balls. "Captain!" Henry bellowed. "Get ready to be underway. Now!"

The captain blinked at him.

"Now!" Henry unsheathed his sword.

The loitering men straightened.

Sailors scurried around them, untying moorings, weighing the giant anchor.

Newt burst onto the docks, long legs pumping.

Behind him surged his pursuers.

"Move it!" Bahir cuffed a dawdling sailor into instant action.

Their oars slapped the water.

"What is it?" Alya popped her head up from the cabin.

"Nay!"

"Get down!"

With a gasp, she ducked out of sight again.

The boat eased away from her mooring.

Newt picked up speed. A mad grin split his face. He hit the end of the dock and launched into the air.

His pursuers slammed to a halt. One of them going over into the murky harbor waters.

Newt pedaled his legs through the air, and slammed into the railing.

Henry grabbed his tunic.

Bahir had him by the belt.

They hauled the addled bastard onto the deck.

Newt dropped over onto his back, a chest clasped in his arms, and laughed.

Arrows whined and thudded into the mast and Henry dropped.

The captain screamed at his men to row faster.

"What did you do?" Bahir crawled across the deck.

Newt rolled his burden onto the deck. "Took back what was ours."

With shaking hands, Bahir opened the chest. "You…"

"You mad sod!" Newt could have gotten himself killed. Henry punched his arm. Then hooked him around the neck and hugged him. "You mad, glorious sod."

Chapter Twelve

Alya sulked below decks. She did not appreciate being yelled at by both Henry and Bahir. She was not stupid, however, and the noises coming from the boat persuaded her to stay hidden.

The boat lurched and she grabbed onto a support pillar to keep her balance.

She burned to know what was happening.

Yells, thuds, the creak of oars, and then nothing.

Straining to hear more she held her breath.

Was that laughter? Aye, it was. Alya stomped onto the deck.

Henry, Bahir and Newt all lay about the deck, laughing. Lying between them was the chest of gifts they'd taken to Ugo.

Henry saw her first and sat up. He grinned at her.

The boat slid through the harbor toward the mouth.

Arrows arced from the dock and dropped into the churning water in their wake.

Bahir staggered to his feet and helped Newt to rise.

Henry need not think he could smile at her and tell her nothing. "What is happening here?"

"We are sailing away, my lady." Newt made a lavish bow. "And not a moment too soon."

"Is that—"

"Aye." Henry handed the chest to Bahir. "Newt took it upon himself to take back what was yours."

She liked that he said yours, and not mine. Many men would now regard all her wealth as theirs. Then again, Henry said he came from wealth. So many questions remained unanswered, so much she did not know about him.

Towers guarding the harbor heads threw dark shadows over the boat. Farewell, Genoa, and farewell any last connection with her father's blood. Ahead of them the sea lay in deepest sapphire expanse, leading her to her uncertain future.

Brisk wind sprang up as they cleared the safety of the harbor, and Alya shivered.

Henry dropped a warm cloak about her shoulders. "You are chilled." His deep voice came close to her ear. Closer than he had ever stood to her, other than those fleeting moments in the church. "Would you go below?"

Below deck. To the intimacy of the small cabin she had occupied alone with Bahir sleeping nearby. Now the space she would share with her husband. The man who had rights not only to the wealth this ship carried, but to her. Every part of her.

"Nay." She swallowed to moisten her dry mouth. "I find it confining. I am enjoying the fresh breeze."

His gaze searched her face and found the truth. His face gentled as he said, "You have nothing to fear from me, my lady."

Nothing to fear? Meaning he would not hurt her, or that he would not lay a hand on her? Or some blurred area in between those two. She suddenly wanted to demand to know what he meant by that. She wanted to know what lay behind his reticence to take her to wife.

She faced the ocean instead. Such a course smacked of almost mind-numbing stupidity. Why pick at a thing that might unravel and reveal a gaping hole? "What do you mean by that?"

Alya wanted to smack her head against the railing. Her impetuous tongue would lead her straight to hell.

Back to the sea, Henry leaned his hips against the railing and folded his arms. "Perhaps you are right, my lady. We should speak of these things."

"Not if you do not care to." Too late for her wits to reassert themselves now.

Afternoon sun tangled golden in his hair. How long would he grow it? She had never seen him with this much hair, never mind long as Newt seemed to favor.

"I mean you need not fear that I will demand from you that which you will not give," he said.

Why not? Did he find her not to his liking? Did his desire run to women of his country? Did he lust for skin like milk, and golden hair? "I still do not understand."

He ran his palm over his head stubble. "We are on a boat, Alya. There is no privacy here. I would accord you the respect of privacy."

She nodded, she had not thought of that.

Bare feet slapping on the deck, a sailor trotted by.

"It is not because you do not find me to your liking?" Her words grew softer and softer.

Henry stepped closer. "Say again?"

The breeze cooled her searing cheeks. "I thought perhaps..." How to put this delicately? And what if he answered aye, he did not find her beautiful? "Never mind."

"Alya." Henry stepped closer, his body warmth a buffer against the sea. "I do mind. Now tell me."

"Do you command this as my husband?" She tried to salvage some pride.

He cocked his head. "Do I need to?"

What edwas that word Newt used? Ballocks! That was it. Well, ballocks to Henry and his clever tongue. Well, let her face her humiliation with her head held high. She raised her chin. "I thought perhaps you found me not beautiful."

Henry laughed.

Dear God. She had to get away. Never had she felt so shamed. She dashed for the cabin.

His arm shot out, and trapped her against the railing. "Where are you going?'

Alya clapped her mouth shut. She would say no more to humiliate herself.

His mouth brushed her ear. "Ask me why I laughed."

She shook her head.

"Ask me?' His voice dropped to a low, rasp.

It stroked like a cat's fur across her skin. "Why did you laugh?"

"When I was your father's slave and there was nothing of beauty in my life, I watched you on the wall. More lovely than the sun setting behind you. More beautiful than all the treasures in your father's house."

His words coursed through her blood. Her knees weakened.

Henry pressed closer. He slid his other arm about her back and caged her close to his heat and the smell of bay and cardamom. "I used to stand in the shadows and watch you stand on your roof at sunset."

"I know."

He tensed. "You know?"

"I wondered why you stood there and watched."

"You never told your father?" His lips brushed her temple.

"Nay." She wanted to turn her head and place her lips against his. Did she dare?

The opportunity passed as he nuzzled her cheek. "Of all the things you may question about me, know that I have never seen a more beautiful woman than you."

"English?" Bahir's voice shattered the spell around her. "I beg your pardon, but we must speak."

* * *

Henry sucked in a great breath of cooling air. Anger and lust pounded with each beat of his heart. Did Bahir think to stand between him and Alya now? The beast in him reminded him constantly that Alya was not yet his. He had made her his bride, but not yet his wife. It thundered through his blood. His beast forgot the boat, the curious sailors, the crude cabin. It forgot the innocence of his bride, and that she barely knew him.

Perhaps it was a good thing Bahir had interrupted them. "What is it?"

"Newt and I have been speaking." Bahir motioned him to the quiet stern of the boat.

Newt waited in the shadows, lounging against a barrel, ankles crossed. He nodded. "Harry."

"You've been speaking?"

Still at the railing, Alya wrapped her cloak tighter around her body. Her raven hair streamed in the sea breeze. Jesu, she had thought he found her not to his liking. God's Balls! Never in his life had he seen a woman such as her. Never would he take from his mind the imprint of her sensuality. Her skin as honey, her eyes of that indeterminate mix of green and brown that tightened a vice around him.

"You listening, Harry?" Newt nudged his ankle with his toe.

Henry dragged his attention back to Bahir and Newt. "I am now."

"The thing with the sailors in Genoa, we did not leave it on the docks," Newt said.

Now he had all of Henry's attention. "What?"

"Newt believes we have ambitious men at sea with us." Bahir folded his arms. Muscle like hewn onyx bulged. Strong as a bull and just as unpredictable, as Henry knew only too well.

Three of them against a crew of close to twelve men. Not the best odds he'd faced, but not the worst either. Bahir would be good for his four, and Newt his. Henry would rip any man asunder who went near Alya. "We will need to keep watch."

"Captain says six days to Lisboa," Newt said. "A lot can happen in six days."

"We are warned." The crew about them became a lingering threat. "We will watch our backs."

Bahir nodded. "I suggest we sleep in turns."

"Agreed." Not that Henry believed he would sleep knowing that at any moment some bastard might like his chances.

"In that case." Newt rose and stretch. "I will grab a quick nap now."

"Why do you sleep first?" Bahir stepped in front of Newt.

"Because, big man—" Newt clapped Bahir on the shoulder "—I do my best work in the dark." He sauntered below decks.

Bahir shook his head.

"You grow accustomed to him." Henry had felt much the same way when Newt had first come to him as squire. Determined to break Newt down and rebuild him in a manner suited to himself, Henry had barely noticed Newt making him more malleable.

Face grave, Bahir caught his arm. "English, do not hurt her."

"I would rather cut my hands off."

"Good." Bahir sniffed. "Because if you do, I will cut them off for you."

* * *

Henry waited for Bahir to return before he took his turn to rest. He left Bahir and Newt to keep an eye on things and went below deck.

To Alya.

He opened the cabin door as quietly as he could. The hour grew late and he did not want to wake her.

"Henry?" She sat up from the mound of blankets on the bed.

"Aye."

Henry found himself standing there with no clear idea of

what to do next. This marriage hung fragile as a spider's web between them. A foolish man would rush through it, destroy it and stamp it beneath his feet.

However, his Alya lounged on her bed in a bronze gossamer thin silk shift. Her bare feet stuck out from beneath. The silk clung lover-like to the long sweep of her legs and creased at her hips. High, full breasts strained beneath their insubstantial containment.

As long as she remained the girl on the wall he could keep his beast in check. Had kept his beast in check in both thought and deed. But here, tonight, this sensual, earthy girl had tumbled from her heights and shimmered within reach.

The jasmine scent of her perfume filled the stuffy cabin.

Henry bent to unfasten his boots. Staring at her wasn't helping any. "I thought you would be sleeping."

"I was waiting for you."

Ballocks! That hadn't made this any easier. "You shouldn't have."

"Why is that?" She tucked her legs up beside her. "You are my husband now."

"Aye." He tugged on a cross garter too hard and it snapped in his hand. Lust was an inconvenient emotion. To think he'd once looked down his nose at Beatrice for allowing her desire for Garrett to rule her good sense. "But we..." How to put this delicately? "What I mean to say..."

"I understand, Henry." Alya patted the bed beside her. "I thought maybe we could speak."

"Speak?" By all means. That should not present a problem. He perched on the very edge of her bed.

Alya settled back and propped her head on her elbow. Ebony hair cascaded over the brightly colored cushions. "Tell me of your family."

Her breasts swelled beneath the shift bodice. A full hand of silky fleshy. His voice came out hoarse. "What would you like to know?"

"You have two brothers and two sisters?"

"Three brothers." Jasmine twined around his senses. "I have a much younger brother named Mathew. My mother had him later in her life. He is slower than other children."

Mathew would be approaching the age when other boys became squires. When last he'd seen Mathew, he had been small enough to upend over your shoulder. A game that had never failed to draw a laugh from Mathew.

The scar deep within him throbbed. He did not wish to speak of his family. "I should rest."

Her face fell. "I understand."

Nay, she did not. Nor could she. The day drew closer when he would see his family once again. For five long years, he had thought it would never come. For his sanity, he had locked the memories and the longing deep within him. He had survived doing what he must to ensure that.

Now life knocked on the door of his mind once again. It reminded him that when a man did more than draw his next breath, then a man felt again.

Alya shifted to make room for him beside her. "You can sleep here."

Reluctant to explain, and not wanting to hurt her feelings by leaving with no explanation, Henry edged into place beside her. Her smooth arm brushed his. Warmth came from her and wrapped around him. Silk, jasmine, and honey, the essence of Alya. So tempting and so near.

Although he did not expect to sleep, Henry dreamed of Anglesea. Saw her great turrets standing proud above the lands she served. He dreamed of his beautiful, gracious mother who knew when a boy needed space and when a boy needed her love. Of his gruff, large father. The way Sir Arthur could scare the life out of a warring baron, yet always had time to patiently teach his sons how to handle their weapons. He saw Beatrice, her face alive with the laughter that always lurked behind her eyes. In his dream life, he begged lovely Faye's pardon. One of their last conversations, he had told her to honor her marriage vows to a man who used his fists on her. So many times, he had lain in his tent with the pilgrim army and prayed for just one moment in time to redeem himself. His dream smelled of the sea, and cool moisture-laden air touched his face. He dreamed of home.

Chapter Thirteen

Over the next days, Alya spent a lot of her time standing at the railing. The boat stayed close enough to land that she caught glimpses of strange places as they slid past.

Henry knew much of the lands they passed, and he told her of them. Strange names like Marseilles, a city of great wealth governed by the Counts of Provence and Cordoba, which in ancient times had been a place of great learning and philosophy. He scattered his speech with English words. Harsh and truncated in her mouth as she tried to form them. Sometimes she mispronounced them on purpose. Henry got such a look on his face when she did. An almost smile with his eyes warm and inviting. He did not look at anyone else like that.

On the fourth day, they passed a great rock rising out of the sea, it's face so light a gray as to be almost white. *Jebel Tariq* Henry called it and the captain judged it ill-advised to land there.

The crew busied themselves for what the captain said could be a tricky crossing. From here they left the Mediterranean Sea and entered the Atlantic. Jebel Tariq sliding past marked Alya's passing from her old life into her new and she kept her gaze on it until sunset brought a low, dense fog. Alya shivered. In the gray gloom, strange and haunting sounds rose and died again.

Bahir joined her at the railing. "And whosoever puts his trust in Allah, then He will suffice him."

She drew comfort from words she had heard so many times growing up. Alya leaned her head against Bahir's shoulder. Bahir would suffice her. She sent a prayer for her father with the wind.

The sea grew rougher in the coming days, limiting the time she could spend at the railing. As they approached the port of Lisboa, Bahir, Henry, and Newt grew tenser. She wished they would share their concerns with her, but in their silence, they stood united. She guessed it had something to do with the crew.

One of the three of them stayed by her side almost constantly and they were always armed.

For her part, she could barely wait to get off the boat and place her feet on something that didn't constantly dip and sway.

With the setting sun barely keeping above the sea their boat slid through the mouth of the Tagus river. Dying rays threw pink light over the great pale keep guarding the city from attack by sea. Bells tolled from the city and reached across the water, signaling the closing of the city gates for the night.

Henry sat on deck sharpening his sword. The dull scraping merged with the raucous squabbling of gulls as they dipped in and out through the ships, falling on scraps and flotsam tossed into the water. The water smelled of waste, fish, and oil and made Alya cover her mouth with her kerchief. "I can scarcely wait to get away from this stench, and onto land."

Rising, Henry sheathed his sword. "My lady." He clasped the railing. "We will not be leaving the boat."

What nonsense was this? Henry must be teasing her. "Why leave this pleasant scent?"

"Lady." Henry grimaced. "It is not safe for you to leave the boat."

Still waiting for him to tell her he jested, Alya stared. She had spent more time on the sea than she had ever wanted to. They had gone ashore in Genoa. She saw no reason for Lisboa to be any different. "Henry?"

"I cannot take the chance that someone will try to get rid of us while we are ashore." He stared at the city. "Or see this as an opportunity to make off with your father's boat, and all it contains."

Lowering her voice because of the sailors preparing the boat to dock around them, Alya said, "Surely if they meant us any harm, they would have used our passage here to rid themselves of us."

"We have been watching them closely," Henry said. "But time grows short now, and desperate men may act."

The sails dropped limp to the deck.

Alya jumped and moved closer to Henry. She did not like to think of any of the men who had come with her from Alexandria wishing her harm.

Still, Bahir stood at the far side of the boat, gaze keen and alert on the sailors.

Close to the stern, Newt sprawled on a pile of coiled ropes. He wore his sword, and his hooded gaze moved constantly about the deck.

"You've been on guard since we left Genoa." She saw it now. The times Henry got up in the middle of the night to join Bahir or Newt on deck. These six nights he had slept beside her for a short time and then left, she had thought he did not enjoy being confined below deck.

He twined his fingers with hers and raised her hand to his lips. "There is no need for undue concern," he said. "But we also do not think it wise to court trouble."

Alya nodded.

A sailor passed her and nodded a greeting.

Could he covet her father's wealth? Did he smile even as he reached for his dagger?

She tightened her grip on Henry's hand, drawing comfort

from his large, still presence at her side. "How long will we dock here?"

"Not long," Henry said. "We will refill our water barrels and provisions. If the wind favors us, we will reach Anglesea in four days."

"Four days?" Her belly fluttered. In four days, she would meet her new family. Henry assured her they would welcome her, but then her father had told her Ugo would open his arms and his home to her. She didn't know whether to pray for favorable winds or not.

The captain shouted and the men dropped anchor.

Night stole across the sky, chasing the last orange smears of the passing day. The wind changed direction and provided relief from the awful stink. Braziers flickered like stars on the city walls. Laughter from a nearby boat drifted over the water.

Henry draped his cloak about her. "You should sleep. We leave as soon as the tide turns."

"You do not sleep?" She turned in his arms.

Shadows caressed the clean planes of his face. "Not this night." He slid his arms about her waist. "But once I have you safe behind the walls of Anglesea, then there will be time for sleep. And other things."

Her heart fluttered in her chest.

Beneath her palms, his heart beat sure and steady. His gaze strayed to her mouth, as his gaze heated.

Alya grew hot beneath the wool of Henry's cloak and she swayed toward him.

Henry growled and stepped away from her. He clenched his fists and took a deep breath. "Sleep well, my lady."

Alya dragged her feet away from him. Suddenly four days seemed way too long to reach Anglesea.

Gaze hungry, Henry watched her go.

In her cabin, she slid his cloak from her shoulders and pressed it to her nose. Cardamom and oranges in a heady combination that clenched through her belly.

A hand covered her mouth. A sharp sting on her neck. "No noise," a man said in Arabic.

The knife at her neck was one of the wicked, curved blades the sailors used to splice rope.

"Slow and careful, woman." The sailor prodded her forward. "We don't want any trouble from the eunuch or the knight."

"What do you want?" Her voice shook.

The sailor shoved again. "Up."

Alya tripped over her gown.

The knife nicked her neck.

"Watch yourself." The sailor jerked her arm. "Maybe your pretty English won't want you when I cut up your face."

"Is this about the cargo?" Henry, Bahir, and Newt were only three against what could be the entire crew.

"Move." He twisted his hand into her hair and yanked. "No talking."

* * *

Henry froze with his gaze fixed on the knife at Alya's neck.

He had known fear. Any man going into battle made it his companion. The day he'd been pulled from his horse in that fateful last battle, he had seen the men surrounding him, known he would not escape and felt the fear for his life. That was nothing compared to the terror that stuck his feet to the deck now.

Bahir hissed.

Newt's hand went to his sword.

"Do not." The sailor pressed the blade into Alya's neck, denting the skin.

"What do you want?"

Thank the Lord Bahir had the presence of mind to speak. Henry's brain rolled like thickening mud.

The captain stepped forward. "We don't want any blood spilled," he said. "Just leave the boat, you three, and we'll let the lady go."

"Then you plan to sail off with the boat and its contents." Newt held his hands up for them to see. "Is that it?"

"No fighting needed." The rest of the crew flanked the captain. "I sailed for her father my whole life. I do not want to hurt her."

Duplicitous sod! Had the captain planned this all along or had they somehow persuaded him to join them? Henry counted heads. Thirteen, including the captain and the whoreson with his knife at Alya's neck. That one died first.

Alya's gaze met his. So much trust it almost brought him to his knees. She believed he would save her.

"How about this plan?" Newt took a careful step forward. "You leave the boat and we don't kill you."

The captain grimaced and then laughed. "I like you, young one. I like one who can make me laugh."

A couple of crew members joined his laughter. Including the one threatening Alya.

"I enjoy a good laugh myself." Newt grinned. "But see, we're at an impasse here." He tucked his hands into his belt. "You could slit Alya's throat, but then where would you be?"

"Eh?" The captain blinked.

Ayla went parchment pale, her hazel eyes imploring first him and then Bahir.

"Mind me well, Captain." Newt shifted his weight onto the balls of his feet.

Henry braced. Here it came.

Bahir frowned. The man was quick witted. He would follow Newt's lead.

"The only reason you're not dead right now is that knife at her throat. Once you've killed her, you're a dead man. And anyone who stands with you." Newt's hand inched across his belt, almost imperceptible unless you knew what to look for.

Jesu, Henry would kill him if he missed.

"We are not pretending." The captain scowled. "We will kill her."

"I believe you," Newt said. "But you should have killed us first."

The knife whistled through the air and found its mark in the sailor's eye.

Alya screamed and dropped to the deck.

Pulling both scimitars from his waist, Bahir charged, bellowing his challenge.

One sailor leaped over the side into the water. Two met Bahir's blade.

Henry sprang for Alya.

Kicking her dead attacker aside, he stood between her and the crew.

Three men shuffled forward. One had an old short-sword, the other two hefted daggers.

Newt hurled two more daggers across the deck.

One pinned the captain through his thick neck. Another embedded in the shoulder of an oncoming sailor.

Henry's sword took the first man at the throat. Blood bloomed over his tunic as he dropped to the floor.

The second came in low, stabbing.

Henry knocked his knife aside and thrust.

Grabbing his gut, the man dropped to the deck.

The third man slipped on the blood pool.

Henry lunged.

He scrambled out of the way of Henry's descending sword.

Not fast enough, and Henry thrust into his chest.

Bracing his leg, he yanked his sword free of the man's breastbone.

Bahir had dispatched one of his opponents.

The other retreated across the deck, reached the railing and vaulted into the sea.

Gazes darting between him, Bahir, and Newt, two more sailors drew back.

They bumped into each other in their haste to clear the railing.

It was over. Blood stained the deck. Moans rose from the two injured men. The one Henry had stabbed wouldn't last the right with that belly wound.

Newt approached the other. He yanked his dagger from his shoulder.

The man screamed. Clapping his hand over his shoulder, he dropped to the deck. Red oozed through his fingers.

Alya huddled with her arms wrapped around her legs.

Henry approached her slowly. The hand he reached for her was covered in blood and he snatched it back. "Alya? My lady? It is over."

She shuddered and buried her face in her knees. "So much blood."

Gore covered the deck.

Newt busied himself hefting bodies over the side.

"Let me take you below." Henry wiped his hands on his tunic. He did not want his killing hands to touch her.

"Nay." Alya took a deep breath and raised her head. As she looked about the gore-splattered deck she paled. "I am not so feeble."

Unsteadily, she stood.

Henry caught her elbow.

She breathed and then nodded. "I am well."

Then she snatched up a bucket and lowered it over the side.

Henry joined her. "Will you not let me take you below?"

"Nay," she hissed as she struggled to raise the full bucket.

Henry leaned over and pulled it aboard.

Alya turned and tossed the water over the deck. Water and blood mingled in swirling patterns about them.

"I am not made of sand." Alya lowered the bucket again.

Henry helped her bring it up.

Again, she tossed water. "I will not fold or falter at the first sign of trouble."

"Lady?" Hands out held, Bahir approached her. "This is not for you."

"Stand back, Bahir." She brandished her third bucket of water. "Or you will get wet."

Somehow, she needed to do this, and Henry motioned Bahir back.

"There." Newt sent the injured men swimming as well. "We seem to be missing a crew." He brushed his hands. "Time for Newt to do what Newt does best."

"And what's that?" Sneering, Bahir wiped blood from his sword with the ragged remains of a sailor's tunic.

"Find things." Newt clapped Henry on the shoulder. "What Newt does best is find things that are missing."

Chapter Fourteen

After Newt disappeared, they finished cleaning the deck. Not wanting to go below and be alone, Alya remained on deck with Henry and Bahir. Always with her best interest at heart, Bahir went below and returned with enough cushions to keep her comfortable for the night.

Lying on her cushions staring up at the star strewn sky she was almost able to forget the last few horrible hours.

Henry sat with his back propped against the mast, his gaze fixed on the quiet dock. Braziers threw off strange and grotesque shadows against the dock. From the other boats the sound of conversation, and sometimes laughter carried across the water.

Needing the contact, Alya shifted closer to Henry.

Glancing down at her, he smoothed a tendril of hair from her face. "Sleep, my lady. I will watch."

* * *

Night dragged on as Alya slept beside him. Neat as a cat she slept with her knees curled into her chest and her hand tucked beneath her cheek. Cool night breeze ruffled her hair and clothes and Henry draped his cloak over her.

The need to protect her fastened around him like an iron claw. She was his to have and to hold, to shelter, and to cherish. He tucked his cloak beneath her chin. If he thought himself still capable of the emotion he would love her as well. Love he might not be able to manage, but he could come as close as he was able.

From the far side of the boat Bahir watched him and nodded before returning to keeping watch.

Dawn ousted the cool night in a gaudy display of red and orange across the horizon.

"Ho! The boat."

Henry must have dozed because the shout from the dock startled him. He stood and joined Bahir at the railing.

A man stood on the dock. A dead sailor dangled from his meaty fist. "Newt said you had a bit of bother. Would this be part of that?"

Grimacing, Alya shuddered. "Is he speaking English?"

"Aye." Henry searched for Newt. The stranger had the looks of a Newt plan all over him.

A grin split the bearded stranger's face as he shook the body. "You seem to have had a lot of trouble."

"Who are you?" The man wore worn but clean tunic and hose, and his large beard and hair were neatly trimmed.

"Smelly Tim." Still fastening his chausses, Newt trotted toward the boat. "Stop scaring them with your ugly face and let me introduce you." He arrived beside Tim and grinned up at the boat. "Sorry I am late. Whoreson drank me under the table."

Henry raised his brow. That took some doing.

"Hand to God." Newt winked and went back to Smelly Tim. "Put that down."

Tim dropped the corpse on the dock with a sickening splat. "The lads thought I should come 'round and see about this boat you were talking about."

"I said I'd bring you." Newt stepped over the corpse.

Tim chuckled. "But why wait. Tide will turn any minute and there was no telling when you'd see daylight again."

Bahir growled. "English, who is this man?"

"A sailor," Henry said. "He's called Smelly Tim and he says he has a crew to take us back to England."

"Why do they call him smelly?" Alya wrinkled her nose. "And he does not seem to mind it."

"Smells like a blasted girl." Newt resorted to French, slapping Tim on the shoulder. "And it so happens that Tim and his lads are looking for a way home."

Stiffening, Bahir glared at the dock. "We do not know him."

"True enough." Tim switched to French and toed the body into the water. "Looks like your crew isn't up to the job right now." Elbowing Newt, he guffawed.

"Can you even sail?" Henry had his doubts.

"Can I sail?" Tim snorted and jammed his hands on his hips. "Can I sail?"

Henry waited for the answer.

"I can sail a sausage around your bathing tub." He eyed Henry with a grimace. "My lord."

"Why would you have a sausage in your bathtub?" Alya frowned.

"Who be that?" Tim jerked his chin. "She your serving girl?"

Bahir put his arm around Alya's shoulder.

Henry blamed himself. He more than anyone else here, knew the battle Alya faced. "Nay." He relished his next words. "She is my wife."

"Wife?" Tim snorted. "Don't make no difference to me, my lord. I just want to get home."

"And how came that to be?" Henry made a show of leaning against the railing as if he had not a care in the world. "What happened to the ship you came in on?"

"Ah." Shifting, Tim put his hands behind his back. "That is a rather long story, and might go smoother with a jug of ale."

"Don't get yourself all excited." Newt motioned Tim to stay put and bounded up the gangplank onto the ship.

"What think you?" Henry turned to Bahir. "We could see what he has to say."

Bahir pursed his lips. "Who are these 'lads' he speaks of?"

"Small group of English sailors." Newt joined them. "I met them at a tavern last night."

Henry had learned to trust Newt's instincts, particularly where it came to people. Having grown up in the gutter, Newt could read people like their intentions were spread on parchment before him. "What do you make of them?"

On the dock, Tim leaned over the water and examined another body.

"Typical dock rats." Newt folded his arms. "But they want to get home."

Of course, news of the ship of treasure could have reached Lisboa long before them. Sailors gossiped more than matrons at a wedding.

"English." Bahir clapped his shoulder. "Let us see what we make of this man before we make a decision."

Dear God, that almost sounded like Bahir suggested they work together. The man must have caught the flat edge of a blade to his head.

Bahir grinned at him as if he could read Henry's thoughts. "We need to get to your home, English. And unless you have been hiding your sailing skills, we are going to need a crew."

Apparently, Bahir had developed a touch of humor. It must be all the time he spent in Newt's company. When Newt had first joined him as squire, Henry had tried to instill a sense of decorum in Newt. Instead, Newt had fostered a healthy dose of irreverence in Henry. Newt had that effect on people.

"Come aboard," he called to Tim.

Tim hitched his chausses. "Right you are, my lord."

Henry turned to Alya. "Perhaps you want to go below?" He didn't want Tim catching an eye load of Alya. Lusty at the best of times, sailors didn't need that kind of temptation. Jesu, Henry didn't need that kind of temptation on a boat in the middle of the bloody ocean where he could do nothing about it.

Bahir and Newt awaited Tim at the head of the gangplank.

"I do not wish to go below," Alya said, so softly he almost didn't catch it.

Politely phrased, aye, but he had not been making a suggestion. "I believe you must."

Alya sniffed. "The battle is over."

By the martial gleam in his bride's eye, Henry gathered the battle was just beginning. Staring into her lovely, challenging face, Henry faced a choice. He could thunder and rail at her, and insist she go below. Except, that approach had never won him many victories over his sister, Beatrice. Instead, he would rant and Beatrice would stick her stubborn chin out and do the opposite. As a sort of atonement to his sister, he took Alya's hand. "I am asking you to go where I know you will be safe."

"Oh." She blinked at him, and glanced at Tim.

Beaming at everyone, Tim hopped onto the boat.

Alya leaned closer to him. "Is that man dangerous?"

"I do not know." Henry resisted the urge to bury his face in the jasmine scent of her skin. "Until I do, I would really like it if you could stay where you are safe."

"I can do that." She nodded, then peered at him with a shy smile. "Thank you for being so concerned for me, Henry."

God's Bones, if only he'd thought to apply that method to Beatrice. Beatrice! Another bridge he needed to rebuild when he returned home. He pushed that thought aside and turned to address Smelly Tim.

"Your lordship." Tim held out a meaty paw. "Pleased to make the acquaintance of another Englishman."

"Indeed." Henry shook the hand. "So, you are offering to crew my ship in return for passage home?"

Tim squinted at the sky. "Tide turns before the hour is up. We'll want to ride that out of here." He shoved his hands into his tattered rope belt. "Especially if the whispers concerning what has your hull riding low in the water are true."

Henry's hackles rose. "What do you know of this?"

"What every dock rat knows by now." Tim met his gaze squarely. "Or believes to be true, which amounts to the same thing. They say you have a ship of treasure here."

Casting his shadow over the smaller man, Bahir moved closer to Tim.

Tim threw his hands up. "Look, your lordship, I'm telling you like it is. I could stand here and pretend I know nothing, but my mam raised me better than that. Honestly, I don't care what you got below decks. All I care about is getting home. Got four young 'uns back in England, and a wife due to drop another any day now."

"How came you to be in this situation?" Like he would an insect, Bahir studied Tim.

"We took passage on a merchantman to Genoa. It was supposed to be heading back for Dover, but when we reached Lisboa, our captain picked up a rich load that needed a way to Damascus. Like I said, my wife is about to birth another one. I want to get home. A couple of the lads wanted the same and we jumped ship."

Henry did not know what to make of Tim's story.

Bahir shrugged.

"There are but five of us," Tim said. "As it is, we are going to need you lads to jump to if we hit a good blow. Judging by how many you sent overboard in your recent...discussions, you have nothing to fear from us." He grinned. "But if you saw fit to show your gratitude when we reach home, the lads and I will not be making a fuss."

Home. The word sent a shiver down Henry's spine. Only four days away now. Hard to believe when he had resigned himself to never returning.

Newt gave him a subtle nod.

"Get your men," Henry said. "We sail with the tide."

Tim's lads turned out to be a scraggly old man, two boys too young for beards, and a round, smooth-faced man who spoke like a woman.

Hard-pressed not to laugh at the look on Bahir's face, Henry greeted them all.

Tim strode across the deck yelling things like "get your fat ass in that rigging, Boils." Boils, Henry surmised was the round man.

Still, he didn't breathe easier until the boat slipped her mooring and slid out of the bay. As Lisboa receded with the stiff breeze filling their sails, he stood at the railing.

"English." Bahir appeared beside him. "Newt and I have the deck."

Henry stared at him, aware he had missed a hint.

Rolling his eyes, Bahir chuckled. "Get yourself below and tell your wife what is happening."

"Indeed." Aware Alya waited below, Henry had been hesitating joining her. Riding him hard was the knowledge he had yet to make his bride a wife. Not for lack of wanting.

"Trust me on this." Bahir slapped his back. "As a man who spent many hours in a harem. You best get down there."

Since the night after their marriage Henry had not spent much time alone with his wife. Wife? Interesting description for the woman who now shared his life. Strangers brought together by unseen twists of fate and now tied together for the remainder of their lives.

He recognized his musings for what they were—a cowardly attempt to ignore the erratic thump of his heart against his breastbone. Although no virgin when he had left Anglesea, he could not claim his brothers' ease with women. William and Roger had dragged him off to meet the village whore, Lilly, when he came of age. Lilly, bless her kind heart, had done the rest. Other than Lilly, there had been a handful of drunken tumbles, and two bored and experienced court ladies.

None of them had made his palms sweat as he contemplated touching them.

Below decks smelled of Alya. Cinnamon and night-flowering jasmine. A heady combination that made his senses whirl. Hand braced against the bulkhead for balance due to his limp knees, he stood and drew it into him. Standing on the roof, watching the sunset, Alya had possessed no unique scent. He had not known the plush pillow of her lips, or touched the cool silk of her skin.

"Henry?" Long hair spilling like ink down her back, she wove into sight. Her silk chemise clung to the dark circle of her nipples and dipped into the shadowed place of wonder between her thighs.

Mouth suddenly dry, he struggled to produce sensible words. "Aye."

"You will sleep here?" In one hand, she held a brush.

"Aye." The need to touch overcame him and he took the brush from her.

She frowned at him.

Henry guided her to the bed and sat beside her. He could allow himself this. "Allow me."

The bed reflected more Alya. Crisp cotton bedding so white it glowed in the dim light. Vivid scarlet, blue, and orange pillows appeared even brighter on its pristine surface.

He slid his hand over the smooth fall of hair, so dark it shone with its own light. Thick and silky, the ends curled about his fingers as if reaching for him and clasping him in a gentle embrace. Beneath the heavy fall lay the vulnerable sweetness of her nape, begging for his lips. His fingers brushed her delicate skin.

Alya shivered. Slowly she arched her neck to the side in a silent plea for more.

Henry let his fingertips linger on the fine arch of sinew. He followed the elegant sweep to her shoulder. Her chemise gave way before his questing touch. Small bones, delicate below her skin, marked her shoulder. He explored them before he palmed the swell of her upper arm. Her skin against his hand was the color of crushed almonds. Would it taste as sweet as the paste they made of almonds, rosewater, and honey?

Beneath his lips, her warm skin begged for the touch of his tongue. Warm, slightly salty and underneath, pure honey.

Alya drew in her breath.

Her chemise slipped over her shoulder and revealed the swell of her breast. A tiny silken bow quivered between her breasts as she breathed. The only thing standing between her and his hungry gaze.

"Henry." She twined her fingers with his around the brush.

With his lips, he followed the path his fingers had taken, moving from her shoulder to her neck. Tendrils of hair stuck to his hair-roughened chin.

Henry closed his eyes and breathed deep.

His girl on the wall. Here. Under his hands. His mouth on her. She was real. "Alya."

Like a cat she arched her neck and rubbed her head against his.

He tightened his grip on her arm. The brush dropped and he took her small hand in his. He ran his nose over the fine line of her jawbone, up over her cheek to her temple. She unmanned him. So achingly beautiful he both dared not sully her with his touch, and was powerless to stop. He kissed her temple.

Boots clumped on the deck above them. A voice called out unintelligible words. A fainter voice answered.

Their breathing mingled.

Henry's fingers found the fluttering bow at the neck of her chemise and tugged.

She gasped. Her chemise slid to her waist.

Dark nipples crowned high, round breasts and he had to touch. His hand shook as he palmed the soft weight.

On a soft moan, Alya arched into his touch.

Dear God, he would spend from touching her alone. Like a man ensorcelled, he brushed her nipple with his thumb.

Her flesh puckered and swelled, demanding more of his attention. Words he formed without awareness whispered from him. "Alya, you slay me."

"More." She pressed her hand to her breast. "I need more."

In this they were very much of one mind. He cupped both her breasts. Full flesh swelled over his hands.

Alya moaned and shifted.

Beneath the chemise pooled at her waist lay more of her mystery. Enslaved by the lure, he slid his hands over the smooth planes of her stomach.

Her muscles clenched beneath his palms.

Fingers brushing her chemise, he stopped. "May I?"

"Please." She wrapped her arms about his neck, pushing her breasts high and baring herself to him.

He touched the coarse curls at the apex of her thighs.

On a murmur, she parted her thighs for him.

Henry slid his fingers into the warm wet heaven. His rod leaped in response. He wanted between her thighs, to join his aching flesh with hers.

From the deck came a coarse bark of laughter, a harsh reminder of where they were.

He could not take her here. Not for her first time. To mark their joining as man and wife he wanted more than a hasty, silent coupling aboard a boat. But he could give her pleasure, and watch her come apart for him.

When he brushed the raised pebble of sensation that would bring her to completion, she started, catching her breath.

Henry dipped back between her wet folds, drawing the moisture over her key.

Her hips picked up the rhythm of his hand, moving against him.

He followed the signals her body gave him, using her soft gasps, the undulations of her hips as his guide. The perfume of her arousal filled his nostrils. Soon, he would bury his face in the honey coating his fingers.

Alya went over the edge with a low keen.

Henry rode the wave with her, bringing her down slowly until she slumped against him.

Powerless to resist, he slid his fingers from her and slipped them between his lips. The taste of her nearly sent him over the edge. Female musk that could drive a man out of his mind.

"Henry?" she whispered, the sound sweet and vulnerable.

Henry wrapped his arms about her and drew her against his chest. He lay down amidst her bright pillows and brought her down with him. With Alya tucked against him, her head resting against his chin, peace washed over Henry. Despite the throb in his braies, he was content to lie here and hold her until the steady rhythm of her breathing told him she slept.

The boat plowed through the waves to Anglesea, but Henry was already home.

Chapter Fifteen

Alya woke with the smell of Henry still on the pillow beside her. She buried her face and took a deep breath. Last night, Henry had opened an entirely new world of experience to her. Speaking of these things with Bahir and other women did not come close to the actual experience.

Her limbs felt loose and easy this morning, and she indulged in a long stretch.

Using the water left for her, she bathed and then took her time dressing. She climbed onto deck with the morning well advanced.

Smelly Tim nodded at her as he passed. A frown marring his smooth brow, the round sailor stopped coiling rope and watched her.

Morning sunlight catching the growing gold of his hair Henry stood with Newt and Bahir. As she approached, he glanced up and smiled.

Alya wanted to drag him back below deck and make him do more things to her. Her thoughts brought happy tingles all over her.

With a knowing look, Bahir crossed his arms.

Heat climbed her cheeks and she chose to greet Newt first.

A wink and a naughty grin from Newt eased her past the slight awkwardness. "How is our lovely Lady Alya this morning?"

"Lady?" A younger sailor stopped and stared.

Henry scowled at the man.

Dropping his head, the sailor scuttled away.

"Did you sleep well?" Henry's warm gaze chased the moment away. He tucked a loose strand of hair behind her ear.

"Perfectly." She could not stop the wide smile that spread over her face.

Bahir cleared his throat. "Tim tells me we make good progress this morning."

"I'm famished." Newt nudged Bahir. "Come along, big man, let's find something for me to eat."

"Do you ever stop eating?" Still grumbling, Bahir followed Newt across the deck.

Alya raised her face and closed her eyes, reveling in the sun and the breeze.

"Alya." Henry's tone sounded grave.

Alya wanted to keep her eyes closed and hold onto her sense of contentment forever. Reluctantly she looked at him. "Aye."

"Newt tells me there has been some grumbling amongst the men."

"Again?" Around them, their small crew all seemed to be busy.

"This time it's not about the treasure." Henry took her hand in his. "I'm afraid some of my countrymen are struggling with our marriage."

"Our marriage?" Alya did not see what they could object to. Then again, her uncle's reaction had taken her by surprise. The truth settled like old bread in her gut. "Let me guess. They do not approve of your infidel wife."

Henry frowned down at her hand. He raised it to his mouth and kissed her fingers. "They fear what they do not understand. Tim remembers the last holy pilgrimage. He even sailed on one of the boats that took us to Damascus."

These damned wars. They had destroyed so many lives, hers included. If not for the wars, her father's life might never have been in danger. She might never have had to run from her home. She would never have met Henry. Which raised a question. "Why did you join the pilgrimages?"

Henry lowered her hand to the railing. Staring out to sea, his face grew thoughtful. "I believed it was my duty as a Christian to bring God's Word to the unbelievers."

Something about his manner made her want to pry further. "And now? What do you believe now?"

On the railing his knuckles whitened. "Now I am not sure what I believe." He scowled. "I have seen things done in the name of God that made me doubt the existence of the very God they were perpetrated on behalf of. I have done things…" He shook his head. When he faced her, his eyes were colder than ice. "I do not speak of it."

Alya wanted to protest the manner in which he had slammed her out of the conversation. To hide her hurt, she changed the topic. "We have never spoken of what your family will make of me."

"My family will accept you." It sounded more like a threat than a reassurance. "You are my wife and you will be treated with the respect that is your due."

The looks on the faces of the men about her did not reassure Alya. Over the day, she noticed how many times their gazes tracked her. The way they bent and whispered amongst themselves, glancing at her. When Henry stood beside her, the men reverted to polite disinterest.

Bahir drew the same covert hostility. Except with him, fear tinged their glances.

Henry had served in her father's home for years, a stranger amongst them with his pale eyes and strange language. In England, she and Bahir would be the strangers, the unbelievers.

How life had turned. It seemed impossible that so much had happened in only a few short weeks.

* * *

By the deliberately casual way Newt approached him Henry guessed that he wasn't going to like what Newt had to say.

Newt leaned against the crate. "Tim tells me we should make England in three days if this wind keeps up."

"Indeed." Times beyond counting Newt had sidled into his tent whilst on pilgrimage, shoved his hands deep in his pockets and cast a disinterested stare in front of him. For a moment, he was tempted to laugh as a string of memories rose. "Well, Sir Henry, there was this mule." Or, "So, Sir Henry, just how attached are you to your surcoat?" And on one memorable occasion, "Now, Sir Henry, is it really stealing when the other person does not even want a thing they have? Especially if I really, really want that thing."

"Spit it out, Newt."

Newt grinned. "I hate how you do that."

Henry waited.

"Bahir and I have been talking."

Indeed! Newt and Bahir spent much time together lately. An unlikelier pair, Henry could not imagine. "And?"

"We are concerned by the crew's reaction to your marriage."

Hot rage surged through him. "The crew should mind their own business."

"Ordinarily I would agree with you." Newt used his best conciliatory face. "However, we are floating in the middle of an ocean, with a king's ransom below decks, and the crew are our best chance of getting home in one piece."

Newt's point hit home. Henry had to grit his teeth to stop from lashing out. "So what do you and Auntie Bahir suggest?"

"Harry, you know me." Newt shrugged. "I've spent most of my life telling the world to go suck ballocks. But we think a little discretion would go a long way to seeing us home without further incident."

"Discretion." The word tasted vile in his mouth. Years as a

slave, with no right to his own opinions and actions, and now again the claws of entrapment rose around him. He ached to tear them away, break free and roar his defiance to God. He steadied his erratic breathing. "What does that mean?"

With those old-man eyes in his young face Newt watched him. "You and Alya are married, the crew know as much. Perhaps it would be better not to push that in their faces."

"I should pretend not to be married to make the crew more comfortable?"

Eyes scrunched against the sun, Smelly Tim stood at the tiller. Another man in control of Henry's destiny. Henry swallowed the impotent rage and managed a nod. Never again. He stared out to sea. At this journey's end, he would make sure he held his destiny in his hands.

* * *

Alya spent most of her time below deck. Henry never spoke of it to her, but something had been said between him and Newt. He didn't spend his nights with her either. She sensed it had to do with the crew. As much as she comforted herself with the knowledge that in a few short days they would be out of her life forever, it did raise uncomfortable questions about her reception in England.

Anglesea. She tried the name out loud. A distant place. Henry's home. What would it mean for her?

She spent the time sewing. Never her favorite occupation but with nothing else to do, she copied the dresses Henry had brought her, using the fabrics in the chests from Father. It made her feel closer to her father. Father had wanted her to take her place amongst his people and she could begin by looking like one of them.

Taking pity on her solitude Newt spent time with her, teaching her new English words and customs. He also had nimble enough fingers to stitch a hem. Although he made her swear on her life never to tell. As Henry's squire, he'd often sewed up the tears and rents in Henry's raiment. He told her stories of Henry as a warrior that made her shudder at times. Henry's fearlessness had often seen him in the midst of battle. She liked better the stories Newt told of Henry's family. What would they make of her?

Chapter Sixteen

Through a low-lying morning fog the battlements of Anglesea wavered into view and Henry held his cloak about him. The tightness in his chest made breathing difficult. She stood on a promontory, surrounded by sea on three sides and declared to all who saw her that she guarded these lands. How is it possible he had forgotten how enormous she was? How impregnable.

Jesu, and he had thought never to see her again.

A stiff onshore breeze pushed their small boat forward. Home.

The sun rose and burned off the fog, and still he stood frozen at the railing, his gaze locked on the great keep. As they drew closer, greater detail came into view. The mighty curtain wall riding the edge of the cliff. Casement openings appeared in the unbroken gray walls. From those casements, the view of the sea was breathtaking, and ever changeable. Did Mother look out of one of those casements and see their small boat bobbing on the blue sea and wonder who she carried?

A warm hand slid into his. Alya. "Is that Anglesea?"

"Aye." He could manage no more words past the lump in his

throat. Alya's hands in his provided the only anchor in his whirling world.

"So huge," Alya whispered. "I had no idea."

The keep of the renowned Sir Arthur of Anglesea reflected her lord. Large, impressive, and ready to do battle with any who would challenge her.

On the tallest tower, Father's colors streamed in the wind. Dragon's head proper upon argent. Henry had marched away with those colors emblazoned across his chest. Proud to declare his allegiance to the world.

Alya pointed to a cluster of low thatched roofs. "What is that?"

"The village of Anglesea," Henry said. "It serves the castle."

"Castle." Alya used the English word, slowly and carefully as if testing it on her tongue. Then she said, "Ang-el-sea."

"Home," Henry said.

"Coming about," Smelly Tim yelled. "Trim those sails."

The prow of the boat slowed in its carve through the water with a slight shudder beneath their feet. Then her nose turned and made straight for the fishing dock that served the village. His village. Would they even know him there?

As if sensing his need for reassurance, Alya pressed closer to his side.

On the end of the dock, two fishermen stopped hauling their nets and turned and watched the boat approaching.

"Ho, the dock!" Smelly Tim called.

One of the fishermen raised his hand in greeting. Reedy and thin with distance, the man called, "Who goes there?"

"Henry." Henry's voice came out as a strangled whisper.

Alya slid her arm about his waist.

"Sir Henry," he called across the water. "Sir Henry of Anglesea."

Both fishermen jerked upright. Their net dropped from their hands.

Henry raised his arm. He searched his memory for the name of the older man. "I see you, Bernar."

"Lord above!" Bernar took a step to the edge of the dock. "God save us all. It is Sir Henry."

Yelling as he ran, the other man took off for the village.

Tim threw the ropes. They hit the dock and Bernar started. He leaped forward before the rope could slide away. Splitting his glance between Henry and his task, he tied the boat off.

Gently, the boat kissed the dock and rocked to a halt.

Tears streamed down Bernar's weathered cheeks. "Saints be praised. It is you. It is Sir Henry."

"Go." Alya gave him a gentle shove. "You are home."

As he leaped to the dock, Henry felt weak as a newborn calf and his legs nearly gave way.

Bernar dropped to his knees.

Henry had no words. Tears dropped onto the deck between him and Bernar. His or the other man's he knew not. Henry knelt beside him. "I am home, Bernar."

Grabbing his offered hand, Bernar squeezed. "We prayed." He cleared his throat. "We prayed and prayed for your safe deliverance. But we never thought...We hoped, but so much time..."

From the village, figures appeared, streaming toward the dock. Voices raised in question. Other voices raised in praise. The dock shook under the combined weight of many feet.

Familiar faces surrounded Henry. The names rose from the dark place in his memory. Hands touched his shoulder, his chest, his arms. It overwhelmed him, and suddenly he needed Alya.

Henry searched through the people until he located her standing beside Newt looking so beautiful. He wrapped his hand about her and tugged her to his side. With Alya beside him, he found the courage to take one step and then another.

Around them people ebbed and flowed.

Clear as the morning about them the village bells pealed. Rising and falling in a continuous carol, the bells declared him home.

Through the village, the tide of people took him. Henry had no chance to look about him and absorb the changes. Up the hill they went and entered the cool, quiet of the beech thicket. Alya walked with him, her head turning constantly as she looked about her. Henry tried to familiarize her with all she saw, but his words stopped and started, stuttered and fell into a confusing jumble.

The beech thicket thinned and the meadow opened before them. Too late in the year for the glorious spring wildflowers, and now covered in thick, golden strands of waving grass. And still the bells pealed out their news.

The crowd around them swelled as folk streamed from the castle to see what brought such joy.

The drawbridge clattered under the tramp of so many feet. Beneath the entrance arch they went, thrown briefly into the shade of the great stone arms protecting Anglesea's front.

The wood gave way to the sand of the outer bailey.

A man pelted though the curtain wall from the inner bailey. The crowd melted away.

Dark hair, broad shoulders, the man stopped.

Henry's feet froze. He met his brother's fierce blue gaze. "Roger."

Roger strode forward, shock and disbelief carved into his hewn features.

Henry lost his hold on Alya as Roger lunged and snatched him into a bone-crushing hold. "Dear God." Roger's rough, deep voice in his ear. "Dear God. Henry."

Henry clung to his brother's tunic, the linen fine beneath his fingers. Roger smelled of horse, leather and ale, the fragrance of home. Henry's knees buckled, his control shattered, and he sobbed.

* * *

Green, everywhere Alya looked and so bright it almost hurt her eyes. The air clung warm and moist to her skin. England smelled of damp earth and growing things. She tried to take it all in as the crowd marched them forward. All attention fixed on Henry, they barely noticed her above the occasional curious glance or whisper.

Newt walked at her shoulder, trying to murmur explanations in her ear but she barely heard anything he said.

The neat village, larger than it appeared from the sea with white houses and what looked like grass on the roofs, flashed past. The women wore skirts as she did, some of them confined their hair beneath cloth. The men dressed as Henry, only not as fine.

Everyone spoke at once, speaking so quickly she barely caught a word above "god" and "Henry".

Henry's hand trembled in hers, conveying tension in his every fiber.

And the bells with that infernal clanging and clanking? A happy sound, but discordant and without established tune, it went on and on and on.

As they marched through the trees, she wanted to stop and touch them. She had never imagined trees could grow so thick and tall, nearly blocking out the blue of the sky. Under her feet, the ground squelched with more plants. How much water did it take to grow this many plants and keep them this green? She liked growing things. That tiny detail gave her the first flutter of maybe this might all be well.

The castle dispelled the flutter. Tall, gray, forbidding and stern it seemed to stare down at her and demand she state her business. *"Please, sir, I am Henry's wife."*

Anglesea loomed, unimpressed by the words she whispered in her mind.

Massive gates guarded the portal, studded with metal and spikes. Surely nobody entered here without permission.

Henry froze.

A man stood and stared at him, painful hope on his face. She would know him as Henry's kin anywhere. The sculpted lines of both their faces marked their shared blood. Tall, like Henry, broad and powerfully built. This man reminded her of the fighting men who had invaded her homeland. The sword strapped to his hip so much a part of him it left no doubt as to his ability to wield it.

He snatched Henry into a hard embrace. Suddenly separated from Henry she almost lost her balance.

Newt caught her elbow and steadied her. "Henry's oldest brother, Roger."

Handsome, but nothing to her Henry, Roger had dark hair with the same intense blue eyes.

Golden hair streaming out behind her, a woman pelted toward them. She overran herself, tripped, but stayed on her feet.

Newt gasped. "Sweet Bea."

"Heeenry!" she yelled. Flushed, sobbing, and battling to catch her breath, she cut through the crowd and flung herself at Henry and Roger.

Henry spun and caught her. She wrapped her arms around his neck and clung, her slim back heaving.

A dark-haired man, not of the same stamp as Roger and Henry, appeared at her side. He said something to her in English.

"This is Garrett," Newt said. "He asked who you were."

Garrett had eyes as dark as his hair and he assessed her keenly, waiting for her to respond.

Carefully forming the English words in her mind first, she said to Garrett, "I am Alya."

"Newt." The man pulled Newt into a hug. He said something in English she did not catch, but it involved more hugging and a few hearty shoulder pounds.

Newt responded in French for her benefit. "I said that I could do it." Color suffused his cheeks. "Garrett congratulates me on finding Henry and bringing him home."

"He sent you to find Henry?"

"He and Roger did. The family feared him dead."

"So." Garrett reverted to French, with a truly horrible accent. "Who is pretty Alya, and what brings her to Anglesea."

"God, Bea!" Henry also spoke French as he pried her arms from his neck. "Let me breathe."

"Nay." Bea shook her head and hung on. "I thought I had lost you. I thought I would never see your stupid face again, and now I cannot let go."

"Bea." Garrett laughed and tugged her away from Henry. "He is home. There will be plenty of time for all that now."

"But I missed him so much." Bea, which she now remembered was what Henry called his sister Beatrice, sniffled, her bottom lip quivering. "I made my peace with his death and now he stands here before me."

"It is a blessed day." Garrett put his arms about Bea. "And we owe our thanks to our old friend, Newt."

"Newt?" Bea scrubbed her eyes. "Is that really you?"

Newt tugged one ear, went bright red and shuffled his feet.

"You've grown so tall." Bea pressed his shoulders back, her gaze roving Newt. "And so handsome."

"Stop it, Bea, you're embarrassing him." Garrett tugged Bea away.

Bea waved him off and her gaze found Alya. "And who is this? Is this your sweetheart, Newt?"

"Um." Newt's head snapped up.

"Nay." Henry slipped his arm about Alya's waist. "This is Alya, and she is my sweetheart. Actually, she's a bit more than that. She's my wife."

* * *

Bea recovered first, and Henry blessed her happy squeal. "A wife? Henry, who would have thought you had it in you."

Whatever Bea meant by that escaped him. "She is still learning English, but she speaks French beautifully."

"Ah." Bea stepped closer to Alya. "Welcome to Anglesea, Alya. What a beautiful name, I've never heard the like."

Bea's happy way of viewing the world used to irk him, now he saw it for a blessing. Bea approached everyone with the same cheerful expectation that they would be friends.

"Lady Alya." Roger bowed over her hand. "Welcome to the family."

"Thank you." Regal as a queen, Alya smiled and Henry wanted to puff his chest out with pride.

"Get out of the way, you lot." Nurse's voice rippled through Henry and he nearly broke down again. "Let me see my boy."

Her boy. Aye, true enough. Nurse had stood as second mother to all of them.

Rotund and grumpy, Nurse came around the much taller Roger and stopped, twisting her hands in her apron. Scrutinizing him from head to toe she nodded. "It really is you."

As she folded like a piece of cloth, Roger barely caught her before she hit the floor.

Everyone seemed to shout at once. People surged this way and that and Henry felt his breath strangle in his throat. Suddenly, it was all too much. His past and future merged in a confusion of sights and sounds, and part of him wanted to grab Alya and run back to the boat with her.

Then Alya was beside him, her small hand slipping into his. "Shall we go inside?"

"At least one of us is thinking straight," Roger said, red in the face from the effort of holding Nurse up. He scowled at Garrett. "Get your ass over here and give me a hand."

The door to Anglesea loomed. Henry could not get his feet to move. Memories rushed out of the dark maw and threatened to bury him. He, Roger, and William running through that door and yelling as they headed to some new adventure. Standing there the night Faye's sons went missing. Mother framed in the doorway, sunlight burnishing her hair to a golden halo. Father bellowing all the way across the bailey at the practice yards.

Roger led the way. He and Garrett carrying Nurse between them.

Bea looked back at him, and smiled. "Are you coming?"

"Aye." Alya answered for him. Tightening her grip on his hand she led him forward.

Henry blinked in the darkness inside the keep. The smell hit him—rushes, the lavender Mother used to perfume them, wood, fire, and baking bread.

Beside him Alya swiveled this way and that, her eyes huge in her face. He should take the time to familiarize her but his brain kept tripping into the past.

A large mastiff dog barked and approached.

Alya shrank closer to him.

"Quiet, Dagger," Roger said. He turned back to them. "My wife's dog."

Wife? "Ah, aye. Newt told me you were married."

Roger stopped and got a sappy grin on his face.

Garrett grunted as most of Nurse's weight transferred to him.

"Aye." Roger helped Garrett seat Nurse in one of the large carved chairs Mother and Father always occupied. "I am married now and I could not be happier."

"Roger?" A lovely dark haired woman entered the hall. "Did I hear true? They say Henry is..." She gaped at him. "It must be true."

Dressed in braies and a fine tunic of scarlet linen, Henry was sure he did not know her.

"Speaking of wives." Roger's chest swelled. "This is my Kathryn."

His Kathryn? They fit together like two puzzle pieces. Henry held out his hand. "I am rather late in offering my condolences on your marriage."

Kathryn laughed, a husky, attractive sound. She brushed past his outstretched hand. "I apologize for this." She gave him a hard hug. "But I feel as if I know you." Flushing, she stepped back. "You have become real to me through Roger and everyone else at Anglesea."

Henry warmed to her immediately. Kathryn met his eyes with her direct gaze. "I am sure only half of what they said was true."

"Oh." Kathryn stared at Alya. "You are...lovely. Beautiful."

Henry liked her even more for her lack of guile or tact.

Alya giggled and squirmed closer to him. "Thank you."

"Get off me." Nurse slapped away Bea's hands and sat up.

Bea tried to press her back into the chair. "Nurse, you fainted."

"Nonsense." Nurse straightened her wimple. "I do not faint." She heaved herself to her feet, and twitched her skirts back into place. Pointing at Henry, she said, "Get over here and let Nurse have a look at you."

Some things never changed and Henry did as he was told.

Nurse took his face in her gnarled, calloused palms. She studied him. "You're thinner," she said. "And I do not care for your shorn head."

Feeling all of five years, he rubbed a hand over his scalp. "They shaved my head to guard against vermin."

"Huh." Nurse continued her examination. She poked his shoulder. "You look stronger, though. At least they fed your properly." Suddenly Nurse clasped her hands around him. She buried her face in his chest. "My boy," she whispered. "My Henry."

Roger cleared his throat. "Mother and Father are at Calder. I have sent a messenger already."

Nurse harrumphed and stepped away from him. She wiped her cheeks with her apron. "Make sure you send riders North. William and Alice will want to know."

Just in time he stopped himself from asking about Alice. With so much to learn and discover in this new version of Anglesea he needed to take it bit by bit. Much would have changed in the years he'd been gone. Most noticeable was that Anglesea was now Roger's keep. Everyone deferred to him as lord. Even knowing as much from Newt, the strangeness of not seeing his powerful, robust father bellowing out orders shook him. Without thought he searched the hall for his lovely, gracious mother.

"There's a lot to take in." Roger squeezed his shoulder. "I'm not sure where to start."

"Sir Roger!" A guard sprinted into the hall, his face flushed. "There's a...man. A big man. He's...he says he is with Sir Henry."

"Aye." Roger glowered at the man, so like their father Henry's head whirled.

The guard squirmed. "It's just...Sir Roger...he's...dark. Very dark. I think he might be a devil."

Henry suppressed the surge of irritation. It was not the guard's fault he had never seen someone like Bahir before, but to assume his dark complexion made him the devil irked Henry no end. "His name is Bahir," he said and looked to Roger. "He is with me."

"Then let him in." Roger shook his head. "Do not leave a guest standing at our gates."

"Bahir stayed behind to watch the boat," Henry said. "We travelled with considerable wealth that belongs to Alya."

"You get to keep your wealth on your marriage?" Kathryn shot Roger a look. "Maybe I should have gone where Alya comes from?"

Roger grabbed Kathryn about the hips and drew her to him. "You're not going anywhere."

"Not yet."

"Not ever."

From the besotted look on Roger's face, Henry judged he'd made a love match.

"Can you fight as well?" Kathryn looked at Alya.

"A bit." Alya shrugged.

She could? Henry knew he stared but he couldn't help himself.

Alya clasped her hands in front of her. "Bahir taught me how to take care of myself."

He had much to learn about his new wife. Here at Anglesea, safe behind her old walls, he and Alya could finally build a marriage.

A commotion followed Bahir into the hall. Behind him, swords drawn, four men-at-arms tripped over themselves to keep him in sight.

"Sir Roger." Bahir approached Roger and executed a flawless bow. "I am Bahir, I serve the Lady Alya. *Assalamualaikum warahmatullahi wabarakatuh.*

"Bahir wishes you peace, blessings, and mercy," Henry said.

"Lord above us." Nurse went to stand before Bahir. She barely reached his armpit. "You're a big lad, aren't you?"

Bahir shot Henry a confused look. That was Nurse for you. "This is Nurse, Bahir. She had the raising of all of us."

Bahir bowed to Nurse.

Nurse ran her hand over his forearm. "I have never seen the like." She rubbed his skin. "I wager you have no trouble hiding in the dark."

"I do some of my best work in the dark," Newt said.

Nurse gasped, then dissolved into an evil chuckle. "Oh, I've forgotten nothing about you young Newt."

"Come." Roger took Father's chair before the hearth. He motioned Henry, Bahir, and Newt to join him. "I need to hear how this all happened." Clicking his fingers at a freckled faced page, he called for wine. Anglesea wine. Henry's mouth watered.

* * *

Up dark, winding stairs, Alya followed Kathryn and the old woman. Did all English hide around in their dark castles? Despite the warmth of the day, the walls held enough chill to make her long for her cloak. Thick grasses covering the floor caught in the hem of her gown.

She stopped, once again, to remove stalks before they pulled the delicate silk.

The old woman tapped her arm. She said something in English. Her accent differed from Henry and Newt and Alya blinked at her, feeling horribly stupid.

The woman rolled her eyes, picked up her own skirts, and jerked her head at Alya's skirts. From this she guessed the woman told her to keep her skirts from touching the floor. Alya could barely look at the floor without shuddering. Dark, dirty, and cold, she did not think much of this Anglesea of Henry's.

The old woman tapped her chest. "Nurse." She then tapped Alya's chest. "Alya."

Kathryn leaned closer. "Everyone calls her Nurse."

Ah! The older woman was trying to tell her what to call her.

"Noose." Alya tried the word out.

Kathryn giggled and shook her head. "Nuuurse."

Alya watched Kathryn's lips form the word. Her cheeks heated, this was like being a child all over again. She copied the movements. "Nuuurse."

Kathryn clapped her hands, and Nurse grinned at her.

"Nurse." Nurse jabbed her thumb at her chest again.

"Alya." Alya jabbed her thumb at her chest.

Then they all grinned at each other. Oh, dear Lord, at this rate in a year or two she might be able to ask Nurse to pass the bread.

She followed Kathryn and Nurse up the stairs to a large open corridor. The air smelled fresher up here, and those horrible grasses no longer littered the floor. Large, colorful tapestries adorned the walls. If she had more light she could examine them better. They marched past several wooden doors before Nurse stopped at one and opened it.

Light poured into this room through huge arched casements.

"Henry." Nurse circled her arm to encompass the chamber. Then she mimed sleeping.

A large bed stood to their left. Wooden beams supported heavy coverings around the bed. Alya had never seen wood of such a rich, deep color. Furs covered the floor. At the fireplace, a young woman dressed in simpler clothing set a small fire. She glanced up and rose when they entered.

More heavy fabric hung on either side of the casements. A deep green that reminded her of emeralds, but with delicate stitchery in gold. Beneath one window a padded bench looked like the perfect place to while away time. Alya approached the casement.

The view took her breath away.

Kathryn showed her how to unlatch the window and opened it for her. "This is one of my favorite parts of Anglesea." She stood beside Alya. "It seems as if you can see right to the end of the world."

"Aye." Cool breeze carrying the tang of the sea caressed her cheeks. Large white birds wheeled and squawked over the water.

Nurse and the young girl spoke behind them. Alya had no idea what they said. She trusted Kathryn to let her know if she needed to mind them.

"Nurse asked if you would care to bathe," Kathryn said.

Bathe? To be truly clean for the first time in weeks. Alya could hardly contain the grin as she nodded. She moved to the hearth. A sweet woodsy smell rose from the fire. They must perfume it with something. Before the hearth two carved wooden chairs stood ready for someone to take a seat and toast their feet on the blaze. The castle depressed her, but this room showed promise. Already she could picture some of the fabrics in her chests turned into bright cushions and drapery. In this space, she could create a bright, happy nest for her and Henry.

Thumps sounded from outside the door, followed by a knock.

Wearing a huge grin Newt entered with her clothing chest. "Bahir is clucking like a mother hen about you, and I came to check on you."

"I am well." Alya wanted to insist Newt sit with her until Henry returned.

"Nurse will take care of you." Newt winked at her. "She's a sour old harridan, but her heart is pure gold."

Three dogs had followed Newt into the chamber.

Alya could scarcely believe her eyes. Neither Kathryn nor

Nurse seemed to be bothered by the dogs. Indeed, one of the dogs came up to Kathryn and nudged her hand.

Kathryn petted the beast.

A dog. A filthy, disease and vermin infested beast that should never be allowed into her dwelling. The enormity of how different things were here in England pressed down on her.

Chapter Seventeen

Nurse and Kathryn left her once they had seen her safely in the wooden bathing tub. Nurse put a few drops of rose-scented oil in the water before she left.

The soap was rich and soft and smelled delightful, something floral, but not familiar to her. How would they feel if she offered them some of her perfumed oils? She washed her hair thrice before the water chilled too much to be comfortable.

Getting out of the bath she nearly stepped on a yellow dog lying before the hearth, keen brown gaze on her. As she stood, so did the dog.

Alya sat down in her bath again.

The dog watched her.

The gap between the door and the dog seemed far too small, and she had seen how fast they could move.

The dog opened its mouth wide, flashing a terrifying set of white, long teeth. Did it mean to bite her with those? Then it lay back down again with a grumble.

Alya nearly laughed. The dog had yawned, that was all.

"You should leave here," she said to it.

The dog thumped the floor with its tail. Ears jerked straight up as if it listened, it raised its head and looked at her.

"Out." Alya used her most strident tone and pointed to the door.

The dog thumped its tail again.

It did not seem to want to attack her. Moving slowly, she rose from the bath again.

The dog watched.

"You eat your own excrement," she said as she wrapped a bathing sheet about her nakedness. "It makes you a filthy animal."

Unabashed, the dog cocked its head.

The door opened and Kathryn walked in. "I thought you might be done."

Kathryn called her beautiful, but Alya had never seen skin so white and delicate as Kathryn's. Certainly not with dark hair and eyes like Kathryn's. Her figure was a little slimmer than most women, but it made her appear strong and healthy. Alya coveted Kathryn's clothes. No stupid dresses trailing in the dirt for her, but instead Kathryn wore much the same thing as Henry, only smaller.

"I see you have company." Kathryn pointed to the dog. She clicked her fingers and the dog trotted to her. Its tongue hung pink and wet out of the corner of its mouth.

Alya shuddered as the dog licked Kathryn's hands. Did Kathryn not know where else that tongue had been?

"I think she is one of Dagger's daughters," Kathryn said. "Dagger has been busy since he arrived at Anglesea."

From her clothing chest, Alya dug out the jasmine oil for her hair.

Watching everything she did, Kathryn perched on the edge of the bed.

Alya did not mind. Had their parts been reversed she would have been curious too and she rather liked the company.

As Alya combed the oil through her hair, Kathryn sniffed. "What is that?"

"Jasmine oil." Alya handed her the vial and Kathryn took a deeper sniff.

"It smells wonderful." Kathryn's pretty face lit up.

"It makes my hair shine." There was something very reassuring about talking about womanly pursuits with another woman.

"Really?" Kathryn peered into the vial.

"I have more if you would like to try it."

Kathryn smiled at her. "I would like that." She nodded. "And I want you to know that if there is anything you need to ask, I would be glad to answer your questions."

The first tendrils of friendship pressed back the isolation and warmed her.

The door opened and Henry entered the chamber. His presence shrunk the space as he stopped and stared.

Feeling suddenly naked before the stark hunger in his eyes, Alya pushed her shoulders back, and held her ground.

"Lady Kathryn." Hot gaze never leaving Alya, he bowed. Like a touch on her skin, his gaze roamed her drying sheet encased form. His voice deepened as he greeted her. "My lady."

And she was. His lady. Henry's lady. Except Alya really did not want to be a lady anymore. She had no fear of marriage intimacy. Bahir had years ago dispelled any fears she might have. Working as a guard in a harem gave Bahir a unique view of women and fleshly pleasures and he shared much of it with her. Although she suspected he kept an even larger portion from her.

"Right." Kathryn's glance bounced between them and she giggled. "I think I will go and find Roger."

Winking at Alya, she scuttled for the door and shut it behind her.

A log popped in the fire and Alya jumped.

Henry stalked her.

Alya stood, a flush spreading over her skin. Under his silent intensity her limbs trembled.

In slow measured steps, Henry circled her.

This must be how the lamb felt trapped in the stare of the lion.

He stopped behind her. Close enough for his heat to prickle along her spine. "Alya."

"Henry." Her breathy murmur sounded nothing like her.

"So beautiful." He tangled his fingers in her hair, and tugged her head back. Neck arched, she was exposed and vulnerable to him. "And here. In my home. In my chamber."

His tone staked a claim on her, so delicious it made her shiver.

"I watched." He stepped closer, his tunic soft against her bare shoulders. "As you stood on the wall at sunset."

"I know." Under his stare, she had wanted to preen.

He chuckled, his breath warm on her neck. "So you said." His lips caressed her neck. "We men and our intrigues and secrets, believing we are so clever to keep them hidden."

"I liked it." Alya's breath sounded loud. The feather-light caress of his lips intrigued, tantalized but fell far short of what she desired. "I liked that you watched me."

"Did you also know how my hands ached to touch you?" He stroked his palm from her wrist to her shoulder. "To discover if your skin was as soft and warm as it looked."

"Aye."

His hand cupped her shoulder and slid forward, his fingertips brushing the top edge of her sheet. "I never dreamed that I would have you here. In my home. My wife."

"Now that you have me here, what will you do with me?" This time she wanted it all. All the pleasure he had hinted at when he brought her to completion with his hand on the boat.

"So brazen." He nipped at her neck. With a snap, he pulled the covering from her.

Alya thrust her shoulders back. Naked before him she felt no shame. Let him look on her.

Henry moved around her, his gaze like a touch against her skin, hot and real. "Jesu, you take my breath away."

"Is this what you pictured, when you looked up at me on the roof?" His desire emboldened her.

He shook his head. "Nothing I pictured could come close to this."

A slight chill in the room pebbled her skin. Still, Henry stood there as if he had taken root on the floor.

"You can touch." Impatience tinged her voice. "I am standing right before you."

He gave her a rueful smile. "I am finding it hard to believe you will not disappear like smoke."

"Henry." Her patience snapped, and Alya wrapped her arms around his neck. "I am here and I am real, and I demand you do something about it."

On a hitched breath, he gripped her hips and pulled her flush against him. "You demand?"

"Aye, I demand." Against her belly, his rod pressed, hard and insistent. "I demand my wifely rights."

He gripped her nape. "Aye, my lady."

At first, he kissed her softly, learning the shape of her mouth. The contact rippled through Alya, so sweet.

His tongue touched her lip and she opened to him. What Bahir had told her of kissing like this had not prepared her for the intimacy. The way the taste of Henry filled her senses, the slightly rough slide of his tongue over hers. He tasted of wine, and cinnamon mixed with the sweet tartness of oranges. She tangled her hands in his tunic, pulling him closer.

Hand thrillingly rough against her skin Henry's stroked the indentation of her waist. The hand at her nape tightened. He deepened the kiss, throwing her into a swirl of sensations that left her boneless and wanting.

His hand found her breast.

Alya moaned against the delicious onslaught. Her nipple pebbled beneath his seeking fingers. Her breasts felt full, heavy, and swollen. Between her thighs heat built and spread through her belly. She pressed into the weight of his rod.

She needed to touch his skin. Her fingers fumbled on his belt. It hit the floor with a clatter. Beneath his tunic his skin was hot and smooth over the hardness of muscle. Alya dug her fingers into his flesh.

Henry broke the kiss. Flushed, his eyes fever bright, he fisted the back of his tunic and dragged it over his head.

Alya took her turn and stared. Henry was beautifully made, a male animal in his prime. A scar cut across his belly and another closer to his collar bone. The body of a fighting man.

Henry tugged her back into his embrace.

The press of skin on skin took her breath away. Rougher hair on his chest abraded the sensitive tip of her breasts. Her softer form cleaved to his, her breasts pressed into the hardness of his chest.

"Let us take this where it belongs." Henry hauled her into his arms.

He placed her on the bed and came down beside her. Propping his head on his elbow, he lay on his side, studying her.

Desperate for the kiss she could no longer wait for, Alya pulled his head down to hers.

Henry slid his thigh between hers.

She parted for him.

His rod pressed into her woman's place. His chausses lay in the way of the contact she craved. Alya tugged at his waistband.

Henry raised himself above her.

Alya wrapped her legs about his hips and tried to bring him back into contact.

"Nay, my lady." The smile he gave her was pure devilment. "I have waited far too long for this to rush now."

His dark head lowered to her breast and took her nipple in his mouth.

Alya's back shot off the bed as the heat and wet of his mouth hit her in one dizzying wave.

He lavished attention on first one breast and then the other. Between her thighs, she ached, restless beneath his unrelenting sensual exploration.

His lips slid over her ribs. Hot kisses traced over her belly. He lifted her bottom and slid his shoulders between her thighs.

Dear Lord, she knew what came next. She had seen this in engravings, heard whispers of it.

His mouth on her drew a cry from her. Nothing had come close to this. His tongue moved on her secret flesh, sure and strong. He found the pleasure place and sucked. Alya dug her nails into his hair, holding him to her, not wanting this to ever end.

Savoring her as if he dined on a great feast, he took his time.

Completion throbbed through her, sharpened and exploded on a cry.

Henry rose above her. He slid off the bed and shucked the remainder of his clothing. Forearms bracketing her head, he pressed her deeper into the bed. "Honey." He framed her face with his big hands. "Every part of you tastes like honey."

His flesh pressed into hers.

Alya opened her thighs wider. She breathed deep as she instinctively tensed at his invading rod. Tilting her hips, she relaxed the muscles that would prevent his entry.

On a low groan, Henry slid deeper into her.

Her slick flesh stretched to accommodate him until he was fully seated within her.

He stilled, pressing his forehead to hers. "Heaven," he whispered. "I could stay here forever."

Slight discomfort receded as she accepted him into her body.

Henry moved with her. Easing out and back in. Chords stood out in his neck, his breath rasped. "I don't want to hurt you."

"You are not hurting me." Alya slid her hands down his back. Thick ridges crisscrossed his sweat-slicked skin as he thrust. Later, she would ask, but not now.

His buttocks clenched with each movement of his hip.

Alya dug her fingers into their firm flesh and pressed him on. Already her body yearned for more.

Thrusting harder, deeper, he responded to her silent demands.

Sensation built from their point of connection. It built inside her, slowly at first, then gathering momentum.

Henry's pace quickened, his breath hot on her face. "You are mine."

"Yours." Alya shattered around him.

On a groan, Henry followed her over the edge. He collapsed atop her, his chest rising and falling rapidly.

Alya folded arms and legs tightly around him. She wanted to keep him in the cradle of her body and hold onto the magic they had just shared.

Sweat cooled on her skin and she shivered.

Henry rolled off her.

At the loss of him Alya, murmured a protest.

Henry drew her into his arms, and pressed gentle kisses to her cheeks, her temples, her forehead. His hand tangled in her hair and pulled her head onto his shoulder. His arms folded strong and sure around her. "My girl on the wall."

Chapter Eighteen

N ot able to sleep, Henry lay beside Alya and watched her sleep. His full mind churned constantly. In a few days, there would be more to absorb when his mother and father came to Anglesea with Faye and Gregory. Roger had sent a message to Tarnwych as well, so William and his wife would make the journey south.

William married, in itself, took some thinking on. Aye, he'd known William had been amenable to the idea of an advantageous marriage. He had left on pilgrimage a few days before Father started his discussions with various bride's fathers.

The threat of him being next on the list had played no small part in his decision to take himself out of his father's matrimonial view.

Alya stirred and huffed in her sleep. She slept with her one hand tucked beneath her head and the other lying on the covers, as if she had been arranged that way.

His family would accept her because she was his wife, but the rest of the Anglesea folk might see things differently. Their reaction to Bahir he should have predicted. He had seen enough of it in Genoa. Most Anglesea folk, for all their inherent goodness, never journeyed further than the next village. Their world was closely confined by the sea, the castle, the fields, and the forest. Father provided well for his demesne, so they had no reason to move on.

More worrisome than Bahir looking different was that he was one of those *heathens* the church had sent its flock to fight.

Careful not to wake Alya, he slid out of bed and pulled his braies on.

Moonlight wavered on the surface of the sea. Trapped in Cairo he had not allowed himself to miss this view. Hardly any stars shone through the heavy blanket of cloud. So different from Cairo, where the stars covered the night sky like chainmail. Unlike Cairo, however, Anglesea had a good, sturdy mead and he could do with some of it.

He opened the door onto the passageway. A large dog stood up from where it had been lying outside the door. With a cursory swish of its tail, it entered his chamber. After a few sniffs the dog strolled to Alya's side of the bed and lay down.

Maybe he should remove the animal? Nay. Growing accustomed to dogs about all the time constituted one of the smaller adjustments Alya had to make.

With only the occasional taper and a splash of moonlight lighting the way the corridor remained mostly dark. His feet took a familiar path down the stone stairs. Things were so familiar and strange all at once. How he fit back into this life remained to be seen.

Hearth fires filled the hall with cheerier warmth. At one of which sat Roger.

Roger looked up as he entered, stared a moment and shook his head. "You are standing right there, and yet my mind still can't quite grasp it as the truth."

Desire for solitude had kept him upstairs with Alya earlier. That and the generous gift of her beautiful body. Other than Roger, the hall lay quiet, and he took the seat opposite his brother.

A sleepy squire stumbled to them. "Can I get you anything, Sir Henry?"

"Sir Henry will have some mead," Roger said. "And be quick about it, Rob."

Roger was not a cruel or harsh man, yet the squire loping out of the hall to the kitchen looked done in.

"For shame, Roger," Henry said. "The lad is young and needs his sleep."

"Aye." Roger scowled after Rob. "Rob over there needs a lesson in manners. His thick skull makes the learning of them all the harder." He grinned and sipped from his goblet. "But the lad has a beautiful way with a longbow. I have never seen such aim. He can pick the pimple off your ass at four hundred yards."

"Impossible." Having something of a way with a bow Henry should know. At least, he used to. It had been many years since he picked one up.

Up went Roger's brow. "Care to wager?"

Just like that they slipped into an old pattern. One that warmed through Henry's chest and made him feel more at home than anything else.

Rob's boots dragged on the floor as he brought Henry a flagon of mead and a cup. "Anything else, Sir Henry?"

"Nay. I thank you." He felt sorry for the lad. "Roger tells me you are an excellent archer."

Rob blushed, the freckles across his nose standing out sharply. "I shoot a little."

"I, too, shoot a little." Henry poured his mead. He took a moment to appreciate the glorious dark honey color. "Perhaps we can shoot together?"

Rob quivered and dropped his head. "I would be honored, my lord. Sir Roger and Sir Arthur have told me much of your skill."

"Get to bed, lad." Roger waved him away.

Rob dragged tired legs out of the hall.

Henry turned back to Roger. "Just how good am I?"

"We may have exaggerated a trifle." Roger squirmed and then gave him a jaunty grin. "Let us say you have a lot to live up to."

This felt right, peaceful. The crackling of the fire, the honeyed bite of mead, he and Roger sitting and not needing to say much. "So." He broke the silence not because it was uncomfortable, but more because they had always spoken this way. "Your luck held when you married Kathryn."

"Aye." Roger managed to look smug and besotted all at once. "Even if she really did not want to marry me at the time."

Mead halfway to his mouth Henry froze and tried to decide if he had heard right. "There was a woman in England who did not want to marry Roger of Anglesea?"

Roger gave him a light kick on the ankle. "In fact, there were two."

"Dear Lord." He kicked back. "How did you bear up under the burden?"

"You have a nimble mouth." Roger smirked. "Care to have me shut it for you?"

"You could try."

"I could succeed."

"Care to wager on that?"

Pounding his fist on his chair arm Roger guffawed. "God's Bones, it's good to have you back, Henry."

Henry shrugged it off, but the warmth in his chest grew and he blinked a couple of times. Not from moisture, of course, merely smoke from the fire. "Much has changed."

"Aye." Roger nodded. "We did not want to overwhelm you earlier, but I have son now."

"Nay." Roger as husband had barely sunk in, and now his oldest brother was also a father. "How old?"

"Nine months." Roger's chest swelled. "We named him Henry."

God's balls! Moisture sprang into his eyes. No doubt from the infernally smoking fires. "I am honored."

"I don't know why." Roger snorted into his goblet. "We named him for the king."

Henry let that pass. "I should like to meet him."

"You will. Only he is sleeping now and Kathryn will eviscerate anybody who wakes him." Roger grimaced. "He is not much of a sleeper, little Harry."

"On the morrow, then."

"For certain."

A large mastiff sauntered into the hall and plopped down before the fire.

"Dagger." Roger pointed. "Kathryn's dog."

"The same Kathryn who did not want to marry you. I sense a story." Henry settled himself comfortably into his chair. The mead spread through him with a comfortable buzz.

Roger told of his meeting with Kathryn. How Kathryn's sister had run rather than marry him. It made a good story, and mellow with wine, Roger made the telling all the better.

"What else have I missed?"

"Let me see." Roger frowned. "William married Alice the winter after you left Anglesea. They now have two children, both boys, and both of them far too much like William for peace of mind."

"Do you think they will journey here?"

Roger's face softened. "Henry, you are our brother. Of course, they will come. We thought you were dead. Only Mother's refusal to hold a mass kept some inkling of hope alive. William will be on his way within hours of receiving the message. I would wager my sword arm on it."

"Tell me of Faye." Henry had to clear the lump lodged in his throat. "She was expecting when I left."

"Aye." Roger nodded. "That would be Bess she was expecting. The babe was safely delivered, and thrives. Then she had another boy and we were all hoping for a girl." Roger shrugged. "We seem to breed boys by the cartload. What with Bea's four—"

"Bea has four?"

"Aye." Roger shook his head. "And she is forever at Garrett for another."

"My coin is on Bea winning that battle."

Roger laughed. "The smartest wager always is."

"Garrett." Henry framed his next question carefully. None of the Anglesea men had welcomed Garrett into their fold. As Bea's choice, they had accepted him, but the man's station lay so far beneath Bea's as to be a jest. "You and he seem reconciled."

"Garrett is a good man." Out came Roger's stone chin, as if daring Henry to say otherwise. "While you were gone, he stepped in as my chamberlain. He helped me out with a situation involving Kathryn's father, and he was also one of the few voices that insisted you would be found."

"Huh?" It did not sound like the Garrett he had known. That Garrett had stayed mainly to himself. Then again, the door to join the Anglesea brothers had never truly been opened to him. It appeared that had changed as well. So much change, so many new things to get used to, whilst all around him the familiar beckoned.

"Of course, now that you are here, we will have to discuss what is to be done about chamberlain."

Henry's tunic felt suddenly too tight about the throat and he loosened it. "There is no rush on that. Garrett has done a good job, let him continue for now."

"Very well." Roger rose, and stretched in a pop of sinews. "I think I shall find my bed."

Henry nodded.

Roger punched his shoulder as he passed. "I am more glad than I can say that you are here."

His boots scraped against stone as Roger left the hall. A keep at night resonated with the small sounds of people sleeping all about them. From without came the steady tramp of guards on the wall, and the occasional quiet call of the hour.

"Henry?" Alya stood at the hall entrance. With the bed fur pulled about her shoulders, hair tumbling down she looked young and fragile.

"What are you doing out of bed?" He rose.

"I woke and was not sure where I was." She motioned the dog by her side. "Then I saw this and I remembered." She tightened the fur about her shoulders. "You were not beside me."

"Nay." He should not have left her all alone like that. "I could not sleep."

She nodded and walked toward him. Her dog companion stuck to her side.

"I see you have a friend." Henry pointed at the dog.

"So it seems." Alya frowned. "I keep telling it that I do not like dogs, but it just stares at me."

"Dogs are loyal like that."

Alya shivered and moved closer to the fire. "Why could you not sleep?"

Henry bundled her in her fur swaddling, tucked her onto his lap and sat closer to the heat. "Things here are the same and completely different all at once." Her hair smelled of jasmine and the scent quieted him.

Alya burrowed deeper into him. "Is it always so cold in England?"

"It is certainly not as warm as Cairo," he said. God help his foreign bride when the winter struck. "Have you ever seen snow?"

"Snow?" She wrinkled her nose at him.

Perhaps he would let the snow make its own introductions. "It rains a lot in England."

"That is why everything is so green." She glanced about them. "What do you call this chamber?"

"The hall," he said. "It is where most of keep life happens."

She lay her head on his shoulder. "Things are very different here."

"Aye."

A guard entered the hall. Alya's dog raised her head and tracked his motions across the hall.

Doing his rounds inside the keep, the guard nodded to them and moved on. A practice Father had insisted on, and Roger continued. Sir Arthur had always said that an attack could come from within a keep as fast as it could from without. Father should know, as he had used this method of attack a few times himself.

Alya shifted in his arms. "Henry?"

Her grave tone caught his attention. "What is it?"

"Now that you are here. Home. Are you sorry you married me?"

So much remained uncertain, but his answer came immediately. "Never."

Chapter Nineteen

Alya woke to Henry gone. Like she did every other morning, she rose alone, dressed and found her own way to the hall to break her fast. After only four days here she had learned her way around Anglesea. A natural result of spending so much of her time alone.

Taking her seat at the table, she smiled her readiness at the serving girl.

The girl flung a full trencher at the table before her.

Alya jerked back before she ended up with skirt full of beef.

"Sorry...my lady." The serving maid sneered and flounced off. Of course, if Henry sat beside her, the same trull—a new English word she rather liked—would wreath her sullen face in smiles and winks. If the servants did not treat her with suspicion and sometimes fear, they resorted to being surly and hostile. Not wanting to burden Henry further, she kept her mouth shut about the hundred different insults peppering her days.

She poked a falling piece of beef back onto her trencher. And why did they eat beef all the time? Unless they ate fowl and Alya could not even think of trying the goose or the peacock. The food lacked flavor too. She itched to take her hoarded supply of spices down to the kitchen and talk to Cook, but the huge woman terrified her. Judging by the way the rest of the household servants treated Cook, it would not be her best idea.

As if her conversation about the weather with Henry had invited in the rain, it had not stopped for four days. A fine mizzle that kept everyone indoors and made her feel as gray as the sky. During the journey, she had not had time to think much on home, but here it crept up on her. The way the bells called the devout to prayer and not the wail of muezzin. The softer light that was like looking through smudged glass. Here the earth smelled damp, not the dry spice-laden dust of home. Perhaps if the wind carried spice aromas, spice might actually find its way into the bland cooking.

As far she knew, Henry spent most of the days with his family. Roger and Garrett showed him around the demesne whilst they waited for his remaining family to arrive.

The bench rocked and Bahir sat down beside her. "You look glum."

"I am glum." She propped her chin on her palm. "Things are so different here."

"Indeed, they are." Bahir pared an apple and handed her a slice. "This is what happens when you get on a boat and travel to a different land." He studied her over his apple. "Things are different."

When Bahir made sense, it made her want to cuff him. "I am homesick."

"I can understand that." Bahir shrugged. "Is Henry good to you?"

Her magical nights with Henry almost made her lonely, long days worth it. Almost, but not quite. As a lover Henry was atten-tive, caring, inventive and gentle and she had no complaints. But he never spoke to her. Oh, he spoke, the sort of everyday pleas-antries expected of two close acquaintances but she stood no closer to the real Henry now than she had on the wall. She wanted to know what he thought, what his opinions might be, what made him angry, what gave him joy. She desperately wanted to know about the scars on his back, but the one time she had brought it up, Henry had changed the subject with a forbidding look in his eye that warned her not to ask again.

And she wanted to understand what drove him out of the keep every day.

Mostly, she wanted to spend less of her day thinking about Henry and what he thought about. Days filled with hiding from angry servants or picking through her chests accomplished nothing, and gave her the fidgets. Her grand plan to sew pillows for their bedchamber had lasted as long as her enthusiasm for needlework, which was about an hour. None of the seamstresses in the keep wanted to help her. In fact, they had been the rudest of all the keep residents.

Beatrice and Kathryn went riding ever morning. Alya had watched them from her casement window. Both mounted on large, glossy horses as they moved beyond the castle walls into the swathe of green forest. Henry had not asked her to stay within the keep but he had appeared nervous when she asked to learn to ride. Perhaps he had the right of it. The longer she stayed at Anglesea, the more she saw the reason for his caution. She was the interloper here, the unknown, and his people did not trust her.

"It rains all the time," she said to Bahir.

"It rains a lot." He sighed. "I never thought one could get tired of rain. But four days of nothing but rain, and they tell me this happens often."

Often enough for her to grow mold beneath her fingernails. "Have they told you about snow?"

"Aye." Bahir raised his brow. "Nurse told me of snow. At first I thought the woman deranged." He snorted. "Ice falling from the sky like feathers. This I have to see to believe." He crossed his arms. "Although I have met traders who come from the north and they spoke of this snow too."

"But you've never seen it?"

Bahir nodded. "I have never seen it."

"It must be cold." Merely thinking about it made her shiver.

The dog stood from where she lay in front of the table and looked at Alya. Pricking up her ears like she did, she whined.

"Is that animal looking at you?" Bahir studied the dog.

"It never leaves me alone." Alya glared at the dog.

The dog cocked its head.

Bahir leaned over the table and peered closer.

The dog pulled its lips back from its fearsome teeth.

Bahir sat back. "It is vicious. I would be wary of it."

"It is not vicious with me. I think they said it was a she." Alya did the same as Bahir had, coming even closer to the dog.

The dog thumped its tail. It stood, trotted closer to the door, sat and cocked its head.

"What does it want?" Bahir looked bewildered.

"I do not know." Did Bahir think she knew dogs? "But it follows me everywhere and when I close the door so that it cannot come in, it merely waits for me until I open the door."

"Is it addled?"

"Nay." Alya rather liked the golden sheen of the dog's fur. It looked like it might be silky to touch. She had seen Roger, Henry, Kathryn, and even Bea and her children caress the dogs that wandered around the keep. For herself, she did not dare get the filth on her hands. "It seems to like to follow me."

The dog whined.

"It looks like it wants you to follow it." Bahir nudged her.

"I have nothing better to do." Alya rose. If the dog had a better idea of how she might spend her day, she was open to hearing it. As she drew closer, the dog thumped its tail faster as if encouraging her. It stood and strolled to the door, looking over its shoulder to ensure she followed.

"I am coming," Alya said.

The dog's tongue lolled out the side of its mouth.

"I hope you are not leading me somewhere quiet where you can eat me," she said.

"Alya." Bahir called from the bench. "You are talking to a dog."

"I know that." She might be talking to a dog but that did not make the rest of her wits missing. "But she seems to understand what I say and she likes it."

"She likes it." Bahir gaped. "How would you know?"

"Because she smiles."

Bahir choked and shook his head. "It is a beast. It does not smile."

Alya did not fancy the argument it would take to convince Bahir the animal did, indeed, smile. Bahir had not seen that look on the dog's face when it first spotted her every morning. Then, the dog smiled in a happy greeting. Sometimes it wagged its tail so hard, it rocked its entire body. Alya had never been that pleased to see anyone, or if she was, had never made absolutely no effort to hide her pleasure.

Dog yipped and trotted a bit faster down the staircase that led to the keep exterior door. Dim light from below provided lighting on the stair treads and round and round Alya went in the dark, grim stairwell.

They reached the outside door and dog trotted into the yard. Steady rain had churned the yard into mud. Cloak raised above his head to keep the rain out a servant scurried across the bailey.

"I cannot go out there," Alya said. "I will get soaked."

Dog whined and sat. The rain did not seem to bother it at all.

"I will ruin my gown." She did not expect the dog to understand the disastrous results of rain and silk coming into contact, but the creature could show some sensitivity. "The rain will make spots on my gown and I will not be able to get them out."

Dog stared at her.

"And what is out there, anyway, that needs us to get wet and cold." She folded her arms so the dog knew she would not be swayed to its pleasure. "I have seen everything there is to see in the bailey. There are horses, which I cannot ride. A laundry where the women glare at me as if I had three heads, and the smithy. He does not like me at all. You saw how he shook his hammer at me."

Dog cocked its head.

"Protect me." Alya snorted. The creature had lost its mind. "How can you protect me against a man so large. And I still do not care to be wet."

Dog whined.

Alya growled her annoyance. The dog was so persistent in her demands. She would not hear nay for an answer.

"At least let me cover my gown." Alya grabbed a garment from a row of pegs beside the door. Bea had told her these would keep the rain out. She slipped it over her head, wrinkling her nose at the smell of horse and unwashed person. "I hope this stings your nose even more than it does mine. The last person to wear this might never have bathed."

Dog stood and waved her tail.

"You had best have something good to show me, or I shall turn you into lion meat."

Dog smiled at her as if she knew Alya could do no such thing.

"Indeed." Alya used her sternest tone. "I might not be able to turn you into lion meat. You have me there, but I still think you are a filthy animal."

Dog wagged her tail.

"No good will come from trying to win me around." Alya needed the animal to understand this. She did not like dogs but she would hate to be responsible for disappointing the creature. "You are a beast that licks its parts in front of everyone."

Dog glanced at her as if to ask where else she should do her licking.

"In private," Alya said. "You should keep your personal grooming to when you are alone."

Shaking her ears, Dog did not seem to agree and increased her pace.

Light rain misted against her skin, and caught in the curls surrounding her face. Her hair would react to all the damp in a crazy display of curls. This, she too, lay at the feet of Dog.

Dog trotted across the bailey to the far side. She led her past the stables and then the barracks to a small gate in the wall.

Hidden by the bulky walls of the barracks, Alya had not noticed this gate before.

Dog stopped before the gate and looked at her.

"You want me to open the gate?"

Dog pawed at the door.

"Where does it lead?" Alya looked about her and tried to get her bearings. The gate definitely did not open on the seaward side of the castle. The main castle gate though, was on the other side of the inner bailey. This gate, it seemed, led to a yard attached to both inner and outer baileys, but tucked in between them.

As if often oiled, the lock turned easily.

Dog surged through before her, brushing wet fur against her skirts. Really, the animal had no appreciation for the cost of silk.

She stood and looked at Alya, wagging her tail and lolling her tongue as if she had done a very clever thing.

And she had. Alya forgot the rain as she stared at the garden about her. Not a large space but filled to bursting with trees and flowers. Grass so green it made her eyes hurt marched in clean lines between the flower beds. And the blooms! Alya had never seen so many colors, in such abundance and in one place before. She did not know the names of any of the plants she looked at, but she itched to.

Dog squatted on the grass and proved to her that she really was a filthy animal. Still, the small enclosed garden lifted Alya's mood.

"All right." She nodded to the dog. "I will concede that I like this place." She shrugged an apology. "I lie. I love this place and you were right to bring me here."

Chapter Twenty

Alya spent the morning amongst the flowers. She located a stick and dug around in the soil. Rich, wet earth coated her fingers. The smell of it settled inside her like contentment. She had always loved growing things.

Pleased with herself, Dog lay in the shelter of a large tree and watched her.

A young boy, they called them pages, found her there. "Lady Alya." He bowed but stared a bit at her filthy hands, wet hair ,and stained dress. "Sir Henry is looking for you. He says you are to come with me."

Dog dropped into place beside her.

The page eyed her askance. "Have you been gardening, my lady?"

"I have been digging holes." Because she could not call her foray gardening. "I am not sure what everything is."

"Really?" The page gaped. "Do they not have plants where you are from?"

"We have plants." Alya had to smile at his wide-eyed curiosity. "But they are not the same at all. Where I come from, it hardly ever rains and the plants need to last without water."

"Huh."

They walked into the bailey. A train of large bullocks lowed and stamped, surrounded by people carrying things into the keep.

"It does not rain much where you are from?" The page frowned. "I could not imagine that."

"Aye." Alya skirted the activity. "It is very different."

Bahir stood at the keep door with a tally slate. He nodded to her.

"I could help you," the page said. He flushed. "With the plants and such. My mum knows a powerful lot about plants and she taught me. I could help you."

The offer wiggled into her heart and lit a small glow. "I would like that," she said. "But perhaps you should tell me your name."

"Oh." He giggled. "I am called Bernard."

"Ber-nard."

"Sort of." He grimaced. "It is more like Bernard, one word. Quick. Not like burr and then nard." He nodded. "Bernard."

"Bernard."

He chewed his lip. "We will work on that. While we work on the plants."

Her first new friend. Other than the furry one who brushed against her skirts. Perhaps she should wear less silk because it looked as if Dog would always be there by her side. Or even better, some of those masculine clothes Kathryn wore from time to time. But that would involve a conversation with the hostile seamstresses and Alya did not fancy that.

When she reached the hall, Bernard left her. Probably following his nose to the smell of baking bread in the kitchen. Surly though she was, Cook did bake the most delicious breads and pies, and Alya could grow fat on the honey cakes.

"Alya." Standing on the far side of the hall with Roger, Henry waved at her and grinned. "Did you get stuck in the mud?"

"Bernard tells me I have been gardening." She rose on her toes and kissed his lean cheek, taking a small moment to draw in the delicious scent of him. Cardamom, bay, and oranges all blended in a unique and wonderful way that she craved a little more every day.

Henry held her to him. "In the rain?"

"Aye." Things always felt less dire when Henry held her. "I gave up on waiting for a fine day."

"Come and see what we have." Henry guided her to a pile of crates, chests, and bolts. More got added to the pile with each new person entering the hall.

Alya poked at the nearest crate. "What is all this?"

"I would think you would recognize your own wealth." Roger joined them, his gaze on the growing bounty. "Bahir had the boat's contents brought up to the keep this morning."

"Mine." Alya snapped her gaping mouth shut. She had no idea of the extent of her father's generosity. Why he must have sent everything he owned with her. Her father. An ache throbbed in her chest. He had known what was coming, and he had sent her away to protect her. He had also ensured that she would want for nothing in her new life. What she wouldn't give to take back that last moment. Kiss him goodbye sweetly and thank him for all he had done.

"Hey." Henry tipped her chin up. "He would be happy to know you were safe."

She snuggled closer to Henry. That he guessed her thoughts brought her closer to him.

Roger cleared his throat. "After Henry and I spoke, I am trying to discover word of your father." He touched her shoulder. "Nobody should live not knowing what has happened to someone they love."

Henry kissed her head. "Now, we need you to tell us what to do with all of this."

"Me?" She wriggled out of his hold so she could read his expression. "Surely that is for you to decide?"

Putting her away from him with a shrug, Henry said, "I cannot tell you what to do with your wealth."

"Mine?" On her marriage, everything she owned became her

husband's property. Could things work differently here in England? "All that is mine is now yours."

Henry grimaced. "By law, I suppose." So things did not work differently here. "But this is yours, Alya. This is all that you have of your father. I would not take that from you."

Honest and noble, her Henry. Had her father read that much in him? "Then let us say this is ours."

"A good solution." His lips lingered on her cheek as if he would go further.

"Dear God." Roger stomped to the nearest chest. "You will give me a toothache if you two persist."

"Stop being grumpy." Kathryn appeared behind Roger. She put her hands on her hips and stared. "Goodness me! There must be a king's ransom here."

"Three kings, at least." Beatrice followed her into the hall. She squealed and darted forward. "Is that silk? Kathryn, come and see this color." Beatrice drew a length of silk from the bale. "Oh, my. I have never seen anything so lovely. It is like spun gold."

"It is spun gold." Kathryn joined her. "Look they have woven gold into the fabric."

"Oh, my." Beatrice stroked her cheek against the fabric. She glanced at Alya, started and lay the silk gently over the bale. "I beg your pardon, Alya. It was so lovely, I forgot myself."

Alya drew the silk from the bale. Yards and yards of fabric gathered in her arms. "Here." She held it out to Beatrice. "It will not suit my complexion."

"Nay." Beatrice snatched her hands behind her back. "I could not."

"Aye, you could." Alya pressed the silk on her. "It is a custom in my country to bring gifts to your new family."

Henry raised his brow at her.

Alya met his challenging look. He said the silk belonged to her. She could stretch the truth a little if she liked.

"If you admire something in an Egyptian's house," Henry said. "It is considered polite to give it to you."

Beatrice laughed. "Then I would wager you must be careful of expressing your admiration." She squeezed Alya's shoulder. "Really, it is not that I do not appreciate the gesture, but this is yours."

"Do you insult my honor?" Alya tried an imperious look Henry could wield like a knife.

Beatrice chuckled. "Oh, Alya, you really must teach me that look. I thank you for the gift, and I mean no insult but I cannot take something so costly from you." She cast a fond glance at the silk. "But I tell you what. Once you have seen all that is here, if you still want to make the gift, I will take enough to make one gown. And then you will let me make you a gown of another silk of your choice."

"Hmm." Alya pretended to give it some thought, but she knew what she wanted in exchange. "I tell you what I would really like. I would like to learn to ride a horse. You can teach me."

Kathryn snorted. "I will teach you to ride a horse."

"I ride very well." Beatrice scowled at Kathryn.

Shuddering, Kathryn said, "You ride like a girl."

"I am a girl. And so is Alya. I will teach her to ride."

"You can watch." Kathryn patted Beatrice's shoulder. "As I teach her how to ride properly." She held up a finger as Beatrice opened her mouth to protest. "And if you behave, I will teach you both to fight with a dagger."

"Sweeting." Grabbing Kathryn by the waist Roger drew her against him. "Perhaps Alya does not want to learn to knife fight."

"I already know how," Alya said. "Bahir taught me."

"Really?" Kathryn perked up. "Did he teach you to fight with one of those curved blades like he carries."

"Aye."

"How marvelous." Misty-eyed Kathryn gazed at her. "I should like to learn how to use one of those."

Roger snorted. "That is all we need at Anglesea. More women flashing metal."

"Roger!" A woman's voice from the doorway acted like a lightning bolt through Roger, Beatrice, and Kathryn.

Henry paled and took a step forward. He froze, hands clenched by his sides.

Without anyone introducing her, Alya knew the older woman who walked into the hall. Her beautiful features so closely resembled Henry's, she could only be his mother. Her mother by marriage. Alya clasped her hands together before she fidgeted. Her palms grew sweaty.

"Mother." Henry blinked rapidly.

Lady Mary stopped within arm's length of Henry. Tears spilled down her lovely face. "Oh, my Lord." Her voice cracked. "They told me—I dared not believe—Henry." With shaking hands, she cupped Henry's face, her gaze roaming his features as if she would press them deep into her heart. Lady Mary folded her much taller son into her arms and held him. "My Henry."

Beatrice sobbed openly, wiping her eyes on her bliaut sleeves. Even Kathryn's eyes glistened.

Roger kept his gaze on his feet.

A bearlike man put his arms about Lady Mary and Henry.

This had to be Sir Arthur. He and Roger looked so alike it was like seeing an older and younger version.

Feeling like an interloper in the tender moment, Alya looked away.

A tall, grave-faced knight stood a little apart from them, his arm about the loveliest woman Alya had ever seen. From her father's readings, she had heard about angels. This lady was like one of those beings of light come to life. Hair a pale gold, eyes even bluer than Henry, her features as delicate as spun sugar. The lady was also crying. Faye, Henry's oldest sister, which made the man by her side Sir Gregory.

With them stood two older boys, a young girl, and an even younger boy. The older boys resembled their mother. The younger children had their dark sire's stamp on their features, softened by their mother's beauty.

What had Henry said on the boat?

The older boys must be Simon and Arthur, Faye's children from her first marriage. Roger had told Henry of Faye's and Gregory's daughter, Elizabeth, whom they called Bess. She could not recall the boy's name.

"Goodness." Lady Mary emerged from the huddle. She wiped her face but kept her hand on Henry's arm. Her gaze fastened on Alya. "You must forgive me, my dear girl." Fresh tears spilled. "I have not greeted you properly."

Faye moved to embrace Henry. Of all his siblings, Henry bore the closest resemblance to Faye.

"Come, Mary." Sir Arthur guided his wife toward Alya. "We must greet our new daughter."

Alya found herself tugged against an enormous chest.

Lady Mary's embrace was a lot gentler, but no less sincere. "Welcome," she said. "My, aren't you lovely. So exotic."

Sir Arthur studied her. Alya had the sense Sir Arthur saw her right down to her chemise. "My son has brought back a true treasure from his pilgrimage."

Henry was hugging his nephews, and being introduced to the members of the family he had never met. He could not come and rescue her.

Beatrice stepped in and hugged her father. "Don't forget your old daughter because you have a new one now."

"Never, Sweet Bea." Her father lifted her off her feet. "Tell me you aren't breeding again?"

"Father!" Beatrice gave him a shove, which did not move Sir Arthur at all. "I am a married woman. You cannot say such things to me."

"I do not care." Sir Arthur crossed his arms in a pose Henry used all the time. "You are still my little girl."

"Give over, Arthur." Lady Mary kissed Beatrice's cheek. "You look well, sweeting."

"I am well." Beatrice glared at her father. "And I am not breeding again."

Sir Arthur smirked. He stopped and stared at the pile of goods. "What is all this?"

Henry rejoined her.

Alya was grateful for his arm about her waist.

"It is Alya's," he said. "Consider it her dowry."

Chapter Twenty-One

Gregory made Alya nervous and that irked her. Not that he did anything to provoke it. Indeed, she had hardly met a more courteous or quiet-mannered man. From what she had seen, he spoke only when he had something of value to add, never raised his voice, barely seemed to grow annoyed and displayed endless patience. Especially with little Bess who appeared something of a handful, and tossed her raven curls to great effect.

Across the hall, he sat with the boys patiently unraveling their fishing string. Beatrice's boys clambered all over him, yelling instructions in their piping boy voices, all of which bothered him not a whit. He nodded, occasionally responded, and kept on with his task.

His size gave her pause. Bigger even than Roger, but with not an ounce of good living to mar the perfection of him. Discipline. It eked from him.

What about him made her fidget?

Gregory glanced up.

Face hot, Alya dropped her gaze. She could not read Gregory. He kept his thoughts close to himself. He reminded her of the first time she had seen the foreign knights. With the intention to parley they had ridden through Cairo to meet with the sultan. Huge men atop snorting, snapping horses, they had worn their metal tunics as if impervious to the glaring sun.

Thrilling as they were, the sight of them had filled her with a cold dread. In the crowd, one of the knights had met her gaze, his eyes cold and implacable, and in that moment, she had known her life would never again be the same. Gregory seemed to possess the same unwavering purpose in all that he did. How she had grown to despise the knights as it had become obvious that war was inevitable. In her mind, they all blurred into that one glance from those ruthless eyes above a metal visor.

Gregory was a knight, and thus she despised him.

Alya jabbed her needle into her thumb. Her lack of sewing talent aside, her thumb injury had its root in her thoughts. She barely knew Gregory, yet she made the assumption that he was a cold-blooded killing beast. In one moment, she had cast aside any personal knowledge of the man and thrust him into a fold with others who bore a resemblance to him. Just as the folk of Anglesea did to her and Bahir.

They looked at her and saw a foreign woman, a woman who represented the same nation they had sent their brothers, fathers, lovers, husbands, and sons to fight. For folk here, the blood of their kin stained her hands. How sobering that she did the same. That which she condemned them for, lurked in her breast.

"You will go wrinkled as a desert crone." Bahir dropped onto the window seat beside her.

His width forced her to inch along and give him space. "I was merely thinking and I did not like the direction my thoughts were taking."

"Ah." Crossing his ankles, Bahir lounged against the casement surround. "Would you like to share your thoughts?"

"Aye." Bahir had much wisdom to offer. "I was thinking how all of us, people I mean, how we look at each other and make judgments based on things that should not matter."

Bahir settled himself more comfortably. "Like?"

"Skin color." She waved her hand at him. "Where we come from. Who our parents were. The languages we speak. Our very differences are what keep us from getting to know each other."

"Wise words, Lady Alya." Gregory moved like a wraith because now he stood beside Bahir. "What led you to this discovery?"

Alya's face heated. Dare she tell him? Except, if she did not tell him, did she not make a judgment that he would be angry based solely on her past experience? "When I was watching you just now, I was thinking how much you reminded me of the knights who attacked my country."

Bahir hissed, and straightened. "She means no insult, Sir Gregory."

"And none was taken." Gregory propped his shoulder against the wall. "You looked at me and assumed I would be capable of the same sort of savagery."

"Savagery?" Leaning forward, Bahir studied Gregory. "You have knowledge of the war."

"Aye." Gregory dragged a nearby stool closer and sat. "I have listened to the stories my countrymen do not always tell."

"You are a man of God?" Bahir seemed to have more knowledge of Gregory than she.

"Indeed." Gregory smiled.

He should do so more often. It transformed his grave features into breathtaking handsomeness.

"For many years, I believed my place was in the church." He winked at Alya. "And then Lady Faye changed my mind."

The wink had her giggling like a silly girl, but goodness, the man's looks were ridiculously pleasing.

"You did not join the war?" Bahir had that look on his face he got when he found something fascinating.

"Nay." Gregory straightened his shoulders. "Many of us did not believe in the holy pilgrimages. Sir Arthur amongst them. We tried to talk Henry out of going."

Now he intrigued Alya. "But Henry went anyway."

"Aye." Gregory drew a line through the rushes with his toe. "The Henry who left here is not the same man who returned. Henry held such strong beliefs at the time. He felt he wanted to go and do his part for God."

"A *jihad*," Bahir said.

Gregory raised a brow in question.

"A holy war," Alya said. "A war against the unbelievers. Or it could be a war within yourself."

"I know a little something of the last part," Gregory said.

Bahir folded his arms. The next sign that Bahir had found something that captured his full attention. "Yet you did not favor this jihad? Even as a man of God?"

"I am a man of war as well, as Lady Alya pointed out. But that was not so much a choice I made, as one made for me," Gregory said. "My size marked me as a warrior and I was raised as such. Still, it did not seem to me that killing people was the best way to spread the word of our Lord."

"Not an opinion shared by many of your countrymen." Bahir snorted.

"Nay." Head lowered Gregory entwined his fingers. "I believe, first and foremost, that all life is precious. The God I serve taught me this reverence for life."

"Huh." Bahir glanced at her.

Alya could not believe how she had misjudged Gregory.

"I would ask you, Sir Gregory, of this god you serve." Bahir spread his arms. "If you would talk to me of this."

"I would be delighted." Sir Gregory smiled. "And in turn you can tell me of the god you serve."

Bahir inclined his head.

"What if they were the same god?" As a Christian in the world of Islam, Alya had grown up seeing both beliefs at work.

Bahir and Gregory gaped at her.

Uncomfortable under their scrutiny, she rose. "It is just that there are a lot of similarities between them."

"You were raised Christian?" Gregory looked taken aback.

Alya pinned him with a challenging stare. "Is that an assumption I heard you make, Sir Gregory?"

He threw back his head and laughed. "A hit, Lady Alya, to be sure."

* * *

Alya waited until Henry joined her in their chamber before she spoke to him. Her conversation with Gregory had raised a few questions in her mind.

Heads together as they talked and talked, Bahir and Gregory had spent the afternoon in the hall. Faye had to separate them to get Gregory to the dinner table.

It did Alya's heart glad to see Bahir relaxed and enjoying himself. As much as she was treated as an interloper here, it was worse for Bahir. He bore it all silently, but it had to make him lonely.

Henry entered their chamber and bowed. "My lady."

It thrilled her each time he did that. Not the courtesy of the bow, but more the wicked gleam in his eyes as he did so.

Already in bed, Alya sat up.

Henry stopped at the foot of the bed, unfastened his sword belt and dropped it to the floor. "Are you well?"

"I am."

Fisting his tunic, he tugged it over his head. "How did you spend this day?"

Dear Lord, he expected her to speak when he revealed all that male beauty for her gaze to feast upon.

His fingers moved to his braies.

"I did some sewing."

He raised an eyebrow. "You hate sewing."

"Aye, but I must do something."

His braies dropped to the floor.

Alya's mouth dried. "I had an interesting talk with Gregory today."

"Indeed."

She gripped her last traces of good sense and forced herself not to stare at the rod rising strong and hard from between his thighs. "We talked of the holy pilgrimage."

"Ah." Henry turned and strode to the washbasin.

His scars nearly made her retreat. This subject matter remained painful for Henry.

Ducking, he splashed water over his head and neck.

As his wife, though, her questions grew with each day and she tried again. "Gregory said your family was not in support of you going."

"Nay." He snatched up a washcloth and rubbed it over his chest and belly.

Frustration forced her lust down to a low simmer. "Yet you went anyway?"

"I believed I did the right thing." He finished washing and rubbed his flesh with a drying cloth.

"You believed you fought for God?"

Henry turned. "What are all these questions, Alya?"

His stern expression gave her pause, but Henry surrounded himself with invisible walls as thick as those guarding Anglesea. "You believed in God enough to go to war for him, and yet you do not pray, Henry. I go to prayers, but you do not come with me."

"Nay." Blowing out a big breath he dropped his head. "I do not."

"Why not?"

He approached the bed and slid beneath the furs. Lying back, he sighed then crossed his hands behind his head. "It is difficult to speak of."

"Can you try?" Alya snuggled down beside him. "For me."

His jaw clenched. Muscle bunched in his arms. "I do not speak of it, Alya. Ever."

As if he slammed a door in her face, she blinked. The hurt took her by surprise. She had sought only to know him better and he denied her that. Good enough to warm his bed, but not good enough to share his thoughts. She turned on her side, and gave him her back. Two of them could throw up walls. "As you wish."

Linen whispered and he touched her shoulder. Leaning over her, he said, "This is our bed, sweeting. This is where I come to forget. I do not want it tainted with speak of war and blood and lost gods. The things I saw...the things I did...I cannot speak of them, and I beg you not to ask me to."

"Was it terrible?"

"Aye." He kissed her shoulder. His arm slid about her and pulled her bottom into the cradle of his thighs. His rod nudged her. Clearly, he had lost none of his interest in their marital bed.

Sliding his hand up, he caressed her breast.

Her body responded, like it always did, to his slightest touch. Alya arched her back, pressing her breast into his palm.

Henry pressed into her bottom. "See now. Is this not a better way to spend our time?"

Doubt lingered in the back of her mind, even as she said what he expected to hear. "Aye."

* * *

Outside Alya's casement sheets of rain poured down and pounded onto the sea. Waves threw themselves against the rocks in a white break of spray. What a surprise, more rain. She turned her back on the view and stomped across her chamber.

She had draped the bed in silks from her dowry in the hope that they would inspire her to turn them into colorful cushions and bed curtains. Her proposed riding lesson had been postponed due to the weather. How could one country have so much weather, all the time?

Arms crossed, Bahir lounged in her doorway. "You are fretting."

"Nay, I am not."

His teeth flashed white in a huge grin. Strolling in, he pointed to the bed. "What is all this?"

"An attempt to amuse myself." A vain one at that. "I thought I might sew some things for the room. Make it feel more like mine."

Bahir winced. "You sew?"

"Precisely."

"But it is a fine idea. You could ask one of the seamstresses to help you." He fingered the edge of a dainty peacock green silk. "These are too beautiful to risk your needlework skills."

All true, but still irksome. She did not want to complain to Bahir about the way the seamstresses treated her. He had enough of that aimed at him. "Did you want something?"

He looked smug. "I saw the rain and I thought of you."

"Maybe I should learn to swim and then I would have more to do here." The sea crashed and thundered below her.

"Swimming is for fish." Bahir went to the door and stretched out of her sight for a moment. He returned with a *dumbec* gripped in his large hand. "Now the *zar* is for everyone... Particularly for grumpy ladies who have many things on their minds."

"I can't dance a zar, here." But even as she said it, her mind whispered, *why not?* To be able to lose herself and her worries in the zar might be exactly what she needed.

Bahir smirked and sat cross-legged on the floor in front of the fire. On the dumbec, he beat the familiar rhythm, *dun-kateka-dun-tek.*

Alya tapped the same beat on her thigh. "What if someone saw me? They would think me even more strange."

Bahir raised his brow. *Dun-kateka-dun-tek.*

"You are going to get me into trouble."

Dog thumped her tail and watched Bahir, head cocked.

Dun-kateka-dun-tek

Beatrice stuck her head in the room. "What are you doing?"

"Nothing." Alya glared at Bahir.

Dun-kateka-dun-tek

"Lady Alya is going to perform the zar."

"Ooh." Beatrice stepped into the room. "What is that?"

Bahir kept drumming.

"Would you stop that?" Already Alya's limbs itched to follow the rhythm, become entwined with it and let it flow through her until her worries disappeared.

"Nay, don't stop." Beatrice clapped along with Bahir. "I like it. It sort of makes you want to move with it."

"That it does." Bahir flashed Alya an evil grin. "That is the entire point of the zar."

Beatrice raised her clapping hands and swayed. "Can anyone do it? Can I?"

"You most certainly can." Bahir closed his eyes as he drummed. His body swayed in time to his hands hitting the hide.

Faye knocked on the door. "Sorry to interrupt but I was looking for...Beatrice what are you doing?"

"The zar." Beatrice grinned at her. "Or I will when Alya teaches me how."

Faye clapped along with Beatrice. "Can I watch?"

"Nay, my lady." Bahir stopped drumming. "The zar is to be performed, not watched. An ancient ritual amongst women."

Faye pulled a face. "I am not much of a dancer."

"You don't need to be." Alya had the feeling she was outnumbered.

Beatrice waved her over. "Come on, Faye, you can do it with us." She stopped in front of Alya. "Show us."

Bahir picked up the beat again.

Alya loosened her hair and motioned Faye and Beatrice to do the same. She dropped to her knees, forehead pressed to the earth.

"Um...what are you doing?" Beatrice crouched beside her.

"The zar," Bahir said. "Do as she does, and let the beat take you where it will."

Alya draped her hair over her head until it curtained her face. She closed her eyes and breathed in the *dun-kateka-dun-tek.*

Head low, she swayed her head. First this way and then that.

Beatrice copied her, her golden hair a stark contrast beside Alya's.

On the other side of her, Faye sat on her knees and watched them. She loosened her braid. "I can do that."

Bahir grinned. "Do it, my lady."

"Just let your head go." Alya's voice fell in with Bahir's drumming. "Let it find the beat and merge with it."

"Like this?" Beatrice whipped her hair around her head.

"Slow down." Alya bit back her laughter. "Slow down and go with the beat."

Beatrice stopped, waited, and then swayed in time with Bahir. "I like this."

"It's a way to release your worries." Alya let her shoulders move with her head. Her world narrowed to the black curtain of her hair. Beside her she was aware of Beatrice and Faye, but they blended into the hypnotic rhythm. Soon she would lose all knowledge they were there.

Her ribcage flexed and contracted in time with her head movements. Her arms came up behind her back and reached for oblivion.

Bahir picked up the beat and her body responded. Her movements grew larger, wilder as the drum gained speed. The steady beats drove her higher on her knees, so she could dip and sway with it. Her heartbeat took up the *dun-kateka-dun-tek*. It pounded through her blood and echoed in her breathing. Her feet took her to standing.

Henry, Anglesea, the rude servants, all of it melted away. Her mind emptied of everything but the steady rhythm of the dumbec. Alya slipped away into the collection of limbs and muscle that moved to the beating of her heart. On and on it went, growing faster and faster, wilder and wilder, drawing her deeper into its trance.

The drum stopped.

Alya opened her eyes.

Her chamber swam before her vision.

Beatrice, breathing hard with her hair a tangle around her head, stood beside her with her eyes wide open and stunned.

Faye's pale skin gleamed with perspiration. Her hair looked like a bird's nest.

All three of them breathed hard.

"Oh, my." Faye giggled and pushed her hair back. "That was..."

Beatrice nodded. "It was indeed."

"Here." Bahir handed them all a goblet. "Drink."

He wiped sweat from his face with his sleeve. But he too wore the vacant expression Beatrice and Faye did. Alya felt certain her face mirrored theirs. "So." The bitter bite of ale quenched her thirst. "That was the zar."

Beatrice drained her goblet. "We should do that again."

"Not now." Faye looked alarmed. She tottered to the bed and sat. "I am worn out. Yet strangely exhilarated."

"This is why the women of Egypt do this," Bahir said. "As a form of release."

"I like it." Beatrice tried to tame her hair.

Faye adjusted her girdle. "I would like to hear more of where you come from, Alya. I know so little of the world beyond Anglesea."

Suddenly the rainy day did not seem so horrible, and Alya did not have that empty ache of loneliness within her. She returned Faye's smile. "I would like that."

Chapter Twenty-Two

Emboldened by her success with Faye and Beatrice, Alya snatched up two of her new silks, gave another two to Bernard, and went to see the castle seamstresses. Dog dropped into place at her heels.

Bernard held the silk gingerly. "Where are we going?"

"Into battle, Bernard." Ayla squared her shoulders.

In a small room on one side of the inner bailey beside the laundry worked the seamstresses. Great vats from the laundry billowed steam into the gray afternoon, and carried the smell of boiling laundry.

A laundress stopped stirring and leaned against her paddle as Alya passed.

"Good day." Alya used English and a pleasant smile.

The woman stiffened, nodded tersely, and worked her paddle through the water again.

Chatter stopped as Alya entered the seamstresses' lair. Light flooded the small chamber and made sewing easier. Three faces turned and stared at her.

"Good day." She did not have many English words but she had drawn a picture of what she wanted. She moved aside an overflowing work basket and put her parchment down on the table.

"Make, please." Henry had stressed the importance of using please. Alya spread her silks on the table, being sure not to let them touch the floor, and motioned Bernard to do the same.

The women glanced at each other.

The older of the trio got up and stared at the drawing. She said something in English and pushed the drawing back at Alya.

"They say they cannot." Bernard translated for her.

She didn't need Bernard to understand the clear message. These women did not want to do her work. Alya pointed to the silk and the drawing. "You make."

Gray Hair shook her head. "Nay."

"Please...why?" Her English improved day by day but she had never cursed her lack of proficiency more.

Gray Hair rolled her eyes. "Silk for pillows. Nay," she yelled.

Did the woman think if she spoke louder, Alya would suddenly understand? "Why?"

"No good." Gray Hair sat down and snatched up her work.

"She says the silk is too good for making pillows." Flushed and frowning, Bernard cast a longing gaze at the door.

"I understood that," she said, but Alya had lain on enough silk cushions in her time to know the woman did not speak the truth. "I want silk."

Cackling, the seamstresses put their heads together.

Bernard gasped and glanced at her.

Alya willed the earth to open and swallow her whole. Or better yet, swallow the cow camels talking and laughing at her. If this were Cairo, Bahir would have whipped them for their rudeness. Then again, if this was Cairo she would know how to speak to them.

"Make." She pushed the silk toward them.

"Nay." Gray Hair shoved the silk back at her so hard it slithered off the table and dropped to the dirty floor.

The seamstresses laughed.

Alya bent to gather her silk. She bowed her head to hide the weak tears pricking behind her eyelids. How dare they treat her as if she did not matter? They did not know her to be so rude to her. They could make what she wanted, but they chose not to.

"Meg." Kathryn's voice cracked from the doorway.

Gray Hair sprang to her feet and curtsied. "Good day, Lady Kathryn."

At least Alya understood that much.

A rapid conversation ensued, too quick for Alya to follow. Based on the way Kathryn stood arms jammed on her hips and the way the seamstresses hung their heads she would wager Kathryn was giving the women a tongue lashing. Good! Let them feel the scald of humiliation.

After a while of Kathryn doing most of the talking and more head hanging on the seamstress's part, she turned to Alya and switched to French. "What is it you wanted made?"

"I thought I could have some cushions and bed hangings made for my chamber."

"With this?" A reverent expression on her face, Kathryn stroked the silk. "It is very fine to be using for hangings and cushions."

"I know that." Alya could feel the seamstresses staring at them. "But my chamber at home was hung with silk. I wanted to make my chamber here feel more like home."

Kathryn's face softened and she touched Alya's arm. "Of course, you did. How foolish of us not to think of that." Face rigid she turned back to the women. "Meg!"

Gray Hair leaped to her feet.

Kathryn spoke rapidly and with heat. When she fell silent, Meg picked up the drawing and the silk. Nodding and bowing her head to Kathryn, she retreated to her friends.

"Come." Kathryn turned Alya out of the room. "They will do it and do a good job or they will have me, and then Lady Mary, to deal with."

"Thank you." Alya was grateful, truly grateful, but still it would have been better if the women had done the work because she asked and not because Kathryn threatened them. Lord alone knew what threat Kathryn had used but it had been enough to keep the three women silent and servile.

As she crossed the bailey, Kathryn strode along beside her. "Have you had this problem before?"

"Problem?" Alya did not want to have this conversation, so she played dumb. In Cairo, she had heard the stinging gossip about a woman who could not control her servants.

Bernard stuck his head between them. "It happens all the time, Lady Kate."

"Thank you, Bernard." Catching her arm, Kathryn drew her to a halt. "Are all the servants rude to you or just those three?"

Alya tried to think of a better answer than the truth. She did not want Kathryn thinking she need fight all her battles for her.

Kathryn growled. "They are, aren't they?"

"The kitchen drudges." Chin thrust, Bernard crossed his arms. "Sometimes they try and drop food on her. Also, the upstairs maids scurry away when she is near. A couple of the stable hands. The—"

"They do not know me. They find me strange." Her cheeks must be searing hot.

Kathryn tucked her arm through Alya's. "Then they should get to know you. Or better yet, accept that you are Henry's wife and should be given the respect your position demands."

That would be nice. Alya nodded.

"Have you told Henry?"

"Nay."

Kathryn stopped, forcing Alya to as well. "Why not?"

"I do not want to be running to Henry over every little problem I encounter."

"Huh!" Kathryn walked them past the horse pens. All the horses were inside on this wet day. "I can understand that, but some problems are going to need some help."

"I will tell him." Maybe.

Laughing, Kathryn tugged her around a large puddle. "Nay,

you will not because you have as much pride as I do. But you must promise to let me help you where I can."

"I promise."

Kathryn snorted. "Liar."

* * *

Henry turned as the pounding of hooves drew closer.

"Look at her." Roger got a dreamy look on his face as he watched Kathryn ride like a berserker across the meadow. "Never saw a woman ride like that."

Henry had to agree. Firstly, because Roger would likely pound his face if he didn't, but more importantly because Kathryn made a magnificent sight on a horse. Low to the saddle, hair streaming out behind her, she moved as one with her horse.

"She trained that horse." Roger glowed as he gazed at his wife. "Raised him from a foal."

"She's remarkable." She'd have to be to bring his big, tough brother to his knees. Of course, Roger had always had that soft spot deep inside.

Kathryn raised her hand.

They waited until she drew abreast. The cool day had whipped color into her cheeks. Mud splattered her boots and chausses. "Henry." She smiled at him. Warm and genuine, it crinkled the corners of her eyes. "I am glad I caught you."

"Is everything well?" Kathryn looked to have business with him.

"All is fine." She waved her hand. "But there is something I wanted to talk to you about. It's to do with Alya."

Henry's hackles rose as his need to defend Alya leaped to the fore. "What about Alya?"

"She is having some trouble." Kathryn brought her mount into line with theirs. She motioned they should walk on. "I thought you should know about it."

Roger frowned at Kathryn. "What sort of trouble? She is not ill?"

"Nay, nay." Kathryn paused as if choosing her words. "It's about the Anglesea folk and mind it is not all of them, but they are not as accepting of her as I would like."

Henry had hoped for the opposite reaction, but he remembered the faces of the Genovese as he walked the markets with Bahir. "Who?"

Kathryn eyed him with a slight frown. "With you looking so fierce, I do not think it prudent to mention names."

"Prudent?" Roger guffawed. "You?"

Kathryn's face reminded Henry of his mother when she was at her most displeased. He tried to motion Roger to watch himself, but his brother continued to laugh. Well, let Roger take his own punishment.

"You will pay for that," Kathryn said to Roger.

Henry felt sure Roger would.

Roger grinned back at his wife, silently daring her to do her worst.

Henry was aware of being the interloper in their exchange. "Tell me what happened."

"She will not tell me the extent of it," Kathryn said. In the fields to their left, serfs took advantage of the break in the weather and moved amongst the growing crops. "But I came upon her trying to get the seamstresses to make some things for her. They refused."

"Bloody hell!" Roger balled his fist on his thigh. "They had best not have. Alya is a lady of the family. They live in the keep at our sufferance."

Henry could not have put it better. "What did you do?"

"I made it clear to them their behavior would not be tolerated. Refusing Alya would be viewed by Roger and yourself as refusing a direct command from Lady Mary."

"My thanks." Henry bowed to his sister by marriage. He would wager she had put a flea in their ears. Still, it rankled that

Kathryn had come across the problem and not him. "Just the seamstresses?"

"I think not." Kathryn grimaced. "Alya would not elaborate, but I have the feeling it has happened before. I would speak to young Bernard. He has been noting the problem."

"You should do something," Roger said.

Henry glared at his brother for stating the obvious. Of course, he would damn well do something, and without being told. Except, he had spent most of his days with his brother and his mother. There did not seem enough time in the day to catch up with all that had happened in his absence. At times, he merely enjoyed sitting with his mother and his sisters as they spoke amongst themselves. He had not thought to hear their light chatter again. He drew comfort from being around his family.

Except he had a wife now and a man's duty belonged firstly to his wife.

They turned and crossed a narrow bridge spanning one of the spider web of smaller rivers that met the sea. Redshanks, oyster catchers, and plovers speckled the sandy banks, digging amongst the thick, silty mud for their dinner.

"I think she is lonely," Kathryn said.

Her words hit him like a fist to the belly.

Roger glanced at him. Reproach seemed to emanate from Roger's averted face.

Was Alya lonely? He asked her every night how she spent her days and she had said naught. Bahir remained at the castle as company for her. Bea and Faye had told him how they liked her. Still, he did not really know how she spent her days, and he should. "I will speak with her."

They returned from their ride with enough time to change before the evening meal. Henry found Alya in their chamber, sitting at the casement and staring outside. She started when she noticed him. "Henry?"

Her surprise acted as another lash. Most evenings he bathed in the barracks, and saw her only at dinner. Knowing it was irrational did not stop his annoyance that she had not come to him and told him. "Why didn't you tell me you were having trouble with the servants?"

He regretted his terse tone the moment the words left his lips.

Alya stiffened. She took a long moment to straighten her skirts. "You have been speaking to Kathryn."

"You should have told me." He yanked off his gauntlets and dropped them on the chest guarding the foot of the bed.

"I did not want to bother you." She turned back to the view outside the casement.

"You are my wife. It is my duty to take care of you." Blast! That had not come out right at all.

Alya raised her brows. "And you are always one for your duty, are you not?"

He had no idea what that meant, but got that sick sensation he had trod up to his knees in some very murky water. "You are my wife. My responsibility."

She shot to her feet. "Responsibility?"

Ballocks. He was making a mess of this. "I want you to be happy in my home."

"Is ensuring my happiness a duty or a responsibility?" She sashayed toward him.

He damned himself for becoming transfixed by the sway of her hips. "It is neither." The gown she wore clung to her full, beautiful breasts. Breasts he loved to caress and take in his mouth. "You should have told me."

"When should I have told you?" She drew closer.

Night-blooming jasmine and cinnamon befuddled what remained of his senses. "Anytime."

"Indeed." She put her hands on his chest. "Should I have told you when you leave before the sun is up?" She shoved him.

Surprised, he tottered back a step. "What—"

"Or perhaps when you are not anywhere to be found." Alya shoved again. "All day." Another shove.

Braced for it this time, he held his ground. His brain finally caught up to the fact that Alya was not just angry. She was livid. "I have been busy." This was his best defense? He fully deserved to be shoved again.

Clearly Alya thought so too, because she got her strength behind the next push. For a woman who barely reached his shoulder, she had remarkable strength. "Perhaps you think I should have interrupted your time with your mother and your sisters. Nay?" She cocked her head. "Maybe I should have followed you and Roger around." Unable to move him, she punched both fists into his chest. "Or perhaps I should have said something in the two heartbeats it takes you to get naked and leap on top of me."

"I do not leap on top of you." Male pride rose to his rescue. He caught her fists and held on. "Are you complaining about my attentions to you, my lady?"

"Nay." Alya flushed, struggling to free her hands. "But you never talk to me. You enter this room, disrobe and…"

"And what?" He snatched up the gauntlet.

Alya glared at him, eyes bright, cheeks flushed, her chest rose and fell with her rapid breathing.

Dear God, she stirred him and he tugged her closer. "You are saying that you do not enjoy my attentions."

She licked her lips. "Nay."

"So you do enjoy my attentions?"

With a strangled cry, she mashed her mouth against his.

Henry lit like bone-dry tinder. He sought to master her with his kiss.

Not so easy as Alya gave as good as she got in a thrilling duel for supremacy.

Bending his knees, he hoisted her up.

Her legs wrapped around his waist. Her hands tangled in his hair, hard enough to make his scalp smart.

In his chausses, his rod pulsed hot and ready. He needed to be inside her now. Sliding his hand between her legs, he found her wet and ready for him. It drew a groan from him. He fumbled himself free of his chausses.

Alya made low, needy sounds in his mouth. She grabbed hanks of his hair and held his mouth to hers.

Henry pressed her against the wall. He found her heat in one hard thrust.

Alya dropped her head back and moaned. "More."

He had more for her, and more, and more. Harder and deeper he thrust. Not a gentle coupling but hard, animal lust. He could barely hold on long enough for her to finish. He was a heartbeat behind her, pressing her into the wall with his final thrust.

Dear Lord. His arms shook and his knees threatened to buckle. Gently he lowered her to the floor. He pressed his sweaty forehead to hers. "Did I hurt you?"

"Nay." She wrapped her arms about his neck. "That was marvelous."

Relief rushed through him and made him laugh.

Alya's laughter joined his.

Through the haze of satiation, an unwelcome thought crept into his mind. Once again, he had not taken the time to speak with his wife.

Chapter Twenty-Three

Alya couldn't say what, but something about Henry was different. She watched him as they broke their fast with the rest of the hall. Something she had said the other evening must have penetrated because he no longer left her right after meals and only saw her at the next one.

He hovered more before going off on his own, which he only did once she assured him she did not need him. It might be annoying, or it might be nice, she hadn't decided yet. Certainly, with her guardian angel beating his wings at her back, the servants at Anglesea twisted themselves about to make her life an easier place. Their eyes however did not change. Suspicion and fear lurked within them just the same.

With him spending so much more time with her now, she also got to know Henry better. Not through lengthy explanations of his childhood but more through the offhand comments he passed throughout the day. There, he had fallen off the wall at eight and nearly broken his arm. On this tree, he had hung his sister's favorite bliaut when she annoyed him when he was ten. In that hayloft, he had snuck his first kiss from a village girl. She liked those parts of his lurking about.

She did not like the loss of freedom, which was strange for a girl raised in Cairo. Within her father's house she had been granted freedom, but outside she had needed a chaperone and a male escort, not to mention being shrouded in the hijab and niqaab. Since Henry had persuaded her to drop the concealing veil, she had relished her liberation. She loved the wind on her face, riffling through her hair. Once the shyness passed, she enjoyed the glances of male appreciation, Henry's especially. That made her a vain girl, she supposed, but she did not really care. The bearing of her face to the world seemed a brazen declaration that here she stood and it made her feel stronger, more present.

"What are you going to name your dog?" Henry pointed to her other shadow who lay under the table, ever alert for dropped food.

Alya peered beneath the table.

Dog thumped her tail.

"Should I give her a name?"

Henry laughed. "If you would like to call her to you, you should."

"I do not need to call her." Alya returned to her meal. "Wherever I am, there she is. She follows me."

"You do not like her?" Kathryn frowned and clicked her fingers for the dog.

She rose and licked Kathryn's hand.

Alya shuddered. "You should wash your hands seven times."

Kathryn looked at Alya as if she might have lost her mind.

"My father considered dogs to be spiritually unclean," Alya said, uncomfortably aware that the attention of most of Henry's family was now on her.

"They do not like dogs were Alya comes from," Henry said.

"Forgive me, my lord." Bahir spoke from beside Kathryn. "It is not that simple. Alya's father as a new convert to Islam did not always appreciate the...complexities. To truly understand the Qur'an can involve a lifetime of study."

"But you're Christian," Kathryn said to Alya. "And Christians like dogs just fine."

"But I was raised in both religions." Alya did not like having to defend herself like this. She and Henry had only been speaking of the dog lying beneath the table.

"Just as you, Kathryn, were raised as both knight and lady." Lady Mary's voice broke the loaded silence. "None of us are simply one thing or the other. I think we should allow Bahir to speak."

"My lady." Bahir bowed low. "The Qur'an expressly forbids the unkind treatment of animals. We consider animals, including dogs, to be part of the greater divine. *There is not an animal that lives on the earth, nor a being that flies on its wings, but forms part of communities like you. Nothing have we omitted from the Book, and they all shall be gathered to their Lord in the end.*"

"The Qur'an is to the Muslim what the Bible is to us." Gregory joined the conversation. He sat beside Bahir. Indeed, since their talk the other day, they were often together.

"So, why did my father consider them filthy animals?" Alya stared at the dog again. She had not seen her do many filthy things, other than the licking of her privates. With the same tongue that had licked Kathryn's hands. Alya suppressed a shudder.

"There is much disagreement amongst our own scholars on the matter," Bahir said. "There are texts that state that to keep company with dogs, voids one of a portion of one's good deeds. Other scholars decry this as not true and point to the many examples of Mohammed's kindness to all animals, including dogs."

"As many of our scholars disagree." Gregory nodded. He turned to Bahir. "So, am I to gather by what you say that the term Muslim is applied not only to humans but to the wider world?"

"Indeed." Bahir's face lit from within.

Kathryn rolled her eyes. "And they are off again."

"Gregory enjoys Bahir's mind and his view on the world intrigues him." Faye smiled fondly at her husband. "He tells me that our beliefs are not so very different after all."

Sir Arthur thumped the table. "That is the problem with war.

We do not stop hacking at each other for long enough to discover our similarities."

The entire family gaped at him.

"This from you?" Roger snorted.

"My father is renowned for being a fierce and indefatigable fighter," Henry whispered to Alya.

Sir Arthur blushed and cleared his throat. "A man can change."

"Indeed," Henry said it so quietly, Alya barely caught the words. He looked haunted by some inner struggle he refused to share.

Kathryn huffed. "Are you going to give the dog a name or not?"

Alya had grown up believing them filthy, but if Bahir spoke true, the decision rested with her. Surely giving a beast a name could do no harm. "What do you suggest?"

Kathryn peered at the dog. "I am sure she is one of Dagger's daughters, given her size and her shape. She's a pretty girl."

The dog grinned at Kathryn.

"I shall call her *Jamila*," Alya said. "Pretty."

"Good." Kathryn pushed away from the table. "Now that we've settled that, I think we should start your riding lesson." She stopped and gave Alya a challenging stare. "Unless you are going to tell me that your father didn't like horses either."

Henry bristled.

Alya put her hand over his. She would not have him fight all her battles for her. "Horses are fine," she said. "The most beautiful horses raised are to be found among the nomadic tribes of my land. Let us see if your horses are a match."

Kathryn glared.

Alya held her stare. If she and Kathryn were to be equals in more than name, then she needed to behave that way.

"Well said." Roger thumped the table and guffawed. "What have you to say to that, my fiery Kathryn?"

"I say you should shut your pie hole." Kathryn scowled at her husband, but humor lit her eyes. "Let us go riding." She raised her brow at Alya. "If you can lower yourself to mount one of our inferior animals."

"I can try." Alya matched her haughty tone.

Kathryn chuckled and tucked her arm through Alya's. "Come along then, you mouthy wench. I'm not sure I did not prefer you when you could barely manage a word of English."

Henry rose.

Alya needed to establish her place here without him. She motioned him to stay. "Finish your meal. I am sure I am in good hands."

He opened his mouth to argue.

"You cannot follow her around like a dog," Kathryn said. "Anyway." She nudged Alya. "She does not like dogs."

"I cannot say I like all dogs." Alya clicked her fingers at Jamila. "But we can agree that my dog is probably superior to most. Come, Jamila."

Jamila trotted over with her tongue lolling.

Kathryn smiled. "That we can agree on."

As they were crossing the bailey, Kathryn glanced at her. "Is Henry looking out for you better?"

"Aye," Alya said. "He wants me to be accepted here. Being by my side makes that easier, he believes."

"Hmm." Kathryn nodded. "I'm glad he listened. When you would not ask him for help, I took matters into my own hands and suggested he spend more time with you."

The words hurt, and they should not because Kathryn meant to be kind. Alya thought Henry accompanied her out of the desire to be with her, or because he had understood her desire to know him better. Instead, he followed her because his sister by marriage had told him he must be more attentive. If Kathryn had said nothing, would he still be at her side?

They entered the cool dimness of the stables. The earthy tang of horse mixed with that of hay. Dust motes danced in the thin fingers of sunlight that pierced the wooden walls.

Kathryn called out, "Peter?"

A stable hand emerged, and tugged his cap from his tousled head. "My lady?"

"Can you please saddle Lady?"

"Not Striker, my lady?" Peter jerked his thumb behind him. "He has been kicking his boards all day, waiting for you."

"I will take him out later." Kathryn smiled. "I raised and trained my horse myself, and he is a little spoiled." She motioned Peter to continue. "Nay, today I am to teach Lady Alya to ride, and she needs a gentler mount if we are not to frighten her to death."

"Lady A-Alya?" Peter glanced at her, then ducked his head.

"Aye." Kathryn linked her arm through Alya's. "She wants to learn to ride and I aim to teach her."

Wringing his cap between his hands, Peter shifted.

"Now, Peter." Kathryn put some steel in her voice. "Thank you."

Peter scuttled off to fetch the horse.

Did he think she would eat the horse? Alya kept her thoughts to herself. She would learn to ride if it killed her. She would do what she must to have people stop looking at her as if she had an extra head on her shoulders.

The lesson went well and took her mind off her other concerns.

Lady, a beautiful bay mare, had endless patience with Alya. Much more so than Kathryn, who rode as if she was part of her mount, and battled to understand how anybody else could not do so.

Peter and two other stable hands appeared at the stable entrance and lingered there throughout her lesson. With their gazes on her constantly, Alya refused to fail. She mastered any fear and kept trying. By the end of the morning, Kathryn had Striker saddled and rode beside Alya and Lady.

"Sit up." Kathryn poked her in the back. "You are not a sack of grain, and Lady is not a beast of burden but a proud stepping palfrey. Ride like that and you will shame her."

Someone snickered from her cluster of watchers.

Alya straightened her spine.

"Tuck your elbows in," Kathryn bellowed from atop Striker. "You look like a scarecrow."

Behaving like the perfect lady she was named for, Lady patiently led Alya around and around the practice yards.

By the time Kathryn pronounced her, "Not terrible," every bone in Alya's body ached, particularly those below her skirts. Gritting her teeth, she dismounted as gracefully as she could.

Without making eye contact, and ensuring his hand did not touch hers on the rein, Peter took Lady from her.

Tired, sore, and more than a little hungry, Alya dug her nails into her palms to stop herself from limping.

"Tomorrow we might attempt a ride outside of the bailey." Kathryn loped gracefully along beside her.

Alya bit back a whimper. "Lovely."

"All in all, I am pleased with your progress," Kathryn said. "You sit your horse strong and tall, and you do not loll around like a poppet."

"My thanks." Alya's legs had turned to pudding beneath her skirt, and her ass ached like Lady and Striker had taken turns kicking it. Ass. Another marvelous English word. If they cooked as well as they cursed, life in England might be pleasant.

Kathryn left her at the hall and went off to the armory to find Roger.

Alya checked to see if anybody was about. The short corridor remained mercifully empty and she allowed herself to hobble to the stairs.

Stopping at the bottom of the stairs, she wanted to snivel like a baby. There were so many of them.

Henry strode out of the hall toward her. "There you are."

As she forced herself to stand straight, Alya bit back a whine.

Henry's blue eyes laughed at her. Breath warm against her ear, he whispered, "I remember what it feels like when you have not ridden before. Shall I carry you up the stairs?"

"Nay." Alya dug her nails into her leg. She would master those blasted stairs. Foot on the first riser she stopped and sucked in a deep breath. "I can do it."

"Uh-huh." Crossing his arms, he glanced up the stairs. "I have a hot bath waiting for you in our chambers. Bahir even gave me some salts to ease your aches."

Up the longest staircase in the history of staircases lay sweet relief and Alya moaned.

Henry slid his hand about her nape. "After I bathe you, I can ease the soreness from your muscles with a special ointment Nurse makes."

He was trying to torture her. Flanks screaming at her, she heaved her second foot onto the riser. Only about six hundred more to go, or at least that's what it felt like.

Tutting, Henry scooped her into his arms. "You, my lady, are too proud for your own good."

Perhaps. Alya looped her arms over his neck. But at least she had not had to ask.

Chapter Twenty-Four

Kathryn bounced into Alya's chamber before the sun had decently crested the horizon, and jerked her awake.

"You must wake." Kathryn hopped from one foot to the other.

"Nay." With Henry in the mood to soothe her riding hurts, Alya had not gotten much sleep the night before.

Alya tried to move. Pain lanced up her thighs and speared her in the belly. Groaning she dropped back onto the bed.

A rumpled pillow the only sign of him, Henry must have left earlier.

"It is fair day." Kathryn bounced closer. "And we are going to take all the children to the village."

"We?" Did Kathryn expect her to move?

"Beatrice, Faye, Lady Mary, me, and you." Kathryn jerked the bed curtains back.

Sunlight jabbed Alya in the eyeballs and she covered her face with her hands. She could barely breathe without pain, let alone make it down to the village. "You go ahead. I will stay here."

"Nay." Jostling her, Kathryn sat on the edge of the bed. "I

have been thinking. Do you want to hear what I have been thinking?"

"Nay." She wanted to crawl back into sleep and stay there until the hurting stopped.

With a nudge to her hip, Kathryn giggled. "I shall tell you anyway. I think the reason people are unfriendly with you is because they do not know you." She spread her arms wide. "Hence, we will give them the chance to know you and then they will love you like we do."

A rosy theory, but not one Alya gave much credence to. "If you love me, you will go away and let me sleep."

"Alya." Kathryn shook the bed. "Get up or I will be forced to set Nurse on you." She stood and jammed her hands on her hips. "We are going to the village for the fair. We are going to have a wonderful time, and you will love it." She spun about and marched out the room.

With a lot of huffing, puffing, and groaning, and, aye, a fair amount of whining, Alya got out of bed. She washed and dressed in one of her Genovese dresses. Like Beatrice, she braided her hair and placed a circlet over her head. Now she looked like any of the other Anglesea ladies. Other than the almond slant to her eyes, and her deeper hued skin.

Did Henry look at her and see the differences? Was it why he kept her at a distance? Maybe the differences between them made him trust her less. Or perhaps they just needed more time to get to know each other. Tired of her own thoughts, she rushed and finished dressing and joined the other women in the hall.

"Alya." Lady Mary's smile lit up her lovely face. "How wonderful that you are joining us. I look forward to showing Anglesea my newest daughter."

Beatrice entered the hall behind her four boys. All four seemed to be heading in different directions and Beatrice looked frazzled.

Faye's oldest boy, Simon, carried little Bess in his arms.

Already tall, Simon apparently closely resembled his father. The younger, Arthur, looked much like Faye.

"Why do you like fairs so much?" Prodded by Kathryn, who had their son in her arms, Roger entered. Little Henry looked so much like Sir Arthur, down to the frown on their faces, it almost made her laugh.

"I do not know." Kathryn sniffed. "But I do, and thus we are going."

"You could go without me." Roger looked hopeful.

"Nay. I cannot." Kathryn poked him in the back. "Because the people will want to see you, and will feel slighted if they do not."

"Garrett is not going." Roger perked up.

"Aye, Garrett is." Garrett joined Beatrice and his boys. He caught Edward and tucked him beneath his arm, and put Geoffrey on his shoulders.

"Wonderful." Sir Arthur rubbed his palms together. "A true family outing."

"Except for William and Alice." Faye tied a bonnet over Bess's dusky curls. "When will they arrive?"

"Any day now." Like a war captain, Kathryn took the lead. "But the weather in the north can be unpredictable, so perhaps it has delayed their travel plans."

The entire family, except Henry. Even Bahir joined them. As usual, he and Gregory had their heads together, faces grave as they discussed.

"Should we wait for Henry?" Lady Mary looked at Alya.

Alya had no idea, and her face heated. Henry had not even mentioned the outing to her. She stood, uncertain for a moment, in a crowd of people who all had someone. Having been stuck to her side for days, he chose now to be missing.

"His loss." Sir Arthur commandeered her hand and tucked it through his arm. He winked at Alya. "I am not stupid enough to let a pretty woman stand alone."

Roger glanced at Sir Arthur, shared a moment, and then the party moved forward.

As they walked to the village, Sir Arthur kept her entertained with all manner of stories. On her last walk this way, she had been too caught up in Henry's homecoming to notice much. Now she took the time to appreciate the natural beauty all around her. Even the sun came out and touched the land with gentle warmth. As if begging forgiveness for all the rain, everything about her threw out its best colors, almost sparkling under the sun,

"Bahir tells me you are raised Christian." Sir Arthur assisted her over a fallen log. "How is such a thing possible?"

"My father is...was...Genovese. He accepted Islam to marry my mother, but insisted I be raised in his faith." So, Henry had not spoken of her with his father. Despite his increased presence by her side, she still felt more separated from Henry than ever. The man at Anglesea differed from the man who had travelled all this way with her. She wished she understood why. At first, she had thought he spent time with his family, to try and recover what they had lost. But Henry spent most of his time alone. To understand him, he would have to speak with her, and he still did not care to do so.

Sir Arthur patted her hand. "Do not fret about your father." He had misread her expression, but she decided against correcting him. "Newt will find some answers for you."

"Thank you."

The villagers cheered as the Anglesea family entered a large green in front of the church. Lady Mary stopped to chat with everyone and, to a person, their delight at seeing her shone from their faces. She asked after children and aging parents, remembered illnesses and strife, and had time for everyone. Kathryn did the same, but she tended to be more direct and less tactful. The people loved her all the same. Swept into a knot of villagers, Beatrice and her children were also clear favorites.

Sir Arthur stepped away to speak with the priest, and Alya found Garrett at her side. He watched Beatrice and his boys.

"They love her here," he said. "Some of them still have long memories about my plot to ruin her."

Alya had heard the story of Garrett and Bea, how he had set out to ruin her to punish her father. Yet, Garrett had fallen into his own trap.

"But you are married now." A couple of hard glances slid over Garrett.

"Bea could have married a man of great influence and wealth." Garrett spoke without rancor. "Some of the villagers believe she married beneath her."

Charming, handsome, clever, sharp-witted, and he adored Beatrice. Alya understood Bea's choice. "What do you believe?"

Garrett laughed. "I know she married beneath her, but that doesn't mean I intend to give her back."

Spritely music came from a group of men near the middle of the green. They played instruments that looked similar to ones she knew. So light and full of vigor, the tunes they played made Alya want to tap her feet.

Gregory led Bahir to the priest, and the two men shook hands. The priest eyed Bahir warily for a short while, but they were soon deep in a three-way conversation. Around the priest, Gregory, and Bahir a clear space appeared.

Gazes fastened on Bahir, some with interest, others with fear, and still others with outright hostility. Perhaps it had not been such a good idea for her and Bahir to join the family today.

"Most of them have never seen someone like Bahir," Garrett said. "All they know are the horror stories from the holy pilgrimages."

She had not realized her thoughts showed so clearly. "Perhaps we should return to the castle."

Garrett considered her words. "I think not," he said. "This way the village sees that the Anglesea family extend their protection over Bahir."

Hostile gazes fixed on Bahir, a cluster of men stood beside a large oak tree. "Will he need that protection?"

Garrett's gaze followed hers. "Ah! Our little group of malcon-tents. The family is much loved here. I would not think any will make trouble."

But he could not be sure. Alya could read the doubt in Garrett's expression.

"Garrett." Bea waved him over from across the green. "Simon would like to show you something."

He excused himself and joined his wife.

In amongst the other castle folk, Alya stood alone for a moment. She wished Henry had joined them and strolled beside her.

Averting her gaze, a young matron clutched her child closer and scuttled past her.

Another older woman nodded a polite but distant greeting.

Alya drifted along in the midst of Henry's family.

Faye tugged her to a woman who sold finely wrought hair combs.

Alya admired the work, and pretended she did not notice the woman subtly pick up each item she had handled and wipe it before placing it down again.

"Henry should be here," Faye said as they moved on. "He should introduce his wife to the village."

Giving Faye a noncommittal smile, she pretended interest in a group of girls dancing to the music. Henry should be here and he had said nothing of leaving her alone today.

As they drew nearer, a group of three women abruptly stopped talking. They greeted Faye and her, but Alya felt their eyes on her back as they passed.

"So dark..."

"...heathen..."

"What was Sir Henry thinking...?"

Each word burrowed its barbed point in her breast. And so did each subsequent whisper she heard throughout the day.

Smiling, even laughing when appropriate, Alya hid her seething, wounded pride. She would not give them the satisfaction of seeing her cry, or let them know how their words affected her.

Beneath the large central tree stood Bahir, a pretty, plump girl speaking to him and tossing her golden ringlets.

With a smile, Bahir shook his head.

The girl grabbed his arm and attempted to pull him into the dance.

"Ann!" A large man marched through the dancers and pulled the girl away. Over his shoulder he shook his fist at Bahir. "Stay away from her, devil."

Bahir had done nothing. Outrage propelled Alya and she hurried over and stood beside Bahir. "Trouble?"

He shrugged. "She is just a silly young girl with a taste for trouble."

When the dancing started, she and Bahir stood to one side. Some older women sat on benches a little way from them and glanced and whispered at them. Alya slipped her hand into Bahir's.

He squeezed her hand back. "Keep your head up, Lady Alya. In their ignorance, they are unworthy of you."

"I hate them all." Angry tears stung her eyes and she dropped her head to hide them.

"Nay." Bahir's deep voice rumbled in the near dark. He spoke in Arabic so only she understood. "You despise their ignorance and hate the hurt and humiliation it causes you."

Alya bit her tongue, because right now she remained certain she hated the entire village. Every whispering, staring, giggling, sign of the cross making one of them. They did not even ask if she shared a god with them. They assumed otherwise.

"Come." Bahir took her arm. "Let us slip away quietly."

Alya was more than ready to do so.

Bahir raised his hand to Gregory.

Clear understanding on his face, Gregory nodded.

"Let us go." Bahir drew her further into the shadows of the green. They left the light and laughter behind them as they hurried through the near silent village. A dog barked at them as they passed.

They made the outskirts of the village unnoticed.

Three young men swaggered toward them on the road leading to the castle.

One noticed and nudged his fellows. All three men stopped, blocking the path.

"Look," the middle one said. "It is our new lady." He drew the word "lady" out with a sneer.

"Lady of what?" The largest of the three grabbed his crotch. "Lady of Sir Henry's cock is all."

The three laughed.

Bahir tensed and dropped into a fighting stance.

"Leave it." Alya grabbed his arm and tugged. "It does not matter what they think, and I do not want to cause trouble." This ended a truly horrible day and she only wanted to get back to her chamber and hide.

Bahir frowned, then nodded. He led her closer to the three men.

Chests puffed like barnyard roosters the men stayed in the path.

"Look!" The loud mouth crotch grabber nudged his friends. "Do you think she is lady of his black cock as well?"

With the ring of metal, Bahir drew his sword.

Fear sent the men stumbling back, tripping over each other.

Alya felt a surge of satisfaction.

"Stand aside," Bahir said. "The Lady Alya and I would pass. Do not make me cut a path through you."

As she and Bahir hurried the rest of the way to the castle, Alya held her emotions inside. Who were they to speak that way to her? She had done nothing to them. Done nothing to all those villagers who would not deign to speak to her or even look at her. Yet they said plenty amongst themselves. They smirked, sneered, and snickered together like she was an oddity to be prodded and poked at. Bahir's humiliation seared through her too. The only reason Bahir was here was because of her. If she had not married Henry, they would both be gone by now. Gone where, she did not know. Her foolish girlish heart had not stopped to consider any of this. Instead, she had gazed upon Henry's beauty and wanted it for herself. The cost was too high.

Bahir stopped her before she could climb the stairs to her chamber. "The problem lies with them, not you."

She nodded and moved her arm free of his hold. Keeping her spine straight and her chin raised, she climbed the stairs. Aye, ignorant, stupid, dirty peasants they were, but they had stood in judgment of her and Bahir and found them wanting. So, aye, the problem might have started with them, but it burned in her belly.

Chapter Twenty-Five

As he walked into the hall, tension slammed into Henry. He had spent the day riding, and eventually stumbled on the manor house Garrett and Beatrice would move into once it was restored. Fascinated by the work, he'd stayed longer than expected. Even shedding his tunic to join in and then spent the remainder of the day working alongside the men. There was something predictable and comforting about working with your strength beside other men.

Roger spotted him first and stood, fists clenched at his side. "Where the bedamned have you been?"

Suppressing his gut reaction to bite back, Henry said, "I spent the day at the old manor house. Working."

"Jesu!" Roger spun about and kicked a stool across the hall. "I could break your stupid head."

Tired, hungry, his muscles aching, Henry nearly took his brother up on the offer.

"It is my fault." Kathryn touched Roger's arm. "I should never have insisted she go with us."

"Do you see that?" Roger bellowed. He charged toward Henry. "My wife is blaming herself for something that is your fault."

"What are you talking about?" Henry glanced at Kathryn.

Grabbing him by the tunic, Roger hauled him onto his toes. "I am talking about your wife."

"Alya." Henry ripped himself free, and shoved away from Roger. He didn't want to fight, but if Roger didn't back down, this was going to end that way. "Get your sodding hands off me and tell me what this is about."

"It's about your wife going to the village and being treated like a diseased dog," Roger shouted, his face going red. "It's about her being there without you to stand in support of her and being treated like she has the pox."

Not really believing what he heard, Henry stared from one face to the other.

Kathryn dropped her eyes.

Beatrice turned away from him and into Garrett's embrace.

Faye and Gregory glanced at each other.

His father scowled.

Mother met his eyes, hers full of a silent rebuke.

"What happened?"

Mother rose and looked at the others. "Let me speak with Henry." She raised her hand. "Alone."

Grumbling, Roger nodded, took Kathryn's hand, and left the hall. The rest of the family trailed behind them.

Henry faced his mother. The disappointment on her face cut deeper than any of Roger's bluster and threats. "Tell me."

In a calm voice, Mother told him about the trip to the village. How the village had rejected Alya, some barely bothering to conceal their antipathy. How they had treated Bahir even worse. Even of the three thugs who had stopped Bahir and Alya on their way back to the keep, and then had told their story about their encounter loud enough for the story to reach Mother's ears. Village rumor now had Bahir as the aggressor in an innocent encounter on the part of the three men. "If I didn't know Bahir, I might even believe them," Mother said.

Henry could barely look at her. "I should have been there."

"Aye, you should have." Mother laid her hand on his arm. "You should have been by your wife's side to make it clear to everyone that she was your choice and you stood by her." She sighed and dropped her hand. "Instead, they saw a foreign woman standing with your family."

He had never lied to his mother successfully, and now struck him as a bad time to start. "I forgot about the fair. I went for a ride to clear my thoughts." His excuses sounded pathetic, even to him. "I thought she would be fine with the family."

"You thought wrong." Mother smoothed her skirts. "You are not a cruel man, Henry. I do not pretend to understand why you left your wife open to ridicule like that. At best, I can hope it was thoughtlessness."

"I apologize." It seemed woefully inadequate, and the insincerity behind it made him flinch. If he could take back what Alya must have suffered, he would. However, if that meant spending the day at the fair with the family, he could not in truth say he would do that. Instead he would have persuaded Alya not to go and remained with her within the castle. Trying to keep up the pretense of his old self was torturous enough before a family he loved. Faced with an entire village, he would crack and they would see the rot that lay beneath the shiny exterior of what used to be Henry of Anglesea.

"We both know your apology is not for me." Mother sighed and patted his chest. "I think you need to speak to Roger as well. He is rather upset with you. He says you are not taking up your duties as chamberlain."

"I have no excuses." Another area in which he failed. All his inadequacies slunk closer and settled about his shoulders, but his old life constricted like a poorly fitting skin.

Finally, she said, "I miss my son." Tears glittered in her eyes. "Nothing can compare to the pain when I thought you lost forever. Yet, here you stand and still I miss my son."

Her son had died on a distant battlefield, trampled beneath the hooves of a destrier and ground into the mud along with the rest of the gore and blood. He had no words to comfort her. Here, in the place where he should feel at home, Henry only felt more lost than ever. Neither Lady Mary's Henry, nor slave, he struggled to acquaint himself with this new man. In the midst of this he found himself now husband to a woman whom he had never thought to have. He woke every morning with the dull blade of dread twisting in his chest. This day would surely be the day she discovered how unworthy he was.

Trying to strip past his armor and see what she sought, his mother studied him.

Henry shrugged.

The sadness on her face another rebuke to add to the stripes across his flesh, Lady Mary stepped away. He failed his mother too.

On leaden legs, he climbed the stairs to his chamber.

A lone taper cast fitful light across the chamber. Alya lay in the bed, fast asleep. Tear stains spotted the pillow beneath her cheek. She had cried herself to sleep. Damn him for having failed her. Damn all of them for having made his Alya cry.

Rage drove him out of the keep. Rage at himself and rage at every accursed, misguided, ignorant pig who had cast a slur upon Alya. Alya was his girl on the wall, his dream, his salvation. How dare they make her cry?

Too impatient to wait for a horse to be saddled, he ran to the village. Sweat streamed down his face, his heart pounded, and still the anger pulsed through him. At the inn, he flung open the door.

Conversation stopped and faces turned toward him.

"Sir Henry." Harrow bowed him into his inn. "Welcome."

Henry nodded. He had come here to find someone.

Hunched amongst his cohorts, Patrick had his head down.

In five paces Henry reached him and ripped him from his seat. Twisting his tunic neck he slammed Patrick onto the table.

Benches and tables clattered over as people scattered.

"You." Henry shook Patrick like a rat.

Patrick stared at him, his face pale, sweat prickling along his brow. "Sir Henry?"

"You dared to speak to my wife in that manner."

Patrick opened and shut his mouth. He glanced toward his friends.

"I will get to them." Henry pounded Patrick onto the table. "Once I have dealt with you. Tell me the names you called my lady. Tell me the things you said to her."

"I...I...did not mean anything by it."

"When you humiliate my lady, you humiliate me." Henry fastened his hand about Patrick's throat. "Is that what you intended, Patrick?'

"N-nay, my lord." Eyes wide with fear, Patrick wriggled on the table.

"Release him, Henry." Garrett appeared at Henry's side. He put his hand about Henry's wrist and tugged. "He is just a boy, Henry. Let him go."

The desire to squeeze roared through Henry, to tighten his fingers and press until Patrick's face filled with blood, then blackened.

"Get off him." Garrett thrust his face in Henry's. "Get off him. Now."

Henry released Patrick.

Patrick rolled off the table and fell to his knees. Coughing and rasping, he crawled away amongst the shocked crowd.

Folk he had known since childhood stared at him as if he were the monster. Silent condemnation. Disappointment in all their faces. Well, he had his own disappointment to air. In all of them.

"I brought my lady to Anglesea where I promised her she would be safe." He met each gaze in turn. Many could not hold his stare and slithered away. "You all made a liar of me. You rendered my vow puny and untrustworthy."

"Henry." Garrett clasped his elbow. "Your point is made."

Turning his back on them, Henry strode into the night.

Garrett followed him. "What the hell ails you?"

Not calm enough to speak yet, Henry breathed deep. He marched through the village, driving his boot heels into the soft earth, wishing he could grind his own stupidity beneath them. Patrick had done wrong, aye, and he deserved to be called to account for disrespecting a lady. But Henry's anger lay not with stupid boys, it lay with himself. More than any of them, he had failed Alya. He had brought her here and left her to their scorn and derision.

He stopped, his breath coming harsh and leaned against the support of an ancient elm.

"What is it?" Garrett joined him. Dark shadows drew pools of mystery over his face, but Henry could picture the concern in Garrett's eyes.

"I should not have done it."

"Nay, you should not have." Garrett put his hands on his hips. "That boy cannot fight you, and even if he could he would not because of who your father is."

"Not that." Henry thudded his head against the tree, wishing he could bash some sense into himself. "Aye, that, but not just that. I should not have let her come to the village alone today. I should have been with her."

Garrett shifted. "Why were you not?"

"I was out pleasing myself."

"Ah." Garrett nodded. "Let us return to the castle. Alya needs you now more than ever."

Henry slipped through the silent castle and into his bedchamber. Not wanting to disturb Alya, he disrobed by the light of the fire and slid into bed.

Alya lay in a tight ball with her back to him.

He eased himself around her, tucking her back against his heartbeat. In his arms, she lay sleeping, so fragile and vulnerable. His to protect, to cherish, to keep. Blast him to hell but he knew not how. He knew not how to be the man she needed. Fear lying just beneath the surface of his skin rose and gained a chokehold about his throat. He had failed when he had gone on pilgrimage.

Failed to see the truth of what he had been a part of until it was too late. Failed to stop the atrocity, failed to prevent the needless deaths. In his failure, slavery had seemed a just and perfect repentance. He had failed his God, failed his family, betrayed his roots, and now he teetered on the precipice of failure once again.

How could a man with no soul be the man Alya deserved?

Chapter Twenty-Six

Alya woke with Henry still beside her the next morning and lay quiet for a moment listening to the steady in and out of his breathing, absorbing the warmth of his body. Like a lead weight in her chest the heaviness with which she had gone to bed the night before lay still within her.

As a girl, she had always known her place in the world, the adored and indulged daughter of a wealthy merchant. Servants had pampered and taken care of her. Her future lay secure in the loving hands of her father.

Between one blink and the next, all that had changed, tumbling her into a series of events that had led to her here now. At Anglesea she had no worth apart from the man beside her and she did not think she had worth for him, other than as a warm body.

"You are awake." Henry's breath stirred the hair at her nape.

"Aye."

Arm tightening about her middle, he took a deep breath. "I heard about yesterday."

"Where were you?" She cursed the peevish tone in her voice.

Propping himself onto his elbow, Henry looked down at her,

his eyes sincere. "Not where I should have been and for that I must beg your pardon."

"They hate me."

"They do not know you." He kissed her temple. "And I am to blame for that as well."

A horn blared from outside the casement.

Henry stilled and listened. With a quick kiss, he rolled out of bed and went to the casement.

Alya took advantage of his naked form. Despite her complaints, she had married a fine-looking man.

"It is William." Henry turned and grinned at her. "My brother William has arrived."

He trotted for the door.

"Henry!"

He stopped and turned to her.

Alya laughed. "Clothe yourself first."

Henry threw on his clothes and hurried from the room.

Alya dressed slowly. She would give him time to greet his brother without her. After yesterday, she found herself less eager to meet the final member of the Anglesea family. Even knowing he would probably be much the same as the others, she harbored the smallest tendril of fear that he would be as the villagers.

Running out of excuses to remain in her chamber, Alya made her way to the hall.

She took a moment at the door without anyone being aware of her.

A tall, dark haired man stood with his arm about Henry's shoulders. That must be William. Beatrice had told her William was the handsomest of her brothers and Beatrice had told no lies. Having inherited the best of both his parents, William was beautiful.

Over Henry's shoulder, William caught sight of her and smiled.

Dear Lord, he must have tossed his fair share of skirts up with that roguish grin.

"You must be Alya." As he sauntered toward her, William held his arms wide. "I am very pleased someone would have Henry. We had our fears you know."

Eyes so blue they made her blink twinkled down at her.

Alya tried to find her words. "G-good morrow."

William swept her into a hug and before she could recover her breath held her away from him and smiled. "Thank you for bringing Henry back to us."

A woman with hair the color of sunrise joined them.

Alya found herself staring again. She had never imagined hair that color. It resembled living flame in its glory. She wanted to touch so badly her fingers twitched.

"I am Alice," the woman said. "I am married to William."

Alice stood half a head shorter than Alya and had a sweet rather than beautiful face.

Alya shook her hand and returned her shy smile.

Next, she met William and Alice's two boys, James and Stephen. Both boys could be no other than William's sons. Although the younger had the same glorious hair as his mother.

"Now we are all here." Sir Arthur clapped his hands. "Tonight, we celebrate."

Oh, dear. Alya tried to smile along with the others. A feast meant people, and people could mean a repeat of yesterday.

* * *

With Alya happily ensconced between his brothers, Henry slipped out of the hall.

The feast had been going strong for the best part of the night. Limited to family and household members, an air of celebration swept everyone in its path. The merrier the mood around him grew, the worse Henry felt.

William led Alya into the center of the hall and attempted to teach her a reel. With her natural grace, Alya picked it up quickly. She looked so beautiful with her flushed cheeks, laughing like she had not a care in the world. It was not an expression he saw often on her face.

Henry took the stairs to the minstrel's gallery. From here he could keep an eye on her and find some peace.

Even his father joined the reel. Sir Arthur danced as if he charged a battlefield, and Anglesea folk were wise enough to give him plenty of room.

Alya wore a gown of scarlet red. Her dark hair flew in an ebony mass as she spun from Father to Roger and William.

"Brooding again, are we?" Newt appeared beside him.

With Newt, Henry did not have to pretend. He shrugged and kept his gaze on the festivities. "When did you return?"

"About an hour ago." Newt watched the scene below them.

His family's happiness was palpable even from here. They celebrated his return and he stood and watched them do it. "You have news?"

"Aye." Newt rubbed his nape. "But let that wait for the morrow. Tonight is for celebration."

Meaning the news Newt carried was ill. Henry nodded, the morrow would be soon enough.

Newt took a seat beside him. "You know when I was a street urchin life was hard but I always knew where I fit."

Beatrice had saved Newt from the stocks as a lad. Since then Newt's path had wound in and out of theirs, until Sir Arthur had sent him to squire for Henry on his pilgrimage. Newt's sticky fingers had been discovered attached to one of the king's deer. Sir Arthur had judged it auspicious to get Newt out of England.

"Would you go back to the streets?"

"Nay." Newt grimaced. "As we both know, I would probably be dangling at the end of the hangman's noose by now."

Beatrice hooked arms with Alya and spun her around and around. Two lovely women, one as fair as the other was dark, they made a pretty picture.

Newt gazed on them with a hunger that matched Henry's. Except Newt's gaze fell on Beatrice.

Catching him watching, Newt hid his expression behind a nonchalant grin.

They knew each other too well for that. "I always suspected that's how the land lay."

"Keep it to yourself then." Newt scowled.

"She's too old for you."

"Aye." Newt leaned his elbows on his knees and gestured to the hall. "And then there is that."

Hands about her waist, Garrett lifted Beatrice off her feet.

Beatrice shrieked with laugher until Garrett brought her down and kissed her soundly.

"He is a good man," Newt said.

"Roger certainly seems to believe so." Henry still could not believe the change in the relationship between Roger and Garrett. When he'd left, they'd barely been able to share a meal without coming to blows. Still, Garrett had filled Henry's shoes as chamberlain well. Very well.

"He makes a better chamberlain than I." With Newt, Henry had always felt free to speak his mind.

Newt studied him for a moment. "That's because he wants to be chamberlain."

Wishing he could cleanse his thoughts and force them into order, Henry scrubbed his hands over his face.

"As much as I would not want to go back to the streets, life was simpler then," Newt said. "I was a gutter rat. I knew it. Everyone else knew it. My place in the world was set."

Dressed in a fine tunic and hose, Newt no longer resembled that gutter rat. "Now you are part of this."

"Nay." Newt shook his head. "I can dress for this world, fight like a knight, and speak like a courtier, but I am no more a part of this than I am of the streets."

Like him, Newt no longer knew his place, and Henry nodded. "You could find another Beatrice and marry her."

"There is only one Beatrice." Newt laughed softly. "And she is not for me."

As squires joined the line, the reel grew more boisterous.

Henry kept his eye on the young men peacocking for Alya's attention.

"Your place is down there." Newt nudged him. "Amongst your family."

"I know that." His curt response surprised him. He softened his tone. Newt was not the enemy. "I know that. And yet I do not feel it. They all expect me to be the Henry they knew. Before."

"Give it time." Newt clapped his shoulder. "And show them the Henry you are now. Your family loves you. They will love this Henry as much as they loved the last one."

"If only I knew who that was."

"Give it time." Newt shrugged. "Not that it matters, but this Henry is far less of a pompous ass than the old one."

Newt could always make him laugh. Tired of talking about it, he turned to Newt. "What of you? You cannot spend the remainder of your days pining after my sister."

Newt snorted. "I never pine, it is pointless." He stared back at the hall. "I wanted to speak to you about something."

"Aye." Henry's nape prickled and he knew he was not going to like what Newt said next.

"I have been speaking with Bahir."

Henry waited.

"He and I are the same."

Henry could not credit his ears.

Newt caught his eye and laughed. "Aye, we are. Both of us cannot return to where we came from, and are not a part of where we are."

Henry was right. He did not like where Newt was headed with this. "Is this where you tell me you are leaving?"

Newt's face grew serious. "Aye, Henry. It is time I find my place in the world."

"Your place is here." Newt had been his anchor even before his slavery.

Truth hanging heavy between them, Newt stared at him.

Newt would never be welcome to court the daughters of the men he now rubbed shoulders with. He would never rise higher than his current station and most still looked at him and saw the gutter rat.

Henry looked away first. "When?"

"Bahir wants to wait for Alya to be well settled before we go."

"You and Bahir?" Henry had trouble picturing it.

"I think we will do well together." Newt grinned. "And at least I never have to fear him stealing my women."

Henry laughed, but the idea of Newt leaving pushed his mood lower. "I will miss you."

"Are you going to get all maudlin on me?" Newt looked horrified.

Henry cuffed the impudent ass.

"Come." Newt clapped his shoulder. "Come and join your family and your lovely wife."

* * *

Alya lay beside Henry in the dark and stared up at the bed canopy. The seamstresses had shown her the new bed curtains and they were nearly finished. They had replaced surliness with an air of cool distance. Perhaps when the curtains were hung this place would feel more like hers.

Again, Henry had disappeared from his celebration for a long time. When he came back with Newt he seemed even more remote than ever. Tonight, he had climbed into bed beside her and kissed her a chaste good night. He still had said nothing to her about the events in the village other than his apology that morning. Even at his remotest before, he had never turned from her in the bedchamber. Did he tire of her? So soon? Her speculation annoyed her. She sounded like one of the women she had despised back in Cairo. They complained, they whined, and their thoughts ran in tighter and tighter spirals.

Something bothered Henry and yet he remained silent with

her. Although he lay perfectly still, she sensed he didn't sleep. Barely two feet separated them and yet they might be on opposite sides of the world.

"Henry?"

"Aye."

"You do not sleep."

"Nay." Bedding rustled as he turned to her and rose above her on his elbow. "You do not sleep either."

"Is something bothering you?"

"Aye."

She held her breath. Here, finally, he would raise his beautiful mask high enough for her to see beyond.

Fingers running over her arm, his expression grew sensual. "Does my wife require my attention?"

The disappointment gouged her middle, and Alya rolled onto her side. "I am tired."

<h1 style="text-align:center">Chapter Twenty-Seven</h1>

Summoned to the hall midway through the next day, Ayla wiped her trowel on her apron and stood. She and Bernard made good progress with their garden. At first, they had made small changes and waited for someone to berate them. As days passed and nobody said anything, their changes grew larger.

She removed her apron and handed it to Bernard. Smoothing her hair, she snapped her fingers for Jamila to join her. With Jamila by her side she never felt completely alone.

On entering the hall Alya read the bad tidings stamped on Sir Arthur and Lady Mary's faces before they even told her. Legs shaking, she drew closer to them.

Jamila pressed into her side and Alya dropped a hand to her head.

"I am so sorry, sweeting." Lady Mary took her hand. "But we have received news of your father."

"He is dead." She split into disparate parts, and her heart froze within her. Strangely, she received the news as if from a great, cold distance. Her emotions felt as if they belonged to a stranger. Like she stood above herself and watched as she nodded, took a seat and smoothed her skirts over her knees. "Do you have any further details?"

Sir Arthur glanced at Lady Mary and took the seat opposite her before the hearth in the hall.

Lady Mary perched on her chair arm. "I have sent for Henry."

"He does not need to come." Henry had left their bedchamber without a word this morning. Since that night she had turned from his advances, he had made no further attempts to touch her. Nor she him. The distance made living here easier. He could not wound her if she stood apart from him. "Tell me."

"We are fairly sure the information is accurate." Sir Arthur motioned his page to her with a goblet of wine. "Newt found an old friend of his in London. One of the sources he used to find Henry."

Alya sipped her wine. For a girl who had grown up not drinking, she had taken to this aspect of life in England.

"Let us wait for Henry." Lady Mary's fingers tightened about her goblet. "I do not want you to hear this news alone."

Alya almost laughed. Other than Bahir, she was alone. Now even more alone than ever.

Her hand shook and wine spilled. A damp spot appeared on her skirt, and she brushed it off. Clumsy to have spilled wine on her new bliaut. She swiped at it. She had to remove the spot. Her vision narrowed on the spot, and she wanted it gone more than her next breath. A tightness gripped her chest, and her breathing grew difficult. She rubbed harder.

"Alya, sweeting?" Lady Mary caught her hand. "We will get someone to get rid of that mark for you."

"But it is new." Alya stared at the stain. She had asked for this bliaut to be made from the fabrics of her dowry. The mark must come out. She could not stain her new dress so. "I have marked it. I have put a mark on my dress."

"It is a lovely bliaut, Alya." Face endlessly patient Lady Mary held onto her hand. "And we will make that go away. Nurse has any number of tricks for cleaning things."

Had the mark spread? No longer able to touch, Alya could not drag her eyes from the blemish. It had definitely spread and she hated that mark. She wanted it to go away. "It must come out."

"And it will." Lady Mary glanced at the page. "Find Sir Henry and Bahir. Now."

"I am so clumsy." Alya shifted her legs so the mark dropped to the side of her knee. From here she did not have to look at it. "Tell me of my father."

"I think we should wait un—"

"Now, if you would." She did not like to interrupt Lady Mary, but she must hear the news and remove this bliaut. Ask Nurse how to remove a wine stain. "I need to hear it."

Elbows on his knees, his craggy face grave, Sir Arthur leaned forward. "Your father was right to send you away," he said. "Newt's friend told him that men broke into your father's house the night after you left."

Ah, perhaps the same men who had chased them in the desert.

"Did they kill him?"

"Aye." Sir Arthur touched her knee, too close to the mark for her comfort. "They burned the house. Newt's friend said they looked for your father's wealth and were angered when they didn't find it."

"I had it." This fabric had come with her from Cairo and now she had ruined it. "How did he die?"

"Sweeting." Sir Arthur flinched. "It is not necessary to know that."

"It is." She nodded to assure him she could hear this. "I would like to know all of it."

"He died by the sword, it was quick. Merciful." Sir Arthur straightened in his seat.

"Nay." She did not know how she knew this, but she did with a cool certainty. "It was not quick or merciful. Tell me."

"Look here is Henry." Lady Mary spoke too loud and too brightly. "He has come."

"Alya." Henry stood by her chair. His hand landed on her shoulder.

He could not see her with her ruined dress. Alya placed her hand over the mark. "My father is dead."

"I heard, sweeting." He crouched at her knee.

Too close to the mark. "Your father is telling me how he died."

Henry and Sir Arthur exchanged a loaded glance.

"Please." They wanted to hide the truth from her. She did not like that. "I would know everything. Please."

Henry nodded at his father. Even now they looked to Henry for permission to tell her what was hers by right to know.

Sir Arthur cleared his throat. "They tied him up. They...um... whipped him. Then they set the house alight around him."

"While he was alive?"

"We cannot be sure. It is very possible he succumbed to his injuries before the fire..." Sir Arthur rubbed his palms on his thighs. "That is all of it. I swear."

He lied. She had heard the rumors around other deaths before she left Cairo. Bad things had happened. Cruel, ugly things inflicted on men because they carried the wrong blood in their veins, bore the wrong color on their skin, spoke with the wrong tongue,

Bahir stood behind Sir Arthur. Big hands folded before him, head bowed in grief.

How odd that Bahir grieved more for her father than she did. Of course, they had always been close. Her father had rescued Bahir from a cruel master and placed him in charge of his household. Bahir had always felt he owed her father a life debt.

"Alya?" So full of regret, so full of pain for her, Henry gazed at her. Now she saw real feeling in his eyes, now when she had no need of it.

"Well." Their heavy emotions weighed on her, pushed against her shoulders like a load of rocks. Bahir in his grief. Henry with his sympathy. Even Sir Arthur had his regret in having to share this with her. "I must change my dress. I have soiled this one."

Lady Mary rose with her. "I shall come with you."

"Nay. I am fine." She motioned her back. "Stay here with Bahir. He feels this keenly."

"Alya." Henry moved to take her arm.

"Nay." She sidestepped him. She needed to change her dress. How did they not understand this? "Nasira can assist me."

Bahir jerked and stared at her.

"Nay, not Nasira." Her head felt so full, too full, jumbled and messy. The stain on her dress had seeped into her head and made everything hazy. "Not Nasira. Nasira is in Cairo. My maid in Cairo. I am sure she perished with my father. She would not leave him alone. She promised me."

"Henry." Lady Mary clasped Henry's arm. "You must go with her."

"Nay." Alya warded them and their crushing emotions off with her hands. If they came close, they would break her beneath the weight. "Stay. I will change my dress. I must change my dress." They stared at her as if she spoke a strange tongue. "See." She held it up to them so they could witness the mark. "I have a mark here on my dress. Marked. Ruined. It is soiled." Moisture dribbled down her cheeks, and she scrubbed it away. Who was crying? Whose tears stained her face?

"Sweeting." Henry strode toward her.

"I am crying." She stared at the dampness on her fingers. "I have stained my dress and I am crying."

Henry enfolded her.

She resisted his arms.

He tightened his hold until she rested against his chest. The need to nestle her aching head against his strong shoulder raged through her, weakening her knees in its implacable demand.

Henry took her weight.

Her legs buckled. Her voice came from outside her. "He is dead, Henry. My father is dead."

"Alya." So much pain, her pain, filled his words. "I am so sorry."

"Henry?"

"Sweeting." He kissed her head.

"I did not say goodbye to him." Her fingers fastened claw like on his tunic. Swift, deadly, the hurt rose through her and she could not stand. "He said he could not protect me. He told me that he loved me. He begged me to forgive him, and I could not."

"You were hurt, sweeting." Henry's heart beat against her ear. "You were frightened that he sent you away with strangers. He loved you, Alya. He loved you enough to know how you felt."

"I did not say goodbye." She hurt—everywhere. Her voice rose on a wail, and she could not make it stop. "I did not say goodbye. I did not tell him I loved him. He died and he did not know I loved him."

"He knew." Henry scooped her into his arms and carried her from the hall.

The only solid thing in the waves welling up inside of her and crashing over her, Alya clung to him.

He lowered her onto their bed and came down beside her. He held her to him as she cried. Tears that would not end, drawn from a hurting that had no bottom.

* * *

Long after the keep had fallen silent Henry entered the hall.

Gregory rose from his seat by the hearth. "How is she?"

"Sleeping." Concerned that she would make herself ill he had almost called for Nurse countless times as Alya wept. Yet, some part of him had understood her need to lance the festering pain within her, and he had let her cry herself insensate.

Bahir had promised to sit with her while she slept and Henry let him do it. Bahir needed to be near Alya, and Henry took pity on him.

Gregory pulled a chair closer for him, and pressed him into it.

A platter of bread, cheese, and cold beef rested before the hearth. "You did not eat."

"Are you my mother now?" Henry's words lacked any heat. More for something to do than any real hunger he picked up the bread.

Gregory shrugged. "Lady Mary waited up for you most of the night. I sent her to bed and promised I would wait. Garrett has the next shift."

Of course, his family would wait to hear how Alya fared. They had drawn her into them, as one of them, and they would not sleep without someone standing watch. He imagined even now, his mother rested but did not sleep. "Her father sent her away to protect her."

"Bahir told me what happened."

"I knew before that it was near certain he was dead." Henry toyed with the bread and cheese in his hand. "Only she looked at me, so desperate for it not to be true, that I could not tell her."

"You left her with hope?"

"I wanted her hope to be true." Henry dropped the mangled mess back onto the platter. "But I knew it couldn't be. They were killing the foreign merchants one after the other. Picking them off like ripe fruit."

Gregory nodded. "I imagine there was a lot of anger in the wake of the war."

"Is war not always mired in anger and fear?" The senselessness of it ripped through Henry. The fear, the anger, the useless, pointless, heartbreaking death.

Gregory nodded. "I remember the day you left."

So did Henry. Down to the last angry words he had spoken in the armory. Filled with righteous wrath and the certainty of his own cause he had faced down his father and his brothers and spoke those haunting words. "If I die in the name of God, then my death will have meaning."

"They forgave me." He shrugged as if the burden of his family's forgiveness did not hound him even into his dreams. "Thus, I know her father forgave her."

"Forgiveness is a strange thing." Gregory stretched his legs out to the fire. Even in midsummer, night chill crept into the hall. Alya was not the only one who missed the Cairo heat.

"We believe it comes from without, but truly it rests here." Gregory touched his chest. "Faye forgave my failure to act long before I was able to."

Gregory's words chilled Henry. They struck so close to his heart that he dug his hands into the chair's arm rest. "Did you forgive yourself?"

"Partly." Grim-faced, Gregory stared into the fire. "There are still times, even now, when I see every mark that bastard put on her. When I feel every tear she shed."

Aye, Gregory had lived beside Faye for all the years of her marriage to a man who took pleasure in hurting her. At her side, Gregory had watched as another man hurt the woman he loved. "They were married. It was not your place to intercede."

"Just as you believed that you acted with God on your side," Gregory said.

"I was wrong." In the end, death was not noble or honorable. It all ended in a gory, writhing mass of blood, piss, and tears and the only meaning it had was to those who loved the dead men.

Gregory nodded. "As was I. I should have broken my vow to Calder and told your father. Hell, I should have gathered her and the boys up and run with her and hidden her. I should have killed him."

This conversation irked him, it scratched at a wound he did not want to acknowledge. "What is your point?"

"My point is this, Henry." Gregory took a slow, careful breath. "We all act with that we know to be true at the time. You are an honorable man, and you acted out of that honor. Now that same honor condemns you to question yourself and demands that you pay penance for having acted thusly." He leaned forward. "Your family loves you. The possibility of your death ripped them asunder. When you returned to them, they did not see your past failings, or even remember the angry words you spoke before you left. They just saw you, and were grateful to have you back."

"I remember."

"Aye." Gregory handed him a goblet. "You remember, and you do not forgive yourself. But you do not yet see that the anger you hold against yourself stands between you and their love. Only you can end the anger, as only you can forgive yourself."

Could he forgive himself? Henry rather thought not.

Chapter Twenty-Eight

While Roger paced the length of the armory and back again, Henry sat beside Garrett and tried to concentrate on a solution. William drank his wine and watched Roger pace. The parchment at the center of the consternation lay crumpled in Roger's fist.

The issue was marriage. His. Or rather his current lack of marriageability. Roger held in his hand a missive from a member of the king's inner circle, Sir James of Fenwick. Though not a royal missive, it was close enough to make Roger flinch. Close enough to believe that the king sought this alliance without appearing to seek this alliance. Sir James had some blood connection to the king. Near enough that everyone knew of it, yet sufficiently removed not to be part of the royal family.

After years of floating on the edge of the king's grace, finally an overture had come.

An offer of marriage between house Anglesea and house Fenwick. They had a suitable daughter, and hunted for a groom. Problem being, Anglesea no longer had any marriageable progeny and news of Henry's marriage had not yet reached court. Once again, he failed his family. He should have grown accustomed to it by now.

"Thoughts?" Roger glanced at William, him, and then Garrett.

Henry tried to look as if he bent his brain to the matter on the parchment. He failed them in more ways than they knew. Not only could he not be the marriageable son they needed, he could not find it in him to take the role assigned to him before he'd left on pilgrimage. In the weeks following the death of Alya's father, he had been granted a reprieve from Anglesea matters and Roger's expectations, but now duty had found him.

Duty! The Henry who had left for Cairo had been an insufferable ass, always berating others in the name of sodding duty.

"No handy bastards running around?" Garrett steepled his fingers in front of him.

"Only you." William grinned and stood. "And as fascinating as all this is, I promised my wife my company." He shrugged. "This might amaze you, but she likes to keep me about."

Given time, William's furtive mind might very well provide a solution, but that was not his role in the Anglesea clan. It fell to Henry to provide the answer, and he had nothing to offer.

Roger punched Garrett's shoulder. "My father did not beget any bastards. And I'd like to see you suggest that to my mother."

Chuckling, Garrett sipped his mead. He'd never developed a taste for wine, and while before, Roger would have mocked his common tastes, now he always had mead stocked for Garrett. Garrett and Roger had fallen into a comfortable pattern and Henry threw off the balance. Two chairs beside the armory hearth, on either side of the table covered with parchment. One for Roger and the other for Garrett, and from there the two of them ran the Anglesea demesne.

Garrett occupied the place Henry should, and Henry had no desire to oust him. Therein lay one of his greatest failures. That and his strained marriage, but he did not know how to close the chasm between him and Alya, and he did not want to cause her more torment.

Since birth Roger, William, and Henry had known their

assigned paths. Roger, the heir, would take over Anglesea and the title. William, as the second son would function as a spare in case Roger did not reach adulthood, but would also be used to strengthen alliances through marriage. Not the heir, yet almost, made him valuable matrimonial property without the Anglesea family having to commit the heir. As for Henry, he could have sought his fortune either in the church, or function as chamberlain to Roger. He favored women far too much for the church, and chamberlain had been fixed. Of course, he would also prove a good marriage resource, but with his older brothers hale and already producing heirs of their own, his claim on the title stretched thinner and thinner.

And thank the good Lord for that. Henry had been happy with his allotted role. Some men hankered for the position of heir, and perhaps as a young boy he'd had moments of coveting the glory of the name, but not since he had grown to see what an ache in the ass Roger's inheritance could be.

Younger sons, especially in a household as loving and indulgent as Anglesea, had far more freedom and were granted greater forbearance than the heir. While Roger spent hours learning how to step into his father's boots, William and Henry explored.

"Anything?" Roger glared at Henry.

Uncomfortable under the scrutiny, and glad Roger could not read minds, Henry tried to find a more comfortable position on the bench opposite Roger. "Well, first we need to inform court of my marriage."

"Really?" Roger drawled. "Why did we not think of that? Bugger it, Henry! We know that. This is about managing this opportunity in a manner that causes no offense and still accepts the hand of friendship extended to us."

If he had any interest in participating, he might have taken offense. "Garrett is the one with the twisted mind."

"Aye, but Garrett will not be here to see this thing play out." Roger pounded his fist into his palm. "Garrett has land he wants to get to. A demesne to run."

"The manor is taking longer than anticipated." Garrett shrugged. "I can stay for a while longer."

"That is not the point." Frustration eking from him, Roger kicked a stool across the armory and stood with his back to them.

"Indeed." Garrett rose and took the parchment from Roger. "I will give this some thought. In the meantime, I will leave you alone."

As Garrett ambled from the armory, Henry braced. Frustration had been building between him and Roger, and the time of reckoning had come.

"I have tried to give you time." Roger clenched his fists. "I have told myself that you merely needed to grow accustomed to being home again, and then things would come right."

Henry had labored under much the same misapprehension. He could no longer lie to himself or his brother. "I know."

"But it is only getting worse." Shoving his hands behind his back Roger faced him. "You show no interest in Anglesea, in being at my right hand."

"Roger." Henry searched for the right words, then gave up. Roger was a direct man, and blunt words would be best. "I show no interest because I have no interest." He raised his hand to stop the storm building in Roger. "Of course, I love Anglesea and want to work to see it prosper. But this." He prodded the pile of scrolls on the table. "And the fine dance of politics is not for me. There has to be another way I can serve you."

"It used to be all you wanted was to be chamberlain." Roger sighed and took the seat opposite him. "I want to bash your head in, but that won't do either of us any good. Speak to me, Henry."

"That man, the one I was when I left, does not exist anymore." The hurt on Roger's face lashed at him. "On a practical level let us examine this new situation. It has been years since I took part in any of the court intrigues. The game changes daily and I no longer even know all the players. What use can I be to you in my ignorance?" He hated what he said next, but it had to be aired. "With my foreign bride, I have become a liability at court. Many will consider Alya to be a female enemy. You saw how the villagers reacted to her. As much as we would like to believe it not so, many at court will see Alya as our weakness and seek to exploit that."

"Henry." Roger stared fixedly at the floor. "Alya is your wife and we accord her that respect."

"Aye, you do." Henry's gut churned. He did not regret his marriage, but he did see the trouble it could cause. Alya and Bahir had paid the price for his naivete in the village, and he would not put them in such a position again. "But in the game of politics, she can be used against us."

"I did not say so." Roger laced his fingers together, knuckles growing white in his tight clasp.

"But I did." Restless with his own thoughts and needing to get all of this said, Henry paced. "I came back prepared to do my duty by you but you already have Garrett. Let us be frank, he makes an excellent chamberlain, and he enjoys the task. His mind bends to these intricacies so much better than mine."

"You are my brother." Roger's loyalty was commendable but misplaced here.

"That does not make me the best person to fill this role." He stared out of the casement. Alya hurried across the bailey with Jamila at her heels. He and Alya drifted about each other like polite ghosts. He did not want to push her in her grief, but the gap between them only grew wider and harder to breach. "I have spent time at Garrett's manor. More time than Garrett, in fact." The idea had grown slowly in Henry's mind. "Put me there. Give me the task of making that demesne profitable. Maybe a little distance is what I need. Perhaps there I can build a future without trying to compensate for an ill-fitting past."

"You mean away from the family."

"Aye." He hated the thought of hurting them, but the weeks stretched on and the situation worsened, until he itched beneath his skin. "I love my family. All of you, but you all look to me to be the same Henry who left here. It weighs on me."

Roger reared back. "Our love weighs on you?"

"Nay." Henry was clear on that. "Your love is even more precious to me now than ever. Having faced its loss, I truly see it for the cherished gift it is. But I have changed, and I need to be the man I am now, not the man I was."

Roger frowned, but some of the grimness left his features. "You think this would be easier if you did not live at Anglesea?"

"Aye." Alya disappeared through a small gate in the curtain wall. Beyond that lay a garden he had not visited in years. "And if Alya and I are going to stand a chance of building a strong marriage, I believe she needs it too. She would be happier away from the center, less in the glare of all eyes."

"Let me think on this." Roger nodded. "I have never considered a time when you would not be my chamberlain."

"Truly?" Henry found that hard to believe. "Even when you had such a frighteningly capable man already in service to you?"

Flushing, Roger dropped his gaze. "I will think on this, but I need something from you in return."

"Name it."

Roger poured wine for them and sat back. "You say you are a changed man, and we all see it. Tell me, Henry. I need to know what happened to you."

Henry's throat tightened around words he had never spoken, holding onto things he could not unsee but also did not want to share.

Roger leaned his elbows on the table. "Tell me."

Henry's hand shook as he took up his goblet. Roger loved him and in the steady, calm of his regard, Henry found the courage to do what he had thought he never could. "We sailed first for Anatolia. We sought to make an alliance there that would prevent us fighting a war on two fronts..."

* * *

Alya shut herself and Jamila into the garden and leaned against the door for support.

"Many at court will see Alya as our weakness and seek to exploit that."

Henry regretted marrying her, and it hurt more than she could credit. Since her father's confirmed death, he had been kind, solicitous, but also distant. A caring stranger now shared her bed. As much as she had felt slighted when he shared only his body with her, now she missed even that.

Duty done, Henry had turned his back on her. Bewitched by his beautiful eyes, and his handsome face and form she had allowed herself to believe their marriage a blessing. All that time traveling together had lulled her into a blissful world of make believe.

The real world bore no resemblance in its cruelty. His family had accepted her with such warmth and now they paid the price for that. No place, person, or family existed separate from the cold world about it.

Beatrice had told her all about the fine edge Anglesea teetered on with their king. Alya did not understand all of it, but things did not change so very much from one place to another. Those who lived in the glow of the palace prospered. Those who did not, suffered. Cairo had been just the same.

As much as Henry's words hurt, there was no point in fighting them. He had married her in a bargain with her father. This was her lot now, and she needed to find a way to accept it.

"My lady." Bernard slipped through the gate, his young face alight to see her. "I was hoping you would come today."

Of course, she had come. Here amongst the growing things she found solace. The simple act of planting a seedling in the damp, rich soil and nurturing it as it grew gave her more peace even than prayer. With the gentler sun and all the rain, things thrived here in England and the joy of it soothed her.

Clasped to his breast, Bernard carried a bunch of tiny green plants. "I brought these from my mum." He looked smug. "I asked her all about what would grow and what wouldn't."

"What do you have there?" This boy and their love of plants provided a bright point in her day.

Even Jamila liked Bernard and nudged his leg for attention.

"I have herbs," Bernard said. "We can use them for all sorts of things." He laid his precious cargo on the ground. "We can cook with them, use them for healing."

Alya picked up a plant with broad, bright green leaves, the veins running purple across its surface. "What is this one?"

"That is sorrel," Bernard said. "And my mother says it is very easy to grow."

Alya pushed her worries aside for later. One thing she knew, is that they would bide their time and be there later. "Then, Bernard, we shall grow sorrel."

Chapter Twenty-Nine

Alya rolled onto her side and tucked her arm beneath her cheek. They could not continue like this. Rather, she could not continue like this. Henry did not love her, but perhaps there could be more for them than the cold, empty silence. As the grief over her father's death eased, the voids in her life, once more, made themselves known.

Naked as he washed, Henry stood in a shaft of early morning sunlight. Better eating and softer living had added more muscle to him. He gleamed with vitality and strength like a pampered stallion. A stallion who might as well be living in another stable for all the attention he paid her.

The emptiness within her nagged at her. "Henry?"

He turned, confident in his nakedness. Indeed, why would he not be?

Alya's physical response quivered low in her belly. Until recently they had no trouble with that side of their marriage.

Henry waited for her to speak.

"What will you do today?"

He looked taken aback. "I...train arms with my brothers. Go to the manor house."

"You go there often." She had his attention and her heart clamored for her to hold it. "What do you do there?"

"I help with the repairs." He cocked his head. "Why do you ask?"

She had no good answer, so she shrugged. "I wanted to know how you spend your days."

"Did you need me for anything?"

Always so polite. *Aye*, she wanted to yell. *I need you to chase away the hollowness inside of me.* "Nay."

As if he might say something, he stilled and then returned to his washing. Pausing with the washcloth midway down his belly he turned to her. "How will you spend your day?"

It was the closest they had come to conversation since her father's death. "The silks are ready for this chamber. I am going to help hang them."

"Ah." He steeped the cloth in the basin, wrung it and washed his belly, his sides, up beneath his arms.

Flesh she had touched, worshiped with her hands and mouth. Between her thighs, she ached for him. Too many lonely nights, and mornings, had passed. It should not be so hard for a man and wife to speak. They shared a bed, and their lives, and yet she could find no topic to keep him in the chamber. "Kathryn says I am ready to ride outside the keep."

"Indeed." He snatched up a drying cloth. Lucky cloth to be so close to the smooth, warmth of his skin, and run unhindered over the ridges and planes of his form. "Would you like to ride with me?"

"When?" She tried not to sound too eager.

"When you are done with your prettifying." He waved his hand at the chamber. "We could go to the manor and I could show you what I do there."

Her day brightened considerably. "I would like that. Very much."

"Me too." He smiled.

It touched the deepest part of her and lit a flicker in the void.

Henry pulled on chausses and a tunic. He belted his sword about his hips. "I will see you later."

"Later." She nodded, her gaze meeting his. So much unsaid hung between them.

Henry nodded and cleared his throat. "Until then."

"Aye."

"Right." He strode to the door.

She did not want to let him leave. She wanted to hang onto the tiny moment. "Henry?"

"Aye." He spun about.

Obeying her impulse, Alya hopped out of bed and ran to him. Rising onto her toes, she kissed him. "Until later."

His arms snatched her to him, pressing her against him. His gaze caught instant fire.

It robbed her of breath. He did desire her, as much as ever.

"I could stay." His lips touched hers, teasing a response from her.

Alya pressed closer. "You could. Stay."

Pounding at the door made her jump. "Henry." Roger yelled from beyond the closed door. "Get your ass out here. I've got a clucking bunch of new boys I need to turn into fighters."

Henry cursed. Indecision all over his face he glanced at the door and back at her. "I promised Roger yesterday I would help him."

"Then that's what you must do." Alya did not want to let him go. She wanted to drag him right back to bed. His reluctance to leave acted like a balm to her disappointment. She kissed him. "Until later."

He returned her kiss, swift, hard, and hungry. "You can wager your life on that."

* * *

Alya dressed and joined the family in the hall to break her fast.

Looking up, Kathryn smiled. "Is that a new bliaut?"

"Nay." Although it was one of her favorites in a deep, rich blue.

Tilting her head, Kathryn continued to study her. "Then your hair is different."

"Indeed, nay." Alya laughed. She wore her hair much like she did every day.

"Huh." Kathryn motioned Alya to join her at table. "Something is different."

"Ah, my girls." Lady Mary swept into the hall. "I see all our men have left us this morning." She glanced at Alya, stopped and looked back again. A sweet smile lit her face. "Ah. I have missed your lovely smile, my Alya."

"Is that it?" Kathryn squinted at her. "Are you smiling?"

"Perhaps." Alya touched her face. It did not feel any different, but she did feel lighter within. "I do not walk about making an effort to smile all day."

"I should hope not." Beatrice snorted and joined them at table. "That would make you appear deranged."

"Who is deranged?" Faye took the seat beside her mother. "You look pretty today, Alya."

"She has found her smile." Lady Mary shared a smug look with Faye.

Beatrice growled. "Well, she hasn't exactly had a lot to smile about lately, has she?"

Lady Mary eyed Beatrice. "Are you expecting?"

"Nay." Beatrice slammed her beaker onto the table. "Why would you ask that?"

"Because you're grumpy," Kathryn said. "You always get grumpy when you're expecting."

"I do not." Beatrice scowled at her.

"Aye, you do." Alice slid onto the bench beside Beatrice. "And I should know because you boxed my ears more than once when you were expecting Edward."

"I did not...perhaps I did. But I am not expecting. And why am I not expecting?" Beatrice raised her voice so it carried to all the Anglesea women. "I am not expecting because my husband will not help me get that way."

Alya flushed. This conversation made her uncomfortable. Perhaps Garrett had problems that he would not want shared about like this.

"Bea." Lady Mary looked pained. "This is not something, that as your mother, I want to hear."

"I have explained to him that I am fully recovered from Geoffrey's birth. I am ready to have another child."

Faye peered at Alya. "We should not talk about this. Alya is embarrassed."

As all the women turned and stared, her face grew even hotter.

Kathryn patted her arm. "We are all married women here. We can speak of these things."

"Aye, but will Garrett want his...I mean...perhaps Garrett would not like Beatrice to share his...er...difficulties."

Clapping a hand over her mouth, Kathryn snorted with laughter. "Why would you think Garrett had difficulties?"

"Garrett has difficulties?" Alice leaned forward to catch their conversation. "What sort of difficulties?"

"The limp kind." Kathryn flopped her hand forward on her wrist and laughed louder.

"Garrett does not have those kinds of difficulties." Beatrice harrumphed. "And I should know."

"Again, Beatrice. Not a discussion I enjoy," Lady Mary said. Then she leaned closer to Faye. "Perhaps Nurse has something for Garrett's—"

"Garrett does not have any trouble with...that." Beatrice's voice rose. "What would possibly give you that idea?"

All eyes turned her way again, and Alya squirmed. Her grasp on English remained tenuous and she'd drifted out of her depth with this conversation. "You said he did not want any more children and would not get you with child."

"So you thought..." Beatrice chuckled. Her chuckle grew into a laugh. "This is how a nasty rumor gets started. Although it would serve him right for being so stubborn about the baby thing." She stopped giggling for long enough to smile at Alya. "Let us be clear. Garrett works perfectly well thank you. He just refuses to provide what I need, when I need it."

That was supposed to make things clearer? Alya looked at Kathryn for an explanation.

"She means Garrett withholds at a certain time of the month."

"Withholds what? His affection?" Could this be why Henry had turned from her?

"Nay." Kathryn flushed bright red. "His seed. He withholds his seed."

That made sense. Henry did things with her that did not always end in his completion inside her. But still she needed more details. "What did you mean about time of the month?"

"Your women's time." Lady Mary made a circular motion. "Do not, for all our sakes, speak to a priest about this, but Bea is speaking of when she is ripe for conception."

Kathryn sat back and gaped at her. "You have no idea what we are speaking of, do you?"

"Did your mother not tell you of this?" Lady Mary frowned. "Or your maid, Nasira?"

The idea of Nasira speaking of anything close to this made her giggle. "Nay. Nasira did not like to mention anything related to women parts, and my mother passed when I was very young. Bahir explained it all to me."

"Bahir!" They may have shouted all at once.

Alya's face heated. "He guarded a harem. He knows all sorts of interesting things about women and...that."

"But not this." Lady Mary inched closer to Alya. "It is not a sure measure against getting with child, but it does help." Lady Mary went on to explain about her courses, the times when she was more likely to get with child and when she was unlikely to.

"So." Kathryn toyed with her paring knife. "If Bahir did not explain about getting with child. What did he tell you?"

"Oh, many things." Alya waved an airy hand. An entire week of excruciating conversation during which she had worn a permanent blush. "But mainly about how a woman can please a man. Perhaps because that is the sole reason for a harem, a man's ultimate pleasure."

Kathryn sat up straight. "Really?"

All five women scooted closer.

Alice leaned all the way over the table, her emerald eyes glittering. "Tell us everything."

* * *

Henry walked into the hall and immediately his nape prickled.

Mother, Faye, Beatrice, Kathryn, Alice, and Alya stared at him. Huddled together over their sewing they wore matching flushed faces and speculative gleams.

Henry checked his tunic for stains. "What?"

"Nothing, dear." Mother rose with a secretive smile. She patted his cheek in passing. "I was merely thinking what a lucky boy you are." She left the chamber laughing.

The other women broke into giggles.

Alya went redder than a cherry. No doubt, the trouble began and ended there.

"I came to fetch you for our ride," he said.

Beatrice snorted. "Did you, now?"

Raucous laughter came from all the women.

Henry cursed the heat crawling over his neck and onto his cheeks. "Are you ready?"

"More than ready." Kathryn nudged Alya.

More cackling from his family crones.

"Come on." Desperate to get out of there with his balls intact, he jerked his head at Alya.

Amidst more giggling, she rose and slid her hand into his outstretched one. "Should I change?"

Her bliaut, although not ideal for riding certainly displayed the swell of her breasts and hips. "Not when you look so beautiful."

"Ah." Kathryn clasped her hands to her bodice. "See how sweet they are."

Enough. Henry tugged Alya out of the hall. Her hand fit perfectly into his. Small and delicate, he wrapped it tightly within his. His to protect.

A page nodded to them in passing. "Lady Alya."

"Good day, Bernard."

"I checked on our sorrel earlier. It looks to be taking root."

"Wonderful." Alya gifted Bernard one of her lovely, unrestrained smiles. Henry had seen too little of those smiles recently. He took for granted that his family would accept her, but what of Alya? Was she even happy here? He fervently hoped so, because the idea of letting her go twisted blade-sharp through his vitals.

Warm sunlight bathed the bailey and Alya turned her face up to it. "Ah! Today it is not raining."

"It does not rain all the time." Although having lived in Cairo, he understood how Alya would miss the near constant sun.

She looked skeptical enough to make him laugh.

"I will grant you, however, that it rains a lot of the time." The longest time had passed since there had been ease between them and Henry craved to hold onto the sensation. He led her to their horses. For Alya, he had chosen a mild-mannered palfrey called Summer. A fitting mount for his sunshine girl.

As always, Jamila joined them. They were not going too far for the dog and she would easily keep up with the horses.

Henry hovered close enough to make sure Alya had control of her mount, but Kathryn had taught her well. As naturally as breathing Alya matched her motion to Summer's. Still, Henry kept their pace sedate. With summer warming the earth and sending up the perfume of a hundred growing things, they had no need to hurry. A gentle breeze kept the heat at bay as they rode north from Anglesea, away from the sea and deeper into the lush farmland of the demesne.

He took her to the place he now spent so much of his time. Five miles from Anglesea stood the beginning of the land Garrett would manage, and here on its southern edge, crowning a rise that provided a clear view of the land about them, lay the old manor house. Far from grand, the sturdy old structure sprawled in a homely tangle across the hill. Originally a wattle and daub hut, generations had added on from the original structure and created the charming clutter of shapes.

Workers clambered all over the manor, slowly putting her back to rights.

Alya sat straight in her saddle. "What is this place?"

"This is where Beatrice and Garrett will live once they leave Anglesea." Henry led her into the busy stable yard. Piles of lumber and heaps of stone sat ready for the men to put them to good use.

"Sir Henry." Chester, the foreman, waved to him from where they mixed mortar. "We have a fair day for it, today."

Henry returned the wave, dismounted and assisted Alya from Summer. "Come, I will show you what I have been doing."

"Come to lend us some muscle?" Chester pumped his hand.

"Not today." Henry gestured to Alya. "I have brought my lady with me to see what keeps me from her side."

"My lady." Chester bowed to Alya. "We have put your husband's strong back to good use. What with all the rain we've had this year, we needed all hands."

Alya threw Henry a naughty glance. "Rain? How unusual."

Chester snorted. "You would not say that if you had lived here longer, my lady."

"I do not want to keep you. I will show my lady about." Henry took her hand.

"Right you are." Chester cracked his knuckles. "Them walls won't get built with me standing here jawing." Shouting to a laborer as he went, he trotted off.

"This will be the hall." Henry led her into a wide space. A large man hammered the roof struts into place. He stopped, looked at Alya and scowled. Henry locked eyes with him and held his gaze. He would tolerate no more of this. "Originally it was four smaller rooms, but we took out the walls to create a larger chamber. It will be a handsome hall once it is done." He pointed. "We are putting in the chimneys to house extra hearths, one at each end and one against that wall more central."

"You like this work." Alya studied his face.

"Aye." Henry felt stripped by her keen gaze, and he looked away. "I learned in your father's house that I like to work with my hands. I find the hard labor soothing." He needed to ease out of the telling moment, and he planted a smile on his face. "Although, if you tell Bahir I said that, I will say you are lying."

* * *

By the time they returned to Anglesea, Alya was pleasantly tired. A day spent with Henry in the fresh air and sunshine had eased the distance between them. Too late for the evening meal, Henry led her straight to the kitchen.

"Late night kitchen raids." He settled her at the table. "My brothers and I used to do this all the time."

"Did Cook not object?" The kitchen lay still all about them. Two drudges slept by the smoldering hearth coals.

"Aye she did." Henry laughed. "But then she always left a little something in the pantry for such an eventuality. I think she conceded defeat in the end."

Henry disappeared into the pantry and returned with a platter laden with cold beef, cheese, fruit, and bread. He laid it on the table with a flourish. "A feast for my lady."

Appetite sharpened by the day, Alya lost no time tucking in.

Henry brought her a mug of ale and sat beside her.

"The manor will be beautiful once it is completed," she said. She preferred it to the grandeur of Anglesea. "When will that be?"

"Chester hopes to have it habitable by the end of the summer." Henry spread cheese over thick slices of bread. Sun had painted color on his cheeks. His hair, now grown longer, looked like spun gold in the amber light of the kitchen.

"And Beatrice, Garrett, and the children will live there?"

"That is the plan." Henry stopped chewing and pulled a face. "At least, that was the plan, but since I am not performing my chamberlain duties adequately enough for him to leave that plan looks to be changing."

Alya sensed much more behind that statement. "You do not perform them adequately?" She struggled to see Henry as anything less than competent at whatever he did. Even as a slave, he'd had the calm air of self-assurance about him.

"Nay." Henry sliced beef and handed it to her. "Roger finds my performance lacking."

"Perhaps Roger should give you a chance."

"Nay." Henry stroked her cheek. "As much as I appreciate your defense of me, he is right. I find myself dodging those responsibilities."

"Why?" Henry did not dodge things.

He ate a slice of beef before replying. "It does not sit well with me anymore. I do not enjoy the games and the intrigues. The thrust and parry of politics bore me."

"Ah." His work at the manor made sense now. "You prefer to work with your hands."

"Something like that." He tore off a hunk of bread and ate it. "Cairo changed me in ways I am only now beginning to discover."

"Not all of it for the worst?" Until she uttered the words, Alya had not understood how much his answer mattered to her.

Henry's expression softened. He cupped her cheek. "Not all of it for the worse. Some of it so much better than I could have hoped for."

The heat in his eyes awakened an answering heat in her. It had been too long since he had lain with her. A day out of the castle had done more than awaken her appetite for food. Alya had other appetites that whispered of being neglected. "You did not ask me what I spoke of to your mother and sisters."

"Nay, I did not." He traced her bottom lip with his thumb, his gaze slumberous and fixed on her mouth.

Alya slid over and straddled his lap. "I spoke to them of Bahir."

At the apex of her thighs, his rod thickened and swelled.

"Bahir?" He slid his hands about her waist, rocking her onto his hardness.

"Mmm." She let the sweet press of him against where she ached most seep into her muscles. "Bahir was a harem guard, you know?"

Henry's pressed his hot mouth against the column of her neck. "I did know that."

"Did he also tell you that what he learned there?" Hungry for the feel of him, Alya pressed her breasts against his chest.

He thrust his rod against her core. "He did not tell me that."

"He told me." Alya's need rose to a sharp hunger to feel him inside her. "He told me all the ways in which a woman may please her man."

Henry groaned.

The sound thrilled her.

"Tell me." His breathing rasped in her ear.

"Nay, Henry." Alya bit the lobe of his ear. "There are some things that must be shown as they are spoken."

Chapter Thirty

Henry stood on the ramparts beside Roger as indistinct figures jogged along in a large group, banners snapping in the morning breeze.

"Can you see who it is?" Roger shielded his eyes from the glare.

"Nay." Traces of Henry's excellent mood still sat in his bones on a low rumble of contentment. He had left Alya still asleep in their bed. Asleep, and wearing the flushed bloom of satisfaction he had put there. This morning, he stood ten feet tall. "Armed?"

"Not for war." Roger frowned. "I see knights, and then palfreys between them."

"Aye." An army moved differently. Faster, with more intent and casting a glitter from armor and weapons. This party moved at a pace more suited to escort women and children.

Dressed with his normal disregard for his status Garrett joined them on the ramparts.

Henry liked that about Garrett. Regardless of who he had married, Garrett stayed true to himself.

"Who have we here?" Garrett peered at the approaching party.

Roger glanced at him. "That is what we are trying to ascertain."

With a jerk of his head, Garrett stilled.

"What is it?" Roger glanced at Henry and then Garrett.

"Roger." Leaning over the parapet, Garrett took a deep breath. "You did send the missive to Sir James, did you not?"

Roger sucked in a breath. "Henry sent it."

The pit of Henry's stomach dropped into his boots. "Nay. Garrett sent it."

Balling his fists, Roger scowled at them. "Tell me someone sent the missive."

Silence.

"God's balls." Roger pounded the stone parapet. "I have two chamberlains, and this is the result."

"Garrett is your current chamberlain." Henry refused to take the blame for this. He had been telling Roger he did not want the job.

With a glare, Garrett jabbed a finger at him. "I am only chamberlain because you were missing. You're back and now you are chamberlain."

"Nay, I am not." Henry refused to back down. "You are the incumbent and far better suited to the job than I. I left the armory and you and Roger said you would deal with this."

"Jesus on the blasted cross." Roger advanced on the two of them. "I could bang your stupid heads together. Are we saying the missive never got sent?"

Henry took a step out of punching range. "I think that is exactly what we are saying."

Garrett threw back his head and laughed.

However misplaced his humor, Henry also saw the amusing side of this.

If his thunderous scowl provided any hint to his mood, Roger, not at all. "So, you are telling me that I have the King's cousin riding to my keep with his daughter in tow. The same daughter whom he proposes as a bride for Henry."

The situation lost any trace of humor. "Except I am already married."

Garrett laughed harder.

With a punch hard enough to shut him up, Roger got to him before Henry.

"Right." Clasping his hands behind his back Roger paced the wall. "We need to make a plan, and before they reach our gates."

"And one that doesn't make Sir James angry enough to complain to his cousin," Garrett said.

"We need time to break the news gently," Roger said. "But with the entire keep knowing of Henry's marriage, we don't have that time."

"You could banish Henry." Garrett rubbed his nape. "Make it appear as if you in no way support his marriage."

"Within the next hour?" Roger glared at Garrett. "And ignoring my open support for Henry's marriage thus far."

Henry knew only one person with the skills for this. "We need Mother."

Relief spread over Roger and Garrett's face. "Aye."

* * *

Mother stared at them. "You had best tell me that again." They had joined her in the armory to find a solution.

Roger stumbled through the explanation a second time. It sounded even worse the second time around.

"What do you expect me to do?" Mother threw up her hands. "Clearly, we have to tell Sir James as soon as we can, and grovel." She fixed Roger with a stare. Her hands flew to her mouth and she gasped. "Dear God."

"What?" Henry knew he was not going to like what came next.

"Sir James lost his son on Holy Pilgrimage." Mother took a shaky breath. "He may not take kindly to the fact that you threw his daughter over for a Saracen."

"I did not throw her over." Even as he argued, Henry knew it made little difference. Neither did the fact that Alya was not Saracen. That is what Sir James would see. "We need to get Bahir out of sight."

Mother rubbed her temples. "Get them here. Bahir and Alya need to be part of this conversation."

The last thing Henry wanted to do was upset Alya further. Not when they had taken a small step toward each other again. "Why?"

"Because." Mother poked his shoulder. "If you are about to decide what is to become of them for however long Sir James stays here, then they should be part of that conversation."

Roger unearthed a page and sent him off.

It took a few minutes to find them. All of which, Roger spent at the casement, calling a rolling report back on the progress the approaching party made.

It made Henry want to tip him out the casement.

"What is it?" Alya arrived, her pretty cheeks pink and a secretive smile just for him.

If only he could scoop her up and return them to the bedroom where their troubles melted away.

"We have a problem." Mother took Alya's hands and led her to the chairs beside the hearth. "It seems we have an unexpected visitor at our gates."

None of this would be happening if he either took his duties as chamberlain seriously or officially handed over the job to Garrett. When Mother finished the explanation, all he had to offer his wife was a shrug and, "I'm sorry."

In a graceful ripple of motion, Alya stood. "So, this man thinks to marry his daughter to Henry. My husband."

"Aye." Mother dipped her head.

"And he hates my people because his son died in one of the wars you brought to our lands?"

The atmosphere in the hall stiffened to rival Sir James's banner in the breeze.

"Lady Mary." On a low bow, Bahir approached Mother. "I think it best if I make myself scarce whilst you attempt to clear up this misunderstanding."

Momentary relief washed through Henry. It would be much easier were Bahir not about to upset Sir James further.

"Thank you, Bahir." Mother took his hand. "We are sorry to ask you to do this. You are a guest in our home, too."

"We are both realists, my lady." Bahir bowed over her hand. "The way the world works is not always as we would like it."

"We will send you to Garrett's demesne." Roger clapped Bahir on the shoulder. "The place is habitable for the most part, and it will only be for a short time. Until we get this goat's ballocks sorted out."

Fists curled into her sides, Alya stepped forward. "If he goes, I go."

* * *

Alya may as well have tossed a viper into their midst.

"Nay." Henry fastened hard hands on her shoulders. "You are not going anywhere."

Had she been any less furious, her heart might have sung at the starkly possessive look he bent on her. Her Henry looking at her like that should have been a dream come true. Instead, she wrenched free of his hold. Her anger came from that aching place within her that had formed on the day her uncle had hurled her into the street. A wound barely healed, when the villagers of Anglesea had torn it open again. A seeping hole that gushed fresh blood every time Henry refused to stand by her side and every time Henry reminded her of her otherness here.

With sad eyes, Lady Mary looked at her. "We meant no offense, sweeting. It is sometimes best not to rub salt in a wound, and Sir James is a proud, arrogant man who has the king's ear."

"If it were not him, it would be another." Too long her anger had festered within her and now demanded it be heard. "There will always be one reason or another why I am not right to be Henry's bride. I do not fit here. Like Bahir. We are as brother and sister, Bahir and I, and if you hide him in shame from those who visit, then you must hide me in shame as well."

Henry frowned. "I think you are overreacting. This is a special—"

"And that is precisely the problem." Alya needed out before she hit someone. "You think I am overreacting every time something like this happens."

Spreading his arms wide, Henry frowned. "Something like what?"

She could not credit he even asked her that. "The way people refuse to accept me."

"They need time." Reaching for her, Henry's tone gentled. "All they know of you is that our nations have been at war. They will come to accept you in time."

"They will come to accept me?" Her! The daughter of one of Cairo's wealthiest merchant. A girl who could have looked high for an advantageous marriage. If she had not been chased out of her home, and chased out because people were angry about a war that men like Henry had brought to her land. Indeed, Henry himself had climbed aboard his huge horse, taken up his steel and wielded it against her countrymen. Here they called her barbarian. They wallowed in their own filth and the filth of dogs and called her savage. Dogs other than Jamila. "Nay, Henry." That she did not shriek her outrage surprised her. "I care not if they accept me. In fact, they can all go straight to hell."

Face darkening, Henry stepped closer to her. "That is enough."

"Nay, it is not." Not even close. "You brought me back to your country as your bride, and now you seek to hide me away."

"Alya." Flushed, Henry glanced about at his family. "We will not speak of this now."

Roger and Lady Mary stood close together, with lowered heads as if they tried not to hear what she said. Impossible as she intended to yell even louder before she was done. "Nay we will not because I will not be here later." Alya stood beside Bahir. "I will be leaving with Bahir."

"Why are you being so stubborn?" Henry grabbed his hair as if he would yank it out by the roots. "You know how my family has suffered in the eyes of the king. I have told you all of this. It is only for a day or two."

"It may as well be for the rest of my life." Hooking her arm through Bahir's she tugged him with her. "I will be with Bahir at the manor until you are ready to acknowledge me as your wife in the true sense."

"I already acknowledge you as my wife." Written clearly in the taut, grim lines of his face and the rigid set of his shoulders was Henry's smarting pride. He would hate that she berated him before his family. "I brought you here, did I not?"

She could not stand here a moment longer and stare at his arrogant face. She felt a momentary twinge that they would now see her as a shrew, but if they could not accept her either, there was no point in keeping their good opinion. Dragging Bahir in her wake, she stormed from the hall.

* * *

"Can you credit that?" Henry stared at Roger and then his mother.

Roger shook his head. "Women!"

"Women?" With an imperiously raised brow that every Anglesea child knew spelled trouble, Lady Mary turned on her oldest son. "What could you mean by that, Roger?"

"Um...not...only that she deliberately chooses not to understand the fix we are in. Bahir understood. You did not hear him flapping his gums."

"Bahir understood perfectly." Garrett smoothed the lie of his tunic. "But it does not mean he accepts what you have decided.

He is merely older and a pragmatist and has lived in this world too long to fight that which he cannot."

Henry had not the patience for Garrett and his riddles. "What, in God's name, are you talking about?"

"The mighty Angleseas." Circling his arms, Garrett encompassed the hall and everyone in it. "The power and might of a family who have always stood foremost in the kingdom. Even in the king's anger, you were not banned from court. You have never known what it is like to be looked at and judged before someone has even learned your name."

Frowning, Roger stuck his hands in his belt. "What are you saying?"

In Henry's memories of Garrett and Roger, this conversation would not be happening and would probably involve fists and boots by now.

"I am saying." Garrett clapped Roger's shoulder. "You have no understanding of what it is to be other. Not only have you always been a part of the herd, you have often been the prime stock in that herd. For people like Alya, Bahir, and myself, the herd is a hostile place."

"You are comparing your situation to theirs?" Henry marveled at Garrett's audacity.

"In part." Garrett shrugged. "And in as much as when you look at me you see first bastard, then blacksmith and finally the man beneath all of that."

* * *

Face expressionless, Bahir watched her pack. "You are sure you would do this, my lady?"

"Of course." Feigning more confidence than she felt, Alya shoved her new dresses into a large chest. If they insisted on sending her from them like some sort of leper, she would take all her pretty things with her. And her dowry. "Are you going to help me?"

"Nay." Bahir rose from the casement. "If I am unable to prevent your foolishness, then I shall not aid you in it."

"Fine." She hopped over Jamila who insisted on lying in the middle of her path. "Could you move?"

Jamila dropped her head onto her paws in silent protest.

"If you keep at this, I shall not take you with me." Her threat lacked teeth, because if she went, Jamila went with her. Jamila thought nothing of the threat either and did not even flick an ear. Ayla stubbed her toe on a smaller chest. "You really will not help me?"

"My lady." Bahir took her by the shoulders. "You are acting out of hurt, and that is never a wise place from which to make decisions."

"Well, maybe I do not feel wise," Alya said. Bahir always had this way of bringing reason to her moods, and she did not want it right now. She wanted to enjoy her anger, let it cocoon her from the hurt throbbing beneath it. "Maybe I want to act from my feelings."

"Aye." Bahir gave her a sad smile. "Except those decisions do not end well."

She was so very tired of going around in the same circles with Henry. First, she believed he valued and cared for her, and the very next minute, she felt shoved aside. Since they had made land in England, they pushed and pulled at each other like two scrapping children. "What should I do then?"

"I cannot tell you that." Bahir shrugged.

Honestly, what good was he when she finally listened and then he would not talk? "But that does not stop you for pointing out my mistakes."

"Alya." Bahir sat her beside him on the bed. "All marriages take time to settle. Two people join their lives and must discover all the ways in which they are compatible and all the ways in which they are not."

"It does not seem as if Henry and I share any similarities." And how could they hope to build a marriage without any common ground? Henry had promised her all those weeks ago on the boat that if she ever really wanted to leave, he would let her go. Would he still let her go? Did she even want to go?

"That is not true." Bahir put his arm about her. "You are both passionate people who believe in things like honor and justice. You both value family and loyalty. I have seen the way he makes you smile and the way he looks at you. But." Bahir's face grew grave. "You have a greater divide to cross than most couples and that will take more patience and tolerance from both of you. Getting angry and storming off will not accomplish that."

"Like I did with my father." Not able to look at Bahir she traced the pattern of birds stitched onto her bed covering. The bed she had shared with Henry, and now planned to leave. It was all so confusing. He said he did not regret marrying her, but sometimes his actions spoke other. Then again, he sent her away to protect her and Bahir as well as his family, and she could not fault him for that. Had she not railed at her father for doing the same and lived to regret it?

"How long do you plan to stay away?" Bahir tugged her closer to him.

"I had not got that far in planning yet." Alya tucked herself into the comfort of him. "All I knew is that I planned to leave Anglesea as fast as I could."

"Ah!" Bahir nodded. "You needed to be seen leaving."

"No wonder they sold you from the harem. Your inability to lie to a woman long enough for her to keep her delusions would have disadvantaged you."

Bahir grinned. "Have you thought what you will do if he does not play his part the way you want him to?"

"Nay." Alya needed to walk. Her head felt as if it might explode with all the conflicting thoughts. "I am not sure if I am even leaving Henry. There is a chance he would not notice if I did. He sends me away—"

"You think to leave me?" Still as a hunting cat, Henry stood in the doorway.

"Excuse me." Bahir left the room so swiftly he almost caused a breeze.

Alya wanted to chase after him and demand he stay with her. Although if she did get past her furious husband in the doorway, she might not return. At least until he calmed down. "You misunderstood what you heard."

"Did I?" Tucking his hands into his belt Henry strolled forward.

He looked so calm and at ease, one could be mistaken for assuming all was well. Until you looked in those eyes, colder than winter well-water. She had not known blue eyes could blaze or freeze before she met Henry.

Wary to keep her distance, Alya backed up a few steps. "I did not say I intended to leave here and never return."

"Nay you did not." Henry rubbed his jaw. "I believe what you said was that you had not yet decided whether you would leave me."

"Why should you care?" Tired of retreating, Alya stood her ground. "And you did say, when you asked me to marry you, that if I was no longer happy I could leave. You are as unsure if you want me here or not."

"I want you here." Silky, his voice held not a trace of warmth. "Make no mistake that I want you here." He circled her, and caught her braid. With a slight tug, he eased her head back. "You are my wife. Your place is beside me. Do not make the mistake of believing this is an open point in our marriage. If you leave, I will bring you back. If you run I will chase." He tugged her head back an inch more. "If you go to ground, I will find you."

This was a ruthless Henry. One she had only glimpsed. This close, the effect was startling in its primacy. She wanted to fight him. She wanted to kiss him. "Let go of me."

"Never." Henry planted a swift, hard kiss on her mouth. "I cannot let you go because you are mine."

She needed to break this hold he had on her. "You said—"

"I care not what I said then." Henry tightened his grip and then let her go. "Now I am saying this."

Trumpets split the tension between them as the gate announced their visitors.

Alya stumbled back.

"You will go to Garrett's manor with Bahir. Stay there until this is over. And then I will come for you and we will speak."

His imperious tone made her angry enough she could barely speak. "I—"

"When I come for you, wife, you will be there."

* * *

Henry could not credit how poorly he had handled that situation. He had gone to their chamber determined to speak with her and try to make her understand that he did not reject her, or judge her. The decision was purely pragmatic and aimed at protecting her.

Instead, he heard her say she might leave him and reason had deserted him. He'd wanted to fill her with the same fear that surged through him, and he had. He had filled his wife with fear for her brutish husband. This issue between them frustrated him and it had spilled into his interaction with Alya. He knew not how to make it go away.

On the ramparts, he stood and let the view soothe him. Compared to the mighty vastness of the sea beneath him petty human worries drifted into nothing. No more than the foam cresting the waves. Soon he would need to change to greet their guests, and that meant braving his bedchamber again and the angry woman currently presiding over it.

When he had left Cairo with her, he had known there would be some resistance to her presence, perhaps even some resentment. But the blanket intolerance with which she was met confounded him. And it truly should not because hadn't he seen the same thing on Holy pilgrimage? Holy pilgrimage! The words scalded his throat and he could not utter them. The things done in the name of God, the atrocities visited on people who sought only to live their lives in peace, content in their beliefs. Their Holy army filled with the very dregs of humanity, interspersed with a few naive souls like he had been, desperate to serve their God and act in His Glory.

Truth be told, when they pulled him off his horse, his first sensation was relief. Relief that the nightmare had ended. Relief that he would not have to return home, tail between his legs, and admit how wrong he had been. Even worse, admit to himself how so much of his life had been a lie. The things he had held dear, the beliefs he had fought for and defended. Those had all amounted to a pile of ashes blown away by the heat of battle, drowned in the sticky stench of blood spilled.

In those early days of his captivity, he hadn't cared what became of him. So mired in his self-loathing and self-pity, his enslavement had seemed a fitting punishment. Perhaps this was why he had not minded when people treated him as other or like he was an animal. In his mind, he had been worth no more and their treatment of him had been only what he deserved.

"Sir Henry?" Roger's page stood a mere three feet away.

"Aye."

"Sir Roger requests your presence in the great hall."

"Sir James is within?" His reprieve had ended. He must change and help Roger disentangle this snarl. Or watch Garrett do it in his effortless ease of reading people and situations.

"He is, my lord." The page bowed and retreated.

Henry looked out over the sea and drew a deep breath. The thing that had changed for him had been his girl on the wall. Sold by his first master, a minor spice merchant, into Bahir's care he had kept his head down for weeks. Then one day, as the sun set behind the minaret, he had looked up and seen the girl on the wall.

Beneath him the postern gate scraped open and three mounted figures appeared, hoods drawn over their heads. But he would know Alya anywhere atop her gentle gray palfrey. He had missed his opportunity to make peace with her. On her left, the taller figure would be Bahir, and on her other side, rode Newt. How many times had Henry tried to cure him of his slump in the saddle? Even learning to ride anything in Sir Arthur's stable had not turned Newt into a natural horseman.

Ayla took his heart with her, and she did not even know it.

From that first moment of seeing her, he had been her fool. The defiant way her slim figure stood against the fierce umbers and scarlets of the Cairo sunset had called to him. A siren song that had grown all the stronger for the knowing of the woman who sang it. He had thought he drew his hope from the girl on the wall, but that figure was as nothing when compared to the fire of Alya in his life. His to touch, love, hold, laugh with and cherish. Except his love left here with no real knowledge of how cherished she was.

"You're not dressed." Garrett wandered onto the battlements beside him, not looking particularly perturbed at finding him tarrying.

"Nay." He willed the middle rider to turn and see him here. In a reverse of their former roles he wanted her to see him on the wall, and experience their connection.

"Ah." Gaze on the riders, Garrett leaned on the crenellations beside him. "I have issued instructions for her other belongings to be sent as soon as they can be packed."

"My thanks." Roger was right. Garrett did make an excellent chamberlain. He thought ahead of others.

"Might I suggest you add your own belongings to the load?"

Henry almost laughed. Garrett's tact could do with some work. "You think I have failed her."

"I think you know you have failed her." Garrett crossed his arms, his gaze a direct challenge. "Just as I failed your sister and continue to do so. We are human. We err. We cannot love perfectly because we are not perfect."

"The bastard philosopher." How Garrett had changed since

those early days. Or perhaps Garrett had remained the same, and Henry now saw him clearer. Even when Beatrice has spoken of her love for him, they had only seen what they wanted to see of Garrett. "I do not suppose you could handle this visit without me?"

"Forget it." Garrett snorted. "Think of it as your last official duty as chamberlain."

"Have we reached that stage in our brotherhood where we tell each other the unvarnished truth?"

Grinning, Garrett punched his arm. "I still reserve the right to lie on demand."

Henry had to laugh. Despite the difficulties of being crammed into Beatrice's family, Garrett had never allowed it to change him. Now, Roger saw the value in the man clearly. Even Father, for all his stubbornness, conceded that Garrett had done right by Beatrice and his children, as well as helped the family out of one or two stickier situations.

"You do not relish the task." Slinging an arm about his shoulder, Garrett steered him off the battlements. "And I, to my eternal surprise, love it. Working with Roger suits me very well, and Beatrice would love to stay at Anglesea, and raise the boys here."

"And I shall become a farmer." Henry allowed himself to be led down the stairs and toward his bedroom.

"It suits you." Garrett chuckled. "And you have put more of your sweat into my manor house than I have." He stopped and turned Henry toward him. Expression grave, Garrett said, "Build something, Henry. From that land build a legacy for you and Alya and your children. Shape that legacy to fit your family." He grinned. "But first you need to turn down a suitor. Gently. For all our sakes."

Chapter Thirty-One

For three days, Alya had no time to dwell. True to his word, Garrett sent the wagons after her and Bahir straightaway. The first wagon rolled into the yard of the manor within hours of their arrival. With them came Bernard and his mother and three sisters.

Shyly they curtsied as Bernard introduced them, but Alya saw nothing but curiosity and friendliness in the glances they threw her. She guessed she could thank Garrett for that as well. For making sure she had friendly faces about her.

With Bernard and his womenfolk putting the livable areas of the manor to rights, she went exploring. Once the work was completed the manor would be a fine home. Not built to be impregnable like the mighty castle, the manor allowed more light and warmth to penetrate her inner halls. With all the fireplaces the men were building, a person would be warm and snug inside. Her beautiful rugs would look perfect on the river stone floor. The wide casements cried out for the adornment of her lovely silks. Aye, she could make a home here.

For the most part, the men still repairing the manor had seen her the day she came with Henry. A couple of them looked up and nodded.

Half-submerged in a drainage trench Chester stuck his head up. He clambered out the trench, wiping his hands on a rag. "Well met, my lady."

Ever vigilant, Bahir shifted closer to her. "Who is that?"

"The one in charge of the men." As she faced the curious faces of the men, Alya was grateful to have Bahir with her.

"God's bones, you're a big 'un." Chester eyed Bahir like he would a side of beef. "Did you come to work or piss about inside like a girl?"

"How does one piss about like a girl?" Rich and infectious, Bahir's chuckle rolled through the courtyard.

Chester joined in, and then a couple other men, and then a few more. Tension dissipated like early morning mist. Except for one man, a round, ruddy faced fellow a few feet behind Chester, who looked annoyingly familiar, but Alya could not place him.

* * *

Had his heart not already been taken, Henry would have been delighted to accept Lady Elizabeth as a bride. With her raven hair and eyes bluer than William's, she was stunningly beautiful. Skin paler than ivory, with a form rounded in all the interesting places and slim in all the others, Elizabeth put even Faye's beauty to shame.

A fact not lost on any of the Anglesea men. On being introduced to her, they had stood to a man, with their jaws hanging open and their eyes starting out of their heads. Probably for the first time in his life, even Garrett was lost for words.

All of her could have been his for the taking, and yet Henry felt not an ounce of regret. Truly there had been a moment of male pride, which had toyed with the idea of being the envy of every other man with such a wifely treasure. But it came and went before Sir James had finished the introductions.

Lady Elizabeth of Fenwick, peerless beauty, with a healthy dowry and a powerful father could seek anywhere for a groom.

However desirous of healing the gap between crown and Anglesea, why would the king hand over such a prize to a younger son?

Mother took the lead, charming Sir James into a lot of shared memories and nostalgic laughter.

As agreed, Henry offered his arm to Lady Elizabeth. Garrett thought it best to attack this from two directions. An outraged father would not be as outraged if his daughter were quite happy not to be marrying Henry.

Even in his youth, Henry had left the swiving and cajolery to William. It had been years since he had tried to speak pretty words to a gently reared virgin. Alya's directness had spared him the trouble of dancing around fragile sensibilities. He led Lady Elizabeth into the garden Alya and Bernard loved so much. Firstly, it made him feel closer to his wife, and on a more pragmatic level the garden lay far enough from the keep to mitigate against Lady Elizabeth taking loud exception to him withdrawing his suit.

Midsummer heat encouraged Henry to get it over with quickly. Underneath his black velvet tunic, emblazoned with his father's arms, sweat slid down his sides.

"Lady Eliz—"

"I'm not a virgin." Lady Elizabeth's beautiful eyes flashed azure as she thrust her chin out and her shoulders back.

Feeling sure he must have misheard, Henry said, "I beg your pardon."

"I am not a virgin." She rolled each word around her mouth before almost spitting it out. "Indeed, I could be breeding right this minute."

"Um..." He had not a word. In all the hasty strategizing between them, neither Roger, Mother, or even Garrett had prepared for this. "You are breeding? Are you to be congratulated?"

"Nay." Lady Elizabeth paled, then looked askance at him. "Why are you still standing here?"

"Should I not be?" Henry felt the tide close over his head and wash him out to a sea of confusion.

Lady Elizabeth stuck her hip out and jammed her fist on it. "You should be storming off to see my father in outrage."

"I see." And Henry rather thought he might. The tasty irony almost made him laugh. "Do you have any idea as to the father of your child?"

"I didn't say I was with child, I said I might be." She tossed her head. "And it could be one of dozens, tens of dozens. Hundreds even."

"You are to be congratulated on your stamina." An evil part of Henry wanted to wait and see how far she would take this. But the better part reminded him that the stakes here were too high for levity.

She stopped and stared at him. "You do not believe me."

"Nay, I do not." Henry pressed her onto a garden bench. "For a start, you're far too young to have amassed that many lovers, and secondly, women of healthy appetites do not blush fire-red when they say the word virgin."

Lady Elizabeth blushed, and looked even lovelier than ever. "Will you tell my father?"

"Nay." Henry eased onto the bench beside her. "Because it turns out, I don't want to marry you either."

Her full, red mouth dropped open. "You don't?"

Aye, she may well stare. The only men who would not want to marry Lady Elizabeth were those who did not like women or those whose hearts were already taken. "I do not. I also have a secret and I propose we join forces to make sure your father's matrimonial desires never come to pass."

"Huh." She fiddled with her skirts. "Before I agree to anything, I would need to know the nature of your secret."

Lady Elizabeth hid a sharp mind behind that beautiful face. "First, you will tell me why you do not want to marry me."

"Then that leaves you holding the higher ground," she said.

"I already do." Henry smiled to soften the blow. Neat as a puzzle piece, the answer to why Sir James was here fit into place. It lay with a certain lovely, but duplicitous young woman. "You have already declared yourself not a maiden. In fact, a bit of a trollop is how you put it."

"You know I was lying." She stuck her chin out at him. "You said so not five minutes ago."

"I know you are lying." Henry paused to make sure she felt the impact of his best weapon. "But your father does not, and I would wager enough suitors believed you to have your father bring you here to Anglesea where we may not have heard the gossip."

Frowning, she chewed on her bottom lip. Then suddenly she tittered. It became a giggle and finally a full-throated laugh. "You are a lot cleverer than you look," she said, still smiling. "I had you pinned as all steel and no head."

"You certainly do know how to get on the right side of a man." She reminded him of Beatrice, tossing herself headlong into trouble. "Now tell me why you don't want to get married."

With a pout, she folded her arms. "I lied. It was just you I didn't want to marry."

"Elizabeth." He used the same tone he would on Sweet Bea.

"All right." It worked better on Elizabeth as she scowled at him. "I do not want to get married because I do not want to be property of some man for the rest of my life."

Kathryn had felt the same about being married, but for very understandable reasons. Her father had been a bully and a brute. Could Sir James be the same? Henry did not sense cruelty in him, but you could not always know. He went for a simple, "Why?" and let her fill in the details.

"Do you want to be somebody's property?" Shoulders thrust back like a wrathful goddess she surged to her feet. "To be told what you must do and when you must do it?"

"Nay." His sisters had railed against this too often for him to disagree. The world they lived in was not fair to women and there was no painting it a prettier hue. "So you have been discouraging your suitors?"

"Aye." She shrugged. "I had to make it compelling enough for them not to see only this." She waved a disparaging hand over her form.

"Or your father's wealth and influence, I would wager." Henry patted the seat beside him. "What would you do if you were free to do whatever you wanted?"

As if nobody had ever asked her that question she gaped at him. "Not very much." Blushing she glanced away. "I do not have some grand dream."

"Tell me anyway." Henry rather liked her, and current situation aside, aimed to see if he could help her.

"I want a cottage." She raised her head, her gaze daring him to mock her.

Henry motioned her to continue.

"I want a cottage and enough land to feed myself. I would like to grow fresh herbs and healing plants." She raised and lowered her hands in a helpless gesture. "I have a gift for healing, and I would like to use it."

"I would see you use that gift, Lady Elizabeth." Henry shuffled closer lest they be overheard. "I think we can help each other. If we do this right, you should get a cottage on my land to practice your healing, and I get to go and grovel before my wife."

Chapter Thirty-Two

Alya jerked awake, ears scouring the night for what had disturbed her. There it came again, voices raised in anger. The steady tramp of feet on cobbles.

Light from torches turned the walls of her bedroom flickering orange.

The door opened and Bahir slipped into her bedchamber. "There are villagers outside. I suggest we send to Anglesea for help."

"Villagers?" Alya hauled a shawl over her nightrail. She hissed a protest as her bed-warmed feet hit the cold stone floor. "What are they doing here?" As she hobbled toward her slippers the rest of Bahir's speech penetrated her sleepy brain. "And why would we send to Anglesea?"

Had the mighty castle not already cast them into hiding? And why was it always so cold in this country? Midsummer they called this and she still needed to wear a thick nightrail to bed. It was fine during the day, but at night, she reached for her furs. Every night.

"Alya." Bahir's face grew graver than she had seen in a long time. "They are armed and look to be ready to make trouble."

That took her mind off her cold feet. "Does Newt know?"

"He does," Newt said, emerging from the dark so suddenly

278

that Alya nearly screamed. "We have one or two guards but they're older and wouldn't be much good against this lot. I've sent Bernard on our fastest horse. This looks like it might get ugly."

"But why?" Alya tiptoed to the casement. Careful to stay out of sight she peered into the courtyard. "What do they want?"

Newt glanced up from strapping on his sword. "That is what I was about to ask them." Missing his usual charming smile, he nodded to Bahir. "Make sure you stay out of sight until we know more."

"You can't go out there alone." Alya caught his arm.

"It is better this way." Newt glanced at Bahir. "Keep her safe. Do what you must."

The crowd reached the courtyard. Alya counted at least twenty heads bobbing in the flickering torchlight. One face jumped out at her, the man she was sure she had recognized the other day. Features contorted into harsh, angry lines, he snarled at his companions.

People around him nodded, renewed purpose in their faces.

As he approached the front door, the man dropped out of sight. Shortly after, pounding sounded down the corridor.

Standing dead still, Alya held her breath to hear better.

Newt opened the door. "Good evening, Miller. What do you mean by this?"

"I want that black devil." Miller grew louder. "I want him strung up for all to see because of what he's done."

Alya glanced at Bahir. He had not been to the village since that night they had sneaked home together.

Frowning, Bahir shook his head.

"You are going to have to provide more detail than that." Newt's voice remained calm but each word held steel. "What is it you think he has done?"

"I do not think it." Shouts of support rose from the crowd in the courtyard. Light flashed off axes, scythes, hoes, and pitch forks. The men of Anglesea village had come armed. Dear Lord let Bernard ride swift and true. Even then it would take the men of the castle hours to arrive.

"You must run." She pinched Bahir's arm to get his attention. "Run and hide. It's you they want. If you are not here they will leave."

"If I am not here, they might turn their anger onto you." Bahir touched her cheek. "And that I cannot risk, habibti."

"But they will kill you." Alya needed him to see reason. The mob outside was beyond that. "You are all that I have. I cannot let them get to you."

"Nay, habibti." He kissed her forehead. "You have an entire family now. You are angry with them currently because you feel they are ashamed of you but you will get past this. They will learn and you will learn."

"I am still waiting to hear about this grievous wrongdoing." Newt spoke from the door. "But I must warn you before you speak. Bahir is my friend and therefore I will hear no false accusations against him."

"Your friend raped my girl," Miller yelled.

The crowd bayed for blood.

"He raped her and put his rotten seed in her."

If she had not been so frightened, Alya would have laughed. The absurdity of it was staggering. Then again, Newt had not known what a eunuch was.

"I am sorry your Ann was hurt," Newt said. "But it is impossible for this to have happened."

"My girl told me which devil did this to her." Miller pounded the door. "And now I want him to pay for what he's done."

"My dear, Miller." Newt gentled his tone. "Let me explain why this is impossible."

* * *

Henry seated Lady Elizabeth at dinner before taking his seat beside her. They had yet to come up with a plan that would satisfy all parties. Her father wanted her safely married and out of the eye of the king's already gossiping courtiers. Elizabeth had no intention of marrying anyone.

A commotion arose from outside the hall. "Boy!"

"Stop!"

Bernard dashed into the hall. Behind him came two of the guards, but the lad was quick and slipped by them. When he spotted Henry, he made straight for him.

"Sir Henry." His thin chest rose and fell rapidly as he tried to catch his breath. "Newt sent me. Must come. Villagers."

"Take a deep breath." Henry grabbed his goblet from the table and held it to Bernard's lips. "Drink."

He forced himself to wait until Bernard had drunk enough and calmed his breathing. For Newt to send a message could not be good.

A frowning Roger joined them. "What is it?"

"The villagers." Bernard's eyes were huge in his pale face. "They marched on the manor. They have weapons. Newt bade me tell you to bring the men. You will need them."

"What is it?" Sir James rose. A man now past his prime but still strong and fighting able.

"Call up the men." Henry looked to Roger. If they touched Alya he would spill enough blood to make the pilgrimage look tame.

Roger turned and bellowed his orders. "I want every man armed and mounted in the bailey. Now."

Kathryn rushed to them. "Is Alya all right?"

"Newt has her and her man in the manor, and he says he will keep them locked inside," Bernard said. "But the villagers are shouting that they want Bahir."

"Dear Lord." Kathryn paled and glanced at Roger. "Alya will never let them take Bahir."

"Who is Alya?" Sir James pounded the table. "And Bahir? It sounds like a barbarian name."

"Bahir is our guest, Sir James." Regal and lovely in dark blue satin, Lady Mary rose. She motioned for Sir James to take his seat. "He joins us from Egypt. He travelled here with my son and his wife."

"Eh?" Sir James allowed himself to be guided into his seat.

"Aye." Lady Mary motioned a serving man to refill Sir James's goblet. "We have something to tell you and you will not be best pleased to hear it."

Lady Elizabeth ran to them. "What is it?"

"The manor housing Henry's wife has come under attack," Kathryn said.

"Henry's wife?" Sir James rose and sat again. "Henry does not have a wife."

Lady Mary murmured to him, and he fell silent again.

"Can I help?" Elizabeth looked at him.

Henry appreciated the offer. "Frankly, my lady. I pray we do not need your help."

* * *

Henry tore out of Anglesea with the men already mounted on his heels. A hard wind at their backs drove them forward as if nature too urged him to reach the manor. He did not have time to wait for the remainder of Roger's men to be ready.

Newt could fight like the very devil but he would not be able to hold off the twenty-odd men Bernard estimated were at the manor.

Sir James rode by his side. His men having not long arrived mustered faster than Roger's. Henry knew not why Sir James joined them, but he needed all the help he could get.

With no guiding light from the moon, they galloped blind. Henry relied on his horse's memory of having travelled this path many times. In amongst the thunder of hooves and the rasp of the horse's breath there was no place for speech.

"Look." Sir James pointed.

An umber smudge stained the broiling clouds on the horizon.

Only fire made that sort of light and it would have to be a big one for them to see it from here. Henry's heart lodged in his throat, and for a moment his vision went hazy.

"Breathe!" Sir James bellowed at him. "You are no good to her if you don't get there in one piece."

As they rode Henry kept his eyes trained on that growing orange-brown stain. He prayed. Disjointed phrases and words he had not uttered in so long tasted foreign on his tongue.

They crested the last rise and the manor wavered into view. One half of the building was alight. As one, they spurred their tired horses forward.

* * *

Alya screamed. Powerless, almost blinded by her tears she scraped up handfuls of mud and tossed them at the last of the departing villagers. The impotence of her actions only made her cry harder. The cowardly whoresons had finally stopped and turned tail with the news that Anglesea came. In her rage, Alya could chase them all back to the village and cut them down. But she had no time. A storm threatened to break and around her the damage wrought by the cowards demanded immediate action.

Stomach churning, she took a deep breath and faced the carnage. Three household guards lay dead or beaten badly enough that they could not rise. Orange and yellow light from the burning manor painted tongues over their inert forms.

And Jamila. Her sweet friend who had tried so hard to stop them. Not caring for her life, Jamila had tried to defend her. A sob lodged in her throat. She could not think on that now. She must help the living and see if she could keep them that way. Did God not know that she had no healing skills, knew barely anything?

Thunder rumbled around her as she dragged her skirts through the churned red-stained mud. Refusing to believe what Newt told them and denying that they could be wrong about Bahir, the villagers had fought savagely.

This England of Henry's might have killed Bahir and she cursed the day she had come here. Cursed the rain and the green, growing things. Cursed the small-minded villagers and their angers and their fears. Cursed them all.

Water! She ran to the well and drew water. Needing both hands, she dragged the heavy bucket to Bahir and Newt.

Stripped, arms tied above him, Bahir bled from countless wounds inflicted on him. His chest rose and fell with his breathing, and she clung to that morsel of hope.

At Bahir's feet, Newt lay, his blood mingling with Bahir's.

He had gone down fighting like an animal. Taking his fair share as he went, eventually Newt had succumbed to the sheer overwhelming numbers.

"Don't you die on me, Newt." Alya pressed her ear to his heart. "I am not from here. If you die, I will dig you up and make you sorry."

Newt tried to smile, but choked and coughed up blood.

Although no healer, still Alya knew that could not be good. Blood seeped from wounds in his head, his belly, his arms, and legs. So much blood that his tunic was sticky and soaked with it.

"God!" She ripped a section of her skirts. "If you are up there and listening to me, I need you to save this man."

Newt caught her wrist. His mouth worked as he tried to produce sound.

Alya leaned closer to his lips.

"Bahir."

"I will check him next." Alya ripped off more of her skirts as she tried to staunch the blood flow. "I need you to stop bleeding so I can do that."

"Like...oblige." A ghost of a normal smile flit across Newt's face and ended in a grimace of pain.

Hanging over them, Bahir dropped his head on a soft groan. She had to tend to him, but hers were the only hands in sight. The other men and servants had run off early in the fight.

Wind tugged at her tattered skirts. Dark clouds boiled overheard. Rain, such a sign of hope in her home country and now she cursed it.

"Nay." Raising her head, she screamed at the sky as if she could stop nature by her force of will alone. She forbade the rain, forbade Newt or Bahir to die.

Using her sleeves, she wiped their faces, pressing the damp cloth to their lips so they could drink. The bindings bit into Bahir's wrists and she wanted to take him down. But she had not the strength to lower him without him falling on Newt.

If she could brace his body somehow, and lower him gently.

Blood seeped through the cloth she had placed over Newt's wounds. Alya ripped another section from her skirts and replaced the blood-soaked cloths. Some of the wounds no longer bled, and she snatched up that tiny thread of hope and clung to it.

Somehow she would get all of them out of this. The villagers would not enjoy the knowledge of having bested her. And when she did recover from this, she would make them rue the day.

More thunder rolled around her and shook the ground beneath her feet. Nay. Not thunder but hoofbeats.

"We are saved." She took Newt's face in her hands. "Do you hear the horses, Newt? Do you hear them?"

Over the rise to the east of the manor they came, so many they stretched from one side of the horizon to the other. Heads rising and falling with the motion of their mounts the men of Anglesea rode to the rescue.

Except they were too late. Newt and Bahir were gravely injured, three good men lay dead, and her Jamila. Alya could not even bear to think what had happened after the man had kicked her and tossed her body across the courtyard.

"Bahir." She pushed his head back so he could see the approaching riders. "See they are coming to our aid."

Too late.

Riders streamed down the rise. In the front, Henry rode bareheaded, his gold hair easily identifiable. Her gaze fixed on him and didn't move.

Before his horse had stopped, he leaped from the saddle. Flinging himself toward her, he did not stop until his hands covered her shoulders. "Are you all right?"

"Aye." Physically she was fine, but now that rescue had arrived all she wanted to do was collapse in a heap and weep until she felt well again. "Newt and Bahir are hurt."

"We see them." Henry wrapped her against his chest and rocked her. "We will take care of them." Strong emotion clogged his voice. "I was so frightened for you. The entire ride I feared the worst."

A beautiful woman appeared behind Henry. "We need to care for these two."

Alya was sure she had never seen this woman before. She scoured her memory for something connected with this woman.

Sir Roger came up beside her. "See what you can do, Lady Elizabeth."

The name of the woman who had come to marry Henry. He had brought Elizabeth here where Alya had known more fear than ever before in her life. Even aboard the ship, when they were attacked had been nothing compared to the unrelenting rage of the villagers. They had wanted to hurt, deliberately and cruelly. After they had overpowered Newt, a couple had sought to punish him for his interference.

Then they had gone to Bahir. Beaten him and tied him up, then stripped him for all to see. And even when the evidence of their error was plain before them, even then the villagers did not relent. Frustrated now and forced to face they were wrong, they turned that fury on Bahir.

Her, they did not touch. A few had murmured how she was Sir Henry's wench and not to be touched. She supposed some part of her was grateful, but she was also guilt-ridden that the anger the villagers refused to demonstrate on her had merely moved to Newt and then Bahir.

"It is not good." Unmindful of the mud and blood, Lady Elizabeth knelt beside Newt. She glanced up and nodded to Alya.

"You did good to stop the bleeding. We will need to get him up and out of the mud. Get these wounds cleaned, with fire if necessary, and sew them up."

Alya wriggled for Henry to free her, but his arms merely tightened about her. "Be still," he whispered. "Later you can be wroth with me, but for now let me hold you."

Men moved before the fire, pulling unburned items out of the path. Steady rain fell, dousing some of the flames and turning the ground to a boggy mud bath.

Standing in Henry's arms, Alya watched as if she stood on the far side of the world. The fire hissed and sputtered along the eastern side of the building, angry its ravenous path had been halted.

This must be how it felt to have nothing. To lose everything you owned. The fire had taken her wealth, the last vestige of her father. She had neither country, nor family and now with the flames having done their damage, she had no home. In that blaze had also gone the closest thing to a friend she'd had since she arrived. The man holding her so close was not hers either. In name, they stood as a couple, but she had never felt further from him than she did then. While chaos reigned about them, and he comforted her for her loss, she felt utterly and completely alone. She felt nothing.

Chapter Thirty-Three

etween Newt, Bahir, and the fire, Henry did not sleep that evening. Even with the rain the flames took hours to douse and even now the men watched for live embers. So much of Chester's hard work gone in a matter of hours.

Standing beside Henry as the sun rose the next morning, Chester stared. The stone walls had survived and stood, charred black like lone gravestones amidst the rubble. Men picked through the rubble for anything salvageable.

"Well," Chester said. "This is not good."

It almost made Henry laugh. "It was a bad night."

"Aye." Chester motioned the stables that had survived the fire. "How fares your lady and her friends?"

"My lady lives." Somewhere inside the walking, talking shell was Alya. When the shock wore off she would be better. "But Bahir and Newt fare badly. Lady Elizabeth does what she can but..." Like a boot to his chest ground the fear for Newt. Reckless, impulsive, irreverent, and vigorous, it did not seem possible that Newt now fought for his life. His friend. His brother in arms who had stood with him through the horror of the pilgrimage. The man who had refused to let him die a slave.

"This is a bad business, Sir Henry." Chester picked up a

broken piece of wood and hefted it in his palm. "A bad, bad business."

Henry nodded because he had no words. All through the endless night his anger had sparked beneath his skin. In a dull, lifeless voice, Alya had told them what had happened. Even Sir James, with his son killed on pilgrimage by men who looked like Bahir, had exclaimed over the rank injustice of last night.

The people who had done this, were people Henry had known his entire life. Some of those men had drank and laughed with him in Harrow's inn. Men he had hunted with, shared their joys and sorrows, the same men who had welcomed him home with tears.

"We are sure it's out now." Sir James strode toward them. Soot stained and dirty, he had worked as hard as any man this night. "I have organized the men into shifts. So some may rest while the others clear away the damage."

"I will make sure they don't do even more damage in the name of help." Jamming his ancient leather cap on his head, Chester marched toward the working men.

Squinting against the rising sun, Sir James folded his arms. "You knew about Elizabeth?"

"I knew some of it." That situation had almost been forgotten. Henry's ability to dissemble crumbled. "I know she does not want to marry me. Does not want to marry any man, in truth."

"Aye." Sir James shook his head. "Such a willful girl. I kept thinking if I showed enough men to her, one of them would catch her fancy."

"Huh." Having grown up at Anglesea, Henry knew a thing or two about willful women. "If it helps, you should know that it would not have worked on my sisters either. When they make up their minds, there is no swaying them."

"I understand it not." Scowling, Sir James rubbed his shorn head. "What woman does not want to settle beside a good hearth with her children clustered about her skirts. She is unnatural."

"She has a vocation." This world made it impossible for any

woman to want anything other than marriage and motherhood. As men, he and Sir James had more choices. Over near the well, Roger and Garrett sat, heads together as they spoke. He guessed last night formed their topic. It was worse for Elizabeth because she was a woman, but they had all been born into their designated places.

Garrett, born a bastard and cast into poverty as a young child, had fought the rigid order his entire life. But even now, people looked at him and saw not a man who had changed his destiny, but saw a man who made them uncomfortable for having moved beyond what they considered right.

Then there was Roger. Born the heir to the mighty Sir Arthur of Anglesea. As the youngest son, Henry, too, had experienced the burden of their father's greatness. It loomed over their heads constantly. Surely the sons of the great Sir Arthur mirrored his greatness? As heir, Roger had borne the greatest burden. His every action scrutinized and compared to Father. Somehow Roger had made the Anglesea legacy his, and not only that which passed to him. Such deep thoughts as he faced this morning and kept him from dwelling on Alya.

As if it mocked them scrabbling about beneath it, the sun rose over the walls and treated the morning to a glorious roseate splendor.

Sir James cleared his throat. "What will you do?"

"I do not know." He would need to speak with Roger and Father. What had happened could not go unanswered but none of the options were easy. Then he needed to find a way to make Alya look at him again. If he could get her to meet his eye, he could explain, apologize, grovel, beg if need be, but get his wife back.

"Will you speak of her to others?"

Momentarily lost, Henry stared at Sir James. The man spoke of Elizabeth and not the events of the night. Every person had their own worries, and to them they were the most compelling concerns. "Nay." The growing morning heat made sweat prickle and itch beneath his hauberk. "If she truly does not wish to marry, why not let her stay here and pursue her healing gift?"

"Eh?" With a grimace, Sir James tugged at his hauberk neck. Chain mail did not make for hours of comfortable wearing. Especially in the heat. "The girl must marry."

"Why?" Sod it. Bending at the waist, Henry wriggled out of his hauberk. Despite the events of the night, he doubted an archer hid nearby, waiting to put an arrow in him. "Anglesea and you can forge an alliance without marriage being involved. Now that the truth is known, we can use that to form the basis of an agreement."

With a look of profound relief, Sir James shed his hauberk as well.

Henry waited while the thicker set man wriggled a bit to get it over his head. Hair standing upright, Sir James stood with a big sigh. "This is not the usual way."

"Nay." Garrett and Roger could take the conversation from here. "But the usual way has cost you a son, and look what it nearly cost me." Henry motioned around them. "One thing you will already know about our family is that we rarely do things the usual way."

* * *

Alya tried to see Elizabeth as the woman who had come to steal her husband, but Elizabeth made that impossible. Beyond devoted to the care of Bahir and Newt, she worked tirelessly through what remained of the night. Eventually Alya gave up the battle, for it existed in her head alone, and she did exactly what Elizabeth asked her to do.

Elizabeth's lovely gown looked ready for the fire, but her beauty remained undimmed. It also became clear as they worked side by side that Elizabeth had no interest in marrying Henry. It might be better for all of them if she did. Although Alya still couldn't bring herself to wish for that. Hurt, and angry with

Henry, she was still not ready to hand him over to another woman.

Which left the question as to what she intended to do with him. As welcome as his rescue had been, a stubborn core within her insisted she would not have been in that situation in the first place were it not for his need to hide her away like the family's darkest secret. If only things were that simple though, and she could block out all the other things he'd said and done. Things that made her think that despite the last few days, Henry did want her. From here her thinking grew jumbled, colored by the constant nagging dread over Bahir and Newt.

Although Henry had brought her to England, he had done so out of the best motives. Henry had been honoring his vow to her father to protect her, and doing so in the best way he knew possible. That he did not need to marry her also occurred to her. Henry had spread his honor over her like a mantle of protection. Only it had not worked.

"He grows feverish." Elizabeth rose from where she bent over Newt. "It is as I feared. Lying in the mud and dirt has set up contagion in the wound."

Her thoughts would wait for when Bahir and Newt were out of danger. And they would be out of danger because she could accept no more loss. Bahir was all she had in the way of family, and Newt was the last tenuous connection between her and Henry. It made no sense, but she felt if Newt died, her connection to Henry would be severed. Already the bond between them stretched to breaking point.

About mid-morning, a young man-at-arms brought them a meal and some ale. He told them they were working hard outside to clear the mess away, after which they could properly assess the damage.

Slumped on an upturned bucket, shoveling bread and cheese into her mouth, Elizabeth still managed to look beautiful. Hair had escaped her braid in wisps about her ivory face. Smears of dirt and blood stained her forehead and cheek. Alya was certain her own looks had not fared as well.

"Who are they?" Elizabeth motioned Newt and then Bahir. "Why did those men do this to them?"

Elizabeth had labored hard enough to earn a full response. As it was easier, she started with Newt. "I am not sure of all of his history, but he and the Anglesea family go many years back. I believe he first befriended Lady Beatrice. Somehow both Lady Beatrice and Lady Faye ended up owing him a huge debt."

"He is not a knight?" Elizabeth pushed Newt's hair from his face and studied it. "He has the fine features of one noble born."

How Newt would laugh to hear anyone say so, let alone such a lovely, high-born lady. "Nay, he is not entirely sure who his mother was, and has no idea as to his father. Beatrice first discovered him locked in the stocks for theft."

"He seems to have made his way to better things from there." Chewing her bread, Elizabeth stared at the sleeping Newt.

"Henry told me he got into some trouble for poaching the king's deer. He called in the debts Beatrice and Faye owed and ended up as Henry's squire."

"He went on pilgrimage with Sir Henry?"

"Aye." Not out of hunger but out of necessity, Alya forced herself to finish her meal. She would need all her strength in the days to come. "He was the last to see Henry alive before his capture and brought the news home to the family. After, he begged Roger to send him back, so he could discover what had happened to Henry."

"He sounds brave." Elizabeth's eyes grew misty.

"He is." If he could see that look Elizabeth bent on him, Newt would be squirming right now. "He is also foul-mouthed, has no sense of decorum, and marches entirely to his own drum. He is very dear to my husband." She needed to go and tell Henry how Newt fared, but she kept waiting to see if she could carry better news.

"And him." Elizabeth rose, and pressed her hand into her

lower back with a groan. With a damp cloth, she bathed Bahir's face, the water making his dark skin gleam like onyx.

"He is the closest thing I have to a father." Alya swallowed past the lump in her throat. "For years, he worked as a slave in our home and my father gave me into his care before I left Cairo."

"He looks too strong and noble to be a slave." Her smile soft, Elizabeth pressed a damp cloth to Bahir's lips.

"I have never known where he came from or how he ended up a slave." So much of her life shared with Bahir and yet she did not even know who his people had been. "He was put into the harem to guard the women as a young man, which is why he could not have done what they say he did."

Elizabeth nodded. She had seen for herself the scarring on Bahir. "I shudder to think of how much pain that must have caused him."

"Aye." For the first time Alya thought about how much those slavers has cost Bahir. The man she had known and who had shared in the raising of her would have made a wonderful husband and father.

Pushing the thought away, she stood and tidied away the herbs Elizabeth used to make the men more comfortable.

A shadow crossed the door and Henry stepped into the stable. How could she be so angry with him and still her heart skipped a beat when she saw him? "My family is here," he said. "We need you to come with us."

Chapter Thirty-Four

Dressed finer than a queen, and so tired she could barely sit her horse, Alya followed Henry and Lady Mary into the center of the village. Around them, armor jingling, leather creaking, the knights of Anglesea rode. For the occasion, every household knight had been roused and dressed in their honors.

Sir James added his men to the party.

They entered the village like an army prepared for war. Drawing into columns on either side of the roadway, they stood as she, Henry, and Lady Mary rode through them to the village green.

From the church scurried the priest, adjusting his robes as he ran.

Lady Mary stopped her horse and sat.

Alya sat beside her.

Henry nudged his horse forward. Closest to him rode the family. Sir Arthur, Roger, William, Garrett, Gregory, all large and imposing men, the threat implicit in their silence.

A mismatched couple of men joined the priest as they walked across the green. From his size and hair color Alya guessed the bigger one to be the blacksmith, Red Alfred. The other man wore the wind chapped visage and bow-legged strut of one who spent his life on the sea.

"The village elders," Lady Mary murmured to her. "They know why we are here."

That made three people who knew more than she did. Lady Mary had summoned her from her nursing duties, and without too much chatter seen her dressed and mounted. All Lady Mary had said was that this ended today, and she would take care of it.

"Sir Henry. My lady." The priest bowed before them.

The other two tripped over their feet to join him.

"You know why I am here." Henry's voice was colder than his blue eyes.

"Aye, my lord," Alfred said, and shoved the priest forward.

"We are horrified, Sir Henry." The priest twisted his hands in his robes. "We cannot express how sorry we are that this has happened."

"You know who did this?"

"Aye." He glanced at the two men with him. "They do not know how they came to act in this terrible manner."

"I see." Henry smoothed the leather of his gloves. "And yet, Father Mark, I find no conciliation in this. I can find no conciliation because three loyal guards are dead and two of my dearest friends, men I regard as family, lie close to death because of what these fiends did."

Father Mark winced. "Is it as bad as that?"

"Indeed." Henry looked over their heads to the villagers clustered on the far side of the green. "I have seen people suffer under the hands of an unjust lord. Indeed, my brother William, had the task of righting what undeserved privilege had wrought on his lands by marriage."

"God bless Sir William." Father Mark's hands shook as he crossed himself.

"I did not know that Anglesea was such a village," Henry said.

"Eh!" The smith frowned and glanced about him. "We are not..."

Henry stared him down. "And yet you raised your hand to me."

Gasps and whispers rose from the listening villagers.

"Nay, my lord." Rulf, a sailor and the third elder clambered to his feet. "They acted without thought, but never would anyone in this village raise their hand against the Angleseas."

"But you did." For all his silky spoken manner, Henry's voice carried a wicked sting. As he looked at the villagers, heads dropped, gazes slid to the side. This was Henry the powerful English lord, a side of him Alya did not often see.

"You deliberately sought to hurt and kill a man I regard as family. In your unfounded fury, you caused damage. Three dead, two injured and my home near destroyed." Henry said. "I am ashamed to claim you as my people."

Father Mark looked ill. "Do not say so, Sir Henry."

"How long did it take you to accept Garrett as Lady Beatrice's choice?" He looked from one villager to another. "And even now there are those amongst you who deny him the respect he so properly deserves."

Garrett's horse shifted beneath him.

"I believed in you." Henry's voice rose. "I believed that in time you would come to love, value, and respect him as we do."

"Lady Beatrice could have married a prince." A male voice rose from the clustered villagers.

"I see you have something to say, Bardolf." Sitting straight in the saddle, Lady Mary barely moved her head. "Step out from behind the others and face me instead of hiding like a sniveling coward."

A tall, rangy man stepped to the front of the villagers.

Alya had seen him in the crowd that attacked the manor. Her gut tightened as the fear memory surfaced, to be replaced by a scalding anger that made her sway in the saddle.

Lady Mary nudged her mount closer to Alya's. "Hold steady," she murmured. "Do not give them the satisfaction of seeing you break."

"Aye, Bardolf." Henry turned back to the man. "Beatrice could have married a prince. To my mind, she did, no matter what his birth."

Expression set and mutinous, Bardolf kicked at the turf.

"I blame myself in part." Lady Mary nudged her horse closer to Henry's. "If I had done years ago what I intend to do today, perhaps you would not have thought it fell within your rights to judge who my son takes to wife, or who this family welcomes into its bosom."

The elders exchanged glances. Father Mark stepped forward. "What do you intend to do?"

"My son brought to his home the woman who had stolen his heart. The same woman who gave him hope and joy through the long, dismal days of his captivity. He brought her to us believing we would welcome her because he loved her at first, and then come to love her as our own."

"Heathen." The insult whispered across the green.

"Heathen." Lady Mary's tinkling laughter seemed horribly out of place. "She is as Christian as you or I. Even more so, because her faith was challenged daily in the country in which she was raised."

"Perhaps if we had seen her at mass." Father Mark ducked his head and fidgeted with his cross.

"She should come to mass in the village?" Henry's voice rang across the green. "So you could shame me once again by whispering behind her back, casting aspersions on her good name, jeering at her and making up stories. She should come to the village so young louts can waylay her and threaten her."

Henry's fiery gaze fixed on the villagers. As if he stopped himself from yanking out his sword and running them through, his fist lay balled on his thigh near his pommel.

"For shame." Lady Mary's voice rang across the green. "With your actions, you have shamed me and you have shamed yourselves. Three are dead and two more good men may die because of this, and the girl I have come to love as one of my own bears a wound deep in her heart."

Tears pricked Alya's lids. All of this and the ring of truth in Lady Mary's declaration made her heart ache. How she still longed for acceptance.

"There are barons in this kingdom who would raze this village to the ground after what you did." Sir Arthur joined Henry and Lady Mary. He waved his hand to encompass the neat, white-washed thatched cottages about them.

From Sir James and his men came a murmur that sounded like they were merely waiting for the sign to unleash their brand of vengeance on the villagers.

"My lord." Father Mark wiped his brow with his sleeve. "You cannot mean to punish an entire village for the actions of a few."

"A few?" Up went Lady Mary's brow. "How many attacked you, sweeting?"

With a start Alya answered the unexpected question. "About twenty."

"Indeed." Father Mark cleared his throat. "I misspoke. But you cannot mean to punish everyone for the actions of some."

"Do not presume to tell me what I can and cannot do." Pure steel ringed Roger's voice as he moved his horse beside Alya. "The actions of last night have shown me clearly on what footing castle and village now stand. You have the twenty to thank for that."

"Then I beg you." Sweat gleamed on his pate and face. "We can all see you have the might to do as you will. I beg you for the sakes of the village innocents."

"Show me these innocents." Lady Mary searched the crowd. "If you have never glanced askance at Bahir, Alya, Newt, or Garrett, step forward. If you have never uttered a bad or judgmental word against either of them, come and stand freely before me and I swear you will come to no harm." She made a graceful, sweeping motion. "Those whose thoughts have never condemned my new family, I invite you to declare your innocence before all."

Father Mark paled. "Surely, the children..."

Villagers shifted. A man near the back of the crowd hurried away from the green. From behind the cottages came the rest of Anglesea's men. On horseback and on foot they blocked any escape. Muttering rose within the villagers, and Alya swore she could smell the sharp acrid tang of their fear.

Suddenly she was not so sure what the family intended. Until this moment she would have sworn the gentle, gracious Lady Mary would not allow her rage loose against the village. Alya was less sure of the calm, poised stranger sitting perfectly still and straight in her saddle. This woman could do anything and the men with her would obey her without question.

Alya glanced to Henry for reassurance, but his face remained stony and blank. William and Roger were no better. She could not condone a bloodbath. Not even for Bahir and Newt. "Roger?"

Under the direct intensity of Roger's gaze, she faltered before she found her courage. "You cannot mean to do here what happened last night."

"Can I not?" Roger raised his brow. "If I do not send a powerful message, then how do I know that next time it will not be one of your children who face mob justice?"

"I understand, but..." But what? Words failed her and she glanced at Henry.

Gaze warming, he nodded his encouragement.

"If we wreak death here, that makes us no better than the cowards who came last night with their axes and their pitchforks." She swallowed to ease the dryness in her mouth. "If we refuse to listen to reason, then we are just as vicious and stupid as they were."

Squabbling gulls sounded loud in the absolute silence over the village green and its people.

"She begs for you." Lady Mary turned to the villagers. "You went to kill her and her people last night, and here Lady Alya begs for your lives."

"My lady." Father Mark had tears in his eyes as he gazed at Alya. "I cannot...no words..." He dropped to a knee.

Rulf and Red Alfred copied his actions.

Slowly and in singles and then groups, villagers took their knees until only a few hardened souls remained standing.

"Here is what will happen." Roger spoke at last. "I want the men who took part in last night's atrocity and I want them now."

As the crowd stepped away from them, Alya's heart hardened again. These faces she remembered, ugly and jeering in their rage and their cruelty. For them, she had no pity. "You were more courageous last night," she said. "Then you did not hide behind women and children."

"Quite so." Henry threw her a hard look, the message clear, to leave this with him.

The men left standing in the center of the green numbered twenty-three, and ranged in age from barely old enough to shave to gray headed. Shoulders thrust back, still not cowed, stood the one Newt had called Miller. The one who had stirred the men to tie up Bahir, and then had carved gashes into Bahir's ribs.

A younger man stepped forward, face pale beneath a mop of brown hair. He dropped to his knee. "I beg for your mercy, my lady."

As if he had opened a floodgate, more men stepped forward and threw themselves before her and Lady Mary.

"Henry?" Roger turned to his brother.

"Hang them." Henry pointed at Miller and two men standing defiant beside him. "Hang them and once they are dead stake their bodies here in the green as a reminder to all of their shame."

One of Miller's compatriots buckled, and dropped to his knees. He gibbered and cried for mercy but Henry barely even glanced at him. "As for the rest of you who took part in last night, you have forfeited your welcome here. The compact between lord and yeoman is clear and you have broken your side of it. Thus, you are no longer welcome to make your living from our demesne, no longer entitled to the protection of the castle, and no longer will you call Baron Anglesea lord."

A woman in the crowd sobbed and prayed aloud.

"So be it," Roger said. "You will leave here today with what you can carry. If your family chooses to go with you, they too are no longer welcome in this demesne. You have until sundown."

Henry picked up his reins. "After that, if I see you, you will be hunted down like the curs you are, and I will unleash the full weight of Anglesea upon you."

Chapter Thirty-Five

Lady Mary tried to insist Alya move back to Anglesea, but she could not. With Newt and Bahir deemed too ill to move, Alya's place was with them at the manor. As damaged as it was, she still felt more at home there, and she clung to that stability.

After they left the village, half the armed party returned to Anglesea and the other half escorted her back to the manor. Henry joined her escort and rode silently beside her the entire way. Bone-achingly tired, she rode into the manor long after sunset.

Fast asleep in her chair, Elizabeth sat beside Newt.

Newt seemed to be breathing easier. His skin was still warm to the touch but he did not seem any worse than when she had left.

Bahir slept as if he might never wake. Once in Cairo, one of the house slaves had fallen from a wall. No bones had been broken, in fact he did not even bleed from any seen wound, and yet the young slave had slept as Bahir did now. A deep, heavy sleep that rested just this side of death. Taking his hand, she sat on the ground beside his cot. He had to wake up and be well again. Surely God could not be so cruel as to take her father, and Bahir, and her dear, sweet Jamila so close together?

She must have fallen asleep because she awoke to Elizabeth moving quietly about.

"You're awake." Elizabeth had tidied her hair and changed into chausses and a tunic. She still looked utterly female, even in men's clothes. In truth, the chausses clung to her hips and bottom like a skirt never would.

Bahir's hand felt less clammy in hers and she rose onto her knees to examine him. "How are they?"

"Not much change." Elizabeth grimaced. "Although Bahir grew a little restless earlier. I don't want to give you false hope, but I believe he might be trying to wake."

False or not, Alya would grasp at any hope.

The door opened and Nurse and Ivy entered.

Ivy went immediately to Newt and examined him.

Nurse gave Elizabeth a top to toe searching look. "Your father seems to think you have a gift for healing."

"I do." Elizabeth raised her chin, then dropped it. Not many managed to stand chin to chin with Nurse and Alya applauded Elizabeth's wisdom. "At least, I believe I do and I would like to learn further."

"Hmph!" Nurse adjusted her constricting wimple. "Tell me what you have done and then we'll decide if you have any skill in this sort of thing. It takes an iron belly to be a healer."

With Nurse and Ivy there, the room was too crowded, and Alya stepped into the stable yard. The amount of work that had taken place stopped her for a moment. Already Chester and his men were stacking new wood to replace what had burned.

On her way across the stable yard she recognized a few faces from the village. What must Lady Mary have promised or threatened to get those here? The fire had destroyed the east wing of the manor house, but fortunately the hall and the still being built west wing had escaped with only some blackening.

Hoping to find something to eat and a change of clothes, Alya headed that way. The aroma of beef and bread cheered her complaining stomach as she entered the hall.

More people than she expected milled about. Some of them sat and ate, others stood about and chatted, still others worked at scrubbing the walls clean again. The new faces also belonged to villagers. A rotund woman offered her a tentative smile and bobbed a curtsy. "Lady Alya. May I bring you a something to eat?"

Hungry or not, Alya did not trust any villager near her food. "Thank you, but nay."

"As you wish, my lady." The woman looked crestfallen as she backed away.

Three more times she was offered food before she made it to the great hearth. There she found her own bowl and ladled stew into it. She waited until she saw someone else chew and swallow before she attempted her own meal.

Whoever had made the stew knew what they were about. Carrots, onions and parsnips added their flavor to the hearty beefy goodness. Not a grand meal but one with working folk in mind, aimed at feeding their tired bodies. With no Cook presiding over this kitchen, she might even add her spices to the meals. Fire had taken some of the storerooms. When she could find the energy, she would check and see what remained of her inheritance.

Finding a quiet corner, Alya perched on a bench to eat her stew.

Glances swiveled her way and turned again. One or two tentative smiles were offered to her, but she did not engage.

A hush fell over the hall when Henry entered.

He spotted her immediately and made his way to her side. Rocking the bench beneath her, he took a seat by her side. "Are you well?"

"I am." Her belly tightened and she had to force another bite down her throat.

A woman approached with a bowl and handed it to Henry. He had no qualms about accepting it and tucking in. Then again, these people had not been intent on his death. "How are Bahir and Newt?"

His question dragged her away from her musings. "Not much change. Nurse and Ivy arrived and are with Lady Elizabeth now."

"Ah." Nodding, Henry chewed and swallowed. "If anyone knows what to do, it is Nurse and Ivy. If Bahir and Newt can be helped at all, those two will do it."

So many unspoken words lay between them and Alya was too tired to even attempt any of them, so she doggedly ate until her bowl was empty. She rose to return it to the hearth.

"Stay." Henry caught her hand and tugged her down to the bench. "So much has happened and we need to speak of it."

"Nay, we don't." Talking had never been a strength between them. Setting all that had happened today aside, Lady Mary, the village, and even the people here now. None of that made a difference if he still could not accept her fully and with no reservations in his heart. He admired her, he gave every indication of enjoying her body, and at times even of liking her company. But for as long as doubt lingered with Henry as to if he had made the right choice of wife, she could not be his wife. "I have nothing left to say."

"Perhaps I have much to say." His blue eyes were solemn. "Would you allow me the opportunity to share what is in my heart?"

Now he chose to share with her. But it was too late. Bahir may have paid the ultimate price, and Newt as well, and Alya did not want to hear it. "Do I have a choice?"

A small frown puckered his brow. "Of course."

"Then I choose not to hear it. Right now, there is nothing you can say that would make any difference. I thank you and your family for today at the village, but it came too late to help me or Newt or Bahir." With nothing more to lose, she did not hold back her words. "I could accept them and their suspicion of me so much more readily if I felt that you were on my side." Shaking off his light hold, she stood. "But you are not wholly on my side." She held up her hand when he would speak. "You brought a foreign wife to your home and now you are not sure you should have done so. Perhaps if you were more sure of your choice, others would not dare to question it."

* * *

Henry visited the infirmary after dinner. He had been cowardly about coming before now, afraid to confirm the worst.

Bandages white against his dark skin, Bahir lay on one cot. Top to tail on a second cot slept Newt. So many bandages covered him it was hard to see skin. Dear God. Henry's stomach churned. Newt must have lost a frightening amount of blood.

Ivy rose from her seat beside the fire and put her mending on the seat. "You have come to see how they fare."

"It looks..." The words jammed in his throat and refused to come out. If he did not say it aloud perhaps it would not be true, but Bahir and Newt both looked dire.

"It often does." Ivy ran a protective hand over the rise of her rounded belly. She and Tom expected their first child in the winter. "But Lady Elizabeth did a good job cleansing the wounds and closing them. There is always hope, Henry. You must know this by now."

Her pregnancy had made Ivy so lovely she was fae-like. It had also made her more hopeful. After checking on both men, she took up her mending and sat down again. "Sit with us for a while."

With the small fire warming his back, Henry took a seat at her feet.

"I remember the day Beatrice rescued Newt." Needle moving swiftly through the cloth, Ivy laughed softly. "Such a strange, ungainly looking boy. I might have left him to his fate, but Bea could never turn her back on an injustice."

"Real or imagined." Henry returned Ivy's smile. Before his pilgrimage, he had deplored his sister's huge heart. Even mocked the passion with which she embraced life. He saw her differently now. Souls like Sweet Bea's were rare and precious. Without their relentless belief in joy, the rest of the world would be a bleak and cheerless place.

"Did you know Newt harbored feelings for Bea?" Speaking to Ivy was safe as keep walls. She never spilled all the secrets whispered to her.

"How could he not?" Ivy chuckled. "She was like a beautiful, golden avenging angel come to save him."

An image of Newt, bedraggled, filthy, and foul-mouthed as he had been then, crept into Henry's mind. And another of the day Newt had stepped in front of Father's destrier and saved Faye's life. Then later still, when he had arrived at the docks trussed and under Gregory's guardianship.

Newt had not wanted to be a squire. Henry laughed at the memory of Newt's angry gaze searing him from above the gag Gregory had put over his mouth.

The anguish caught him by surprise. One heartbeat he was laughing with Ivy and the next the pain near doubled him over. "He has to live, Ivy."

Ivy smiled, kind but sad, and continued her sewing.

"When Father first sent him to me, I couldn't fathom what he was thinking. The lad didn't know the ass end of a horse from the mouth. He had no skill with weapons and had a deplorable habit of relieving other knights of their valued possessions."

Ivy laughed and bit her thread. "He tried to teach me once, that quick fingered knack of his."

"I swear he could take the tankard out of your mouth before you had taken a swallow." Those early days with him and Newt had been a running battle. Strange, in hindsight, they had kept him from dwelling on the atrocities taking place all around him in the name of the Lord. Over time he and Newt had become a sort of island, relying on each other in an increasingly insane world.

Once he decided to apply himself, Newt had mastered the sword well enough to spar with him. Newt must have fought fiercely to save Bahir.

"How is Tom?" Fond of Tom though he was, Henry asked after Ivy's husband more to take his mind off the present.

"He is well." She threaded her needle with red thread. "He fusses over me getting too tired, and I'm sure will march up here tomorrow to make sure I am eating and sleeping properly."

No doubt, Tom cherished his wife. Which brought Alya to mind again. He had made such a dog's ballocks of his marriage. Smug in his rescue of her, he had taken for granted she would adapt herself to his life. On his arrival home, he had spent his time nursing his wounds and searching for his sense of purpose. All the while leaving his beautiful, courageous wife to fend for herself.

His family had tried to tell him, but he had blocked his ears. Perhaps he had not changed as much as he believed he had. He still had the ability to render himself deaf to all but what he wanted to hear, and blind to that he did not want to see.

"Ivy?"

"Hmm?" She glanced up from her sewing.

"Have you ever been so angry with Tom you doubted you could forgive him?"

Ivy stared at him, until he wanted to fidget like a small boy. Then she nodded. "Aye." She shook out Tom's chemise and folded it. "When he first met me, all Tom could see of me was that I was a whore."

Henry winced. He hated that word and doubly so when applied to Ivy. "But you had no choice. You were sold into it."

"Indeed." Ivy took out another of Tom's chemises.

Did Tom wrestle wild boar in his clothes?

"But it did not change what I was. And Tom had difficulty seeing past that. For as long as he saw me as a whore, he would not allow himself to love me." She threaded her needle again. "I think he used it as an excuse not to love me. Tom loved me from the first, and that frightened him, so he found a reason to keep me at a distance."

Ouch! Her words found their mark and smarted. He circled around and around the word love with Alya. He described her as his hope, his light, his girl on the wall. Like a wild yearling, he refused to acknowledge her as his love.

Then when they had arrived at Anglesea and the opposition to his bride had built, he'd shied even further from a love that grew increasingly inconvenient.

"You look as if you are sucking lemons," Ivy said.

"I feel that way." Henry shook his head in disgust at himself. "How did you forgive Tom?"

A truly wicked smile crossed Ivy's face. "He groveled."

Henry left to find Alya and commence the groveling. He was halfway across the yard when Gregory hailed him.

"I came as soon as we heard." Gregory and Faye lived at Calder Castle. The news must have traveled like a hare. "I am to report back. How is Newt?"

Henry shook his head.

"He died?" Gregory paled and stepped back.

"Nay." Henry grabbed the bigger man's arm and steadied him. "I meant there has been little change in his condition."

"Thank you, God." Gregory lifted his gaze skyward. "For a moment there..." He shook his head. "Faye and I are very fond of Newt."

Newt had played an important part in Faye and Gregory's scramble to find each other. The path to love had been rocky for all his siblings. Arrogantly, he had assumed it would be different for him.

Gregory caught his shoulder in one giant hand. "We should pray for them."

"It has been a long time since I prayed." Henry could not keep the bitterness from his tone. "It has been even longer since I have found God in the actions of men."

With a nod, Gregory squeezed his shoulder. "You are not the first to come back from pilgrimage and think so. I fear there is nothing of God in what happens there."

"This from a man of God?" Gregory's words stopped Henry in his tracks. Of all the folk at Anglesea, it had been Gregory who had most readily accepted Bahir. Doing what none of them would and asking questions and discovering the man for himself. There was more of God in Gregory than in all the armies of God under the sun.

"And how fares my friend, the wise Bahir?" Gregory showed true to form. A good man to his marrow. "I will pray for him too. Although he might prefer if I prayed to his Allah." Gregory looked around them warily. "I suspect there is not so much different between his God and ours as we would like to believe."

A statement so close to heresy that Henry held his breath, half expecting a lightning strike to singe Gregory.

"Will you pray with me, Henry?" Gregory stared at him.

"I..." Henry searched for the right words and then went with the truth. "I fear I cannot."

"Ah." Gregory steered him around the side of the manor to where the noise and people thinned to nothing. Poised on the edge of a river, the back of the manor provided a pretty view. If a man believed in God, he might find Him in such beauty. Leading the way to the river, Gregory said, "I lost God once."

"You?" Henry found that impossible to believe. "You are the Godliest man I know."

"Hardly." Gregory pulled a face. "I have more questions than I can voice in this lifetime."

"And yet, you still believe?"

"Aye." Gregory nodded. "If I had all the answers and all the proof, then it would not be faith."

True enough. Henry chuckled. "What made you lose God?"

"Faye." Gregory grimaced. "After one beating, Calder left her bleeding on the floor of their bedchamber. I had to wait for him to leave before I could get to her." Gregory stared over the river, his face haunted by the past. "I counted the heartbeats until he left the castle. When I found her..." He cleared his throat. "When I found her, it was so much worse than I had imagined. And I had spent hours torturing myself with my imagination."

Another of Henry's regrets was his treatment of Faye. She had come to her family begging for help, but only after her brute husband nearly destroyed the Angleseas. He had told her that her place was with her husband. "I should never—"

"I know." Gregory sat on a log worn smooth by the river at high tide. "And Faye knows. You were a different man then."

"Perhaps." Not by his reckoning he wasn't. "I often wondered how you kept your faith through all that happened to you and Faye."

"I didn't always." Gregory selected a flat pebble and sent it skimming over the water. "I bore so much anger toward God, I think that is why they never admitted me to the monastery."

"That and the way you were in love with my sister," Henry said.

Gregory's serious face relaxed into a brief smile. "And that."

The river rushed over rocks in a soothing whisper. The sinking sun gilded the water and cast soft light on Gregory's harsh features.

"I prayed all the time when I was first on pilgrimage." A sense of relief swept through Henry. Speaking of this no longer came with jagged edges. "But what I saw there. What those people did in the name of God. At first I was confused, thinking I must not understand. Then I was angry at them. And finally, angry with God for allowing it."

"I was angry at God for not smiting Calder." Gregory skimmed another pebble. "I stayed away from Faye out of obedience to God, and still, he allowed Calder to hurt her."

"Clearly, you and God have reconciled." Henry counted three skips of Gregory's next pebble.

"For the most part." Gregory smiled. "I still have my questions, but He is fortunately patient with me. We have found a rocky sort of common ground."

"How?"

Gregory smiled and said, "I realized that we do not need God's help to do the evil we do. God had no part in what happened to Faye, just as he had no part in what happened here, or what happened on pilgrimage."

Henry needed to think on that. His anger had kept him company for too long to be discounted in mere moments. "Why do you care if I pray or not?"

Gregory shrugged. "I do not, Henry. But I care that you hold so much anger and regret inside you it blocks the light from entering. Perhaps I see you making peace with God as a step toward making peace with yourself." Crouched, Gregory sifted through the pebbles for another flat one. "You have a beautiful new wife who deserves a full man by her side, and not one who is still mired in the bitter past.

And suddenly Henry needed no other reason. "Do you still believe He hears you?"

"Always." Gregory smiled. "And how could our prayers hurt at this point?"

True enough. "You begin."

Gregory bowed his head. "Heavenly Father..."

Chapter Thirty-Six

Alya drifted around the manor like a ghost. Henry tried to reach her but was met with cool distance. Even anger would have been preferable to her serene indifference. The only time she seemed to be alive was when she nursed Bahir and Newt. She spent as much time there as Nurse would allow.

Gregory stayed for two days and left to report to Faye, whom he claimed would kill him if he did not return home soon. Faye was far too enamored of her huge husband to do more than huff at him.

Bahir's wounds healed but he showed no sign of waking. Nurse feared for him the most because injuries to the head, she had always said, were a mystery and the outcome near impossible to predict.

Elizabeth hovered over Newt near constantly. Henry answered her questions as patiently as he could, but one always seemed to breed twenty more. Perhaps if she had met Newt before his injury she would not have declared she would never marry. Then again, knowing Newt as he did, perhaps not. Newt could talk most women into lifting their skirts, but with a woman like Elizabeth that would not suffice.

More villagers joined the effort to restore the manor by the day. Frightened by his family's anger and mired in shame, the villagers now sought to make amends.

Alya drifted past them, oblivious to their efforts. In an odd twist, the more she ignored them, the harder they worked to please her. Already repairs to the burned section of the manor proceeded faster than even Chester had dreamed possible. The women had sorted through Alya's dowry and carefully salvaged as much as they could. Her cushions and bedcurtains had been brought from Anglesea and now adorned their chamber.

Their chamber? Henry snorted beneath his breath. If she could oust him from there, she would. Thus far, he survived by pretending not to notice how much she did not want him sharing thc chamber with her.

"Sir Henry." Bernard led a knot of boys toward him. Two of them fosters at Anglesea, and the other three, he knew from the village. They hid something in their midst.

"What is it?" He wanted to catch Alya as she took her turn beside Newt. Pathetic as it was, it was the only contact she allowed him and he guarded it jealously.

The older foster, Abel, stepped forward. "We have something here for my lady."

"Lady Alya?"

"Aye, my lord." Abel blushed. "Only we do not know how to give it to her."

Henry strode to them.

The youngest boy held a puppy in his hand. No more than eight weeks old if Henry had to guess, and a similar color to Jamila. Henry had found Jamila's body behind the manor and buried her quietly. The dog Alya had never wanted, but had wheedled her way into Alya's heart anyway.

The boy turned big brown eyes up at him. "My dog had pups and when I heard about Lady Alya's dog, I thought she might like a new one. But...she seems so quiet and sad, and I did not want to make her sadder."

A sentiment Henry supported wholeheartedly. "Wait here. I will fetch her for you."

* * *

Alya bathed Newt and then Bahir in tepid water as Nurse has instructed her.

The door opened and Henry entered.

Tall and beautiful he stood in the doorway and stretched out a hand to her. "Come with me."

"I cannot." Her heart urged her to take his hand, but her trust felt as lacerated at Bahir's ribs."

Henry smiled. "Please."

"Why?" Already her feet moved her closer to him.

"Come." He wrapped her hand in his strong, roughened grip. "You will not be sorry, I promise."

"Run along, dear." Nurse shooed her. "You are only disturbing my patients with your arguing."

A group of boys waited for them outside. They stopped talking and watched her approach. Excitement eked from them.

"What is it?" Alya turned to Henry for her answer.

Henry motioned the smallest boy forward. "They have something for you."

The last time someone from this place had something for her, it had come from the sharp end of a pitchfork. "What?"

A small boy stepped forward. In his arms, he held a tiny bundle of flaxen fur. Two soft brown eyes blinked up at her as the boy brought the bundle to her. "Everyone knows Jamila was killed," he said. "And my old dog died last year and they leave a hole right through the middle of a person when they go. I know she's not your Jamila, but one of my da's bitches had a litter and she might look a bit like your Jamila when she grows."

Alya's brain stuck and refused to start again. The boy held a puppy and he was offering it to her. She had never thought of a dog as anything other than a filthy animal before Jamila had forced her way into her life and heart. Then Jamila had proved her nobility, fearlessly and without hesitation, giving her life to save Alya. How could this small beast replace that bond? "You are giving me this puppy?"

"We can't bring your friend back." Bernard took the puppy from the boy and placed it in her arms. "But a new friend can help heal the pain."

The puppy wriggled in her arms and yawned, displaying her tiny white teeth and pink tongue. Alya had never held something so sweet and fragile. The trusting way the puppy nestled against her astounded her. This baby animal had no protection from life and yet it gave its trust so willingly. "Jamila was my first dog."

"Aye." Bernard nodded. "And she was a great dog. Maybe in time this one will grow to be a great dog too."

"I know nothing about puppies."

"Bernard can teach you." Henry put an arm about Bernard's shoulder. "It will give you both a task until we can get your herb garden established."

Her herb garden? Alya had not considered the future much, past getting Bahir and Newt well.

* * *

Later that day Bahir woke first and in typical quiet, composed Bahir fashion. According to Nurse, who had been the only one present, he opened his eyes and looked about him. Sore, confused, and missing pieces of his memory, but still Bahir.

Alya rushed to see him. One look at his open eyes and she burst into tears. Noisy, snotty sobs that would not stop. She had to stop when Nurse threatened to lock her out for upsetting the patient. Still sniveling, she sat beside Bahir with the puppy on her lap, and his hand in hers. He drifted back to sleep. An easier, more natural slumber this time.

Not even Nurse could oust her now. Bahir, her anchor, was alive and she needed him more than ever. Henry snarled her in knots within knots. She loved so much about him, but being with him demanded that she become someone else, or pretend to be that which she couldn't be.

A groan drew her attention to Newt. He tossed his head to the side and groaned again.

Alya ran to the door and threw it open. "Nurse! Ivy! Elizabeth!"

Ivy came running.

Newt had tossed his coverings to the floor and Ivy replaced them without a blush. But Newt...well, there was yet another reason he was popular with the ladies.

Ivy put her hand to his forehead. "I think he wakes. His skin is cooler."

Alya touched his shoulder. His skin did feel cooler.

"Newt." Ivy leaned over him and raised her voice. "You will rip your stitches if you do not keep still."

Groaning, Newt attempted to roll away from her.

Ivy held him still, motioning Alya to help her. "Newt." Ivy raised her voice. "You must lie still. Can you hear me?"

"Aye, I hear you. You are yelling in my face." Breathy and raspy, Newt's voice brought more tears. Hers, Ivy's and after she entered, Nurse's as well. Even Elizabeth seemed moved.

Bahir made an excellent patient. He took what herbs were given to him, lay quietly and slept in between being tended to and ate or drank whatever was given to him.

Newt did not. He complained near constantly about being kept confined. He could barely contain himself from scratching at his stitches and his scabs. Gruel and beef broth set up a whining litany that had them all ready to smack him.

Alya spent even more time in the infirmary now. Outside repairs to the manor continued but her world had shrunk to Ivy, Nurse, Elizabeth, the two invalids and Amira, her puppy who had so much quiet dignity she could only be named a princess.

Henry floated around the periphery. Her attempts to get him

to leave their bedchamber had ended in a stalemate of him sleeping on the floor in front of the fire and her on the bed.

Fortunately, after a couple of horribly awkward mornings he got up with the sun and left before she woke.

They could not continue like this indefinitely.

Chapter Thirty-Seven

lya took pity on Elizabeth and pressed her arm. "For as long as they stay here, they will always be seen as different."

"I do not understand." Elizabeth stamped her foot. A habit Alya was amazed Sir James tolerated, but then Sir James seemed to tolerate much when it came to his only daughter. In the weeks following Newt and Bahir's wakening, he had even agreed to allow her to stay at Anglesea and learn from Nurse and Ivy.

"If they go to Lord alone knows where, they will be strangers there too." Elizabeth paced to the hearth and back again. "Why not be strangers here amongst your own people?"

"These are not my people." Newt resumed his packing. He and Bahir would travel light, taking only what they could on their horses. "I fall betwixt two worlds and neither is comfortable to own me."

"It's not like that at Anglesea." Elizabeth snatched a cloak out of his hands and tossed it on the floor. "People here love and respect you."

"They love and respect me so much, they nearly vivisected me." Newt picked up the cloak and folded it.

Alya let them argue it out. Elizabeth had a strange fascination with Newt that made her dizzy with how fast it swung from one emotion to another. "Bahir?"

Quietly to one side of the big manor table, Bahir also went about his preparations. "My lady?"

The smile he gave her, a combination of pride, sadness, and love, near broke her heart.

She had been thinking on this for the last three nights now. Since Nurse had declared Bahir and Newt well enough to travel. She said it fast before her heart caught up with her brain and stopped her. "Take me with you."

"What?" Bahir spun and gaped at her. "Did you...?"

"Aye." She shuffled closer to him, out of earshot of the rest of the hall. "I cannot stay here without you."

"My lady." He put his folding aside and took her hands. "You are married now. That is no longer a decision you can make."

"Henry will not care." Saying the words stripped the new skin off the wound to her heart. "He will be glad to be rid of me."

"Alya." Bahir's face grew stern. "You are not a child anymore to play these games. You may very well be with child."

"I am not."

"Your time for these silly games is over. If you want to know if your man loves and cherishes you as you wish him to, then ask him."

Her cheeks burned with mortification. "I do not—"

"Do not run away with Newt and me and trust he will come after you. What if he doesn't?"

"Then I am better off without him." Bahir's words hit too close to home for her comfort.

"What if he sees your leaving as a sign that you do not love him and that is why he does not pursue?"

"I..." Henry did have his pride. "Do you think that might happen?"

"I don't know, Alya." Bahir went back to his packing. "But I do know that playing childish games will only cause chaos."

"Are you saying I cannot come with you?"

"Alya." He grabbed her shoulder and gave her a small shake. "Wherever you go in this life, I will find you and make sure you are well. If coming with me is what you really want, then I will take you. But I am not sure it is what you really want."

Alya cuddled Amira close and took a moment to think that through. Around her the manor came to life again. Villagers, who before the attack would not pass her on the road, now flocked here to help. But her resentment still burrowed deep. If Lady Mary had not threatened their lives, would these people be so eager to serve her? They had not given her a chance when she needed it, and now she was not inclined to return the favor.

"I am decided." Even as she said the words, doubt flickered in her middle. "I want to come with you."

"Nay." Henry appeared behind her.

Alya started and faced him.

Standing taut, Henry said, "Your place is with me."

His certainty almost made her laugh. If it had not made her want to cuff him. "My place is with you?" She took a step closer. "Only you do not want me there, because there is no place for me with you."

"What are you talking about?" Henry reared back. "You are my wife. Of course, there is a place for you."

"As your wife?" It hurt more than she could say, and she refused to let on. "Your duty and your responsibility."

"Well...aye." Henry glanced at Bahir and shrugged. "Of course you are my duty and my responsibility. I swore these things before God."

"I think she waits to hear about the other things you swore before God." Bahir folded another chemise and stuffed it into his pack. "If I might offer a word of advice, I would take some time on the love part."

Ayla could not credit her ears. She stared at Bahir, not sure who this traitor was.

"That goes without saying." Henry frowned.

"I think not." Bahir straightened and pinned him with a stare. "A woman needs to hear it."

"But of course, I love her, honor her, all of that." Hands spread, Henry shrugged. "How can she doubt it?"

How could she doubt it? *How could she doubt it?* Alya thought her head might come off her shoulders. "I doubt it because your actions show me otherwise."

"Like what?"

Beatrice said one needed to explain things carefully to a man. "Everything you have done since you brought me here has shown me that you are ashamed of me. That you regret marrying me and now wish you hadn't."

Henry gaped at her, glanced at Bahir and shook his head. "Are you addled?"

Alya hauled back her arm and punched him. Her fist connected his shoulder. Pain burst up her arm but Henry remained unmoved. "You never talk to me." Alya cradled her hurt hand. "You never tell me what you are thinking or feeling. You go off alone to places and leave me. You are never beside me in front of others—"

"Stop." Gently Henry took her hurt hand and kissed it. "I did not talk because I did not understand all the things swirling through my mind. How can I share that which I do not understand?" He pressed her hand to his chest. "Besides, what right had I to complain when you had so much to worry about?"

"Henry." She wanted to cling to her anger but the sincerity on his face crept around her walls.

"How could I hope to keep my beautiful girl on the wall when inside I was dead?" He stepped closer. "How could I hold something so pure with the taint of blood and dishonor all over these hands?"

She cursed the tears that stung her eyes. "I saw only a man I admired and could love."

"But I did not." He took her hands and kissed one and then the other. "All I saw was a man shamed and whom I despised."

That he saw that in himself baffled her. Since the day they left Cairo, he had behaved with honor and nobility. Even in his silence and refusal to let her see within him, Henry had behaved like the knightly code that he upheld. "What do you see now?"

"Now?" Henry smiled his beautiful smile that lit his eyes from within. "I see a man who is still not worthy but will spend every day of his life trying to be."

"Oh, Henry." Her heart begged her to take what he offered, but her mind still needed more clarity. "You withheld so much from me. You shut me out and left me in the dark, feeling like you were ashamed to call me wife."

"Never that." He cupped her cheek. "That you married me is a miracle, and that I stand here and call you mine is so incredible to me that I still cannot quite believe it."

He had such a clever tongue, her Henry. Even her mind wavered and slunk a little closer to her heart's view of the situation. "I needed to understand you, and you would not let me."

"For that I can only beg your pardon on the basis of being a man. We are not good at sharing that which we hold within. Give me another chance and I will tell you anything." He pressed his forehead to hers. "Ask me anything and I will give you an answer."

"Will you tell me of the pilgrimage?"

"Now." Straightening, Henry rubbed the back of his neck and took a deep breath. "Where would you like me to start?"

"Another time." Alya did not resist as he threaded their fingers together. She had wanted to know if he would speak to her, and now that he would, the details did not seem to matter so much. Until the words left her lips, Alya had not thought to utter them. "Are you sorry you married me?"

"Never." He wrapped an arm about her waist and pulled her to him. "You are my everything. In Cairo, you were the hope I clung to. Here, you are my heart, my soul, and my very being."

Alya's knees turned to water. He said such things that she had never even dared hope for, and he meant them. His gaze met her directly and full of love. "Do you love me?"

"How can you doubt it?" He tugged her closer. "And if I have not spent enough time convincing you of that, I ask for a lifetime to do better."

"If I really wanted to go, would you let me?" Alya did not know how she wanted him to answer that question. Aye could mean he did not love her enough to fight for her. Nay could mean he did not want what was best for her.

A haunted look crossed his face. "If you could not stay here, then I would let you go."

Alya near buckled under how much that hurt.

"But." Henry's face hardened. "Then I would have to come with you. You go nowhere without me, Alya. Not since the priest joined us, not now, and not in the future. If you leave Anglesea, I go with you. If you want to explore foreign lands, I will be your shadow."

"You would leave your family." She gestured the hall. "And all this to come with me?"

"In a heartbeat." He drew her closer to his hard chest. "None of this means anything without you."

"Thanks." Roger had entered the manor and now stood beside Bahir. "Nice to know how much we mean to you." But his eyes twinkled and he winked at Alya. "I'd help him pack if it came to that." He raised his brow and crossed his arms. "Is it going to come to that?"

"I—"

"Do not leave, my lady." A serving woman sidled up beside Roger. "I be begging you to stay and give us all a chance to make you welcome here."

"We beg you." Bernard and his mother joined the woman.

Bernard's knot of friends flanked them. "And us."

Bernard pointed to Amira. "What will happen to her if you leave?"

"And the new ground we plowed." Chester tugged his cap off his head. "We turned the sod on the eastern side of the manor for your flowers and your herbs."

Meg, the gray-haired seamstress slunk around Chester. She held up a pair of braies and a tunic like Kathryn sometimes wore. "And we made these for you. Bernard said you admired Lady Kathryn's so." She laid them gently on the table beside Bahir's pack. "And we checked your silks. There are more left than we thought and with a bit of clever cutting we can make bed hangings and cushions for this entire manor."

"What say you, sister?" Roger cocked his head. "We will make things right for you, if you allow us."

"And me." Henry whispered in her ear. "I will spend my life making sure you are happy here, but if you still want to leave, then that is what we will do."

So many faces in the hall, all turned her way and waiting. She glanced at Bahir for guidance.

He shrugged.

The choice was hers to make. First, she needed to know something. Taking Henry's lean cheeks between her palms she stared deep into his eyes. "I need to know that you accept me as I am. That you do not wish me to be anyone other than who I am."

"Alya." He placed his hands over hers. "Why would I want anything else when what I have is perfect?" He dropped a soft kiss on her mouth. "That is if I still have it. Do I, sweeting? Do I have you?"

She could not be surer of her answer. "Always."

fternoon sun hit Mary's face with the benign warmth of late summer. Voices carried from the terraced gardens Roger had added on the landward side of Anglesea. The outer bailey, once a cluster of cottages, now spread before her in a gentle rolling green interspersed with bright bursts of flowerbeds.

The brightest blooms in the garden her grandchildren, and the newer crop of great-grandchildren. The family gathered to celebrate with Roger as he attained his earldom. Baron Anglesea, Earl of Devon, but still her Roger. Now almost entirely gray-haired, but still as tall and strong as the young man who had strode through the halls challenging his sire. He'd done well with his stewardship of the great demesne. Not a man of war like her Arthur, but a man of his time who understood how to take what his father had bequeathed him and build it into a strong political force.

Somebody shrieked and Mary opened her eyes. A fierce wooden sword fight, looking more like an all-out rout took place about twenty feet away from her. So many boys. Mary shook her head. Nurse had bemoaned the lack of female offspring with the birth of each new male child.

Beatrice had given up on a daughter after eight boys. Faye had given them sweet, lovely Bess, but followed her with another three boys. William's Alice brought them another six boys and only one girl. Fiery, tempestuous Prudence, who joined the sword fight with as much vigor as her brothers and male cousins.

Roger and Katherine had brought the male tally up again with three boys before a stillborn fourth had meant the end of sons for the couple. Henry and his sweet Alya, had sadly never had a child of their own. Nurse had done all she could, but some things were never meant to be. Instead Alya filled the manor house with dogs of all shapes and sizes.

Even two years after her death, Mary could not reconcile Nurse being gone and she spoke to her as if she were still there. Nurse had passed one night in her sleep. How she would have delighted in the new bellies swelling around them.

"Maybe we'll get those girls now, Nurse," Mary said to the empty chair by her side.

How Arthur would have beamed with pride today. The demesne he had fought so hard to build, had shed blood and sweat to establish, would now become one of the most powerful earldoms in the Kingdom. They called Roger the aye-sayer. The king made decisions, and the court looked to Roger for endorsement.

William, still so devastatingly handsome, strolled across the sword-fight and disrupted it. He laughed off the shouts of protest, throwing back his now silver head and laughing. His startling blue eyes had lost none of their impact over the years, and several female eyes followed him. They wasted their sighs. William had never had eyes for any other woman but his Alice. His wife, now grown plump in her middle years, but still the tiny fury at the center of William's life.

In the shade of a large oak sat their Sweet Bea, chatting to lovely Faye. Arthur's beloved daughters, his pride and joy, and the source of endless hours of pacing and worry.

"They turned out well, my darling." Gone six years now, and

his absence a gnawing ache that dulled but never fully left her. As if half of herself was missing. Her love, her Arthur. In her moments of whimsy, she liked to think that Arthur was now with their Mathew. The pain of losing a child never eased, and for her late born son who had passed in his twenty-second year, the wound still throbbed.

Arthur had given her all of this. That night, so many years ago, when she had made sure she would marry him. He'd been so angry with her for putting them in a compromising position. Mary smiled as his handsome, furious face rose in her memory. His shock at her sneaking into his room.

A clever woman arranged matters to suit herself, and so she had. Two strong wills, she and Arthur had had their share of battles over their many years together. But she'd never regretted her actions that night. One look had been all it took for her to know there stood the man for her.

Tomorrow Roger would be Lord Devon. "Imagine that Arthur, Lord Devon." Mary chuckled. "You would have loved to be called that." She swept her arm over the happy throng enjoying the summer afternoon. "But here is your legacy, Arthur."

A soft breeze caressed her cheek, and Mary closed her eyes. Lately, Arthur's spirit stood right beside her, waiting for her on the other side. The veil between this life and the after thinned to the point where at times she caught glimpses of him on the other side. He waited, tall, handsome, strong and looking as he had the day she had first cast eyes on him. How she longed to be with him again. Lately, she thought she could see Mathew and Nurse beside him.

"I will see you soon," she whispered.

The breeze traveled up and up, over the ramparts and up again to where the pennant hung from its pole. The breeze rippled the pennant and then snapped it straight until it streamed against the blue sky, dragon's head proper upon argent.

* * *

You've reached the end of Sir Arthur's Legacy. The series consists of five books; ***Sweet Bea, My Lady Faye, Conquering William, Defying Roger,*** and ***Henry's Honor***. Although…I do think—at some point—Newt deserves a story of his own 😊 Give me a shout at sarah@sarahhegger.com if you agree.

* * *

For first dibs on news, deals, and giveaways, and so much more, join the @Home Collective

Or if Facebook is more your thing, join the Sarah Hegger Collective

Anything and everything you need to know on my website http://sarahhegger.com

About the Author

**Sarah Edwards is also published under the name
Sarah Hegger**

Born British and raised in South Africa, Sarah Hegger suffers
from an incurable case of wanderlust. Her match? A hot
Canadian engineer, whose marriage proposal she accepted six
short weeks after they first met. Together they've made homes in
seven different cities across three different continents (and back
again once or twice). If only it made her multilingual, but the best
she can manage is idiosyncratic English, fluent Afrikaans,
conversant Russian, pigeon Portuguese, even worse Zulu and
enough French to get herself into trouble.
Mimicking her globe trotting adventures, Sarah's career path
began as a gainfully employed actress, drifted into public
relations, settled a moment in advertising, and eventually took
root in the fertile soil of her first love, writing. She also
moonlights as a wife and mother. She currently lives in Ottawa,
Canada, filling her empty nest with fur babies. Part footloose
buccaneer, part quixotic observer of life, Sarah's restless heart is
most content when reading or writing books.

Praise for Sarah Hegger

Drove All Night
"The classic romance plot is elevated to a modern-day,
wholly accessible real-life fairy tale with an excellent mix of
romantic elements and spicy sensuality."
Booklife Prize, Critic's Report

Positively Pippa
"This is the type of romance that makes readers fall in love not
just with characters, but with authors as well."
Kirkus Review (Starred Review)

"What begins as a simple second-chance romance quickly
transforms into a beautiful, frank examination of love, family
dynamics, and following one's dreams. Hegger's unflinching,
candid portrayal of interpersonal and generational
communication elevates the story to the sublime. Shunning
clichés and contrived circumstances, she uses realistic, relatable
situations to create a world that readers will want to visit time and
again."
Publisher's Weekly, Starred Review

Hegger's utterly delightful first Ghost Falls contemporary is what other romance novels want to grow up to be." – Publisher's Weekly, Best Books of 2017

"The very talented Hegger kicks off an enjoyable new series set in the small Utah town of Ghost Falls. This charming and fun-filled book has everything from passion and humor to betrayal and revenge." –
Jill M Smith, RT Books Reviews 2017 – Contemporary Love and Laughter Nominee

Becoming Bella

"Hegger excels at depicting familial relationships and friendships of all kinds, including purely platonic friendships between women and men. Tears, laughter, and a dollop of suspense make a memorable story that readers will want to revisit time and again."
Publisher's Weekly, Starred Review

"...you have a terrific new romance that Hegger fans are going to love. Don't miss out!"
Jill M. Smith – RT Book Reviews

Blatantly Blythe

"Ms. Hegger has delivered another captivating read for this series in this book that was packed with emotion..." Bec, Bookmagic Review, Harlequin Junkie, HJ Recommends.

Nobody's Fool

"Hegger offers a breath of fresh air in the romance genre." – Terri Dukes, RT Book Reviews

Nobody's Princess

"Hegger continues to live up to her rapidly growing reputation for breathing fresh air into the romance genre." – Terri Dukes, RT Book Reviews

"I have read the entire Willow Park Series. I have loved each of the books ... Nobody's Princess is my favorite of all time." Harlequin Junkie, Top Pick

335

Also by Sarah Edwards

Sarah Edwards also writes as Sarah Hegger

Urban Fantasy

The Cré-Witch Chronicles

Prequel: Cast In Stone

Vol l: Born In Water

Vol ll: Purged In Fire

Vol III: Raised In Air

Vol IV: Cradled In Earth

Vol V: Joined In Spirit

Sports Romance

Ottawa Titans Series

Roughing

Contemporary Romance

Passing Through Series

Drove All Night

Ticket To Ride

Walk On By

Ghost Falls Series

Positively Pippa

Becoming Bella

Blatantly Blythe

Loving Laura

Willow Park Romances
Nobody's Angel
Nobody's Fool
Nobody's Princess

Medieval Romance
Sir Arthur's Legacy Series
Sweet Bea
My Lady Faye
Conquering William
Defying Roger
Henry's Honor

Love & War Series
The Marriage Parley
The Betrothal Melee

Western Historical Romance
The Soiled Dove Series
Sugar Ellie

Standalone
The Bride Gift
Bad Wolfe On The Rise
Wild Honey

www.ingramcontent.com/pod-product-compliance
Lightning Source LLC
Chambersburg PA
CBHW071205210726
48293CB00002B/289